Brendan's e powerful.

It swept through N her whole body wa he was.

A life force. Compelling. All-encompassing.

And that was before his kiss deepened. Taking her. Capturing her. Promising her. Making her believe in the breadth and depth and pure power of love.

She broke away from him and stood staring at him, her chest heaving, her mind whirling, her soul on fire.

She didn't want to believe! Belief had left her shattered. Her belief in such things had left her weak and vulnerable and blind.

And she was doing it again.

HOW TO MELT
A FROZEN HEART

BY
CARA COLTER

MILLS & BOON

First published in Great Britain 2013
by Mills & Boon, an imprint of Harlequin (UK) Limited,
Eton House, 18-24 Paradise Road, Richmond, Surrey TW9 1SR

© Cara Colter 2013

ISBN: 978 0 263 90131 3
ebook ISBN: 978 1 472 00511 3

23-0813

Harlequin (UK) policy is to use papers that are natural, renewable and recyclable products and made from wood grown in sustainable forests. The logging and manufacturing processes conform to the legal environmental regulations of the country of origin.

Printed and bound in Spain
by Blackprint CPI, Barcelona

To my favorite animal lover, Margo Jakobsen,
and her beloved, the true Prince of Pomerania, Phaut.

CHAPTER ONE

BRENDAN GRANT AWOKE with a start. At first he heard only the steady beat of rain on the roof, but then the phone rang again, shrill, jangling across his nerves. His eyes flicked to his bedside clock.

Three o'clock.

He felt his heart begin to beat a hard tattoo inside his chest. What good could ever come of a 3:00 a.m. phone call?

But then he remembered, and even though he remembered, he reached over and touched the place in the bed beside him. Two and a half years later and he still felt that ripple of shock at the emptiness. Becky was gone. The worst had already happened.

He groped through the darkness for the phone, picked it up.

"Yeah?" His voice was raspy with sleep.

"Charlie's dying."

And then the phone went silent in his hands.

Brendan lay there for a moment longer, holding the dead phone, not wanting to get up. He didn't really even like Charlie. They were going to start breaking ground on the lakeside living complex, Village on the Lake, tomorrow. His design had already attracted the attention of several architectural magazines, and based on the plan, the project had been nominated for the prestigious Michael Edgar Jonathon Award.

Still, as always, before they broke ground, and even after, he struggled with a feeling of it not being what he had wanted, missing the mark in some vague way he could not quite define. He recognized the stress was beginning. He was a man who needed his sleep.

But with a resigned groan, he sat up, swung his legs over the side of the bed, and sat there for a moment, his head in his hands, listening to the rain on the roof. He was so sick of rain. He certainly didn't want to go out in it at three in the morning.

Then, with a sigh, Brendan reached for his jeans.

Ten minutes later, he was on Deedee's front stoop, hammering on her door. Her house was a two-minute drive from his. Brendan turned and looked out over his neighborhood. They both enjoyed locations on "The Hill," still Hansen's most prestigious neighborhood, and even on such a ghastly night the views were spectacular.

Through wisps of mist, he could see the whole city, pastel-painted turn-of-the-century houses nestled under mature maples, clinging to the sides of steep hills. Beyond the houses and the cluster of downtown buildings, lights penetrated the gloomy gray and reflected in the black, restless waters of Kootenay Lake.

Brendan turned back as the door opened a crack. Deedee regarded him suspiciously, as if there was a possibility that by some mean coincidence at the very same time she had called him, a home invader—Hansen's first—was waiting on her front stair to prey on the elderly.

Satisfied it was Brendan Grant in the flesh, she opened the door.

"Don't you look just like the devil?" she said. "Coming out of the storm like that, all dark menace and bristling bad temper. I used to say to Becky you had to have Black Irish in you somewhere. Or pure pirate."

Brendan stepped in and regarded his grandmother-in-law with exasperated affection. Only Deedee would see a devil or a pirate in the doer of a good deed!

"I'll try to contain the bristling bad temper," he said drily. The darkness he could do nothing about. It was his coloring: dark brown eyes, dark brown hair, whiskers blacker than night. It was also his heart.

Deedee was ninety-two, under five feet tall, frighteningly thin. Still, despite the fact it was 3:15 in the morning and her cat, Charlie, was dying, she was dressed in her go-to-church best. She had on a pantsuit the color of pink grapefruit. A matching ribbon was tied in a bow in her snow-white curls.

Would Becky have looked like this someday? If she had grown old? The pain was sharp, his guilt so intense it felt as if a knife had been inserted underneath his ribs. But Brendan was accustomed to it coming like this, in unexpected moments, and he held his breath, waiting, watching himself, almost bemused.

Pain, but no emotion. A man so emotionally impoverished he had not shed a single tear for his wife.

Sometimes he felt as if his heart was a tomb that a stone had been rolled in front of, sealing it away forever.

"I'll get my coat," Deedee said. "I've already got Charlie in the cat carrier."

She turned to retrieve her coat—pink to match her outfit—from the arm of a sofa, and he saw Charlie glaring balefully at him from a homemade carrier that looked like a large and very ugly purse.

Charlie's head poked out a round hole, his ginger fur stuck up in every direction, his whiskers kinked, his eyes slit with dislike and bad temper. He made a feeble attempt to squeeze his gargantuan self out the tiny opening, but his quick resignation to defeat, and the raspy breathing caused by the effort, made Brendan aware that tonight was the end of the road for the ancient, cranky cat.

Deedee turned back to him, carefully buttoning her coat around her. Brendan picked up the cat carrier with one hand and crooked his other elbow. Deedee threaded her arm through his, and he nudged open the door with his knee, trying not to be impatient when the rain sluiced down his neck as she handed him a huge ring of keys.

"Lock the handle *and* the dead bolt," she ordered, as if they were in a high-crime area of New York City.

Both locks were sticky, and Brendan made a note to come by and give them a squirt of lubricant the next time he had a chance.

Finally they turned toward his car, inched down the steep stairs that took them from her front stoop to the road. When they reached the flat walkway, he tried to adjust his stride to Deedee's tiny steps. He was just under six feet tall, his build lithe with a runner's sleekness rather than a bodybuilder's muscle, but Deedee made him feel like a giant.

A bristling pirate of a giant.

Brendan found himself wishing she would have called one of her children to accompany her on this late-night trip to the vet's office. But for a reason he couldn't quite decipher—it certainly wasn't his graciousness—it was him she turned to when she needed anything, from a lightbulb changed to her supply of liquid meal replacements restocked.

Deedee was not a nice little old lady. She was querulous, demanding, bossy, ungrateful and totally self-centered. It had occurred to Brendan more than once that she called him because no one else would come. But Deedee was his inheritance from his late wife. Becky and Deedee had adored each other. For that reason alone he came when she called.

Finally, he had both the cat and Deedee settled, the animal on the backseat, the woman in the front. The carrier did not look waterproof and he hoped the cat would not have an accident that would bleed through to the seat. Of course, with Charlie it might not be an accident. It might be pure spite.

Regardless, the car was brand-new, all plush leather and purring power. Had Brendan bought it hoping to fill some emptiness? If so, he had failed colossally, like putting a pebble in a hole left by a cannonball. Brendan shook off the thought, annoyed. It was the lateness of the night, the strangeness of being awake at what seemed to him to be the witching hour, that made him vulnerable to uncharacteristic introspection.

He got in the driver's side and started the engine, glanced at Deedee and frowned. She looked quite thrilled to be having this middle of the night outing, not like an old woman making the painful final journey with her cat.

"Which vet are you using? Is he expecting us?"

"I'll give you directions," she snapped.

It was the tone of voice she used right before she

pronounced you an idiot, so he shrugged and put the car in drive, and pulled out into the wet, abandoned streets of Hansen.

He was determined to be patient. It was one more loss for her. Putting down her precious cat. She was entitled to be crabby tonight, and he did not want her to be alone at the vet's office as the needle went in. He did not want her to be alone when she came home without her cat.

She gave him directions, and he drove in silence, the mountains on either side of the valley making the night darker, the water hissing up under the tires. The cat's breathing was labored.

Deedee issued shrill commands for Brendan to slow down and squinted at the signs on every crossroad. Finally, she fished in her purse, took out a piece of paper and held it very close to her face.

"If you give me the address, this new car has GPS."

She contemplated that, deeply suspicious of technology, then reluctantly gave him the information.

He put it in his system. They were headed into the neighborhood that bordered Creighton Creek. A stone's throw from Hansen proper, the area was rural residential, with a collection of small, neat acreages. Because of the great location, and the land, it was a sought-after area for young professionals who had a dream of children, a golden retriever and a horse or two.

All Brendan had ever wanted, growing up the only child of a single mother, was that most elusive of things—normal. And when he'd been almost there, in a blink, everything was gone. There must have been something he could have done. Anything.

He felt the pain again, of being powerless, and again

felt himself watching, wondering if at some unexpected moment he would just break open. If he did, he was certain it would shatter him, that the pieces would be so small there would be no collecting them and putting it all together again.

But no, he was able to focus on the small, old houses of Creighton Creek, which were slowly but surely being replaced with bigger ones. Brendan's firm, Grant Architects, had designed many of the newer homes, and he allowed himself, as they drove by one of his houses— one with a particularly complicated roofline—to be diverted from the painful realization of the life he was not going to have by the reality of the one he did.

The house was beautiful. The home owners loved it. Again, he had to try and shake that feeling of having *missed* something.

"I don't recall a vet located out here," he said. "In fact, didn't I take you and Charlie to Doc Bentley recently?"

"Dr. Bentley is an idiot," Deedee muttered. "He told me to put Charlie to sleep. That there was no hope at all. 'He's old. He's got cancer. Let him go.'" She snorted. "I'm old. Are you just going to let me go? Put me to sleep, maybe?"

Brendan cast Deedee a glance. Carefully, he said, "Isn't that what we're doing? Taking Charlie to have him put to, er, sleep?"

Deedee cranked her head toward him and gave him a withering look. "I am taking him to a healer."

Brendan didn't like the sound of that, but he carefully tried to strip any judgment from his voice. "What do you mean, a healer?"

"Her name's Nora. She has that new pet rescue place. Babs Taylor told me she has a gift."

"A gift," he repeated.

"Like those old-time preachers who laid their hands on people."

"Are you kidding me?" He began to look for a place to turn around. "You need a vet. Not a nut."

"What I need is a miracle, and Dr. Bentley already told me he can't give me one." Deedee's voice was high and squeaky. "Babs's niece volunteers out there. She said somebody brought in a dog that was deader than a doornail. And Nora Anderson brought it back to life. With her *energy*."

Brendan felt his mouth tighten in a hard line of cynicism. One thing Becky and her grandmother had had in common? They loved all things "woo-woo." They actually believed in what they called psychics and mediums, had frowned at him when he had made disparaging remarks about fortune-tellers and gypsies.

An unfortunate mental picture of Nora was forming in his mind: dangling earrings, wildly colored head scarf, hideous makeup, dark blue eye shadow, a slash of blood-red on her lips.

"Can you keep a secret?" Deedee didn't wait for him to respond, but lowered her voice conspiratorially, as if dozens could hear. "Clara, over at the post office, told me she thinks from the mail that she gets that Nora is Rover. You know, from the column? *Ask Rover?*"

He didn't know.

"You can tell when you read it," Deedee elaborated, still whispering. "Nora gets right inside their heads. The animals."

"That must be helpful, so that she knows where to

send the energy to," he said, his tone deeply sarcastic. Deedee missed the sarcasm entirely, because she went on with enthusiasm.

"Exactly! I'm a great fan of *Ask Rover,* so I knew she was the one who could help Charlie. I don't drive anymore," Deedee said, as if Brendan, her favored chauffeur, didn't know that, "and I can't hear properly on the phone, so I wrote her a letter, and brought it right to the post office so I knew she'd get it the next day. She wrote me back right away saying she would send me—Charlie—some energy."

Brendan felt a kind of helpless fury claw at him. Deedee nursed the worry that Hansen's first home invader would target her. She double-locked her doors. She was suspicious of the checkout girl at the grocery counting out the wrong change! How could she fall for this?

"It worked," Deedee whispered. "Charlie got better. But then he got worse again, and she wouldn't answer my letters. I phoned, too, even though I can't hear, but I got an answering machine. I hate those. No one returned my calls. Then tonight, Charlie's breathing changed. I'm scared. I know he's dying."

Brendan hated it that she was scared, and hated it more that her fear had made her so vulnerable. "Did you send money?"

The silence was telling.

"Did you?"

"A little."

His GPS system startled them both by telling him to turn right at the next crossroad. Suddenly he wanted very much to meet the person who would use an elderly woman's fear over losing her beloved pet to bamboozle money out of her.

All the better if they rousted her from a deep sleep in the middle of the night!

He turned right; they went up a road he had never noticed before, and passed under an archway that spanned the road.

A sign hung from the archway, letters painted in fresh, primary colors. Nora's Ark.

At any other time, he might have thought it was clever little play on words. Or maybe not. He didn't like *cute*. He was an architect. He liked calculation, precision, math. He liked figuring out how large a load a beam could carry, and how to make a wall of glass that was structurally sound.

He liked the completely balanced marriage of art and science that was his work. If at the end of the project he always felt, somehow, he had missed the mark, wasn't that part of what drove him to do even better the next time? To try again for that thing, whatever it was, that was just out of his reach?

Brendan considered himself pragmatic and practical, perhaps with a good measure of cynical thrown in. He was the man least likely to give himself over to whimsy. But given that it seemed to have been raining for forty days and forty nights, he felt a strange shiver along his spine that he was arriving at an ark of any sort.

Below the sign Nora's Ark was a smaller one, announcing they were supported by the Hansen Community Betterment Committee.

His company was one of the charter members!

He shook off his annoyance, and drove over a wooden bridge that spanned a creek that was still raging with spring runoff, though it was the last day of June. Up ahead, carved out of the mountainous wilderness all around, a white house—almost a cottage—was illuminated in his headlights, surrounded by a picket fence and a yard where yellow climbing roses rioted.

Through the grim, pelting rain a light shone, warm and inviting, from inside, and the house seemed like a welcoming place, not the kind of place where a charlatan who cheated vulnerable old women would live.

Was someone awake? It was probably a good time for chanting and consulting cards. Though why do it if the mark wasn't there?

Behind the house and yard, barely visible in darkness that was slowly giving way to a soggy predawn, he could see the huge silhouette of a barn.

"Oh, we're here," Deedee breathed happily. "It looks just the way I thought it would."

That explained the appearance of the place. Homey. Welcoming. Like the old witch's cottage in *Hansel and Gretel.*

All the better to dupe people, to lure them closer.

"You wait here," Brendan said, and cut off Deedee's protest with a firm slam of the car door. He walked up a path that smelled of perfume as he crushed damp fallen rose petals under his feet.

Then, out of the corner of his eye, back toward the barn, he saw a light fly up, heard the high-pitched whinny of a horse, and, straining against the sounds of the storm, he was sure he heard the startled cry of someone in trouble. A female in trouble.

CHAPTER TWO

TURNING FROM THE house, adrenaline pumping, his instincts on red alert, Brendan Grant ran toward the barn.

At first, he thought it was a pile of old rags in the churned-up mud of the paddock adjoining the barn. The pile was faintly illuminated by the fallen flashlight beside it. Then it moved. Heedless of the mud, he put one hand on the fence, leaped it, landed, raced to the still form. It looked like a child facedown in the mud.

His sense of urgency surged as he squatted down. He knew better than to try to move whoever it was without assessing the injuries.

"Are you all right?"

Movement from the heap of rags and a squeak of distressed surprise were a relief to Brendan. Then the pile of rags flipped over.

It was his turn to be shocked. It wasn't a child, but a woman. Her hair reminded him of Charlie's—ginger, sticking up all over the place, except where a clump of mud had flattened it to her skull. But even the mud that streaked her skin could not hide the exquisite loveliness of her pale face.

Her nose was dainty, faintly dusted with copper freckles. Her lips were plump and pink; her chin had a little jut to it that hinted at a stubborn temperament. A goose egg was rising alarmingly above her right eye.

Her eyes were amazing, wide-spaced, unusually large in the smallness of her face, a color of jade that flickered with light in the grayness of the night.

If this was Nora she was an enchantress of the kind who would have no need of makeup to weave her spell.

She was obviously very woozy, because she looked at him quizzically, and then oddly, reached up and touched his cheek, a faint smile on her face, as if she did not see a dark devil arrived on the tails of the storm, but something else entirely. Something that she recognized and welcomed.

His feeling of being enchanted—however reluctantly—increased.

Then abruptly she came to her senses. She seemed to realize she was flat on her back in the middle of the night, in the mud, with a strange man who oozed menace and bristling bad temper hovering over her.

Her eyebrows knit together in consternation and she struggled to sit up.

"Hey," he said, his attempt at a soothing tone coming out of his mouth like rust, a hoarse croak. "Try not to move."

She looked as if she had no intention of following his well-meaning instruction, so he laid a hand on her shoulder. It was tiny underneath a thin jacket that appeared to be soaking up rain rather than repelling it.

He could see a little bow on what could be her pajamas at the V of her jacket.

She shook off his hand, sat up, wincing from the effort. He'd been right about her chin giving a clue to her temperament. She was stubborn.

"Who are you?" she demanded. "What are you doing out here, on my property, at this time of night?"

He was annoyed with himself that the tone of her voice increased the sense of enchantment weaving through this miserable night. Despite the lack of welcome in her words, her voice reminded him of maple syrup, rich and smooth and sweet.

She scanned his face, that initial reaction of trust, of welcome, completely gone. Now she looked wary and stubborn and maybe just a little frightened.

What she didn't have was the look of a person who would be trying to dupe an old lady out of her money.

No sense putting off the moment of truth.

"Are you Nora?"

She nodded. He let that sink in. No head scarf. No dangling earrings. Certainly no blue eye shadow, or slash of red at her mouth.

Brendan was aware that in a very short time he had started to hope the woman in a vulnerable little heap in the mud was not the same woman who had written Deedee a letter promising to heal her cat. With energy. For a fee.

He looked at her fresh face, tried to imagine dangling earrings and heavy makeup and the gypsy scarf, and found his imagination didn't quite go that far. But fresh faced or not, she'd duped Deedee. He was already disillusioned by life, so why be disturbed by the gathering of a little more evidence?

Still, for the moment she looked faintly frightened, and he felt a need to alleviate that.

"I brought a cat out," he said. "I heard a ruckus out here, saw a light and came to investigate."

She considered his explanation, but looked doubt-

ful. He suspected he didn't look much like the kind of
guy who would be attached to his cat.

"I heard you were a healer." He tried to strip judgment from his tone, but he must have looked even less
like the kind of guy who would put any kind of faith in
a healer than one who would be attached to a cat, because her doubtful expression intensified.

"Who did you hear that from?" she asked uneasily.
Her eyes skittered toward the fence, as if she was going
to try and make an escape.

"Deedee Ashton."

The name did not seem to register, but then she
might be struggling to remember her own name at the
moment.

"Can you tell me what happened?" he asked.

She put a hand to the goose egg above her eye.

"I don't know for sure," she said. "The horses might
have knocked me over."

He scanned the corral. Three horses were squeezed
against the back fence, restless and white-eyed. He
didn't know much about horses, but these ones seemed
in no way docile.

He told himself firmly that it was none of his business what kind of chances she took. He didn't know
her. He certainly didn't care about her. Still, there was
a certain kind of woman that could make a man feel he
should be protective. That was the kind you really had
to guard against, especially if you had already failed
in the department of protecting the smaller and weaker
and more vulnerable.

Brendan ordered himself not to comment. But, of
course, his mouth disobeyed his mind.

"Given you're about the size of a peanut, doesn't it

seem a touch foolhardy to decide to come mingle with your wild mustangs in the middle of the night?"

She glared at him. Her look clearly said *don't tell me what to do,* which was fair.

"Unless, of course, you hoped your *energy* was going to tame them?"

Those amazing eyes narrowed. "What do you know about my energy?"

"Not as much as I plan to."

"Why does that sound like a threat?" she asked.

He shrugged.

She tossed her head at that, but he saw a veil drop smoothly over the flash of fire in those green eyes, as if *he* had hurt *her* by being a doubter. You'd think, in her business, she would have developed a thicker skin.

But he would have to deal with all that later. She had begun to shiver from being wet, but when she tried to move, a small groan escaped her lips.

He knew he shouldn't move her. But she was clearly freezing. Now was not the time to confront her about any claims she had made to Deedee. He shrugged out of his coat and wrapped it around her.

She looked as if she planned to protest his act of chivalry, but when he tucked his coat around her, he could clearly see the warmth seduced her. She snuggled inside it instead. She looked innocent, about as threatening as a wounded sparrow.

Stripping away any censure he felt about her claims of extraordinary power, he said, "Can you move your hands? How about your feet? Can you turn your head from side to side for me?"

"What are you? A doctor?" Despite the protest, she tested each of her body parts as he named it.

He touched the ugly-looking bump rising above her right eye. She winced.

"You're not lucky enough to have conjured up a doctor. You'll have to work on your conjuring a little. I'm an architect. Luckily, I have a little construction site first aid experience."

As he had hoped, at the mention of his profession—oh, those professional men were so trustworthy—her wariness of him faded, though annoyance at his conjuring remark had turned her green eyes to slits that reminded him of Charlie.

He picked the flashlight out of the mud and shone it in her eyes, looking for pupil reaction.

"Tell me about your cat," she said, swatting at the light.

"So you can send him energy?"

"Why are you here, if you're so cynical?"

He felt a shiver along his spine, similar to what he had felt when he passed under the ark sign. What if he hadn't come along when he had? Would she have lain in the mud until she had hypothermia? Would the horses have trampled her?

But he was certainly not going to let her see that for a moment he was in the sway of an idea that some power he did not understand might have drawn him here at the exact moment she needed him.

Ridiculous. If such a power existed, where had it been the night Becky had needed it?

He actually saw Nora flinch, and realized he had grimaced. It no doubt gave him the pirate look that Deedee had seen earlier.

Keeping his tone level, Brendan said, "I'm here as

the result of a comedy of errors. I thought I was on my way to a legitimate practitioner of animal medicine."

"With your cat."

He nodded.

"You don't really look like a cat kind of guy."

"No? What do cat kind of guys look like?"

She studied him, the eyes narrow again. "Not like you," she said decisively.

"So, what do I look like? A rottweiler kind of guy? Bulldog? Boxer?"

Her look was intense. If a person believed that energy crap, they would almost think she was reading his. He raised the light again, shining it in her eyes, hoping to blind her. He was not sure he liked the sensation of being *seen*.

"You're not a dog kind of guy, either."

Accurate, but not spookily so.

"In fact," she continued, "I'd be surprised if you even had a plant."

Okay. That was about enough of that.

"I never said it was *my* cat." He turned off the light and put it in his pocket. "I don't think your back is injured, so I'm going to pick you up and carry you to the house."

"You are not picking me up! I'll walk." She tried to find her feet, and glared at him as if the fact that it was his jacket swimming around her stopped her from doing so. "If you'll just give me your hand—"

But Brendan did not just give her a hand. It wasn't the jacket. The small effort of trying to get up had made her turn a ghostly white, the freckles and mud standing out in stark relief. So he ignored her protests, slid his arms under her shoulders and her knees and scooped her up easily.

She was tiny, like that wounded sparrow, and despite the barrier of his jacket, he was aware of an unusual warmth oozing out of her where he held her against his chest.

Was it because it had been so long since he had touched another human being that he felt an unwelcome shiver of pleasure?

CHAPTER THREE

UNEASILY HOLDING A beautiful stranger in his arms and feeling that unwanted shiver of something good, Brendan Grant was aware it was what he had wanted to feel when he had purchased the car. Just a moment's pleasure at something. Anything. With the car, he had not even come close.

He should have already learned *stuff* could never do it. An unwanted memory came, of standing in front of the house he now owned, with Becky at his side, thinking, *This is the beginning of my every dream come true.*

"Put me down!"

Nora's hand, smacking hard against his chest, brought him gratefully back to the here and now.

"You couldn't even stand up by yourself," he said, unmoved by her tone. "I'll put you down in a minute. When I get you to the house."

Her expression was mutinous, but she winced, suddenly in pain, and conceded with ill grace.

He strode to the house. The woman in his arms was rigid with tension for a few seconds, then relaxed noticeably. He glanced down at her to make sure she hadn't passed out.

Wide green eyes stared up at him, defiant, unblinking. If ever there were eyes that could cast a spell, it would be those ones!

Just as he got close the porch light came on, illuminating the fact that Deedee had grown tired of waiting, had exited the passenger seat of the car and was feebly trying to wrestle her cat carrier out of the back.

A boy, at that awkward stage somewhere between twelve and fifteen, who also had ginger hair like Charlie's, exploded out the front door of the cottage, and the woman in Brendan's arms squirmed to life.

His architect's mind insisted on filling in pieces of the puzzle as he looked at the boy: too old to be hers.

"Put me down," she insisted, then shook herself as if waking from a dream. "Honestly! I told you I could walk."

The boy looked as if he had been sleeping, his hair flat against his face on one side and sticking straight up on the other. But he was now wide-awake and ready to fight.

"You heard her," he said, "put her down. Who are you? What have you done to my aunt Nora?"

Not his mother. His aunt.

The boy dashed back into the house and came out wielding a coat rack. He held it over his shoulder, like a baseball bat he was prepared to swing. His level of menace was laughable. Brendan was careful not to show that he had rarely felt less threatened.

Still, he couldn't help but admire a kid prepared to do battle with a full-grown man.

Brendan closed his eyes, and was suddenly aware he didn't feel the weight of new cynicism. Instead he was acutely aware of how the sweet weight in his arms and the woman's warmth were making his skin tingle. He was aware that the air smelled of rain and rose petals, and that those smells mingled with the clean scent of her hair and her skin.

Two and a half years ago, in the night, a phone call had changed everything forever. He'd been sleepwalking through life ever since, aware that he was missing something essential that other people had. That it was locked inside the tomb, and that even if he could have rolled the rock away, he was not sure that he would.

And now, another middle of the night phone call, leading to this moment. He was standing here in a stranger's yard with a woman who either was trouble, or was in trouble, in his arms, an adolescent boy threatening him with a coat rack, Deedee oblivious to it all, struggling to get her dying cat out of the car.

Brendan was aware that the rock had rolled, that a crack of light had appeared in the darkness. He was aware of feeling wide-awake, as if he was a warrior waiting to see if it was a friend or foe outside.

For the first time in more than two years he felt the blood racing through his veins, the exquisite touch of raindrops on his skin. For the first time in so long, Brendan knew he was alive.

And it didn't make him happy.

Not one little bit.

Instead, he felt deeply resentful that the prison of numbness that had become his world was being penetrated by this vibrant, demanding capricious energy called life.

"Put me down!" Nora insisted again, hoping for a no-nonsense tone of voice that would hide the confusion she was really feeling.

She looked up into the exquisite strength of the stranger's face. Through the fabric of the expensive rain jacket he had wrapped around her, she could feel the iron hardness of his chest where she leaned into it. His arms, cradling her shoulders and her legs, were bands of pure steel.

She should have fought harder against being picked up and toted across the yard like a sleeping baby. Because it was crazy to feel so safe.

The stranger had a certain cool and dangerous aloofness about him. He had already made it clear he had heard some exaggerated claim about her energy that had allowed him to put her in the category of gypsies, tramps and thieves.

So the feeling of safety had to be attributed to the terrible knock on her head. Being in his arms made Nora achingly aware that she had been alone for a while now. Carrying the weight of her world all by herself. It was a relief to be carried for a change. A guilty pleasure, but a relief nonetheless.

Now, looking up at him, she could feel something shifting. His hands tightened marginally on her and some finely held tension played around the corners of his sinfully sensuous mouth.

The soft suede of his deep, deliciously brown eyes had not changed when he had called her a healer, his tone accusatory, but now they had hardened to icy remoteness and sparked with vague anger.

Well, he had come to her rescue and was being threatened with a coat rack. Naturally, he would react.

But now he was not the man she had awoken to, one with something so compelling in his face she had reached up and touched...

She shook that off, striving for the control she had lost when she'd accepted his arms around her, accepted being cradled against the fortress of his chest, accepted the comfort of being carried.

She could not be weak. She had to be strong. Everything was relying on *her* now. She was completely on her own since her fiancé had said, "Look, it's him or it's me."

Surely, when her sister had appointed her guardian of then fourteen-year-old Luke she had not expected that turn of events! Karen had thought she was entrusting her son to a home, to a stable, financially secure environment that would have two parents, one her sister, Nora, affectionately known within the family as "the flake," the other a highly respected stable person, a vet with his own practice.

But the highly predictable world Karen had envisioned for Luke didn't happen. When everything had fallen apart between her and Vance, Nora had risked it all on a new start.

She *had* to be strong.

"Look," Nora said, "you really have to put me down."

The man ignored her, looking flintily past her to Luke.

To get his attention off her nephew, and to show she meant business, she smacked the stranger hard, against the solid wall of his chest. It felt ineffectual, as if she was being annoying, like a bug, not powerful like a lioness.

Still, when his arm slid out from under her knees, and she found herself standing, albeit a bit wobbly, on her own two feet, instead of feeling relieved she felt the oddest sense of loss.

He had carried her across her yard with incredible ease, his stride long, powerful and purposeful, his breath remaining steady and even. It was the kind of strength a person might want to rely on.

If that person hadn't made a pact to rely totally on herself!

Get a grip, Nora ordered silently, moving away from the man. She was genuinely relieved that Luke dropped the coat rack and came to her side.

Casting a look loaded with suspicion and warning at the man who had carried her, Luke got his shoulder under her arm and helped her toward the house.

"What happened? Did he hurt you?"

"No. No. It wasn't him. I couldn't sleep and I went to check the animals. One of the new horses must have spooked and knocked me over."

"Why would you go out in the corral by yourself?" Luke asked.

"My question precisely." The man's voice was deep and calm, steady.

"Those horses were wild when they were brought in," Luke said accusingly. "That one took a kick at the guy unloading him."

She didn't like it one little bit that it felt as if the two were forming an alliance against her!

Why had she gone into the corral when the horses were so restless? Probably she hadn't even thought about it, overly confident in her ability to calm animals.

Since she was a little girl she had found refuge from her mother and father's constant bickering by bringing home broken things to fix. Tiny wounded birds, abandoned cats, dogs near death.

Inside, Nora was still the girl who had been seen

by family and school chums as an eccentric, a kook, and she was more comfortable hiding her gifts than revealing them.

Which made her very uncomfortable with whatever this stranger thought he knew about her.

Would Karen have ever made her guardian of Luke if she knew Vance would not be in the picture? Probably not. She would have known her sister could not be trusted to control impulses like jumping into a corral full of flighty horses in the middle of the night!

Nora was solely responsible for Luke. What if he'd found her out there in the mud? Hadn't he been traumatized enough? She was supposed to be protecting him!

Still, it was unsettling to her that what she remembered, in far more detail than her lapse of judgment before entering the corral, or the moments before being knocked over and knocked out, was the moment after.

Coming to, Nora had opened her eyes to find this man bent over her. His expression was intense, and he was breathtakingly handsome. Dark, thick hair was curling wetly around perfect features—a straight nose; whisker-roughened cheeks; a faintly cleft chin; firm, sensuous lips.

A raindrop had slid with exquisite slowness down his temple, over the high ridge of his cheekbone, onto his lip.

And then, in slow motion, it had fallen from his lip to hers.

Perhaps it was the knock on the head that had made the moment feel suspended, made the raindrop feel as if it sizzled in the chill of the night. Made her reach out with the tip of her tongue and taste that tiny pearl of water.

Perhaps it was the knock on the head that made her feel like a princess coming awake to find the prince leaning over her.

Through it all, Nora had been caught hard by eyes that mesmerized: velvet brown suede flecked with gold, a light in them that was mostly solid strength, with just the faintest shadow of something else.

Something she of all people should know.

Woozily, she had reached out and let the palm of her hand caress his bristly cheek, to touch that common ground she recognized between them.

He had gone very still under her touch, but he did not move away from it. She had felt a lovely sense of safety, that this was someone she could rely on.

But then the wooziness was gone, just like that, and she'd remembered she was in her paddock. And that she was alone out there with a man who had no business being on her property at this time of the night.

Nora's instincts when it came to animals were beyond good. Some people, including her ex-fiancé, Dr. Vance Height, whom she had met while working as an assistant in his veterinary practice, were spooked by what she could accomplish with sheer intuition.

But Vance was a reminder that Nora's good instincts did not extend to men. Or much else about life. With tonight being an unsettling exception, her perception was fabulous when it came to dealing with hurt, frightened animals.

Or writing her quirky, off-beat column *Ask Rover,* a column she had never admitted she was behind, because she had come across Vance reading it in her early days at his office, and he had been terribly scornful of it.

The intuition was not so good at helping her stretch her modest income from the column to support both the animal shelter and Luke. Thankfully, as the shelter became more established it was starting to receive financial support from the community of Hansen.

Her intuition was also not proving the least helpful at dealing with a now fifteen-year-old nephew who seemed intent on visiting his hurt and anger over the death of his mother on the whole world.

Feeling foolish now for that vulnerable moment when she had reached up and let her hand scrape the seductive whiskery roughness of the stranger's cheek, and more foolish for allowing herself to be carried across her yard by a perfect stranger, Nora shook off Luke's arm. She was supposed to be protecting him, not the other way around.

She turned and faced the man, folding her arms over her chest.

She had been, she was certain, mistaken that they shared anything in common. Looking at him from this angle, she found he looked hard and cold, and she had, as was her unfortunate habit, given her trust too soon.

"Where did he come from?" Luke asked in a suspicious undertone.

For all she knew he could be an ax murderer! Anyone could say they were an architect! She ran an animal rescue center. Anyone could say they had brought a cat.

She knew he wasn't a cat person, one likely to be ruled by the kind of sentiment that would drive him out on a night like this for the well-being of a cat.

But behind the man, she suddenly became aware of an old woman in a ghastly pink outfit. As Nora watched, the woman gave a grunt of exertion and freed a large container from the backseat of a car that was as gray as the night and sleek with sporty expense. The man turned to her, stepped back and took a large carpet bag from her.

Nora registered two things at once: how protective he seemed of that tiny, frail woman, and that there was indeed a cat! Its head was sticking out of a kind of window in the side of the carrier. One didn't have to have any psychic ability at all to know the cat did not have now, and probably never had had, a pleasing personality.

"I'm Brendan Grant," he said.

The name seemed Scottish to Nora, and with the rain plastering his hair to his head, running unchecked down the formidable, handsome lines of his face, it was just a little too easy to picture him as a Scottish warrior. Strong. Imperious to the weather.

Determined to get his own way.

What was his own way?

"And this is my grandmother, Deedee, and her cat, Charlie." The faint hiss of angry energy seemed to intensify around him. His mouth had become a hard line. He was watching Nora closely for her reaction.

"I'm sorry?" she said. What on earth was he doing here at this time of the night with his grandmother and her cat?

Still, whatever it was, it did dilute some of the threat she felt. Though not an expert, she was still fairly certain architect ax murderers did not travel with an entourage that included grandmothers and cats.

His voice calm and ice-edged, he said, "Deedee has been made certain promises concerning Charlie. And she has paid in advance."

Nora didn't have a clue what he meant. But she did realize the threat she felt was not of the ax-murderer variety.

It was of the raindrop-falling-from-lips variety. She was aware her head hurt, but was not at all sure this feeling of being caught off balance was caused by the knock to her head.

"I don't know what you're talking about," she said firmly.

She became aware that something rippled through Luke. She felt more than saw his discomfort. She cast her nephew a glance out of the corner of her eye.

Uh-oh.

"Look," the man said quietly, the commanding tone of his voice drawing her attention firmly back to him. "You may be able to pull the wool over the eyes of an old woman, but I'm here to look after her interests. And you should know that if you've swindled her, you can kiss the support of the Hansen Community Betterment Committee good-bye."

Kiss the support of the Hansen Community Betterment Committee good-bye? Nora couldn't let her panic show.

"Swindled your grandmother?" she asked instead. Below the panic, she could feel the insult of it! His caustic remarks about her energy and her being a healer were beginning to make an awful kind of sense.

"I wouldn't be surprised if the police became involved," Brendan said, the quiet in his voice making it all the more threatening.

CHAPTER FOUR

THE POLICE? NORA felt a sense of panic, as if her world were tilting.

Still, she could not cave before him. She was about to insist that he was the one trespassing on private property, except that at the mention of the police, she realized she wasn't the only one panicking.

Nora saw Luke go rigid.

There'd been an unfortunate incident at school involving the police way too recently.

Luke claimed to have *borrowed* a bicycle. Apparently without the full understanding of the bicycle's owner, which was why the police had become involved. Luke had talked to the other boy, and the whole thing, thankfully, had blown over.

Now her nephew met her eyes, pleading, and then ducked his head, drawing a pattern in the wet ground with his bare toe.

Nora glanced back at Brendan Grant and saw he had not missed a thing. He was watching Luke narrowly, and her sense of him being a warrior intensified. His look did not bode well for her nephew.

What had Luke done now? She was acutely aware of having failed in her responsibility to her nephew by going into the corral by herself tonight. Now every protective instinct rose in her.

"Nobody swindled me," Deedee said plaintively. "She sent me energy for Charlie."

"For a price," Brendan added softly.

Nora knew she had not sent anyone any energy. And certainly not for a price! But Luke was squirming so uncomfortably she wanted to hit him with her elbow to make him stop drawing attention to himself.

Because no matter what he had done, Luke was no match for Brendan Grant. Not in any way. Not physically, nor could her poor orphaned nephew bear up under the anger that sparked in the man's eyes.

Taking a deep breath, she said brightly. "Oh, I remember now. Charlie."

Luke cast her a glance loaded with gratitude and relief, and she might have allowed herself to relish that, especially coupled with the fact he had taken up a coat rack in her defense. Moments when her nephew actually seemed to like her were rare, after all.

But Brendan Grant looked hard and skeptical, and she needed to stay focused on the immediate threat of that.

She put together the few clues she had. One of her gifts was an acute ability to focus on detail. Brendan and Deedee had arrived in the middle of the night. From what she could see of the cat, he was ill, the lateness of the hour suggested desperately so.

"Charlie's been sick, right?" she said.

"That's right!" Deedee said eagerly.

Brendan's expression just became more grim.

"You said you'd send him energy," Deedee reminded her. "You said to send money. I sent fifty dollars."

"Fifty dollars?" Brendan snapped. "Deedee! You said you sent a *little* money."

"In terms of what my cat is worth to me, that is a small amount." The woman gave him a look that was equal parts sulk and steel.

"So there you have it," Brendan said to Nora, exasperated. "If you play your cards right, she'll sign over her house to you. You won't need the support of the Hansen Community Betterment Committee. Is that how this operation of yours works?"

"Of course not!" Nora said, feeling the heat rising in her cheeks. "I'm sure it was just a mistake. I must have thought the money was a donation."

She tried to keep her voice steady, but was not sure she succeeded.

"Uh-huh." He sounded cynical, and rightfully so.

Nora wanted to whirl on Luke and shake him. She had never even raised her voice to him, but their whole future was at stake here. And worse, if he had sent that letter, and taken that money—and who else could it possibly be?—he had stolen from a vulnerable old woman. How could he? Who was he becoming? And why couldn't she stop it?

Again she felt the weight of responsibility for her choices. Karen would have never entrusted her to raise her nephew alone. She would have been able to predict this catastrophe coming.

With great care, Nora kept herself from looking askance at her nephew.

"Let's get in out of the rain," she suggested, trying to keep her voice steady. Because he had given her his jacket, the rain had soaked through Brendan's shirt, which was now practically transparent.

She was aware she didn't really want Brendan Grant, with his bristling masculine energy and wet, clinging shirt, invading her house. She'd been here only a little while, but it had quickly become a sanctuary to her. On the other hand, she desperately needed to buy some time, to take Luke aside and figure out what he had done.

And fix it.

Yet again.

But a glance at the unyielding features of the man who had made her feel momentarily so safe told her this might not be so easy to fix.

The house was not what Brendan expected of a charlatan's house. There were no crystals dangling in the door wells and no clusters of herbs hanging upside down from their stems. There was no cloying scent of incense.

"Lovely," Deedee breathed with approval, standing in the doorway, taking it in.

"Disappointing," Brendan said.

In fact, he found the house was cozy and clean. An uneasiness crawled along his neck as they passed through a living room where a pair of love seats the color of melted butter faced each other across a coffee table where some of those yellow roses from the yard floated in a clear glass bowl.

"Disappointing?" Nora asked.

"No black cat. No cauldron on the hearth."

Nora shot him a look. She really was the cutest little thing. Again he had that feeling of coming awake. He didn't want to notice her, but how could he not? Her hair was a mess, standing straight up, strawberry-blonde dandelion fluff. Her eyes were huge in a dainty mud-streaked face. She looked more frightened now than when he had first found her.

The scam revealed. But her shock seemed genuine, and so did her distress.

"Look," Nora said in a defensive undertone, "I take in sick and abandoned animals. I don't claim to be a healer."

Her nephew snorted at that, and she shot him a glare that he was completely oblivious to.

Deedee, deaf anyway, hadn't even heard.

"As for black cats and cauldrons, I certainly don't do witchcraft!"

Her muddy, soaked clothes, and his jacket, swam around her, and he guessed she would be determined not to remove her coat and reveal the pajamas underneath.

He wasn't sure why. The pajama bottoms, which he could see, were filthy, but underneath the mud they were plaid. Utilitarian rather than sexy.

They came to the kitchen, and Nora turned on a light to reveal old cabinets painted that same cheerful shade of yellow as her sofas and roses. The floor was old hardwood planking that gleamed with patina. He smelled fresh bread.

There was a jar full of cookies on the counter, and notes and pictures were held by magnets to the front of a vintage fridge. There was a wood-burning stove in one corner, and an old, scarred oak table covered with schoolbooks.

The uneasiness returned. He thought of those wonders of granite and steel that people wanted for their kitchens these days, that he designed, and suddenly he knew what the uneasiness was. They somehow had all missed the mark.

For all the awards that decorated the walls of his office, he had never achieved *this*. A feeling.

He shook it off, looked back at Nora. The caption under her high school yearbook picture had probably read "Least likely to bamboozle an old woman out of her money."

But somebody had. The nephew? The kid practically had a neon sign over his head that flashed Guilty, but on the other hand, didn't all kids that age look like that? Slinky and defensive and as if they had just finished committing a crime?

What surprised Brendan was that he was interested at all in who did it. And if it was her nephew, to what lengths she would go to protect him.

But that's what happened when you came alive. Life, the interactions of people, their relationships and motivations interested you.

It was a wound waiting to happen, he warned himself.

"Put the cat there." Nora pointed to a kitchen island, a marble top fastened to solid wooden legs, and he set the cat carrier down, surreptitiously checking the bottom for any dampness that might have transferred to the seat of his new car.

He knew it said something about the kind of person he was that he was relieved to find none.

"He's been very sick," Deedee said. "Just like I told you in the letter."

"Maybe you could remind me what you wrote in your letter."

In the light of the kitchen, Brendan could see a knob

growing alarmingly on Nora's forehead. She was wet
and covered in mud.

And Brendan Grant was surprised there was a part
of him that still knew the right thing to do. And was
prepared to do it.

"The cat will have to wait," he heard himself say
firmly, in the tone of voice he used on the construction
site when a carpenter was insisting something couldn't
be done the way he wanted it done.

And the people in the room reacted about the same
way. Deedee swung her head and glared at him. Nora
looked none too happy, either.

"I want to take a look at you," he insisted. "If you
don't need a trip to the emergency ward, you certainly
need a shower and a change of clothes before you check
out the cat."

"I can have a look at the cat first."

So she wanted what he wanted. For this to be quick.
Look at the cat. Tell them what they all already knew
about Charlie's prospects for a future. Of course, what
they wanted parted ways at finding out who was guilty
of taking money from Deedee, and what the consequences were going to be.

Still, handled properly, the whole drama could un-
fold and conclude in about two minutes, in and out.

Heavy on the out part. He wanted to head home and
go back to bed.

His old life—that cave that was comforting in its
lack of intensity, in its palette of grays—beckoned to
him. But it seemed to him that nothing was going to
go quite as he wanted.

Which he hated in and of itself. Because one thing

Brendan Grant wanted, in a world that had already scorned his need for it, was control.

"You first, then the cat," he told Nora.

Deedee, in typical fashion, appeared annoyed that her agenda was being moved to the back of the line. But Nora looked annoyed, too. It told him a lot about her when she folded her arms over his coat.

Independent. Possibly newly so. No one was going to tell her what to do. Brendan wondered again what the pajamas she was so determined to hide looked like.

"You already told me you aren't a doctor," Nora said.

"Doctor or not, a head injury is nothing to take lightly. They can be sneaky and deadly. It will just take me a minute to look at you."

"I'm fine."

"Deadly?" The boy got a panicky pinched look around his eyes. "Let him look at you!"

Nora, seeing his distress, surrendered, sinking onto a kitchen chair with ill grace.

"That was quite a hit to your head. Do you think you were knocked out?" Brendan moved close, brushed her hair away from the rapidly growing bump.

Every part of her seemed to be either wet or covered with mud. How was it her hair felt like silk?

"I'm fine."

"That's not what I asked," he said mildly.

"I don't think I was knocked out." She offered this grumpily.

"But you can't say for sure?"

She didn't want to admit it, but Brendan could tell she didn't remember, which was probably not a good sign.

Nora knew what date it was, her full name and her

birthday. He noted that she was twenty-six, though she looked younger. He also noted, annoyed, that he was interested in her age.

And apparently her marital status. There was no ring on her finger, no signs—large shoes, men's magazines, messes—that would indicate there was any male besides the boy in residence.

Brendan hated that he was awake enough to notice those things, to wonder at her history, what had brought her and her nephew to this remote corner of British Columbia.

Doing his best to detach, he asked more questions. She remembered what had happened right before she was knocked down and right after, though she did not remember precisely what had knocked her down. She could follow the movement of his finger with her eyes.

"You seem fine," he finally decided, but he felt uneasy. A concussion really was nothing to fool around with.

"She is fine," Deedee snapped. "Meanwhile, Charlie could be expiring."

"I'll just have a quick look at the cat," Nora said.

"He's lasted this long. I'm sure he can wait another five minutes. You need to go have a shower and put on something dry."

"Are you always this bossy?"

He ignored her. "If you feel dizzy or if you vomit, or feel like you're going to be sick, you need to tell me right away. Or Luke after I leave. You may have to get to the hospital yet tonight."

She looked as if she was going to protest. And then she glanced down at herself, and surprised him by giving in without a fight.

"All right. Luke, come with me for a minute. You can see if you can find a shirt that will fit Mr. Grant. He's soaked."

That explained her easy acquiescence. She was going to go talk it over with the kid. They were going to get their stories straight and figure out who had done what.

Brendan already knew precisely what she was going to do. She had already started to set it up when she'd said the money had been taken by accident, mistaken for a donation. She was going to take the blame.

Personally, Brendan was strongly leaning toward the conclusion her nephew had done it. How could she possibly think that not letting him accept responsibility was going to do the boy any good?

"Brendan?"

He turned to Deedee, impatient. Was she really going to insist that cat come first again? She did love to have her own way, largely oblivious to the larger picture.

"I'm not feeling well," she said.

He scanned her face. She loved to be the center of attention. But the fear he saw was real.

"My heart's beating too fast," she whispered.

He crossed the room and lifted her frail wrist. Her pulse was going crazy. She searched his face, ready to panic, and he forced himself to smile.

"Let's make it a double header," he said. "We'll take you to the hospital and they can check out Nora at the same time."

He cast Nora a look.

Her protest died on her lips as she read his face and then glanced at Deedee.

"You're right," she said. "I think I need to go to the hospital."

CHAPTER FIVE

AT HIS AUNT's declaration, panic twisted the boy's features, but only for a second. He took in the situation in the room, his gaze lingering on Deedee. Brendan saw calm come to him, almost as if he had breathed in the truth.

"What about Charlie?" Deedee half whispered, half sobbed. "I can't leave him! Not when he's—"

The steadiness remained in the boy's eyes as he looked to Brendan and then his aunt. "I got the cat," he said, and Deedee relaxed noticeably, slumped against Brendan.

Ninety-two. Deedee could die right now. She could go before the cat. Life liked to put ironic little twists in the story line.

Becky, young and healthy, gone at twenty-six. To this day, it seemed impossible.

A week before she had died, she had said to him, out of the blue, "If I die first, I'll come back and let you know I'm all right."

"You won't be all right," he'd said, uncomfortable with the conversation, pragmatic to a fault. "You'll be dead."

So far, she hadn't been back to let him know anything, even how to keep on living. So he'd been right. Dead was dead.

And he'd been prepared to deal with it tonight with Charlie. Not Deedee. Not on his watch. With a sense of urgency he was trying to disguise, and feeling somewhat like the ringmaster at a three-ring circus, Brendan pulled his cell phone from his pocket and herded all his charges back out the door into the rain.

"Can you get in the back with her?" he asked in an undertone. "Kick my seat if anything changes. You know how to monitor her pulse?"

Nora nodded and climbed in the backseat of the car with Deedee. Luke and the cat got in the front with Brendan. The car smelled of new leather and luxury. It screamed a man who had arrived.

The type of man who would never see anything in the slightly eccentric owner of a struggling animal shelter.

Not that she cared who found her attractive and who didn't! Good grief! The lady beside her could be having a heart attack. This was not the time or place!

Starting the car, Brendan never lost focus. He tucked the phone under his ear. "Hansen Emergency? It's Brendan Grant here. I'm on my way in. I have a ninety-two-year-old woman who has a very fast pulse. No history of heart problems. No chest pain. I also have a young woman who has had a head injury. Who's the doctor on call tonight? I know you're not supposed to tell me, but I want to know."

Nora took it all in. How his name had been recognized, how the name of the on-call doctor had been surrendered to him with a token protest only.

She took in his confidence as he dialed another number. "Greg? Sorry to wake you. Becky's grandmother is not well."

Becky? She'd thought it was *his* grandmother!

"Who's Becky?" she asked Deedee.

"My granddaughter. Brendan's her husband."

Married. Why would that feel the way it did? Like some kind of loss? Why didn't he wear a ring? Nora hated married men who didn't wear rings. They were sneaky, they were looking for—

"She died," Deedee said tiredly.

"I'm so sorry," Nora said, and thought of what she was sure she had seen in his eyes when he'd first leaned over her. The common ground. Now she understood it. Sorrow.

"In a car accident," Deedee went on. She was talking too loudly, the way people who are hard of hearing did. "Brendan doesn't talk about her. I need someone to cry with sometimes. But he never will. He didn't even cry at the funeral."

It was said like an accusation, and so loudly the man in the front seat could not miss it. Nora watched his face in the light coming from the dash. He didn't even flinch. It was as if he was cast in stone.

But she had seen the pain spilling into his eyes in that first unguarded moment when he had stood over her in the paddock.

"People all grieve in their own way," Nora said, and saw him cast her a quick glance in the rearview mirror before he reached for his phone again. "And it seems to me maybe he's there for you in other ways that are just as important."

Not everyone would be chauffeuring an elderly

woman and her sick cat around the country in the middle of the night!

"Of course, you're right," Deedee murmured, and leaned her head on Nora's shoulder. Nora had her hand on the woman's wrist and noticed, gratefully, the pulse was slowing to normal.

She listened to the deep gravel of Brendan's voice as he spoke on the phone.

"And I have a head injury, too. I think mild concussion, but a confirmation would be good. See you there. We're five minutes out."

He clicked the phone shut and stepped on the gas. The night was wet and the roads had to be slippery, but he oozed calm confidence as he navigated the twisty, mist-shrouded road into Hansen. The powerful car responded as if it were a living thing.

The way a man handled a powerful car told you a lot about him. The way a man handled an emergency told you a lot as well. Not that they were tests, but had they been, Brendan Grant would have passed with flying colors.

His calm never flagged. Not on the wet roads, not as they pulled into Emergency, not as he helped his grandmother out of the back of the car. There were obviously benefits to being emotionally shut down.

"What about Charlie?" Deedee wailed again.

"I'll stay with him," Luke said. "Out here. I'm not going in there."

Nora doubted that he was ever going to get over the thing he had about hospitals. He'd spent too much time in one while his mother was sick. He hated them now.

Brendan didn't question why, just flipped a set of keys at Luke. "Her house is three blocks that way. The address is on the chain. I presume you have your cell phone with you and that your aunt has the number?"

"Why can't I stay here?"

"Because if that cat pees in my car," he said in a low tone that Deedee didn't hear, "it really isn't going to survive the night."

Nora was appalled, but it was a guy thing, because Luke chuckled. Then he sobered. "You're trusting me to go into her house?"

Brendan's eyes locked on his. "Is there any reason I shouldn't?"

Luke ducked his head and didn't say anything.

"I don't know how long we'll be here. Get some rest. Let the cat out of that purse, near his litter box if you can locate it. If your aunt is released, you're going to have to look after her for the rest of the night."

Luke glanced at the address on the key chain. "I hope none of my friends see me with this dorky thing," he muttered, but Nora did not miss the fact that he looked pleased—if somewhat guilty—about Brendan's trust.

"I could drive him," she said tentatively, "and come back. I really don't need—"

Brendan gave her a look that was so don't-mess-with-me it made her stomach feel as if it was doing a free fall from ten thousand feet. She just didn't have the energy to take him on.

In the hospital, she had that same sense that you could tell a lot about a man by the way he handled an emergency. Again he passed. He handled the nurse with confidence that was palatable, not the least intimidated by her officiousness. In fact, the exact opposite might have been true. He was obviously well-known in the community, and respected. The nurse treated Brendan as if he was part of that inner circle of the emergency ward.

Interestingly, Vance had been terrible at emergencies. He became so flustered if a badly injured animal was brought in that he could not inspire confidence in anyone. You would have thought with practice he would have gotten better, but he never did. He liked catering to the pudgy poodle set, doing routine checkups and giving shots, neutering, and cleaning teeth.

In fact, he'd opted for regular hours only and hired a young vet to handle the nighttime emergencies, and finally any emergency at all.

A few weeks ago, Nora had heard he was engaged to that young vet. Up until then she had nursed a secret fantasy that he was going to show up on her doorstep, confess the error of his ways and beg her to take him back.

She shook it off. For whatever the reason—she suspected because Brendan Grant made things happen—she found herself ushered into an examination room in record time.

In short order, a young doctor was in, a nurse at his side.

"How's Mrs. Ashton?" Nora asked.

"Old," he said with a resigned smile. "We're going to keep her for observation. So, Brendan says a bump on the head? Maybe knocked out?"

"Maybe," Nora admitted.

"How do you know Brendan?" he asked.

"It's a long story."

The doctor laughed. "That's what he said. He designed our house and supervised the build. He's an amazing architect."

Great! In her weakened state, Nora just had to know Brendan Grant was an all-around phenomenal guy.

The doctor repeated some of the questions Brendan had asked her earlier, shone a light in her eye, got her to follow the movement of his finger.

"I should keep you for observation, too."

"I can't!" she said. "I have animals that will need feeding in—" her eyes flew to a nearby clock "—two hours."

The doctor sighed. "He said you'd say that. I'm going to send you home, but with strict instructions what to watch for. And what to do for the next few hours. Any dizziness, any nausea, any loss of consciousness, you come right back in. I'll give you a handout with symptoms you need to watch for over the next few days. Sometimes even weeks later symptoms can come up."

After having the nurse go over the sheet with her, they let her go. Brendan was in the waiting room.

"You didn't have to wait."

"Uh-huh. How were you going to get home? And collect your nephew?"

"Taxi, I guess."

"And would the taxi driver be watching you for signs of concussion?" Brendan held up duplicates of the instructions the doctor had given her.

The truth was she was glad she did not have to worry about a taxi right now, or how to find Luke. She was glad this man was in charge. And she might have a concussion, so it was okay to be weak. Just this once. Just for tonight.

The animals needed to be fed in a few hours.

She felt like weeping.

Brendan was watching her closely.

"Are you okay?"

"Yes," she said firmly.

But just as if he hadn't heard her, he slipped his arm around her waist, and just as if she hadn't claimed she was okay, she leaned heavily into him.

They collected Luke and, since no one had any idea when Deedee would be home, recaptured Charlie. Nora tried to stay awake and couldn't. She awoke to find herself in Brendan Grant's arms for the second time that night.

There was absolutely no fight left in her.

None.

Because Luke was bringing Charlie into the house instead of out to the barn. She didn't allow any of the animals in the house. How could she? If she did, soon they would be overrun!

But she just didn't have the energy to make a fuss about it right now. Instead, she snuggled deep into Brendan's reassuring strength and let him carry her into her house and up the stairs to her room.

"Is she okay?" Luke asked, pointing Brendan to a room on the right of a narrow hallway. He disappeared with Charlie and the cat carrier into a doorway farther up the hall.

"She's just done in," Brendan assured him. He nudged open the door and hesitated on the threshold of Nora's room.

It was confirmed she was completely, one hundred percent single. No man could be trusted with so much white: white walls, white curtains, white pillows, white bedspread. Her room reminded him of innocence. There was something alarmingly bridal about it.

And that was the last thing Brendan wanted to be thinking of as he carried Nora Anderson across the threshold!

He looked down at her and felt a wave of relief. Still wrapped in his too large jacket, mud from head to toe, she was the world's least likely bride. In fact, her bridal vision of a room was about to be damaged by her muddy little self.

Brendan took a deep breath, stepped in, and quickly made his way to the bed, where he set her on the edge.

Luke appeared in the doorway. "Anything I can do?"

"Oh, Luke," Nora said. "Where did he come from? You know the rules. We can't have animals in the house."

Brendan turned, expecting to see Luke had Charlie. Instead, he had a black-and-white kitten riding in the palm of his hand.

"This one's different," Luke said. "I'm calling him Ranger."

"We don't name them!"

Luke looked mutinous. "I'm keeping him. For my own."

Nora chewed her lip. "We need to talk about that," she said.

"But not tonight," Brendan said firmly. "Luke, can you get rid of the kitten for now, and find me a flashlight?"

He disappeared and came back, with no kitten, but a flashlight.

"Shine it right in your aunt's eyes. Do you see what it does to her pupils? That's called dilation. It's very important that both her pupils are dilating in the same way. I need you to try it."

The boy grasped the flashlight without any hesitation. Brendan was going to take it as a good sign that Luke was not nearly as rebellious as his aunt was.

"Yes, her eyes are doing the same thing. The black part is getting smaller when I hold the light up."

"Don't talk about me like I'm not here!"

"Good. That's exactly what you are looking for. You need to wake her up every hour after I leave and check her eyes. If you see a change you need to call 9-1-1."

"There's no need to frighten him!" Nora protested.

"I'm not frightening him. I'm asking him to step up to the plate. I'm treating him like a man."

Luke puffed up a bit at that.

"Well, he's not a man."

And then deflated.

"He's not a child, either."

The boy puffed up again.

"Either he checks you or I stay for the night."

She blanched at that, then folded her arms over her chest with ill grace and glared at him. That settled, Brendan conducted some very simple tests on his unwilling patient while Luke watched.

"The doctor already did this."

"Luke needs to see what to do."

Finally, Brendan was satisfied. "Do you need anything? A drink of warm milk, maybe?"

"Oh."

There was something kind of sweet and kind of sad about her surprise that anyone would look after her.

"That would be nice," she said shyly.

"Luke, can you go warm some milk?"

Luke left and Brendan leaned over and pulled off her shoes. Gently, he tugged the jacket off her.

"I can do it!"

"It's not as if you're in a see-through negligee."

She scowled at him, but let him free each of her limbs from the jacket.

He pretended not to notice her pajama top at all, but it was adorable. How was it a pink pajama top with kittens on it that said Purrfectly Purrfect Me could be more sexy than a negligee?

"Stand up for a minute," he ordered. She did, and he deftly pulled back the white quilt. Surprise, surprise, pure white sheets.

He guided her under the covers. She sank into her bed, then struggled to sit up. "Set the alarm. I have to be up. I have to feed the animals in two hours."

The clock was holding down some papers on a bed-side table. He could tell now wouldn't be the best time to relate what the doctor had told him. She had to rest. Completely. For at least twenty-four hours. She wasn't even supposed to look at a computer screen or read. So he pretended to set the clock.

He looked back at the bed, and her eyes were already closed, her breath coming out in soft puffs.

So much for the warm milk.

He went and looked at her. He felt the oddest desire to kiss her, not passionately, but a good-night kiss, like a father might give a child. Protective. Happy she was safe.

Happy he had managed to keep at least one person safe from the perils of life.

Brendan went down the steps. The kitchen was empty; no milk was out or on the stove. Luke was stretched out on the living room couch.

The empty carrier was beside him, and Charlie, a cat

who hated both animal and man equally, was stretched out over the boy's chest. The black-and-white kitten, Ranger, was curled into Charlie's belly. They were all fast asleep.

Brendan moved closer. Charlie didn't even look like the same cat. He certainly didn't sound like it. The death rattle Brendan had heard earlier was gone.

Maybe he had died. Brendan reached out uneasily and touched him. The cat's fur was warm beneath his fingertips and the animal sighed.

He yanked his hand back. There was no such thing as a healer, he told himself, annoyed. Nora had barely glanced at the cat, anyway.

The boy's cell phone was on the coffee table, and Brendan picked it up and checked. Sure enough, Luke had set the alarm to go off every hour on the hour. But the boy couldn't be trusted to cook milk. Besides, he looked exhausted, with dark circles under his eyes, his face pale and taut, even in sleep.

Brendan suddenly knew he couldn't leave them alone with this.

He could feel it. Around the boy. And around her. They'd both been carrying it for too long.

Brendan flicked through the settings on the phone, turned off the alarm and slowly climbed back up the stairs to Nora's room.

CHAPTER SIX

OUTSIDE THE DOOR of that terrifyingly bridal bedroom, Brendan flicked open his own cell phone.

Logically, he knew he could not take this on right now. He had a deadline coming up. Village on the Lake was an amazing opportunity, and he knew the condo project would be the most prestigious of his career to date.

But once before he had chosen work when there was another choice to be made. He had been driven by his need to succeed, driven to outrun the ghosts of his own childhood, driven to be worthy of a wife who came from far different circumstances than he had.

He had needed to be something, or prove something, to have something he didn't have, and he had made a choice that had left him with nothing at all.

That choice had left his heart trapped behind a wall, in a yawning cavern of emptiness.

Could you come to the same fork in the road again? And make a different choice? Not one that would change what had been, nor could alter what had already transpired, but one that changed who you could be?

He shook off the thoughts, finished dialing. His secretary's voice came over the answering machine.

"You've reached Grant Architects. We can't take your call right now, but we'll get back to you as soon as we can."

"Linda, I won't be in today." Added to all the work that Nora and her nephew undoubtedly did themselves, Deedee was in the hospital. She would need company. And word-search books and updates on Charlie. Brendan had no doubt she would be the world's most impatient patient.

"There is a possibility—" horrible as it was, he recognized it was a real possibility "—that I might not be in this week. Send—" he named a junior architect "—to supervise the Village."

And then he closed his cell phone and contemplated the magnitude of what he had just done. He didn't miss work. Not ever.

And then, anticipating it would start ringing right at seven—with fires to be put out, clients, construction site foremen, Linda protesting time off was impossible—he shut it completely off.

He knew there were going to be a lot of questions about his absence. Saying it was uncharacteristic was an understatement.

There were going to be a lot of questions.

And he was not at all sure he had any answers. Because niggling at the back of his mind was the thought that he didn't want to be there when they broke ground on Village on the Lake. He didn't want to be there as his plan took on life. He already knew that his feeling of dissatisfaction would grow in proportion to the buildings taking shape, becoming more and more real.

He slid through the door of the bedroom. There was a chair—white, of course—beside her bed and he took it, a bit guiltily, because his clothes were a little the worse for wear also. He was tempted to put his cell phone back on to use the alarm, just as Luke had intended to do.

And then Brendan was annoyed with himself that he had lasted less than a minute without wanting to rely on his cell phone, so stubbornly didn't turn it back on.

It was part of that relentless busyness that had helped him survive. Just like putting even more ungodly hours in at work than he had before the accident.

Something in him *wanted* to stop. That astounded him. Something in him wanted to rest, and be introspective.

Was part of him ready to heal, to crawl back into the light, shielding his eyes from the brilliance? And maybe, just maybe, was this a place where things like that happened? Where something that was dead in a man could be resurrected?

Maybe it was. Look at that cat down there.

Honestly, Brendan could not believe he was entertaining such thoughts—totally unfounded in any kind of science, totally whimsical, the magical thinking of a little boy.

Mommy, I'm going to buy you a castle someday. I promise.

The memory of those words shook him, and he shivered as though someone had walked across his grave. Hadn't he known from the minute he had driven under that sign that things were about to go sideways?

Annoyed with himself, he sought refuge in the way he always had, but on a point of pride would not turn on his phone to check the weather or the stock report. He prowled restlessly. Starting with the virginal whiteness, the room told him things about her that she might have preferred he didn't know.

There was a picture of her and Luke on her dresser. But none of a man. There was a stack of bills there, too. Why would she have those in her room, unless she wanted to worry over them in private, protect the boy from anxiety?

There was a laundry basket on the floor, full of neatly folded items. She would have been devastated that her underwear was on top. It reminded him of her pajamas, utilitarian, not sexy. There was no jewelry on the dresser, no nod to that feminine longing for the pretty and the frivolous.

If he was a man who felt things, he might have felt a little sad for her and what the room told him about her. Snowed under with responsibility, alone, and sworn off the small pleasure of celebrating her own prettiness.

And then his eyes went to the papers stuck under the alarm clock. They looked like letters, and he shifted over and cut his eyes to them. He wasn't going to read personal mail.

Only they didn't look personal. In fact, the letter on top began "Dear Rover."

Intrigued, remembering Deedee had said something about Nora being *Ask Rover,* he picked up the letter.

"Dear Rover," he read, "I have a new boyfriend. He is everything I ever dreamed of. Handsome. Funny. He has a good job. There is only one problem. I have a thirteen-year-old malamute cross named Sigh. They hate each other. What should I do?" It was signed "Confused."

The handwriting changed. Though still feminine, it was Rover's—make that Nora's—response, Brendan realized. Further intrigued, he saw she had answered and then crossed it all out. He took the chair next to the bed and squinted to read through the scribbles.

Dear Confused,
Though dogs are capable of such emotions as jealousy, quite often they are better judges of character than human beings. What effort has your prince made to win over your dog? Has your new love been sensitive to the fact your dog is aging, and you might have to soon say good-bye? Has he done one single thing to make that moment easier for you? I'm afraid, from a dog's point of view, he sounds like a jerk. I think you would be better off without him. I am not sure I could be trusted not to bite him, possibly in a place that would make it difficult for him to reproduce. Thank you for your question, though really questions where the answers are of such a life-altering nature might be better answered by your best friend, your mother or your priest. Best barks, Rover.

This was crossed out, but it seemed to him with a certain reluctance.

Brendan felt his lips twitching. He flipped to the next page.

Dear Confused,
Thirteen is very old for a malamute. Do you want to make such a weighty decision based on a dog who will not be with you much longer?

This, too, had been crossed out.

He flipped the page, looking for her answer, but instead found a different letter.

Dear Rover,
My dog, an English bulldog named Petunia, won't come in the basement laundry room. She sits outside the door and howls and shakes. Do you think I have a ghost? —Haunted

Again, there were two replies. The first, with a big X through it, said:

Dear Haunted,
English bulldogs are known for many lovely traits, intelligence not being among those. Your laundry room is unlikely to be haunted so much as presenting a myriad of smells and sounds beyond poor Petunia's ability to comprehend them. This situation is unlikely to ever get better, so you could save yourself a great deal of frustration by leaving Petunia upstairs while you go to the basement to do laundry. If you give her a chew bone before you go, there is a good chance she won't notice you are gone until you get back.

The second response was measured, and made no comments about the intelligence of bulldogs. It explained that laundry rooms had strange sounds and smells, that Petunia needed to be introduced to the elements separately and slowly, and that dog treats would help.

Still smiling, Brendan set the papers back on the table.

It penetrated his exhaustion that something was different than when he'd arrived.

For a moment he couldn't figure out what it was.

And then he did: it was absolutely quiet. He got up and went to the window. It wasn't just that night was melting into daybreak. The rain had stopped. And on the horizon was something he hadn't seen for forty days and forty nights.

He blinked like a man emerging from a cave.

Or maybe he hadn't seen it since the night his wife and his unborn child had died.

On the horizon, the sun was coming up.

"Hey, sweetheart, what's your name?"

Nora shook herself groggily. She stared up at the man looking at her, felt his hand on her shoulder.

"Not sweetheart," she said, certain it was a dream and closed her eyes.

That hand on her shoulder, a light in her eyes, "what day were you born?" and then wonderful sleep claiming her again.

"Just for a second, follow my finger with your eyes."

Nora awoke with a start. Sunshine splashed across her bed. Sunshine! The warmth of it was a delight.

All night she had had strange dreams that Brendan Grant was in her room, but now she glanced at the chair where she was sure he had sat, and could clearly see it had been but a dream. The chair was empty.

Sunshine! She looked at the clock. It was noon!

"Oh goodness! The animals!" She sat up too quickly and it made her feel dizzy. She was aware her head hurt, and other parts of her felt bruised.

How was it possible to feel so good, filled with wonderful dreams, and so bad at the same time? Physically aching, sick that she had slept through looking after her animals.

She lay back down, just for a moment.

"Hey."

Brendan Grant was standing in her doorway. Despite the fact he was in the same shirt as last night, and it had been wet, and dried wrinkled, and his hair was rumpled and his face becoming shadowed with whiskers, he looked amazing. Handsome, oozing confidence, one of those superannoying guys who took charge.

Superannoying unless you happened to be in need of someone to take charge!

"Don't sit up. Doctor's orders. You have to rest. All day."

She couldn't let on for a single second that, in her weakened state, she found that take-charge attitude ever so slightly attractive.

"I can't rest all day! I have to look after the animals."

"I've got it covered."

She scowled at him so he would never guess how much those words meant to her.

"You sat with me all night," she said. She knew she should be appreciative. It came out sounding like an accusation.

"I did."

"That's an unexpected kindness to the stranger you think swindled your grandmother."

"I was hoping you'd talk in your sleep."

"Did I?" she asked, aghast.

"What are you afraid of? A confession? Don't you remember? I asked you questions every time I woke you up."

"Yeah, like what my name was. And my birthday."

He slapped himself on the forehead. "Shoot. I didn't take advantage."

For some reason she blushed, as if he meant taking advantage in a different way. He lifted an eyebrow.

"I didn't take advantage like that, either," he said softly.

"I wasn't suggesting you had," she said primly. Feeling terribly vulnerable, she pulled her quilt up around her chin. "If you'll excuse me, I need to get dressed. I need to look after my animals."

"They're all looked after."

"But how?"

"Luke helped."

"Oh," she said uneasily. She didn't really like the thought of Brendan being alone with Luke, interrogating him.

"Don't worry, he didn't tell me a thing."

She didn't like that she was transparent, either!

"Even though I shamelessly tried to pry information out of him."

"About?" she asked, attempting a careless tone.

"I started small, building up to the big question. I asked where you were from, and he said from a nice place, not a dump like this. I asked how long you had been here, and he said too long, and I asked how old he was and he said nineteen."

"We're from Victoria, we've been here six months and he just turned fifteen."

"Then I asked him who took the money from Deedee."

She held her breath.

"He said lots of people open the mail. The place is

practically overrun with volunteers. He said he thought some of those old ladies were pretty shifty looking." Brendan was watching her way too closely. "Are they?"

She felt backed into a corner. Of course her volunteers were not shifty looking! But she wasn't calling Luke a liar, either. She fidgeted with the quilt and didn't answer.

"I thought I'd better find out for myself who looked shifty. So I had Luke call some of them to come help with morning chores. Funny, I can't really see any of the ones who showed up stealing from my grandmother, but I interrogated them, anyway."

"You did not," she said skeptically.

"I did. They all admitted to opening mail. None of them looked guilty, though. None of them remembered a letter from my grandmother. Of course, I'm not sure any of them would have remembered what they had for breakfast this morning. Don't you have a system for dealing with mail? It doesn't seem very efficient that anyone who feels like it, or wanders by the mailbox, opens the letters."

"Systems are not my strong suit."

"Neither is volunteer selection. If the ones who showed up today are any indication, it's kind of like having my grandmother for a volunteer. The old biddy brigade."

Now he sounded like Luke!

"They are invaluable to me!" The truth was Nora needed some young, strong people to volunteer, but they just weren't who showed up when she put an ad in the paper. She hated it that the weaknesses in her organization were so blatantly apparent to him after an hour or two.

"But you can't let any of your current volunteers near a large animal. They can't do any heavy work. One's afraid of dogs and one is allergic to cats. They all hate the parrot. Who bites."

"That's Lafayette. Did he bite you?"

"Of course he bit me. Luke says he bites everyone. Before saying things that would make a sailor blush. In three languages."

"Did you put antiseptic on it?"

"Who's looking after who?"

He was gazing at her keenly. She had sounded way too much like she cared. He was a tyrant, obviously. He'd waltzed in here and completely taken over. She couldn't just let him!

"I don't want to get sued. After infection sets in and your finger falls off. Then you sue me, and at your recommendation, I've lose the funding from the Hansen Community Betterment Committee."

"I haven't decided about a recommendation to the HCBC. Yet."

"And please don't alienate all my volunteers."

"I couldn't alienate your volunteers if I tried, and believe me, I did. But oh, no, they came around the barn after me, promising me cookies, brownies and roast beef dinner. And talking about what a nice girl you are. And available. 'What a shame. No boyfriend. And so pretty, too.'"

"I don't have a boyfriend because I don't want one," Nora told him, and felt a crimson blush go up her cheeks.

"Some jerk broke your heart," Brendan said, and his tone was light, but his eyes were not. They darkened with a menace that made her gasp.

He was seeing way too much, and it had to stop!

"Get out of my room. I need to shower and get dressed."

He sighed theatrically. "It's as hard to pry information out of you as it is out of your nephew. Do you need help?"

Her mouth fell open. She gasped like a fish on a bank.

He laughed, backed into the hall, his hands in cowboy surrender, and shut the door. But he had to get in the last word.

"If you're dizzy or feel like you're going to vomit, call me. Even if you're naked."

CHAPTER SEVEN

NORA WAS GLAD Brendan Grant was on the other side of that door and couldn't see her face. *Even if she was naked?*

He was trying to shock her, and she was not going to give him the satisfaction of responding.

"Especially if you're naked," he called through the door.

So much for not giving him satisfaction. Nora picked up her shoe from where he had pulled it off her foot last night. She hurled it at the door and heard his hoot of pleasure that he had gotten to her.

She looked around her bedroom. Her world felt like a big mess, with chaos everywhere! Even her beautiful Egyptian cotton sheets, one of the things she had treated herself to before she became guardian to a very expensive fifteen-year-old, were dirty. Her sense of messiness increased when she went into the en suite bathroom and saw herself in the mirror.

Her hair, face and clothes were smudged with mud. She looked like a terrible cross between a cast member of *Oliver* and, with the lump rising over her eye, Quasimodo. Luckily, she told herself, she was not in the market for a man, and especially not a man like the one who had totally invaded her world.

Still, it did not feel lucky at all that *that* man was intent on invading her world when she looked like this! Somehow around a guy like that, a woman— any woman, even one newly sworn to fierce independence—wanted to look her best.

She desperately needed these moments to collect herself. The water of the shower was an absolute balm. She told herself it wasn't weakness that made her apply the subtlest hint of makeup. It was an effort to regain some confidence. And hide her bruises. And erase first impressions!

After showering and applying makeup, with far more care than she would have wanted to admit, Nora chose a flattering shirt, short-sleeved and summery as a nod to the sun finally making an appearance, and designer jeans, remnants of her old life when she'd bought designer things for herself and never worried about money.

She convinced herself the makeover worked. She convinced herself she felt like a new woman.

She felt ready to battle for her independence! Ready to fight any inclination to lean on another!

Brendan was alone in her kitchen. She paused in the darkness of the hallway before he knew she was there.

Despite her vow to be unaffected by him, it was hard not to take advantage of that moment to study him.

There was no doubt about it. Brendan Grant was a devastatingly attractive man with that dark hair and matching eyes, the slashing brows and straight nose and strong chin. He radiated a subtle masculine strength, a confidence in himself that was not in any way changed by the fact he was in a wrinkled shirt or his hair was roughed or the planed hollows of his cheeks were darkening with whiskers.

The annoying fact was her kitchen was improved by a man standing at the counter, supremely comfortable in his own skin, eating cookies.

"Sorry," he said, when he saw her. "I helped myself."

"No, that's good. I should have told you to make yourself at home."

But she was stunned by the longing that statement awakened in her. A man like this making himself at home? The image somehow deepened her definition of home, made it richer and more complex, and filled her with yearning.

She recouped quickly. "Speaking of which, you need to go home. You must be exhausted. And want a shower. And a change of clothes. And don't you need to check on your grandmother?"

"But who is going to make sure you don't do anything you're not supposed to do?"

"Luke will. Where is Luke?"

Brendan nodded toward the living room, and she went and peeked. Luke was sitting on the sofa, feet on the coffee table, head nodding against his chest. Charlie was sprawled out across his belly, kneading, the way contented cats do. The kitten was perched on his shoulder, batting at a strand of his hair, and Luke swatted it as if a fly was bothering him in his sleep.

"If only such cuteness could last," she said ruefully.

Brendan came and stood beside her. She could feel his presence, even though he didn't touch her, energy tingling off him.

"Ditto for Charlie," he said. "It's not as if he's a nice

cat. He's waited under Deedee's sofa and attacked my ankles. You think that doesn't make you nervous?"

Brendan chuckled. And so did Nora. It was a small thing. A shared moment of amusement. It made her need to get rid of him even more urgent.

As if he sensed the danger of the moment as acutely as she had, he frowned. "Charlie seems way better than he was last night. Are you, er, doing something?"

"No. There's nothing to do, I'm afraid. How old is he?"

"Seventeen, I think."

"That's pretty old for a cat," she said carefully.

"I think so, too. Unfortunately, Deedee has a friend whose cat made it to twenty-three."

"I wouldn't tell her Charlie is feeling better," Nora suggested.

She knew it was an opportunity for him to make a crack about her missing an opportunity to get some more money out of Deedee, but he didn't take it.

"Okay, I won't tell her. Though it is obvious, even to me, a tried-and-true cynic, that he is feeling better." He added, "I'm going. Do not do a single thing today. Do you hear me?"

"Are you always so masterful?" she said, raising an eyebrow, unimpressed.

"Why?" he asked softly. "Do you like masterful?"

"No!" She'd better be careful. She didn't have a shoe handy to throw. Instead, she quickly changed tack. "I'll catch up on some of my inside things."

She was giving in just a little, to make him go.

"You're not even supposed to read. Except your symptom sheet, which tells you not to read. And don't use the computer. No answering *Ask Rover*."

She stiffened. "What do you know about *Ask Rover?*"

"There were some letters beside your bed."

"You read my mail!"

"It was lying out. I had to think of a way to stay awake. Sorry." He didn't sound contrite.

She *hated* that he knew.

And then she didn't.

Because he said, "I liked the first response better. The dog knew the guy was a jerk." And Brendan smiled at her, as if he actually *liked* it that she was *Ask Rover*. "Is that the one you'll use? About biting him where it counts?"

Nora could feel her face getting very red. That had not been meant for anyone to see.

"No," she said, "it won't be."

"That's a shame."

And it sounded as if he meant it!

"I'll be back," he said.

"No!"

That sounded way too vehement.

"You've done enough," she amended hastily. "I'm very appreciative. Really. But I can take it from here."

"Uh-huh," he said, without an ounce of conviction. He gave her one long look, and then patted her shoulder and was gone.

And suddenly she was alone, in a house that was changed in some subtle and irrevocable way because he had spent the night in her bedroom and eaten cookies at her kitchen counter.

And just as she had a secret side that answered letters to *Ask Rover* exactly the way she wanted to, she had a secret side that listened to his car start up and said,

Usually when a man spends the night something a little more exciting happens! Maybe next time.

"There isn't going to be a next time," she informed her secret side.

But, of course, there was. Because he had said he was coming back, and he did. One of the volunteers must have told him when they did evening chores and feeding, because he was there promptly at seven. Nora peered out the living room window at him getting out of his car.

He was dressed more appropriately, in a plaid jacket, and jeans tucked into rubber boots. Really, the ready-to-grub-out-pens outfit should have made Brendan less attractive. And didn't. At all.

Nora breathed a sigh of relief when he made no move toward the house. Luke, bless his heart, was already at the barns. She was glad to be rid of him, too. He had absolutely hovered all day, Charlie in his arms and Ranger on his heels.

She knew, somehow, she should have insisted he take the cats with him when he went to do chores, and leave them in the barn, but she hadn't.

Charlie didn't like her, and had retreated under the sofa as soon as Luke left, then slunk off up the stairs, probably to Luke's room. It didn't matter. She didn't have to lay her hands on him to know his life force was leeching out of him. The antics of the kitten entertained her, but didn't occupy her enough for her to outrun her own thoughts.

Which let her know her relief that Brendan had headed for the barns instead of the house was pretended relief. Part of her wanted him to come up here. Which probably explained why she was still in the designer jeans and top, and not her pj's despite a full day of doing nothing.

Unless you counted catching up on movies. She scowled at the TV. Since he'd arrived—since she knew he was out there—she had no idea what was going on in the movie.

Then she heard them coming. She felt like a high school girl waiting for her prom date. She checked her buttons. Ran a hand through her hair. Tried to pull her bangs over the bump on her forehead. She tried to decide how to sit so that it looked as if she was completely surprised and a little bored by the fact Brendan was coming to her house.

Luke let him in, so he didn't knock.

And then he was standing there, filling her space, gazing at her, and her silly heart was beating way too hard.

"How are you feeling?" he asked.

If she told him the truth about her racing pulse, she'd probably be whisked off to the hospital, just as Deedee had been. "Bored."

He looked past her to the TV. "What movie?"

Why hadn't she thought of that when she was preparing to see him again?

She snapped it off. "Something silly. I just turned it on to keep from going crazy."

"Uh-huh."

"It's that pirate one," Luke said, coming back with Charlie. "It's for babies, but she's seen it three times. Because of Johnny Jose." He rolled his eyes disparagingly.

Brendan's lips were twitching as if her crush on

Johnny Jose was amusing. "So you're feeling all right? No signs of dizziness? Not feeling sick?"

"I'm fine." If he said uh-huh she was going to scream. Instead he stuck his hands in his pockets and rocked back on his heels and studied her. She tilted her chin defiantly.

"This is cool, Auntie Nora. Brendan gave the old lady a tablet so she can see some video of Charlie while she's in the hospital."

How, exactly, could you steel yourself against something like that?

Or what followed. Luke put down Charlie, got out a piece of string and tied a lump of hay to it. "This is a mouse," he narrated. Then he pulled it across the floor.

The black-and-white kitten exploded across the room after the hay. Luke shouted with laughter. It was the most animated she had seen her nephew in a long, long time. And then he went and dangled the string in front of the couch, where Charlie had retreated.

A ginger paw came out and swatted. Then swatted again. Then both paws shot out, and Charlie grabbed the "mouse" with such strength he pulled it from Luke's hand, yanking it under the couch with him.

Brendan lowered the phone that he had been recording the scene with, and stared at the place where Charlie had disappeared. "That is like the old Charlie," he said uneasily, "the one who likes to attack ankles."

"Did you get it?" Luke asked, then sighed. "Not that Mrs. Ashton will be able to figure out how to open it. Auntie Nora wouldn't be able to."

Why don't you just tell him all my secrets? Crush on Johnny Jose. Computer illiterate. Ask Rover. *He's going to know me better than I know myself if this keeps up.*

Brendan still looked faintly dazed. "I'll go see Deedee and make sure she got it. I can show her on my phone if she didn't figure it out. I'll be back first thing tomorrow for chores."

Nora opened her mouth to protest. First, she didn't think it was a good idea for him to show that footage to Deedee. Second, she didn't think he should come back here.

But she saw Luke's quick look of pleasure before he masked it by snaring the mouse from under the couch and getting Ranger going again.

He liked Brendan. He wanted to believe the cat was getting better. Couldn't she just let life ride, for once?

"Good job with the horses," Brendan said to Luke. "Remember not to let your aunt anywhere near them. And be sure and check her one more night. Can you do that?"

"You had me at the deadly part," Luke said, glancing up from the kitten, and he and Brendan exchanged a grin.

Three days later, Brendan was still showing up to do chores. Nora had started to do a pretty good job of hiding out, which was necessary because chores always finished with Brendan and Luke coming to the house to produce a new video of Charlie. Not only was the aging cat alive and well, but he seemed to be improving.

Deedee was home from the hospital, but confined to bed. She was so impressed with the changes in Charlie she hoped to leave him at Nora's Ark a bit longer.

But enough was enough! Nora was completely recovered. Really, there had been nothing to recover from.

A whole lot of fuss about nothing.

And she'd had enough of hiding out in her own

home. It was time to tell Brendan Grant, nicely, that he had to exit her life. Goodbye. Nice meeting you. Get lost. Could he take Deedee's cat home to her at the same time?

Charlie was in the house. Luke was getting way too attached to him—he seemed to like him even more than the kitten—and Nora seemed to be the only one determined to remember that there was going to be no happy ending for the old cat.

It was way too obvious to her that there were no happy endings, period, and it was a crazy thing to hope for.

She wasn't hiding out today. She was waiting in the living room, her plan firmly in place. She was getting rid of them—the cat and Brendan Grant. And at the same time, she was getting rid of this part of her that wanted so desperately to attach itself to the possibility of happy endings.

She rehearsed from the moment she heard his car. *Thanks so much. Quite capable. Very independent. Lots of volunteers. No room for the cat. Vamoose, both of you.*

And then the door opened, and Luke and Brendan didn't come into her space so much as they spilled into it, like sunshine piercing the dark. Brendan's head was cocked to Luke. She heard his low laugh at something her nephew said.

Her plan faltered.

Brendan Grant was here to help. She wasn't sure if he had intended to help her nephew, but it was certainly a possibility. Look how good he was with his grandmother. Still, whether it had been his intention or not, she saw subtle changes in Luke with this positive daily male influence.

When, she wondered, had she become this woman? So interested in protecting herself that she thought she didn't have to show one speck of gratitude to someone who was helping her. And helping that tiny two-person unit that was her family.

She was Luke's main role model. She had a responsibility. Was that what she wanted to teach him about life? Protect yourself at all costs?

So what if she found Brendan attractive? Surely she could control herself! It would be akin to meeting Johnny. You wouldn't be helpless. You wouldn't throw yourself at him. You wouldn't embarrass yourself or him.

You would act as though your heart was not beating a mile a minute. As though you were a mature woman capable of great grace and confidence.

You would step up to him and look him in the eye. And smile.

"Hi, Brendan," she heard herself say, calm and mature, a woman she could be proud of. "Thanks so much for all your help around here. I really appreciate it."

That would have been good enough. More than good enough.

So why did she have to add, "I made lasagna tonight. There's extra. Do you want some?"

"Aunt Nora makes the best lasagna. Lots of cheese," Luke said, and his hope that Brendan would stay was somehow heartbreaking.

Too late, Nora wondered what she was letting them in for.

Particularly when Brendan said, "It would take a better man than me to turn down homemade lasagna. Especially the kind with lots of cheese."

CHAPTER EIGHT

WHAT THE HELL was he doing? Brendan asked himself as he sat at Nora's table for the second night in a row. Lasagna last night. Meat loaf tonight.

"You wanna stay and play Scrabble?" Luke asked, oh so casually, as if he didn't care what Brendan's answer was.

And out of the corner of his eye he watched Nora, as he always watched Nora, and saw her tensing, caught just as he was between wanting him to go and wanting him to stay.

"Scrabble?" he said. "I'm not staying to play Scrabble."

Luke tried to hide how crestfallen he was. Nora got a pinched look about her mouth and eyes.

It should have confirmed he could not stay here to play Scrabble. Instead he heard himself saying, "Don't you know how to play poker?"

And when they both shook their heads, he said, "I guess it's about time you learned."

An hour later Luke was rolling on the floor laughing. Brendan's own stomach hurt from laughing so hard. The rock had been rolled away and light was penetrating into every corner of that cave.

He needed to stop. He needed to ponder hard questions. He needed to slow down, roll the rock back in place, regroup, retreat, rethink.

Why was he doing this? The truth? Something in him was watching that damned cat getting better and better. Something in him was surrendering, resisting his efforts to be logical, telling him that if that cat could be healed, maybe he could, too.

Healed from what? he asked himself. Until he had passed under that Nora's Ark sign, hadn't he been blissfully unaware of his afflictions?

No, that wasn't true. There hadn't been one blissful thing about his life. It had been cold and dark and dank and gray. Certainly there had been no moments of laughter like this.

He had managed to avoid his demons—guilt, dark despair, crippling loneliness—by filling the confines of the space he had chosen with ceaseless work, by never stopping.

He had thought if he stopped he would find his afflictions had run along with him, silent, waiting.

He thought if he ever stopped, those tears that had never been cried would begin to flow, and would flow and flow and flow until he was drowning in them and in his own weakness.

His hardened heart behind its wall, a life that yawned with emotional emptiness, that had protected him.

And now Nora's laughter was lapping against it, like water against a refuge built of mud, lapping away, steadily eroding the defenses.

How could you defend against moments like these?

"You are," he told her, "without a doubt the worst

card player I have ever seen. Give that deck to Luke before you mark it so badly I'll own your house."

"What do you mean, mark it?"

Luke took the cards from her. "See this bend you made here? Now everyone knows that's the ace of spades."

"Oh," she said, the only one who didn't know.

And she simply didn't have the face for poker! She frowned at bad hands. She chewed her lip if they were really bad. Her eyes did a glow-in-the-dark thing if it was a good hand.

"Your aunt is a wash-out at this game. You have some promise, though. You have to have some ability to lie to be a good poker player."

Luke flinched as if he'd been struck. He ducked his head. He dealt them each a hand and glared at his. And then he set them down, face up. He cleared his throat and looked Brendan right in the eye.

"I did it," he blurted out. "I opened the mail. I sent Deedee the letter. I took the money."

Honestly, Brendan did not want to like this kid.

But coupled with the defense of his aunt with the coat rack, and how hard he worked out there in the barn every day, how good he was with that cat and all the animals, the confession meant there was some hope for the boy.

If Nora didn't manage to kill him with kindness first.

Because his aunt put down her cards—a royal flush, not that she would recognize it—and glared at Luke, ready to fight for him, ready to believe in him. "Luke! No, you didn't!"

"Let him do the right thing," Brendan said quietly.

The words made Nora want to weep. It confirmed

what she already guiltily believed. She was making the wrong choices for Luke over and over again.

Nora hated that Brendan was right. And she hated that he had come into her house and her life and had taken control as naturally as he breathed.

But most of all, she hated the sense of relief she felt that she didn't have to figure out how to fix it. She hated what it said about her that she had been prepared to lie to protect her nephew. And she hated, too, that she felt the same way she had felt in Brendan's arms. Not so alone. Carried.

"Why don't you tell us what happened?" Brendan suggested.

Nora appreciated his tone. Mild but stern. Not about to take any nonsense.

Luke glanced at her, and she nodded, not missing the look of relief on his face. He'd been carrying the guilt for too long.

"I was opening the mail for Nora's Ark and found Deedee's letter. She didn't say Charlie was dying. She just said he wasn't feeling well. I decided to play along. So I wrote her and said sure I'd send some energy. But that she should make, er, a donation."

"You told her to send money," Brendan said flatly, not willing to allow Luke to sugarcoat it.

"Okay. I did."

"But why? You have money," Nora asked plaintively.

"I didn't have enough."

She felt herself pale. Enough for what? Why did a fifteen-year-old boy need fifty dollars that he couldn't ask her for?

Cigarettes? Alcohol? Drugs?

Karen, I have failed. Colossally. Why did you leave me with this?

Given the road she was going down, at first she thought Luke's answer was a relief.

"The police were hassling me about the bike. The guy I borrowed it from, Gerald Jack-in-the-Box—"

"Jackinox," she corrected automatically, thinking, *It's about the bike. Not drugs.*

"Whatever. He said he'd make it go away if I gave him fifty bucks."

Her sense of relief evaporated. "That's blackmail! Tell me you didn't ask Mrs. Ashton for fifty dollars to give to him! Oh, Luke, why didn't you come to me?"

He at least had the grace to look a little shamefaced. "I asked her for fifty bucks. Cash. In the mail. When the money actually came, I was shocked. And I felt guilty. So I sat down and thought I'd send her stupid cat—I didn't know him then—some energy."

"What do you mean by that?" Brendan asked, his voice stern.

"Well, just the way my aunt does it."

"And what way is that? That your aunt does it?"

"That's not important!" Nora said. Her way with animals had always made her a bit of a novelty—and not always in a good way—to those who knew about it. Brendan Grant already knew way too much about her. He'd guessed she'd been betrayed. He knew she had a secret crush on Johnny Jose. He'd read *Ask Rover* and knew she wrote it. Enough was enough!

But annoyingly, Brendan trumped her with Luke. By a country mile.

"She puts her hands on the animal and then closes her eyes and goes all quiet. So that's what I did. Only

I had to pretend the cat was there. I sort of imagined light going around him. It was dumb, because I didn't have a clue what the cat looked like. I didn't picture him being so ugly. I mean, not that he's ugly once you get to know him."

"That's the same with all things, and people, too, Luke," Nora said, not wanting to miss an opportunity to help him see things in a way that would make him a better person.

Luke and Brendan both rolled their eyes.

"Right," Luke muttered. "Anyway, it freaked me out because I got all warm, like the sun came out, and it was pouring rain that day. It freaked me out even more when Mrs. Ashton wrote that it worked, so I just threw out her letter. And erased her messages. Geez, she called about a dozen times a day. I was a wreck trying to get to the answering machine before my aunt."

Nora cast Brendan a glance. He didn't look at all sympathetic to Luke feeling like a wreck trying to keep his treachery hidden.

"Why," Brendan asked carefully, "did it freak you out when you thought it worked? You could have been into some real cash."

"I didn't like the way it felt."

Nora's sweet sensation of relief was tempered somewhat when Luke shrugged and sent her a look. "Who wants to be like her?"

Even though she was used to his barbs, it hurt. And even though it was the story of her life. She was careful not to let how badly it hurt show.

Over the years, some people saw what she did as a gift, but most saw it as just plain weird. She was cautious about showing people that side of herself. Even in the column, she didn't reveal she wrote it, didn't always say exactly what she wanted to say, tempering it with what people wanted to hear.

Nora glanced at Brendan. He was watching her. She had the uneasy feeling he saw everything, even the things she least wanted to reveal.

Again she had that aggravating feeling. Instead of feeling exposed, she felt in some way not alone.

She tore her eyes away from him, forced herself to focus on her nephew. "Luke, do you understand how terrible this is? You gave false hope to a poor little old lady—"

"No one would resent being called old more than Deedee," Brendan said mildly, "and we won't even go into the poor part."

"The point is she was afraid to lose her cat, and Luke played on her fear and took her money."

"I needed the fifty bucks!"

"You allowed that boy to blackmail you! I have to call his parents."

"That's why I didn't tell you! Dammit, Auntie, I didn't really have permission to borrow his bike. Do you have to be so gullible?"

Brendan's tone remained mild enough, but there was steel running through it. "You don't use language like that in front of women. And your aunt is not the guilty party here. You are. What really happened with the bike?"

Nora was aware she should have said that, not him. She felt it again, though. The tempting weakness of liking the fact she was not handling this alone.

"I took it," Luke said, jutting out his chin defiantly. "I stole Gerald's bike because he was mean to me. He made fun of my hair in front of the whole class. You think it's not hard enough being new? And everybody knowing your aunt does voodoo?"

"Voodoo," Brendan said, with just a trace of approval.

"What do you mean, everybody knows I do voodoo?" Nora asked, horrified. "I don't! I run a shelter for abused and abandoned animals. That's all!"

"No, it isn't," Luke said wearily.

And suddenly she wondered if it had been about Luke's hair at all. Or if it had been about her.

"Anyway," Luke continued, "Gerald said he'd back my story that I borrowed the bike if I gave him fifty dollars."

"You've made everything worse," Nora said, but not too strongly. It was bad enough Luke was being teased about his hair. He was being teased about her, too! She was an adult and she could barely handle the mockery. That was why she wrote her column in secret.

"I think the question now is how are you going to fix all this?" Brendan asked.

"Naturally, we'll give your grandmother back her money," Nora said, hearing the resignation in her voice.

"No. *You* won't," Brendan said.

"Excuse me?"

"Luke did it. He needs to figure out how to make amends to her."

"What's amends?" Luke asked suspiciously.

"Just what it sounds like. You broke something, you mend it."

He pondered that. "I don't know how."

"I'll give you a chance to figure it out."

Luke seemed to be back to his old self, arms folded

over his narrow chest, bristling with barely contained hostility.

Take charge, Nora ordered herself, so she added, "Figure it out. With no computer. And no cell phone."

"That sucks," the boy said, and got up from the table and marched away.

"You're bossy," Nora said to Brendan, feeling somehow she had to hide the fact that she was so grateful someone was helping her through this.

"You've already said that."

"Sorry to bore you by repeating myself." She needed time to gather herself. Needed to show leadership, and wasn't. She was letting Brendan take charge.

Only because it had been a strange week. She'd been injured. She'd let down her guard around Brendan. Invited him into her life.

Still, it was a new blow that Luke was being teased at school because of her.

"Tell me what you've heard about me," she said to Brendan.

"Deedee heard you were a healer. She was making biblical references, about the laying on of hands. She's expecting a miracle."

Nora groaned softly. "I'm sorry. Do you think that's what Luke's classmates are hearing about me, too?"

"I assume some version of that. You bring a dead dog to life, and you're the talk of the town."

"I didn't bring a dead dog to life!"

"You're not used to small towns, are you?"

"No."

"It's like that game you played in junior high school. The teacher whispers, 'The green tree on Main Street is dying,' to the first kid in the line, and they whisper it to the next. But twenty kids later it has become 'Mrs. Green killed her husband on Main Street with a tree branch.'"

"We never played a game like that in school."

"A shame. The power of distortion would not be such a surprise to you. What really happened with the dog?"

"He'd been hit by a car. He was knocked out. Not dead."

"Technicalities. So, you have no gift with animals?"

"I didn't say that. I've always liked animals, sometimes a whole lot more than people. There is an energy element to animals that is very strong, and I seem to be able to connect with that. But I'm not a vet, and I don't try to take the place of one."

"Ah."

She had said enough. But despite her vow to herself to keep the barriers up between her and Brendan, it felt strangely and nicely intimate to be sharing her kitchen with him, telling him things she didn't always feel free to say.

"What I have no gift with, I'm afraid, is adolescent boys," she added, since she seemed bent on confessing private things about herself.

"I see cookies in a jar and good food on the table every night. There are drawings on the fridge and homework being done. Where are his folks?"

She could not quite keep the shaking from her voice. "My sister died."

"And his dad?"

"He went before Karen. Luke's never said anything to you? You guys have been doing chores together for days."

"Yeah, well, you know guys."

But she didn't. She didn't know guys at all. That was probably part of the problem with Luke.

Brendan sighed. "We don't talk about *deep* things. Discussion runs to who is the best hockey player in the world. Last night's baseball scores. Who can clean a cat cage the fastest and with the least gagging."

Nora really didn't want to confide one more thing to this man. But she heard herself saying, "I'm not sure that Karen would have trusted me by myself with this. She saw my fiancé, Vance, as the stable one, a vet with a well-established practice. I'm afraid I've always been seen as the family black sheep."

"It seems to me your sister would think you were doing well at making a home for your nephew."

"So, now you know! I'm an orphan," Luke exclaimed from the doorway. "Doesn't that just suck? Who even knew there was such a thing anymore?"

Nora hadn't seen him reappear, but there he was, bristling defensively.

"And you think that isn't bad enough?" Luke continued, jerking his head toward her. "She was going to get married. And then Vance wouldn't marry her. Because of me."

CHAPTER NINE

NORA'S MOUTH FELL open. Her eyes clouded with tears. She'd had no idea Luke knew about that awful conversation between her and Vance.

"Just because I glued his stupid golf clubs to his golf bag."

"Why'd you do that?" Brendan asked mildly.

"He didn't want Auntie Nora to get me a skateboard, because I'd been suspended from school. So she didn't. So I glued his golf clubs to his bag. Super Duper Gobby Glue works just the way it says in the commercial."

"I'll remember that," Brendan promised.

"'It's him or it's me,'" Luke quoted. His mimicry of Vance might have been hilariously accurate, if it wasn't for the context. "She picked me. Dumb, huh?"

And then Brendan said, his voice steady as a rock, "I don't think it's so dumb."

Despite the fact Nora could have done without her whole life story being exposed, she could have kissed Brendan, she felt so grateful.

Unfortunately, that made her look at his lips.

The thought of kissing Brendan Grant made her dizzier than the bump on her head.

"You don't think it was dumb that she picked me?"

Luke said, and the hopeful look in his eyes tugged at her heartstrings. He quickly covered it. "Sure. I just took money from your grandmother."

"You know everybody makes mistakes. Your aunt Nora when she got engaged to a jerk."

Her heart filled with the most unreasonable gratitude that someone saw Vance's defection as a statement about him, not about her.

"He was a jerk," Luke said. "A sanctimonious, know-it-all, stuck-up jerk."

Nora's mouth fell open. First of all, she'd had no idea Luke's dislike of Vance had run so deep. Second, she had no idea that he could use a word like *sanctimonious* correctly.

"She should have asked Rover," Brendan deadpanned, and then he and Luke cracked up. Brendan must have caught her disapproving expression, because he sobered.

"So, everybody makes mistakes," he said. "When you took that money from Deedee, it was a mistake. What matters is whether you choose to grow from them or not."

"What kind of mistakes have you ever made?" Luke challenged, not laughing anymore. Nora could tell he wanted to believe there was hope that a mistake could turn out okay, and was afraid to believe at the very same time.

Which she understood perfectly, of course.

Brendan hesitated. He tossed his cards down on the table. For a moment, it looked as if he wasn't going to say anything at all.

Then, his voice so soft she felt herself straining to

hear it, he said, "My wife died because of a terrible mistake I made. She was carrying our baby."

Nora laid her hand on his, almost unbearably grateful that Brendan had seen how great Luke's need was. And possibly hers. That he had overcome so tremendous an inner obstacle and given something of himself to both of them confirmed that her instincts had been right, after all.

There was a common place between them.

But it seemed to her that common place was the most frightening thing of all. It asked her to put aside her past injuries and her petty fears. It asked her to think less about protecting herself and more about reaching out to another human being.

Reaching out to animals was easy. Human beings were far more complicated.

She wasn't ready. She ordered herself to withdraw her hand.

And yet her hand, as if separate from her mind and linked to her soul, stayed right where it was.

Brendan could not believe he had said that to Nora and Luke. What if these were the words that broke open that dam of emotion within him?

But no, the dam was safe. He had not cried then, and he would not cry now. Still, there was nothing he hated more than sympathy. He waited for her to say something that would make him regret confiding in them even more than he already did.

But Nora said nothing at all. Instead, with a tenderness so exquisite if felt as if the dam of emotion was newly threatened, she laid her hand on top of his.

For a moment he felt only the connection, her small

hand covering part of his larger one, the softness of her palm against his toughened skin.

But then he was stunned by the warmth that began to pour from her hand, some energy vibrating up his wrist into his arm. It felt as if his whole body was beginning to tingle.

And suddenly, the world's greatest cynic believed what he had only suspected until now.

She could heal things.

The light shining in her eyes almost made him believe she could heal the most impossible thing of all: a heart smashed to pieces.

For a stunned second, he felt his throat close. But then he fought it.

Because who would want that fixed? For what reason? So that it could be smashed again? So that a man could face his impotency over the caprice of life all over again?

He jerked his hand out of hers, and she stiffened, guessing it, correctly, as rejection. Then she had the good sense to look relieved. She actually glared at her hand for a minute, as if it had mutinied and acted on its own accord.

She turned rapidly from him, ran a hand over her eyes, winced when she touched the bump on her head.

"I should get some footage of Charlie for Deedee and then go," he said.

Luke, looking pensive and solemn, went and got the cat.

Nora was completely composed when she turned back to Brendan.

"Thank you for telling us. I know it was hard for you.

And yet he needed to hear it. He's known you only a short time, but he looks up to you."

Brendan shrugged, withdrawing, uncomfortable.

Luke came back with Charlie and set him on the counter.

The cat gave a yowl of indignation and made for the edge, as if he fully planned to leap to the floor.

Brendan stared. This was a cat that had barely been able to lift his head a few days ago. "What are you feeding him?"

Luke made a quick grab and caught Charlie by the back of the neck. The cat hunkered down, resigned but unhappy.

"There's no cure for old age," Nora told Brendan gently. "There's nothing that stops life from unfolding in its natural order."

As Luke lifted his other hand so that both of them rested on the cat, Brendan was aware again of that vibration, of an energy he didn't understand. It was almost as if the light in the room changed.

The cat stopped struggling. It was as if Charlie had been tranquilized. He closed his eyes and a deep purr came from him.

Luke jerked his hands away. He took the cat off the counter, set him on the floor, watched him scoot off. Uncaring that there would be no pictures tonight, he shoved both hands in his pockets. His face was white and his voice was brimming with anger.

"Life's natural order?" he spat out. "My mom was thirty-four. What's natural about that? Oh, and Aunt Nora is a healer, all right. Ask anyone. My mom always talked about my auntie Kookie, how her room was filled with mice and birds and cats and dogs, and she could heal them all."

"Luke, that's an exaggeration. I liked animals. I couldn't—"

But he cut her off. "I was here when they brought that dog in. It was dead."

"It wasn't," Nora said. "Obviously it wasn't."

"And then she puts her hands on it, and *poof,* he's alive and wagging his tail. And in three days he's running around the yard, bringing me sticks to throw.

"But when it really counts? When it's cancer? Forget it! Who would want a gift like that, anyway? That's why I don't want to be like her! You can't change anything that matters."

And then he spun on his heel and followed the cat, and Nora and Brendan stood in frozen silence as he thumped up the stairs.

"How did he know Charlie has cancer?" Brendan asked.

"He doesn't," Nora said too quickly, her troubled eyes on the empty doorway her nephew had gone through. "His mom—my sister—died of cancer. I'm sorry, I don't think there's anything more I can do for Charlie. You should take him home to Deedee. She can spend his last days with him."

Brendan could feel weariness like a dull ache in his bones.

Not just because it was late, either.

It was the weariness of it all.

A boy who had lost everything and who already knew you could not change anything that really mattered. A woman who was trying desperately to help him through it, even though she had lost, too.

Brendan realized he had actually been thinking that cat was getting better. Had been bringing Deedee pictures, instead of preparing her to face yet another loss.

This was the truth he had been doing his best to outrun for two and a half years. It was just as Luke had said. When it really counted?

A man was powerless.

And there was no feeling in the world quite as bad as that one.

Luke came back down the stairs. He looked as if he had been crying, and Brendan almost envied him those tears, the release they brought from the inner storm.

The boy's face was white and strained with the manful effort of trying not to let everything he was feeling show. He had Charlie tucked under his arm, an unwilling football.

"I'm going to fix him! And I'm going to pay you back your money, too!" Luke stomped back up the stairs.

Nora bit her lip, sent Brendan an imploring look.

He shrugged. He wanted to be a dyed-in-the-wool cynic, but the past few days had challenged that. The aunt had something. He had felt it when she'd touched his arm.

And Luke had something, too. That cat was acting better, even if he wasn't actually getting better.

Though that something that Nora and Luke had—that gift with things wounded—was not necessarily what they needed.

Despite the shrug, he knew his indifference was pretended. Caring had crept up on him.

Brendan recognized their lives were a web he could get tangled in.

Was already tangled in, whether he wanted to be or not. And he didn't want it. He'd spent a long time locked in his lonely place, avoiding entanglement.

He walked out the door, refusing to look back at Nora. Free of the enchantment of her house, walking through the warmth of the early summer evening to his car, Brendan Grant vowed to himself he wasn't coming back here. Not until it was time to pick up Charlie.

Dead or alive.

Nora loved the barn. It had taken a dozen volunteers and a hundred man-hours to make the falling-down old structure into an animal shelter, but now it was perfect. She was in the small-animal section, two rows of roomy cages facing a sparkling clean center aisle.

After a night like last night, she needed the peace she felt working alone here. She had a rock-and-roll station blasting, music from the fifties. It was partly to keep her moving through the exhaustion after twenty-four hours of being woken every hour on the hour. It was partly a nice distraction from her whirling thoughts.

But the animals loved music. Humming along, she reached inside the rabbit cage, picked up a droopy-eared bunny she had named Valentine, and tucked him into her bosom.

He wriggled against her, snuggling deeper.

"You want to dance, sweetheart?"

"Sure."

She whirled. Brendan was standing there, watching her. The rabbit must have taken the sudden hard beating of her heart as a warning of imminent danger, because he scrambled out of her arms, over her shoulder and down her back. He hit the floor running.

Brendan reached behind him and closed the door to prevent bunny escape, then turned back to her.

How unfair that he looked even better in the pure afternoon sunshine streaming through the windows high up the walls than he had looked last night.

He must have come from work. He had on a white shirt and gray pants. A tie was loosely knotted at his throat. He looked handsome and sure of himself, a model for *GQ,* only more real.

And she still had a lump the size of a baseball on her forehead, and was wearing a charming blue smock of the one-size-fits-all variety that swam around her.

"I—I haven't seen you for a few days," she stammered. She hoped there was nothing in her voice that revealed how she had waited. And watched.

And hated herself for both.

"Busy at work," he said.

"What are you doing here now?"

"Deedee insisted. Luke's been sending her pictures, but she had to come see for herself."

Nora had no idea Luke had been sending on pictures of the cat. She probably would have asked him to stop, if she knew. What did they all think was going to happen?

"Yesterday he sent a video of that old cat playing with a ball."

She looked closely at Brendan. "Please tell me you don't believe that animal is going to get better?"

He shrugged. "I don't know what to believe, Nora. The thing is, *I'm* getting better. And I never believed that would happen."

"What do you mean, better?" she whispered.

He rolled his shoulders. "I've been in total darkness. I can feel the light trying to get through. There are cracks in the wall and light is seeping in, and every time I patch one crack, another one appears."

It felt as if she couldn't breathe. As if she was going to cry. It felt as if she could run to him and put her arms around him and whisper him home.

To her.

"But the walls have become who I am, so when they crumble, will I crumble, too?"

"No," she whispered. "You won't."

"Uh-huh."

The feelings were too strong. To hide how totally vulnerable she felt, Nora got down on her hands and knees and looked under a set of cages. Valentine stared back at her.

And then Brendan was on the floor beside her. His scent, clean and masculine, overrode every other smell in the building. It was not lightening the mood, having him so near, though he, too, seemed to want to back off from the intensity of the previous moment.

"I think he stuck his tongue out at me," he said.

"Like life," she said. "When you most want control, it will stick its tongue out at you."

"Oh boy," Brendan muttered, "I can see it coming now. *Ask Valentine.*"

She laughed and he smiled.

"There he is." He reached under the row of cages; his shoulder brushed hers; Valentine hopped away.

Nora shot back before she did something really dumb, something she would regret forever, and crawled along the floor. "Valentine," she crooned, "come here."

"I dropped Deedee off at the house. Luke said you were down here."

Did that mean Brendan *wanted* to see her? She

glanced sideways at him, just as he shoved himself under the bank of cages.

"You're ruining your clothes," she said.

He ignored her. "I'm being outsmarted by a rabbit."

Valentine hopped from underneath and took off down the row.

Brendan crawled out, dusted himself off, stood up. "Can't you call him back with your energy?"

She glanced at him, annoyed at the barb, and then saw the little smile playing across his face. He was teasing her. Something dangerous rippled down her spine.

The awareness of him shivered more intensely around her. It was nice to be teased by him.

For a moment, she was going to fight it. The intensity, the subtle invitation to bring him into the light.

And then she found she couldn't. By his own admission he had been in darkness. By his own admission he had come here to her.

With an inner sigh of surrender, Nora decided to play. To be the one thing she never was. Totally herself. She had been so serious for so long. She could not resist the temptations of this moment.

CHAPTER TEN

NORA PLACED HER fingers on her temples, squinched her eyes shut tightly and hummed. "Uzzy, wuzzy, fuzzy bunny, let this poem call you home."

She opened one eye when she heard Brendan snicker. "Is it working?"

"That is the worst spell I've ever heard."

"Oh," she said, widening her eyes innocently. "Have you heard many?"

"Thankfully, no."

"Why don't you try?"

He seemed to debate for a moment. Why did her heart begin to beat faster when he gave in to it, too? To the invitation of life not being so serious. A smile tugged at the corners of that sinful mouth.

"How about a carrot instead of an incantation?" he suggested.

"If he was starving, we might have a hope. As you know, since you've been doing it, he's quite well fed. Still…" she went to the fridge at the end of the aisle, removed a bag and handed Brendan a carrot "…we can try. If it doesn't work today, it might work by midweek."

They went back down the aisle, her on one side, him on the other, peering under cages.

"Now that Deedee's feeling better, is she going to make a decision? Is she going to take Charlie home? Or to the vet?" Nora asked.

"She has her own ideas, as always, none of which involve relieving you of Charlie. She seems to have come for a visit. Luke and she were in deep conversation when I left."

"Luke and Deedee? Seriously?"

"Seriously. Hey! Here he is! Here bunny, bunny, bunny." Brendan was down on his knees again, peering under a sink. As she watched, reluctantly enchanted by a man willing to wreck a thousand-dollar suit for a rabbit, he held out the carrot in the palm of his hand. Valentine edged toward him, he made a move to grab him and the bunny leaped sideways and hopped away.

"He's waving his tail at me. Like a middle finger. Wow. Even I can read his energy."

Nora giggled. Brendan turned and glared at her, but a smile lurked in his eyes. "Let's see if he'll fall for the bait again."

Really, she knew if they left the rabbit alone, he'd eventually get hungry and come out. But it was too fun trying to catch him with Brendan.

Together they chased that bunny all over the barn, acting silly, making faces, doing voices, crawling under cages, and in and out and over obstacles. They called suggestions to each other, and whispered plans, as if he could overhear them, and they laughed at Valentine's impudence.

Finally, they had him.

"Companies pay money for this," Brendan said. "It's called team building."

It occurred to her they had been a team. And it had

felt good. Why was it every time she was with him something happened that made her feel the delicious if guilty pleasure of not being alone?

Now she focused on him and the bunny. She could tell a lot about a person from how he handled an animal.

For a moment Brendan looked as if he intended to hand Valentine to her.

But then his expression softened, and he held the bunny firmly in the palm of his hand, his fingers tapered over the rib cage. He pulled him in close to his chest, stroking Valentine's snubby little nose with one gentle fingertip.

There was something about watching a strong man with a fuzzy bunny that could melt a person's heart. Nora felt some terrible weakness unfurl in her at his tenderness with Valentine, in his decision to come into the light. She was annoyed with herself for feeling as if she had unintentionally given Brendan a test, and she was just as annoyed that he had passed.

"Okay, I think I remember where the little monster lives." He put Valentine back in the cage, closed the door and turned to her.

"Deedee's not going to take him home. I figured it out. She can't bear the thought of being with Charlie when he dies. Though I guess we're all wondering if he's going to die at all. He keeps improving."

"It's temporary."

"You sound certain of that."

"I am. I wish Luke wouldn't have taken it on. He's setting himself up for heartbreak."

"And he's had enough," Brendan guessed softly. "And so have you."

The look in his eyes was the one she had seen that

rainy night when she had come to in the horse pen, when she had reached up and touched his cheek in welcome.

A person could drown in a look like that, throw herself willingly into those deep pools of understanding.

Instead, she congratulated herself for trying to back off.

"When you work with animals that are unwell, you expect a certain amount of grief. I've developed strategies for not getting attached. I don't name any of the animals."

"You named Lafayette."

She could say he had come named, but he hadn't. "Who would get attached to *him?*" she said, a bit defensively.

"How about Valentine?"

"Okay, so the odd one slips by my guard. But now that I have this beautiful facility, I don't ever let animals in the house. To prevent attachment, and also, where would you draw the line?"

"But Luke has Charlie in the house. And Ranger."

She bit her lip. "I know I should be stricter."

"But you took it as a good sign that he cared about something," Brendan guessed, and then reached forward and brushed her hair away from the bump on her head. "He cares about you. He told me he woke you up every hour on the hour."

"He did."

"And how are you feeling?"

"Exhausted."

"Funny, you didn't look exhausted when I came in."

She blushed, remembering that he had caught her dancing.

"In fact," he said, cocking his head, listening to the music blaring, "don't we have some unfinished business? Didn't you ask me to dance?"

Her mouth fell open. Of course she had not asked him to dance! He knew she had been talking to the bunny! What was he doing?

What was *she* doing? Because she found herself playing along, again. Boldly, almost daring him, she held out her hand.

Come, then, into the light.

And felt as if the bottom was falling out of her world when he took it. Because it was only then that she recognized what darkness she had been in.

Grieving her sister. And Vance's abandonment when she'd needed him most. Weighed down by extra responsibility. Wanting desperately to be everything Luke needed, and knowing in her heart she had been falling short.

She took Brendan's hand and smiled at him, and it felt as if for the first time in a long, long time that smile was coming straight from her heart.

What was he doing? Brendan asked himself.

Ever since that first smile had tickled her lips, a desire had been growing in him, and it felt as if his fate was sealed when she'd giggled today. When she'd laughed, chasing that bunny through the barn.

Brendan was not sure he could ever find his way to the light, or if the light could ever penetrate the darkness around him. He was not even certain he wanted it to, because it could mean the loss of the grip he had on the pool of pain inside of him.

Still, watching the cat change, watching Charlie

playing, seemed nothing short of a miracle. What had he started to believe?

However nebulous he was about what he wanted for himself, Brendan was aware of what he wanted for Nora. He wanted to make that light go on in her. He wanted something in her life to be fun and carefree.

It hit him like a ton of bricks what she needed, and why he felt so compelled by her need.

She was in the same situation his mother had once been in, a single parent struggling to be both parents, struggling to do everything right.

His mother's struggles had shaped Brendan, made him driven, made him want things for his own family that he and his mother had not had, and could not have even dared to hope for.

Now, looking at Nora, he could see the strain in her face, the stress in the droop of her shoulders.

It looked as if it had been a long, long time since she had laughed, or had anything approaching fun in her life.

The weight of the whole world seemed to be on those slender shoulders

It was not his job to lift it, Brendan Grant told himself. He'd managed to not get tangled in the web of life for a long time. Yet the last few days...

But that begged the question about the kind of man he had become. Hadn't he said to the boy last night that a mistake could be turned into an opportunity? To become something better?

Brendan had made a terrible mistake that night two and a half years ago.

He'd let Becky drive alone on a bad night. He should

have been with her. She had begged him to go. She'd been so excited.

A pressing project at work. No, no, I'll meet you there. I'll come up later tonight. You'll wake up to my handsome mug in the morning. I promise.

He hated these thoughts. He hated that he was questioning himself. That he could see light, and was being drawn toward it. He hated it that he was coming back to life.

There was no reason he had to be here anymore. Nora didn't need him.

Except that she did.

Life was asking more of him. And there was that ironic twist again. It was asking him to show someone else how to lighten up, how to have fun. But in doing so, he was coming closer to finding his own light. What if this time it broke down the walls all around him and pierced his heart like a lightning bolt?

It would be so easy to walk away from a challenge like that! But if he let the legacy of his love for his wife be bitterness, somehow he had failed.

If he could ignore the need of these two people, in a situation so like the one his mother and he had once been in, it wouldn't matter how many beautiful houses he designed and built.

What if the child Becky had carried had already been born? What if he'd had to figure out how to make a life for both of them *and* deal with his grief?

That's the situation Nora was in. She was grieving her sister and trying to make a life for her nephew.

If he didn't do a single thing to lighten that burden when her need was so obvious to him, Brendan was not sure he would ever get the bitterness of failure off his tongue.

"So," he said, making a decision, cocking his head to the music. "Do you know how to jive?"

Ridiculous to feel as if it was the bravest and most risky thing he had ever done.

"No!" she stated, then asked skeptically, "Do you?"

"Of course not. Well, maybe a little. From high school dance class."

"Interesting school you went to! Word games *and* dance class," Nora said.

"Let's teach each other," he said. And then he pulled her in close to him. She put her hands up, pushing away from him, keeping a small barrier between her and his chest. She was tense and unsure.

Well, she should be. Maybe she was asking the question he needed to ask.

So he lightened her burden. And made her smile. Then what? What happened next?

But this moment stole his questions about the future. Her huge green eyes locked on his face, her pulse beating harder than that rabbit's in the delicate hollow of her throat.

"Relax," he heard himself say softly. He was still holding her hand, and rested his other hand on the soft curve between her rib cage and her hip.

She did relax, looking at him with fearful expectation.

"Okay," he said, "just like dance class. One, two, three, one, two, three."

They shuffled along the aisle between the cages. She looked down at her feet, her tongue caught between her teeth.

"I'm surprised you asked me to dance," he said. "You aren't very good at it."

"I thought I was pretty good when it was Valentine I was dancing with!"

"Uh-huh."

"I was. Not so inhibited."

"There's no cause to be inhibited," he said.

"Yes, there is! I'm going to step on your toes—"

"I can handle it. Steel toes." The truth was he'd had to force himself to go to work today. He had wanted to be here instead. He had missed it here as he had not missed getting to Village on the Lake every day.

She glared down at his feet. "They are not!"

"Specifically made for construction sites. They are."

"I'm going to look foolish."

"There's no one here to worry about."

"What about you?"

"I'd love to see this—" he pressed a finger into the little worry line in her forehead "—disappear. Just give yourself to it. Just for a minute."

She hesitated, then he felt the exact moment she surrendered shiver up the length of her entire body.

"Now," he said softly, "you should try moving your hips."

"You first!"

"Just us and the bunnies. And a few cats."

"And a parrot who swears."

"Ah, Lafayette, the finger eater. Hard to find a home for him, I assume?" The distraction of talking about the parrot worked. Brendan was moving and she was going with him.

"Hard to find a home for him? Impossible. Except for young men of a certain age who would take him to use as a novelty item at their frat parties. I couldn't allow that."

"That sounds just a bit like, um, attachment."

"Well, it isn't. That horrible parrot is probably going to teach Luke new words."

"There are no words that are new to a fifteen-year-old boy."

While she contemplated that, Brendan decided to up the difficulty level.

"I'm going to pull away from you, but keep holding your hand. Up in the air like this. Walk beside me."

"This isn't a jive," she said. "I think it's a minuet."

"Nope. No hips in minuets."

"Did you learn that in dance class?"

She was becoming quite breathless. He pulled her back to him, put his hand on her waist, leaned his forehead to hers. "Get ready to spin under my arm."

She did.

"Now spin back. We're good," he declared.

"We're not. We're terrible."

"Ask Valentine if you don't believe me. Get ready for the dip."

"Dip? No! Brendan! We'll fall."

CHAPTER ELEVEN

"FALL? ON MY watch? I don't think so. Relax. Trust me."

Nora giggled. Then relaxed, and then trusted him.

And at that exact second of giving her trust completely, his arm went behind the small of her back and she was literally swept off her feet.

Just like that she found her back arched, totally supported by his strength. Just like that they were in balance. In harmony. He held her suspended there. She gazed into his eyes. And then he pulled her in hard to his chest.

She leaned against him, feeling the steady, solid beat of his heart. They were both breathing hard, and she started to laugh. She laughed until the tears flowed.

"OhmyGod," she said. "I haven't laughed like that for so long!"

He was watching her intently, a little satisfied smile playing on his lips.

As if he had planned this. Give the poor beleaguered aunt a break from the monotony of her life.

It had been a nice thing to do.

But while she'd been losing control, he'd been gaining it.

And that was enough of that.

"Brendan, that was so much fun. I hardly know how to thank you."

Except that she did. She knew only one way to bring him totally into this place of light with her.

And before she could stop herself or think of the consequences, letting the momentum of the dance carry her, she was on her tiptoes, taking his lips with hers. And that's when the bottom really fell out of her world.

Brendan Grant's lips were like silk warmed through with honey.

Nora considered herself something of an expert on energy, but nothing could have prepared her for this exchange.

His energy was pure and powerful.

It swept through her, until it felt as if every cell in her whole body was vibrating with welcome for what he was.

A life force. Compelling. All-encompassing.

And that was before his kiss deepened. Taking her. Capturing her. Promising her. Making her believe…

…in the breadth and depth and pure power of love.

She broke away and stood staring at him, her chest heaving, her mind whirling, her soul on fire.

She didn't want to believe! Belief had left her shattered. Her belief in such things had left her weak and vulnerable and blind.

And she was doing it again.

Love! How could the word *love* have entered the picture? She hadn't given it permission! She hadn't invited it into her life! If anything, she was actively avoiding such a complicated twist to her already overwhelming life.

Realistically, she knew next to nothing about this man.

Except that he had known sorrow.

And that he was good to his deceased wife's grandmother.

And had given her nephew a chance.

And could hold a bunny with tenderness.

And could turn an ordinary moment into a dance.

And had made her laugh.

And was afraid of crumbling along with the walls that came down.

The truth was that Nora felt she knew more about Brendan Grant in less than twenty-four hours than she had known about Dr. Vance Height in more than two years.

"I don't know wh-what got into me," she stammered, and could feel the heat moving up her cheeks. She had kissed a stranger. It didn't matter that she felt she *knew* him. That was crazy. That was the illusion!

"I need to go. I need to go check on Luke. And Charlie. And your grandmother. And—"

"Hey!" He stepped in close to her, touched her cheek, looked deep into her eyes. "Don't make it more than it was. A spontaneous moment between a healthy man and a beautiful woman."

She stared at him.

It was nothing to him. Well, of course! No matter what she read into it, they did not know each other. While she was falling in love, he was building his walls higher.

"I—I'm not beautiful," she stammered. Of all the things she could have said, why that?

"Yes," he said, his voice husky, his thumb moving down her cheek and scraping delicately over her lip. "Yes, you are."

Because she had *needed* to hear that. Had needed someone to see the woman in her.

And for a moment she thought he was going to kiss her again. And she knew, despite her attempt at resolve, she would not do a single thing—not one single thing—to stop him.

But then he stepped back from her, shoved his hands into his pockets.

"How about if I start on the chores? While I wait for Deedee?"

Pride and a need for self-protection made Nora want to refuse. But if she said no, he would know that something he had dismissed as nothing had shaken her right to her core.

And practicality took over. As he had pointed out, her volunteers were largely little old ladies. Here was someone who could do the heavy work. She couldn't turn it down.

"Do you think I could get you to move some hay bales?"

"Sure, just show me what you need done."

Trying to shake off that awareness of him—a need that he had unleashed within her and that she intended to fight with her whole heart—Nora led him through the small-animal section.

She was going to pretend nothing had happened.

But it was harder, as she watched him walk through her world with easy familiarity, pausing to scratch a cat's ear, to stick his finger through mesh to tickle a kitten. Even the hamsters seemed to recognize him, and scurried to the wire to say hello.

They stopped in front of the colorful parrot, which at once swore loudly at Nora, using a term so derogatory to females it made her flush. Then the parrot switched to French.

Brendan's lips twitched. His voice stern, he said, *"Lafayette, fermez la bouche."*

"Ooh," she teased, unable to resist, even though she knew the dangers of teasing, "you speak French. What did you say?"

"Romantic gibberish," he said, wagging a fiendish eyebrow at her. "It means shut your mouth."

And the tension that had been building between them since their lips met exploded into laughter once again.

"What do you do with animals like Lafayette?" he asked when the laughter stopped. "The ones that won't be adopted for whatever reason?"

"I'm pretty new at this. I've only had the shelter open for six months. Demand for adoptable pets has outstripped animals coming in. I even found a home for a white rat! So far, that's a decision I haven't had to make."

"Maybe you should have a plan," he suggested.

She decided it would make her feel way too vulnerable to let him know how she dreaded the day she would have to make that decision, let alone plan for it.

They continued through the barn, and the dogs went crazy when they saw Brendan. With easy confidence, he moved into each pen and opened the door out to the run.

There were three dogs in residence, a black Lab with only three legs, which had been found out wandering. The cocker spaniel, Millie, had been brought in because her owner couldn't afford the diabetes medication. The puppy was of an unknown breed. A week ago he'd been a matted and flea-infested mess, wary of people. Now he gamboled after Brendan.

"I don't suppose you want to take one home?" Nora asked ruefully. "The dog with three legs?"

"You had me pegged right as a guy who wouldn't even have a plant."

It was a warning to her, whether he knew it or not.

Not a man to pin any kind of romantic dream on.

But she already knew that. She was so done with romantic dreams. Though there was something about being dipped over a man's arm that could breathe them back to life in anyone, even a more hardened soul than her.

And there was something about seeing him with animals that told the truth about who and what he was, even if he didn't know that himself.

"You'll have no trouble finding a home for this little guy," he said of the enthusiastic puppy. "I'm not so sure about Long John Silver over there. Really, you should have a plan."

"I don't want a plan!" she said. "What? After six months get rid of him? How could I walk by that cage every day if time was counting down?"

"That sounds a bit like attachment to me."

"Well, it isn't!"

It felt so much more powerful to be annoyed with him than it had felt being in his arms.

Finally, they arrived at a large stack of hay, and without being told, Brendan got a wheelbarrow and began to pull bales down. Nora went back to cleaning cages, putting in food and changing water.

Her annoyance, unfortunately, could not be sustained in light of how hard he was working for her.

The awareness was roaring in her ears, sizzling through her veins. She could not help sneaking peeks at him. There was a certain poetry to a male body hard at work, and she was sworn off romance, not dead! Still, these kind of temptations—dancing, laughing, watching him pull eighty-pound bales down and shift them effort-lessly to the wheelbarrow—were going to chip away at her resolve.

Thankfully, her cell phone buzzed, and when she took the call there was a rescue she needed to go to. That was going to do double duty by rescuing her from the tingles on her skin and on her lips.

"Gotta go," she said, her tone deliberately breezy. "Iguana found on the loose in Hansen Lakeside Park." She ordered herself to thank him, and then to tell him not to come back. Diplomatically, of course. *Nothing here that Luke and I can't handle, especially now that school is out for the summer.*

But, weakling that she was, she found herself look-ing at Brendan's lips. She decided she needed to think about it before doing something rash and irrevocable.

Which probably described her decision to kiss Bren-dan Grant! Rash and irrevocable. Everything she did around him, from here on out, had to be measured and thought out carefully.

Everything she did around him now? From here on out? Hmm, not exactly the thoughts of a woman who was going to look at a man and tell him never to come back!

Three days later, Nora was scowling at her computer screen. Iguanas *did* eat dark, leafy greens. Except not the one she had. He was probably ill, and his owner had not been able to afford the vet bills. She made a note to pack up the iguana to take to her appointment with Dr. Bentley this afternoon. The vet was good enough to donate a few minutes to the animal shelter one day every week, and could also be counted on for emergencies.

She was aware that even as she did these routine tasks, her mind was not on them.

It was on Brendan Grant. He had brought his grandmother out every day for a few minutes, quite early in the morning, before he had to be at the office.

Nora couldn't very well tell him to stay away when Deedee wanted to see Charlie, refused to take him home, and couldn't drive herself.

Without being asked, without checking in, Brendan headed for the barn, and every morning after he left, Nora went out to see all the bales moved, the horse pen cleaned, the large bags of dog food organized, the aisle swept.

He didn't come to the house.

And she didn't go out. In fact, knowing now what time he came, she would sometimes scurry for cover just as he was pulling into the driveway.

Though it felt as if she was fighting her inner demons. That spontaneous dance haunted her. As did the laughter. And his lips on hers. He was out there right now. She could just go down…

She heard the front door open, flicked her curtain back. She saw Deedee making her slow way back to the car, Luke holding her arm and helping her in. Brendan was nowhere in sight, but if she waited just a minute, Nora knew that he would be.

Then Luke came back in the house, and she heard

him taking the stairs two at a time. She quickly flicked the curtain down and stared at her computer screen.

He stopped off in his room, and when he came up behind her a minute later, Charlie was drooping over Luke's crossed arms as if doing an impression of a leopard in a tree.

"Do the animals ever talk to you?" her nephew asked in a troubled voice, scratching Charlie's ears. "I mean, not in words, but you get, like, a feeling from them and know exactly what they're thinking?"

"Give me an example."

He took a deep breath. "Charlie is ready to go. He's tired. And he hurts. And he's a cat. Cats are clean. He doesn't want to be losing control of himself, if you know what I mean. You know why he's staying?"

She shook her head.

"Because he loves her. Deedee. And she's not ready to let him go."

In the past few days it was becoming apparent to Nora that Luke shared her gift, only his was a more intense version. Were animals really talking to him? Or was it just one more example of how her crazy decisions were affecting him?

Karen would not have approved of Luke being certain he knew what animals were thinking! She had certainly never approved of Nora's abilities.

"Remember Mr. Grant said I had to make a mend?"

Nora nodded, not correcting him that it was "amends."

"That's how I'm going to do it. By getting her ready."

"How are you going to do that?"

"I don't know. But she thinks it's by mowing her lawn. I'm going to bring Ranger with me."

Nora gazed at her nephew, and he had a look of resolve on his face. Not like a boy, but a man.

For the first time in a long, long time, Nora didn't feel worried, even though to someone looking in it might seem as if she should.

Luke was communicating with animals! Or thought he was. That probably needed a psychiatrist, not what she was feeling.

He was taking on the gargantuan task of getting Deedee ready to lose her pet. It was a failure getting ready to happen.

Protect him.

But this was probably why her sister had wanted her and Vance as Luke's guardians. Because Nora felt proud of him for taking on the impossible. And as if there was a slim hope, after all, that her nephew was going to leave the world better than he found it.

Somehow the changes in Luke and her own feeling of optimism seemed linked, not to the wonderful summer weather they were suddenly enjoying, but to this man who was in her life while not being in it.

It was all beginning to feel like the scariest thing that had ever happened to her. In that nice scary way like anticipating someone jumping out from behind a bush at you on Halloween, or riding the biggest roller coaster at the amusement park.

Luke went to the window. "Brendan's coming up from the barn now. I'll catch a ride with him into town and mow Deedee's grass."

Nora wanted to scream no, the very same way she wanted to scream no as the roller coaster was inching up that final climb. But just like then, it felt as if it was already too late. She could see all their lives getting more and more tangled together.

Besides, when she looked at the simple bravery revealed in her nephew's face, Nora knew she had to be as brave as he was.

She joined him at the window and saw Brendan striding across her yard.

"He must change for work later," she said out loud, admiring the way faded jeans clung to his legs, to the leanness of his hips. A plaid shirt was tucked into his belt, but open at the throat. Her eyes skittered to the firm line of Brendan's lips.

She had to be brave. Whether she wanted to be or not.

"It's Saturday," Luke chided her.

"Oh. Now that you're on summer holidays, I forget sometimes."

"That's my flaky aunt. Who doesn't know what day it is?" But he said it with gruff affection, then added, "Gotta go. I'll call you later."

Luke put his hand on her shoulder, dropped a casual kiss on her cheek. He squinted at the computer screen.

"It's not because we're giving him the wrong diet. Iggy ate something," he said.

"Iggy? Luke, we try not to name the animals."

"It's not really a name, just short for iguana. Dr. Bentley's going to have to x-ray him. How could an iguana swallow a house?"

And on that note, her nephew was gone, Ranger peeking out his hoodie pocket. He went back outside, and moments later, she heard him calling, "Brendan? I'll come with you. I'm going to mow Deedee's lawn. That's if Deedee can look after my kitten."

Nora twitched back the curtain just in time to see Luke hand Ranger to Deedee.

The old woman stared at the kitten. For a moment, she looked mad, as if she might give it back. But then her face softened, and she tucked Ranger into her breast and got into the car.

Brendan looked up at her, as if he'd known she was watching all along. He gave her a small smile and a thumbs-up. As if they were raising this boy together. She let the curtain fall back into place.

CHAPTER TWELVE

MIDAFTERNOON, NORA WAS thinking of Luke's words while she stood in Dr. Bentley's office looking at the X-ray of Iggy's digestive tract, and not his words about mowing the lawn, either. About how an iguana could swallow a house. The X-ray clearly showed a little toy house lodged in the reptile's digestive system.

"An iguana will eat anything," Dr. Bentley said.

The vet donated many of his services to the animal shelter, but was not volunteering an operation on an iguana, and she couldn't ask. Now what? They had a reserve fund, but to use it for an expensive procedure for an animal she had no hope of finding a home for?

She remembered being thankful, just days ago, that she had never had to face this situation.

Maybe you should have a plan. She hated it that Brendan Grant had been right. He had that look of a man who was always right. Who was logical and thought things through and never did anything impulsive or irrevocable.

We would be a well-balanced team, she thought, before she could stop herself.

"I need a minute to think," she said.

"Take your time."

She wrestled Iggy back into his cage and lugged him out to the waiting room. She had three choices. She could bring him home to die. She could have the vet speed up the process, which would be more humane. Or she could find the money for the procedure.

Her cell phone rang and she looked at the number coming in.

"Hey, Luke," she said, trying to strip the conflict she was feeling from her voice.

"It's not Luke. I borrowed his phone."

"Why?" It was him, the one who was always right. Maybe she'd call him that. Mr. Right. Then again, maybe not. She did not want to be thinking of Brendan Grant as Mr. Right in any context.

There was no Mr. Right! It was a fairy tale to keep females from empowering themselves! Ditto for thinking she was falling in love with him. Just another fairy tale.

"Because we're standing out in Deedee's yard and he handed it to me." A pause, and his voice lowered. "And because I wasn't sure if you would answer if you saw it was me."

"What would make you say that?" she said cautiously.

"I thought you were avoiding me."

Was she that obvious? It was embarrassing, really.

"Why would I be avoiding you?" she asked.

Silence. She thought of the boldness of taking his lips with her own, and shivered. She thought of the word *love* coming unbidden to her after she had kissed him.

He moved on without answering the question. They both knew exactly why she was avoiding him.

"I told Luke I'd take him for a milkshake. He did Deedee's lawn and then started on her shrub beds. They're pretty overgrown. He's worked really hard. I can't believe you've lived here six months and not been to the Moo Factory. His exact words were '*we never do anything fun.*'"

"We do fun things," she protested.

"Oh, yeah? Like what?"

We played a few hands of poker, once.

She knew it said something simply awful about her life with her nephew that, aside from that, nothing came to mind.

"We rented *Star Wars* last week."

"Really? That sounds like fun redefined."

"Are you being sarcastic?"

"It comes naturally to me, like breathing."

"We play Scrabble," she said triumphantly. "When I can get him away from the computer." Too late, she remembered they had invited Brendan to play Scrabble. He'd been unimpressed.

"Fun intensified."

She remembered his face that evening Luke had suggested Scrabble. But she was on a mission now to prove they had fun.

"And Luke showed me how to play virtual bowling!"

"Wow!"

It let her know how wise her avoidance strategy was. He was sarcastic. It was hard to hold that fault in the forefront, though, in light of his good deed. He was taking her nephew for ice cream.

"I bet you threw the bowling ball backward."

"How could you know that?"

"Psychic. That should help me fit right in on the farm."

"Oh!"

"I warned you. Sarcastic."

"How did you really know? About the bowling ball?"

"I've played that game."

"Oh, so *you* threw the ball backward?"

"No." Suddenly he seemed impatient with the conversation. "Anyway, I thought I should ask your permission before I took Luke for ice cream."

It was so respectful it could make a woman forgive sarcasm. Or at least one who did not have her guard way up.

"That wasn't necessary. Of course you can take him." Ridiculous to somehow feel deflated that she wasn't being invited.

Then Brendan said, "Luke would like you to come with us."

Not *him*. Luke.

She looked at the sick iguana. And suddenly was overcome by weakness, not wanting to have to make this decision herself.

"I'm at the vet's office with Iggy, an iguana who has eaten something."

"Iggy," Brendan repeated slowly. "I thought you told me you didn't name them?"

"Who would get attached to an iguana?" she said, but the truth was maybe she already was. She didn't want to bring him home to die. Or put him to sleep.

She told Brendan what was going on. It was his chance to say *I told you so,* but he didn't, and she felt it was another test he'd passed.

Another one that she hadn't meant to give him.

"You have a contingency fund?" he asked.

"Yes, but Brendan, that money would be so much better used educating people not to buy iguanas as pets. And the contingency fund isn't huge. What if I spend it on him, and then have an emergency next week?"

"On something with a little more of a cute factor than an iguana?"

She didn't mean to, but she started to cry. And she wasn't sure if it was because of the damned iguana that she'd been foolish enough to accept a name for, or because Brendan had gone virtual bowling with someone else who had thrown the ball the wrong way.

Or because it wasn't his idea to ask her out for ice cream.

It was Becky he'd played that silly game with. At a Christmas function? Everyone having hysterics at her lack of coordination.

He realized, holding the phone, that this was the first time he'd had a memory of Becky that made him *feel* anything. It was as if, after she died, he had started focusing on his failure to protect her, and that had erased all the good things from his mind.

But somewhere, had he also thought that thinking of the good would be *that* thing? That thing that would break him wide-open?

His contemplation of his treacherous inner landscape was cut blessedly short when Brendan heard a soft snuffling noise on the other end of the phone line. He tried to dismiss it as static, but the hair on the back of his neck prickled.

Maybe he *was* psychic. "Are you crying?"

The truth was his inner landscape seemed less treacherous than that.

The truth was he knew Nora Anderson had been avoiding him. And the truth was, he knew it had been a good thing. For them to avoid each other. Look at how quickly his intention to be a Good Samaritan by making her laugh had become complicated. By her hips under his hands. And then by her lips. On his.

"N-n-no."

But she was. Crying. Was it over an iguana? He was pretty sure she had said she was used to dealing with tragedy with animals. She had strategies for not getting attached.

Not that she seemed to stick to any of them!

An awful possibility occurred to him. Maybe it was because he had just thought of his wife that he was suddenly aware how quickly things could go sideways.

"Have you been having outbursts since you hit your head?" he asked.

"I am not having an outburst!" Now Nora was insulted.

Brendan was astounded that he felt guilty. When he'd been dancing her down the aisle of the animal shelter, he really should have been asking her concussion-related questions. And instead of doing the easy thing, and avoiding her and all the complications that her lips had caused in his uncomplicated life over the last few days, he should have been evaluating her medical condition.

"Have you been to see a doctor?" he asked.

"I don't need a doctor!"

"Look, outbursts can be a sign of concussion—"

"I am not having an outburst!" Each word was enunciated with extreme control, and then the phone went dead in his hands. Nora Anderson had hung up on him!

It seemed to Brendan that hanging up on someone could be evidence of an outburst.

Luke, flushed from heat, his hair flattened by sweat, came out of the flower bed, a tangle of bramble in his gloved hand. "Is Aunt Nora coming with us? For ice cream."

"I'm not sure what your aunt is doing." Except he was sure she was crying over an iguana. "Has she, er, been having outbursts?"

"What does that mean?"

"Crying. Snapping."

"Oh. You mean PMS."

Brendan wasn't sure if he should reprimand Luke or not, but a look of such deep masculine sympathy passed between them that he just couldn't.

Luke seemed to contemplate the fact his aunt might be a little off today. "Maybe just bring me back a milkshake," he muttered, and disappeared into the garden again.

Then he peeked back out. "Can you get something for Deedee, too? And just a little dish of vanilla for Ranger. I'll pay for it." He glanced toward the house. "She's trying not to. But she likes him. Ranger."

There seemed to be a bit of that going around. People trying not to like each other, and liking each other anyway.

Luke was a prime example. It was damn hard not to like this kid.

And that went ditto for his aggravating aunt.

Knowing she wasn't going to appreciate it one little bit, Brendan made his way to the vet's office.

Nora was sitting in the waiting room, doing her best to look like a woman who would not cry over an iguana. The iguana was in a cage at her feet. It had a ribbon around its neck. Who tied a ribbon around the neck of an iguana they planned not to get attached to?

When she saw him, she folded her hands over her chest.

"I. Can. Handle. It. Myself."

"Uh-huh." It was the first time he'd seen her in a dress. Or in clothes that fit, for that matter. It was a denim jumper. She had amazing legs. It was kind of like Ranger, hard not to like something so adorable.

He ignored her glare and took the seat next to her. "Have you decided what to do then?"

He slid her a look. She gnawed her lip. He knew darn well that meant she hadn't. He remembered how her lip tasted.

What was he doing here?

Trying to do the right thing, he reminded himself sternly. Brendan took one more quick look at her, and then got up and sauntered past the receptionist and into the back to talk to Herb Bentley.

"Okay," Brendan said, coming back into the waiting room. Nora was fishing through her handbag, looking for tissues. "Let's go for milkshakes."

While she was sipping her shake, he could grill her about concussion symptoms. He would look up a complete list of them on his iPad while waiting in line. There was always a line at the Moo Factory on Saturday.

She looked stubborn. "In case you've forgotten, I have to make a decision about the iguana."

"I've already made it," he said. He picked up the cage and put it on the receptionist's desk.

Nora bristled, balled up a tissue in her fist. "You made the decision? But you can't!"

It wasn't exactly an outburst, but it certainly seemed as if she might be on the edge of one.

Patiently, Brendan told her, "I told Doc I'd pay for the operation. Let's go have ice cream."

"I didn't tell you about Iggy because I needed you to fix it!" she said.

"Whatever."

"No! It's not whatever! I told you because I needed a little tiny bit of feedback. I needed to not feel so alone. I trusted you. I didn't tell you because I needed the decision made for me."

She looked as if she wanted to stick her fist in her mouth after she admitted that. About not wanting to make the decision by herself. She had let it slip how alone she felt in the world.

He looked at her lips.

Well, that shouldn't last long. Her being alone. At the moment, she was the best kept secret in Hansen. When word got out, every unattached guy for a hundred miles would be beating a path to her doorstep. Brendan didn't even want to question the hollow feeling that realization caused in the pit of his stomach.

But only, he told himself, because he knew she'd made a bad choice once. Only because he knew it would destroy that kid up there slaving away in his grandmother's garden if Nora did it again.

Why was he worried about her? She claimed not to like attachments. On the other hand, she was already attached to the iguana, and God knew there were lots of lizards around.

"My paying for the procedure is no big deal," he explained patiently. "You could be having cognitive difficulties, postconcussion, that were making it hard for you to make a decision."

"I don't like iguanas. But that doesn't mean I want to have the decision whether he lives or dies in my hands."

"Well, now it's not. There. Solved."

"Oh!"

"Irritability," he said sagely. He knew it would be wiser to keep that observation to himself, but he was surprised to find a part of him was actually enjoying this little interchange.

"I am not having cognitive difficulties! And I'm not irritable."

He raised an eyebrow.

"It's justified irritability, not knocked-over-the-head irritability!"

"It just seems a teensy bit out of proportion. I mean, I thought you'd be—" he considered saying grateful, and then said "—happy. I just don't see that it's a big deal."

"You paying is a big deal. I'll pay you back," she said stubbornly.

"Consider it a donation."

"No."

"You really need a board of directors to answer to."

"And it's you making the decision that's a big deal."

"Wouldn't it be forgivable if I made the decision based on the presumption you might be having cognitive difficulties? Even if you weren't?"

He blinked at her. He happened to know he had eyelashes women found irresistible. He wasn't opposed to using them as a weapon when backed into a corner.

She stared at him. Blinked herself. Looked away.

"Talk about cognitive difficulties," she muttered. He was pleased that she suddenly lost her desire to argue with him. Still, she couldn't just give in! Let him have the last word!

"I will pay you back."

"Fine. I'll take it out in milkshakes. A lifetime supply. I like licorice."

"A lifetime supply? How much *is* the procedure going to cost?"

Seeing the worry creasing her brow, he cut the amount in half and was rewarded for his little lie when she looked relieved.

"There is no such thing as a licorice milkshake," she said.

"That just shows you've never been to the Moo Factory."

"Besides, if you think other people making decisions for you is no big deal, *I'll* pick the flavor of your lifetime supply."

It was all turning lighter. He could tell it was against her will. Maybe she *was* experiencing cognitive impairment!

"Have at it," he said drily. "I've never met a flavor of ice cream I didn't like."

"Apparently," she muttered. "Licorice? Yuck!"

He held open the clinic door for her and she went outside to the parking lot, eyed his vehicle suspiciously. "Where's Luke?"

"At the last minute, he said he didn't want to come. He asked us to bring something back for him so he could keep working. And he asked me to bring something back for Deedee, too. And Ranger. He said he'd pay for theirs."

"My nephew, Luke Caviletti, said he'd pay?"

"Yeah."

"You're sure? He's the kind of gangly kid with red hair."

But her attempt at humor was meant to cover something else and it failed. Her face crinkled up. She did a funny thing with her nose and squinched her eyes hard.

The facial contortions didn't help her gain control. He could tell she was making a valiant, valiant effort not to cry again. The tears squeezed out anyway.

He wanted to just shove his hands in his pockets and wait it out. But he was helpless against what he did next.

"Maybe...I...am...having...just...a...little...bit... of...cognitive...impairment." She was scrubbing at her eyes with that balled up tissue.

He went to her and pulled her against him, wrapped his arms around the small of her back and held on tight.

He could feel the wetness soaking into his shirt.

And the warmth oozing out of her body.

And her heart beating below his.

Now, for his own protection and for hers, would be a great time to confirm that emotional changeability was definitely a sign of concussion.

But somehow those words about the proven correlation between concussion and emotions got trapped in his throat and never made it to his mouth.

Somehow his one hand left the small of her back, went to her hair and smoothed it soothingly.

That feeling was back.

Of being alive.

Only standing there in the vet's office parking lot, with sunshine that felt warmer after the months of rain, with her body pressed into his, Brendan was aware he didn't feel resentful of waking up, of being alive. Not this time.

Not at all.

CHAPTER THIRTEEN

"OKAY," BRENDAN GRANT said, consulting his iPad. "Are you getting headaches?"

"You are spoiling the best milkshake I have ever had."

"Just answer the question, ma'am," he said, in a voice that reminded her of a policeman.

Nora leveled him a look that she hoped would get him to stop. He *was* wrecking a perfect moment. They were sitting at a picnic table across from the Moo Factory, in Hansen Lakeside Park. Iggy had been granted a stay of execution. Luke had actually offered to spend his own money buying another human being—and a kitten—ice cream.

The sun had brought everyone to the park. Children were screaming on nearby playground equipment, some boys were throwing a Frisbee, a young couple was pushing a baby carriage. Nora watched the small family and identified the emotion she was feeling as envy.

"They look like they would provide the perfect home for a three-legged dog," she said to Brendan when she saw that he had noticed her watching them.

"Now who is spoiling the moment? Can you stop worrying about your animals for one minute and focus on the question? Lack of focus! It's on this list of symptoms!"

"I seem to be getting a headache right now." Nora was trying so hard to steel herself against him, but honestly, when he turned on the charm? It was nearly hopeless. That thing he had done with his eyelashes? The big, innocent blink?

Criminal, really.

"I'm being serious!" he insisted, glancing at his iPad and then scowling back at her. As long as he didn't blink!

"So am I!"

"You have a headache?"

"Yes."

He scrutinized her, and looked as if he was going to scoop her up and rush her off to the hospital. Really, she didn't quite know what to do with all this chauvinistic caring.

What if she just surrendered to it? She'd had a bump on the head. She could be forgiven a weak moment.

"Could be brain freeze. From the milkshake," she told him.

"Ah." He looked genuinely relieved, but she wasn't letting him off the hook yet.

"Of course, it could be from being nagged by an exceedingly annoying man!"

His lips twitched a little, with amusement, not annoyance. He didn't look the least contrite. In fact, he consulted his tablet again. "I'm not being exceedingly annoying. I'm being mildly annoying. For your own good."

She rolled her eyes and took a long sip of her milkshake. Huckleberry Heaven really was heaven. But to be sitting across the table from a man like this on such a gorgeous summer day, and be asked about your cognitive function?

"Are you having any foggy feelings? Like you can't concentrate?"

Only when you blink at me.

"Would that be the same as lack of focus?"

He considered this thoughtfully.

"Can I taste your milkshake?" she asked him.

"I'm going to put yes for that one. What does tasting my milkshake have to do with feeling foggy?"

"I've never tasted a licorice milkshake before. I've decided to live dangerously, since a blood vessel in my head may be perilously weakened, getting ready to explode as we speak."

He glared at her.

She put a hand to her forehead, swayed. He furrowed his brow, baffled.

"My best impression of pre-aneurism," she told him.

She wasn't sure what it was, but he brought out something zany in her, a kind of lack of inhibition that she had not experienced often.

She liked it, especially when he shoved his milkshake across the table to make her stop. Before he gave in and laughed.

She put his straw in her mouth. She was way too aware of the fact that her lips were where his had been. She thought maybe he liked it, too. He suddenly didn't seem nearly so interested in his silly questions. Instead, he watched her suck on his straw, and there was something so intense in his eyes it made her shiver.

"Whoo, that's cold," she said, to explain the shiver. She suspected he was not fooled. She pushed the shake back across the table at him. "Not to mention surprisingly good."

Deliberately, his eyes still locked on her, he took the straw. He was caressing the damn thing with his lips.

It was the closest she'd ever been to being kissed without actually being kissed. What he was doing with that straw was darn near X-rated. She shoved her milkshake across to him.

"Want to try mine?" she asked softly. She was encouraging him!

Apparently he did want to try hers. Intensity sizzled in the air between them as he grasped her shake, lifted it to his mouth, took the straw between his teeth and nipped before closing his lips over it.

"What else do you want to do?" he asked softly. "To live dangerously. Before the blood vessel in your head lets go."

The thing was, he was kidding. But the other thing was it was no joke. Life was not predictable. Her sister the health nut, dead in her early thirties. His wife in a car accident.

Suddenly, it seemed to Nora that she had not taken nearly enough chances. That she had not lived as fully as she should have.

If it was all going to be over, what had she missed?

It was easy to see the answer right now, with him sitting across from her, doing seductive things to her straw. The sun was gleaming in his dark hair; the faintest shadow of whiskers were appearing on the hard-honed planes of his cheeks.

She had missed the glory of being with a man like this.

And just letting go.

Enjoying wherever life took them, even if it was dangerous. Especially if it was dangerous!

"I want to rent one of those things down there." Nora pointed to a colorful booth and a dock. Parked beside the pier were flat-bottomed boats that had pedals in them.

She realized she wasn't kidding. She wanted to forget Iggy and a three-legged dog she could not find a home for. She wanted to forget an old lady whose cat, despite a reprieve, was going to die. She even wanted to forget poor Luke and the weight of her responsibility to him. She wanted to forget she had *Ask Rover* columns due, and bills to pay that relied on that column to pay them.

She just wanted to go out on the water and play.

"I think," she said slowly, "I want to live as if I'm dying."

"That's a song," he said.

She looked at him. She screwed up all her courage. "So, do you want to sing it with me?"

"Sure," he said, and it didn't even reduce her pleasure when he added, "So I can watch for more symptoms."

While he went down to the dock and arranged to rent the boat, Nora called Luke to tell him his milkshake was going to be late.

He said it was okay. He and Deedee had gotten tired of waiting and were eating pie, anyway.

"Don't ever eat pie cooked by someone really ancient," he warned Nora in an undertone. "I don't think she remembered to put sugar in it. It might be really old, too, like it's been in her fridge for three weeks."

"Don't eat it!" Nora declared.

"I can't hurt her feelings," Luke whispered, and then said good-bye and hung up.

She was still contemplating that when Brendan returned. Luke didn't want to hurt someone's feelings. It really was shaping up to be a perfect day.

"Okay, sailor," Brendan said, coming up to her and passing her a life jacket, "let's go."

Nora wondered if it was because they had been trapped inside so long because of the rain that they gave themselves so completely to an afternoon of playing on the water in the sunshine.

The boat, if it could be called that, was an awkward contraption. It was propelled forward, ever so slowly, by two people side by side, pedaling with all their might. Steering took some getting used to. There was no steering wheel. In order to turn the boat, one person stopped pedaling and the other kept going. The boat would start doing a painfully slow arc.

With much shouting and laughter she and Brendan headed out of the bay into the lake. They had not counted on the wind coming up and creating a tiny bit of chop. They had rented the boat for an hour, but by the time they got it back to the dock they had been wrestling with it, trying to get it back to shore against a headwind and a small swell for over two hours.

"Oh, boy," he said, "if that was your idea of living dangerously, I'd hate to see dull."

"It wasn't dull! It was fun!"

"Uh-huh."

"So, you pick something dangerous then, if you're so great."

"All right. I'll come for you tomorrow at ten."

"We're going to do something dangerous together? Tomorrow at ten?"

"Unless you're too chicken."

But she wasn't. She felt as brave as she ever had. That feeling lasted until the next morning, when precisely at ten, Brendan roared into her yard.

He was on a motorcycle.

It was dangerous all right, Brendan thought. They had taken the ferry across the lake and he was navigating the road that twisted along the north shore. It wasn't dangerous because the road had more dips and hollows and rises and falls than a roller coaster. It wasn't dangerous because of the tourists pulling trailers or boats backed up the traffic, and the locals took incredible chances getting by them.

No, it was dangerous because Nora Anderson was curled against his back, holding him hard and tight, so close that he doubted a piece of tissue paper could be inserted between them. It was dangerous because instead of being the least frightened, she was shouting with laughter and egging him on to new feats of daring.

They stopped for lunch at a pub midway down the lake, and when she pulled her helmet off and freed her flattened hair, her nose was sunburned and her cheeks were rosy from the wind and she was shining with happiness.

She looked carefree and young, and he found himself wishing that she would look like that all the time.

Over steak sandwiches, on a deck that stretched over the blue waters of the lake, they talked of Iggy's recovery and laughed about Luke eating Deedee's pie. Brendan told Nora about something funny that had happened at work, but was aware of not saying a single thing about Village on the Lake, which was supposed to be a pinnacle point in his career. She shared some of her ambitions for Nora's Ark with him.

It wasn't so much what they said as how he felt. Relaxed. At ease. As if he had known her forever, and she was the easiest person in the world to spend time with.

She sipped a beer; he stuck with water. Navigating the road, and his growing feeling for Nora, was going to take him having complete control of his senses! No impairment of any kind.

"You know what I did last night?" he asked.

"Cleaned licorice splotches off your shirt?"

"After that."

"Worked?"

He realized he was surprised that the answer to that was not yes. He always worked. But he hadn't last night.

"I looked up back columns of *Ask Rover* on the internet."

She blushed scarlet and took a swig of her beer. "Why would you do that?"

"Curious."

The blush deepened. "So, now you know. Nut job."

He frowned. "Are you kidding?"

"No. I never let anyone know I write that."

"But why?"

"All I ever wanted was to be normal. Not be laughed at. Not seen as eccentric or weird. I wanted to be popular and surrounded with friends. Instead, I had this thing, a strange ability to offer comfort to injured animals. My family used to tease me that I would have been burned at the stake if I'd lived in a different age.

"I can connect better with animals than people. It's

kind of like mind reading, only without words. I pick up on the animal's energy. My family thought I was strange. The kids I grew up with thought I was a woo-woo. I learned to keep all that stuff that is outside the norm pretty secret."

"So, when you write *Ask Rover,* are you picking up that energy thing, even from a distance?"

She scanned his face, saw he wasn't mocking her at all, but genuinely interested. "I'm not sure how much of it is picking up something from a distance, and how much of it is reading those letters really carefully."

"There are a lot of letters," he pointed out slowly, "from satisfied readers who are amazed by how applicable your advice is to their situation. How could you know that dog that had been shaking for a week had a broken tooth? How could you know that missing cat had gone in the appliance repairman's van?"

"They're just educated guesses…and a feeling. My weird little gift to the world. I hope you won't tell anyone it's me." She saw something in his face that looked stubborn. "It's for Luke's sake, too. So he can have a normal life here."

"What do you want for him?"

She sighed. "The things I couldn't achieve for myself. Popularity. A house full of friends. I don't want the fact that I do something different to make people laugh at him or judge him."

"You know, Nora, people make judgments. For instance, you know that dark period of history your family talked about, where they burned witches at the stake? They associated cats with witches, so they killed them, too.

"And when they killed the cats, the rat population

exploded. And rats carried bubonic plague. Before that was over, twenty-five million people were dead."

"I'm not sure I get what you're saying."

"People make judgments. Lots of those judgments they make are just plain wrong. Somehow, we all have to find our own truth."

He hesitated. "I liked *Ask Rover,* but I *loved* the crossed out rough drafts that I read beside your bed that night. Does any of that stuff ever make it past the final cut?"

"No. Never."

"I wish it did."

She laughed, self-deprecating. "I don't think the world is ready for *Ask Nora.*"

"That's where I think you are wrong. The world could use a little more Nora at her brilliant, funny, insightful best. The world could use a little more of the real thing."

"If I cry are you going to ask if I'm h-having an outburst?" she stammered.

"No," he said. "I'm going to do this."

And he did the most dangerous thing of all. He kissed her. He kissed her long and hard and deep. He kissed who she really was, not the tiny piece of herself that she chose to show the world.

"I shouldn't have done that," he said, pulling away from her.

"But why?" she asked, her eyes round with wonder and wanting.

He shrugged. "We should go."

"No. I feel as if, when you read the columns beside my bed, you uncovered part of my heart, whether

I wanted you to or not. That's not fair. Not unless you show me something of yours."

Brendan looked at Nora, and struggled with it. To show her who he really was. To crawl out from under the crushing weight of his guilt.

Her hand was suddenly on his. He could feel that energy of hers. Promising to lead him out of darkness toward the light, to roll the stone away from the entrance to the cave once and for all.

He still might have resisted.

If she had not proved one more time her intuition was uncanny. Nora said, "Tell me something about you. That's secret. Not just any secret. Your deepest secret."

He was torn completely, between not wanting to trust and for once letting his guard down. He had told her the world needed what was real about her. Could the same be said for him?

Nora knew things. She knew how to heal things. Look at Charlie. Just from being around her, under the same roof as her, the cat was pulling further away from dying every day.

So why had she asked this question? About secrets? The light in her eyes beckoned him in the direction he would not have chosen to go. The light in her eyes made him brave when he wanted to turn tail and run.

The long season of rain was over, and the sun had come out. Could his life be the same?

He took a deep breath. He told her something no one knew about him.

"I feel like a failure as an architect," he said.

"But you're very successful."

"I've never, ever, not even once stood in front of a

house I've completed, and felt pride. I've always felt like I missed something. So there you have it, my secret."

She studied him for a moment. And then she said, "That's not really the secret. It's just the first layer of it."

"What?"

"I'd be willing to bet my newly repaired iguana that that sense of not being good enough has a root somewhere."

"It's not like I feel *I'm* not good enough!" he protested, but her gaze called him out.

He realized he hadn't even told Becky all of it, but been vague about his beginnings. Wasn't that part of how he had failed her?

"My mom was never with my dad," he said, and had to clear his throat to go on. "She got pregnant, he didn't care. She never said it, but I suspect it was a case of unrequited love that culminated in a one-night stand. Who knows? Maybe she even used the pregnancy to try and trap him. But if she did, it backfired badly and left her young, uneducated and totally on her own. She was tired and bitter toward every man in the world except one, and that was me."

He shrugged, tried to laugh it off. "So there you have it, a genuine bastard."

There was something fierce in the way Nora was looking at him, as if she was seeing more, much more than he had intended for her to see.

"No," she said softly, "That's still just a layer of it. There's more. Tell me the rest."

This was her gift, then, unveiled. Her intuition calling to the broken place inside of him, coaxing it toward her light.

"We were poor," he heard himself saying. "There

seems to be this little trend where its popular to say you were poor, poor meaning you didn't go out to restaurants to eat, or you didn't get forty gifts under the Christmas tree, or you didn't have the cool designer label clothes like everyone else.

"People who were really poor? They don't brag about it."

There. That was enough. He'd told her he felt dissatisfaction with his work. That he was illegitimate, and that he'd grown up poor. Those were his secrets.

But not all of them. And she knew. He could feel her energy pulling the words from him. Or maybe they had just wanted out for so long, they could not be stopped now that they had started.

Like the tears, if he ever let them fall.

"We were the desperate kind of poor. My mom worked as a maid at a motel, and in private houses, in the mornings, and a waitress in the evenings. Every penny counted. Sometimes we didn't have food. Sometimes we got evicted because we couldn't pay the rent.

"I grew up knowing it would be up to me to make my mother's every sacrifice worthwhile. She managed somehow—I have no idea how, and probably would have rather she put food on the table—to squirrel away a little money for me to go to university. I worked three different jobs. I got scholarships. She lived long enough to see me graduate.

"Once she died, I moved across the country to Hansen. There was a small architectural firm here. I told myself it was for a job opportunity, but I think it was to leave all that behind.

"And then I met Becky. To tell you the truth, I couldn't believe a girl like her would look at a guy like me. She had grown up extremely well-to-do, the daughter of one of Hansen's old rich families. She was the swimming pool in the backyard, vacation home at Vale, finishing school in Switzerland kind of rich.

"I slammed the door on who I used to be," he said. "I was ashamed of it. I didn't tell anybody what I'd come from, let alone this rich girl who was crazy in love with me. I thought if she knew it all, she'd never say yes when I asked her to marry me."

"But didn't she ask?"

"Of course she asked. I think, at first, she thought it was part of my mystique that I didn't say much about my past."

He stopped himself. He was revealing way too much. No one cared about this stuff! But he looked at Nora, and he could see she cared. And he could see that the light in her eyes was not going to let him go, that he would not feel released until he told all of it.

"I felt I had to be worthy of Becky's faith in me. It wasn't enough to pay the bills every month. No. I had to succeed. I had to have all the trappings of success.

"When my boss decided to retire, we worked on my being able to buy the firm from him. And then, at the very same time, Becky's family home came up for sale. It was exactly the kind of house my mom had cleaned when I was a kid. She called them castles."

It was really time to stop. But it seemed as if that little boy who had promised his mother to buy her a castle was talking, and wasn't going to be quiet until he'd said it all!

"Sometimes if school was out for the day, or I was home sick, I got to go with her to those fancy houses.

"For a kid who was living in a two-room shack on

the wrong side of the tracks, that kind of house was a castle. A special room for dining? Four bathrooms? Hardwood floors and Turkish rugs and good art, and amazing chandeliers. The kids had bedrooms decorated in themes. In one house, the boy had a pirate room and the girl a princess room. I grew up on the phrase 'when my ship comes in.'"

It seemed to him he could stop right there. That he should stop right there. But it was as if a dam had broken inside him, as if something toxic was flowing out and with each word he spoke he felt cleaner and freer.

It was a free fall. He was free-falling into the light in her eyes, trusting that he could survive the landing. He took a deep breath. He was going to tell it all.

CHAPTER FOURTEEN

"BECKY, QUITE SINCERELY, didn't care if we bought that house. But I cared. I felt responsible for keeping her in the style she was accustomed to.

"I was stretched way too thin. I didn't want her to go to work. I felt that would make me a failure, mean I couldn't provide for her. I started working all the time, trying to make it all happen.

"She was becoming increasingly frustrated, trying to get through to me. She was beginning to see what she had mistaken for mystique was my inability to connect with her. She told me I wasn't fun anymore. That nothing was fun anymore."

And here it was, finally, the worst of it. The part where he'd killed a good woman who had done nothing wrong but love him.

"I didn't want to have a baby," he said, his voice hoarse from talking too damn much. "I thought it would just be one more stress. I didn't know she was beyond caring what I wanted. She was trying to save *us,* and I didn't even know we were in trouble.

"She'd booked us a ski weekend. Was I happy about it? No. Annoyed. Why was she spending money on frivolous things?

"But she wanted us to do something fun. She wanted us to be romantic. She had some big news to tell me. News worth celebrating. News worth spending money on.

"The day we were supposed to go, something came up at work. It seemed urgent at the time. Now I wonder if I made it urgent so that she would know I was still annoyed about spending money and taking the weekend off from work. I told her to drive up to the ski hill without me, that I'd meet her there later that night.

"She was upset with me when she left. It started snowing hard while she was on the road. She lost control of the car, skidded off the road and hit a tree. She was killed instantly. I found out her big news, the reason for our celebration, from the coroner. That she was pregnant. The baby died, too. She had stopped taking the pills. I know because I found them in our medicine cabinet after. When I was wondering if there was anything strong enough in there to end my misery, to end the endless question I asked myself.

"*Was* the fact that she was upset with me a contributing factor in the accident? Probably. And if work was everything before that, it was even more after. Aside from pills in the cabinet, it was the only way I could stop the guilt. The only way.

"You know, a week before she died, she said to me, 'If I die first, I'll come back and let you know I'm all right.'

"And I didn't hear the love in that. I just said, 'You won't be all right. You'll be dead.'

"She never has," he heard himself whisper. "She never has let me know she's all right. Because she isn't. And it's my fault that she isn't."

He waited to feel sorry that he had told Nora, sorry that he had exposed so much of himself to her, sorry that just as he now had a better idea of who she was from reading her column, she had a better idea of who he was.

He waited for her to say the wrong thing.

That he should absolve himself, or that Becky *was* all right, or that it wasn't his fault at all.

But she said nothing.

Nora didn't even look at him; she was looking out over the mirrorlike, serene waters of the lake. Her eyes were pools of deep calm.

He had to let her know who he really was. He had to. It was a compulsion he couldn't stop.

"I've never cried for her," he said. "Not the night they told me. Not at her funeral. Not once."

He thought that would make Nora yank her hand from his. But instead, her grip tightened. She left her hand where it was, and her touch had energy in it. Acceptance. Strength. Healing.

Suddenly Brendan felt an enormous sensation of freedom. He was still free-falling. It was the same as flying.

He had expected telling her would bring him to his knees, unleash that bottled-up torrent of grief.

Instead, it had given him wings.

From that moment of trust, an unexpected bond grew between them, and together they flew into the sun of summer.

They simply could not get enough of each other. Luke was part of the magic, somehow. Over Nora's sputtering protests, Brendan taught him how to ride the motorcycle in her driveway. And then he taught her. Just as with poker, Luke had potential, she had none.

The three of them sneaked away in the heat of the day to go to the beach and swim and play in refreshing, icy waters. They rented kayaks, which were more fun than the cumbersome pedal boats. They took the three-legged dog for long hikes in the cool of the forest.

With Iggy recovering under the kitchen table, and Charlie on Luke's lap, they played poker in the evening. Brendan even let himself be talked into Scrabble.

Increasingly, Brendan and Nora found ways to be by themselves. He took her to enchanted places, like the waterfall that cascaded out of the rocks on the Hidden Valley Trail. They ate picnics, and lay out on the grass, sometimes staying late enough to watch the stars pop out in inky skies.

Village on the Lake seemed the least important thing Brendan had ever done.

Important was reading over Nora's latest draft for her column. Important was taking Luke and Charlie to visit Deedee.

It was on one of those occasions that Brendan decided it was time to address the Charlie issue.

"Maybe it's time for Charlie to come back here to Deedee's. He's getting better." Brendan and Luke were doing dishes. Nora and Deedee were outside on her porch in the rocking chairs, Charlie on the elderly woman's lap.

"No," Luke said, and cast a troubled look through the screen door. "No. He's not getting better. He's holding."

But given what Charlie had looked like just a short time ago, wasn't "holding" a miracle?

Brendan smiled to himself. He had gone from being the world's biggest cynic to believing in miracles.

That was a miracle in and of itself.

And wasn't that what love did? Create miracles? Turn the ordinary into the extraordinary?

Love.

Brendan contemplated that word, shocked by it.

But what else could make everything ordinary feel as though it was infused with light?

Even the hunger he felt for physical connection with Nora—holding her hand, brushing her hair away from her face, touching her lips—was a miracle of feeling alive, of feeling eager about life.

He took pleasure in showering her with little gifts: a gold necklace with two hearts entwined, a set of tiny silver hoop earrings. Girlie gifts that she was so uncomfortable accepting and then wore with such feminine pleasure.

He took her to public places, like Shakespeare on the Lake, in the natural amphitheatre at Lakeside Park. He had a barbecue at his house and introduced her to his friends and business associates. She still wouldn't let him tell anyone she was *Ask Rover,* though.

And it hit him right then, as she was standing at his kitchen sink, after all the guests had gone.

He went and put his arms around her, and breathed in deeply of her hair. She turned and caught him hard and they clung to each other.

And then she stretched up and he stretched down.

And their lips met right in the middle.

And he knew.

In the depth and passion and soul of that kiss, Brendan Grant knew the truth. He loved her. And he put her slightly away from him and he saw the truth shining in her. She loved him, too.

"I want to stay the night," she whispered.

But he knew that would never work for him. And it would never really work for her, either.

What he was feeling for Nora wasn't a one-night-stand kind of thing.

There would be people who said it was too soon, and that he couldn't possibly know, and that he was rushing things.

But it wasn't too soon. When he counted back the days, he realized he had known her for six weeks. Somehow they had become the best six weeks of his life. He did know, and in this life, where things could turn around so quickly, was there ever a moment to waste?

He had never in his whole life so badly wanted to do something right. He put her away from him. "You need to go home."

She looked wounded, and he touched her swollen bottom lip with his thumb, nearly caved in with yearning. Gave in to the desire to kiss her one more time.

This time when they pulled away they were both panting. His shirt was tugged out of his slacks where her hands had crept under it, splayed themselves across his flesh with an urgent wanting.

He broke away from her. "Go home."

Tomorrow he would go out to Nora's Ark with his motorcycle and pick her up. He would have the most gorgeous ring he could find in Hansen in his pocket. He would have champagne and strawberries, and he'd carry them to a viewpoint in the mountains where he could show her the whole world.

And then he'd ask her to marry him.

But for now? She had to go home before he did something that disrespected her and the enormous love he felt for her.

"Go home," he said gruffly.

He lay awake for a long time that night, thinking that soon his bed would not be empty. That soon his life would not be empty. He lay awake thinking of how he would propose. The exact words he would say.

He lay awake picturing the light that would come on in her when he went down on bended knee in front of her....

When he finally slept, he dreamed.

Becky had finally come to him. She was in a meadow filled with brown-eyed, wild sunflowers. She was in long skirt, and she was dancing, just like Nora had been dancing that day with the bunny. There was a blanket spread out in the grass, and a baby was sitting on it, his pudgy fist full of wildflowers.

And Becky was holding something, too, just like Nora had been holding Valentine.

Her face shining with joy, Becky whispered, "We're all right. Can't you see that we're all right? All of us."

And he moved closer to her, wanting to see her, wanting desperately to tell her how sorry he was for not knowing what he had when he had it. He moved toward her, needing to see the baby on the blanket and the baby she was holding.

But then he stopped short.

Because it wasn't a baby she was holding so tenderly to her bosom.

It was Charlie.

Brendan woke covered in sweat, to the sound of the

ringing phone. He knew before he picked it up exactly what had happened. He actually considered not answering.

All this time he had been free-falling. Now he considered the possibility he was not going to survive the landing.

He picked up the phone. As he had known, it was Luke.

"Charlie's gone," he said.

Brendan almost said, "I know," but he didn't.

"You don't have to come," Luke said.

But he did. He had to go and be with them.

"I'll be there in a few minutes."

When he arrived, Luke was holding Charlie, with Nora sitting beside him, holding his hand.

She gave Brendan a beseeching look that said, *Take this pain away,* and he felt all the angry impotence of not being able to.

"I'll go out and dig a hole," he offered.

"No, I'm taking him to Deedee's." Luke said. "I made a box for him." He got up, carrying the lifeless cat, cuddling him against his narrow chest.

He brought back a box clumsily made of wood, the corners painstakingly sanded. It had a picture of Charlie lacquered onto the lid. Beneath the picture Luke had carved Charlie's name.

It was not a box that had been whipped up in the less than an hour since Charlie had died.

Nora lost control when she saw it.

But Luke didn't. He opened it up and laid the cat on the soft white towel inside. He put on the lid, and turned to Brendan, who felt as if his control was an elastic band being stretched thinner and thinner.

All this time, while he'd been having fun and romancing Nora and convincing himself love could fix everything and that the cat was going to get better, Luke had been getting ready for a different ending. A realistic one.

"We need to take him to Deedee's," Luke said. "I'll call her and let her know we're coming."

Considering how Deedee had had issues around being there when the cat died, Brendan wasn't so sure that was a good idea.

"We'll bury him there," Luke stated, as if it was all decided. Brendan might have suggested they bury the cat here, but he was terrified if he opened his mouth all that would come out would be a wail of fury and impotence.

Silently, with Nora beside him crying helplessly, Luke in the back, quiet and pale, with the cat in the box on his lap, Brendan drove them to Deedee's.

She was waiting, dressed in black. Luke gave her the box, and she stared at it, ran her fingers over the carving of the cat's name, bent and kissed the picture. And then they all followed her out to the yard.

Brendan saw that while he'd been laughing, and packing picnics and buying trinkets, and watching stars come out, Luke had not just been bringing back a neglected flower bed. He'd been preparing a resting place.

The bed that had been such a mess was now fully weeded. Underneath a rosebush, Luke had dug a square hole. It had been there for a while; white rose petals had fallen inside.

Luke took the box from a quietly weeping Deedee and gently laid it in. A shovel was set unobtrusively against the fence, and he went and got it and began to fill the hole.

Deedee wailed.

It reminded Brendan of how she had sounded when they had buried Becky, that day he had stood there and not shed a tear.

Nora put her arm around those thin, caved-in shoulders of Becky's grandmother.

"Let's go in," she said. "I'll make you a cup of tea." They moved toward the house. Brendan stayed outside with Luke.

"I'll do it," Brendan offered, moving to take the shovel from him.

Luke's grip on it tightened. "No," he said, his voice fierce and strong and determined. "I have to finish it. I'm making a mend."

Brendan shoved his hands into his pockets and rocked back on his heels. He was so aware of his own stupidity. Over the last while, his guard had come down. He had let himself hope that everything could be all right.

In a world where it never was.

He listened to the steady thump of dirt hitting the top of that painstakingly crafted wooden box. He thought of Charlie inside, still and silent. Had he actually thought the cat was going to live?

Dead was dead.

He thought of how powerless he had been to stop anything.

Even falling in love, when that was what he knew he could not do. He knew he could not do it, because the light had broken through the cracks in his cave, undermined the strength of the walls.

Everything felt as if it was shattering around him.

Luke glanced up. "Are you okay?"

The youth was watching him way too closely, with that look so much like his aunt's. You could hide nothing from these two; they *saw* you, right to your soul.

Brendan pinched the bridge of his nose. He swallowed hard. He tried to breathe, and when none of that worked, he spun on his heel and walked away.

"Go home," Brendan had said to her. His face had been ablaze with love and with promise for a future.

But that had been before Charlie died.

She tried to think if he had said a single word at that solemn, sad little ceremony in Deedee's backyard.

Nora didn't think he had. And then he had left without saying goodbye.

There was no way she could have known that those last words to her had stopped short of the future. What he must have meant was go home, go away, it's over.

Those magical days ended as quickly as they had begun. Just like that, the phone stopped ringing, the motorcycle stopped appearing in the yard.

What had changed? Charlie had died. That meant they needed him more, not less. At first, Nora felt furious with Brendan for letting them down.

This was when Luke needed to know he could count on someone else.

She needed to know that.

She had phoned and left Brendan a message. Had practically begged him to be there for her nephew. Had hoped he would hear her own unspoken need.

But he had not come.

Like a lovesick teenager, she had waited by her

phone for him to call and offer some explanation, but no call came because there was no explanation.

Trying to protect Luke, she went through the motions. She even managed to rise above her own pain to think of Deedee.

She was bringing Deedee a casserole as Brendan was leaving. He saw her and searched for a way to escape. There was none.

He looked awful, as if he wasn't eating or sleeping. There were dark circles under his eyes and it made her want to go to him, wrap her arms around him and hold him.

But he was glaring at her, and then he crossed his arms over his chest, waiting, his face a mask. Holding him would be like trying to hold a porcupine.

She had to fight such weak impulses in herself, anyway. He had broken her heart. He had broken Luke's heart. And she wanted to comfort him?

He needed to be brought to task, and she was just the woman to do it!

She didn't bother with the niceties. She didn't say hello, or ask where he'd been or why he hadn't called.

She said to him, her voice low with fury at his betrayal of her and her nephew, "What are you hiding from?"

He smiled a tight, horrible, icy smile. "I don't know what you mean."

"You made a mistake," she said. "But not the one you think."

"Excuse me?"

"You think the mistake was letting Becky drive that night. But you had started to make the mistake long before that."

CHAPTER FIFTEEN

"WHAT ARE YOU talking about?" Brendan said.

She could hear the coolness in his voice, but he wasn't shutting her down or shutting her up. He was the one who, over the summer, had given her a voice, and now he would just have to live with the consequences of that.

"She wanted to love you. While you were busy trying to impress her with someone you weren't, she wanted to love you. That's why she got pregnant. She sensed you pulling further and further away. She wanted you back."

"You can't know that."

"I can."

"Stop it. You don't know anything about me."

"I know you're hiding. From pain. From life. From love."

For one full minute she held her breath. He was hearing her. He was leaning toward her. He wanted it all: that place of refuge, the home, the love.

He wanted it all, and she could tell the exact moment he remembered the price. His face closed.

"That's rich," he said coldly. "This from the woman who never tells anyone who she really is?"

And then he turned and walked away.

The fury dissipated a bit that night as she contemplated that. She had taken a chance through these long days of summer. She had shown him who she really was. She had been zany and carefree, and she had let her intuition out.

Though maybe never quite so much as she had on Deedee's front steps this afternoon.

And she thought he had liked who she really was. Maybe even loved it.

But then, softly, it came to her. The point wasn't really what he liked or didn't like. The point was that *she* had liked it! She had loved it. She had loved living in that place of freedom, without masks.

As long as she was hiding any part of who she really was, she recognized she would never have power.

She recognized something Brendan Grant might not have known.

You could protect yourself by being alone. But that required nothing of you. Life required something. And that was that you become who you really were, under any circumstance.

Life went on. Nora had a boy to raise. School was starting again soon. He needed school supplies and clothes. She needed to get on with the business of living.

She had even stopped writing *Ask Rover,* and now was very aware she needed to start again.

So on that first day of school, after Luke had gotten on the bus, Nora went through the piles of letters she'd received, and she didn't pick a single easy one. She didn't pick one that said, "Sambo will not stop pooping on the floor," or "Buffy attacks the mailman."

She picked one that said, "My dog is sick. Do I spend the money to make him well, or do I give up?" She picked one that said, "My kids want a dog so badly, but I'm a single mom and I feel overwhelmed already." She picked one that said, "I work long hours and am never home. Is this fair to my dog?"

She picked them, and with Iggy, the most lovable iguana ever born, snoozing on top of her feet, she answered them, from the place deep in her heart that had always whispered to her.

That place that other people didn't always understand, because it was so pure and uncorrupted.

It was a place of untainted instinct and uncontaminated intuition, and it was who she had always been and who she wasn't going to be afraid to be anymore.

And when she was done answering them, she changed her byline. It said *"Ask Rover, by Nora Anderson."*

When she was finished, she went out and visited with her volunteers, telling them there would be a meeting soon, and to please bring ideas about better organizing the jobs and having systems in place for dealing with difficult situations like Iggy.

When Luke came in, she was busy making cookies for him.

"How was your first day at school?"

"It was okay."

But she could tell it wasn't. "What happened?"

"Gerry wanted another fifty bucks."

"I'm calling his parents! This is outrageous. I should have called them—"

Luke put his hand on her shoulder. She realized she was looking up at him, and that he had grown a lot over the summer.

"I went to the police station at lunch hour. I told them the truth. I told them I stole the bike."

Her mouth fell open. He had grown a lot in every way.

"Did you tell them that boy is extorting money from you?" she sputtered.

"No," he said. "I just took away the reason he could extort money from me."

"I'm going to call his parents."

"No," he said, "you're not. I'm not giving it one more ounce of energy. It's finished."

"Are you going to be charged? For stealing the bicycle?" She could feel that old, desperate worry clawing at her. That she was doing it all wrong.

That she had let Brendan into their lives, trusted him, and now Luke was dealing with the loss of a male he had looked up to. And he was trying to navigate difficult situations on his own. Why had he gone to the police? He should have talked it over with her! What if he was charged?

"The sergeant I talked to said it was unlikely I would be charged."

Something was different about Luke since Charlie had died. Instead of tearing him down, it was as if the death of the cat had helped him come into his own, and in such a genuine way that not seeing Brendan did not seem to be bothering him.

Luke had used the word *energy* so easily a moment ago, and suddenly, just like that, she could see his, and feel it.

Just like that, she knew who her nephew was, and who he would always be. She knew she had not done things wrong, after all.

Except maybe for one thing.

She realized he could handle an adult discussion. "I'm sorry about Brendan," she said. "I'm sorry that I let you become attached to him, and that he doesn't come around anymore."

When Luke looked at her, she realized he did so with eyes that were wise, the eyes of an old soul.

She knew in that second it was never going to be what she had hoped for him.

He was never going to be the popular kid, the one who laughed lots and was at the heart of all the fun.

It was never going to be like that.

It was going to be better.

He was introspective. Somber. Strong. Intuitive.

"Brendan not coming here is not about me," Luke said slowly. "It's not about you, either."

"What's it about?" she whispered.

"It's about hope. He hoped he didn't have to hurt anymore. When Charlie died, it reminded him he did. He was crying when he left Deedee's that day we buried Charlie."

Nora felt herself go very still. "Brendan was crying?"

"He didn't want me to see, but I did."

The words hit her like hammer blows. She'd been making it all about her. While she'd been breaking free, Brendan had been building up the walls of his prison.

And she had let him. She had accepted his strength. Accepted the fact that he wanted to be responsible for her and for the whole world. She had leaned on that, and come to depend on it.

She'd let him believe he was in charge of the whole world. She had relished that sense of being looked after!

And then Charlie had died, reminding him that protecting everyone and everything was a hopeless job. One he could not do. He withdrew, nursing the sense of failure and powerlessness that he'd had to face for the first time when his wife died.

"How'd you get to be so smart?" Nora asked Luke softly.

He snorted and was just a fifteen-year-old boy again, not a wise sage who had been born again and again and again.

"If you think I'm so smart," he said, snatching a still warm cookie from the sheet, "tell my math teacher."

Brendan stared down at the plan. It was after ten and he was still in the office. One of the fluorescent lights had started flickering a few hours ago, and now it felt as if his headache was flickering in unison with it.

He heard a door open somewhere in the building and ignored it. Janitorial staff.

He scowled at the plan, dissatisfied.

"You look happy."

He stiffened at the sound of her voice, straightened and glanced at the door. She was there. Her ginger hair caught the light and looked like a flame around her head. Her eyes were deep and soulful, and filled him with a sense of regret for the choice he had made.

To walk away. It was as if he had walked away from a pool of water beckoning a man who had crossed the desert.

But of course, he had walked away because he understood the nature of a mirage.

Even though he turned from her swiftly, masked that reaction of pleasure at seeing her, she did not go away.

She came and stood beside him, so close he could smell that cinnamon-and-citrus smell that was hers and hers alone.

He inhaled it as if it were that pool of water and he was that man dying of thirst.

"That's a pretty house," she said, looking down at the plan.

He ordered himself not to be drawn into discussion. To fold up his plan, fold his arms over his chest and drive her away.

But a man, any man, was only so strong.

And loneliness had made Brendan weak. He would just drink in her scent and her presence for a while longer. A few minutes.

"The house is okay," he said.

"Really? What don't you like about it?"

It's not what he didn't like about it. It was what he didn't like about *him*. He used to focus only on the house, and the function of it. He had never wondered about the lives that would be lived inside.

"It's a pretty house, for a lovely young couple."

"And?" she prodded.

"They've never known a moment's agony over anything."

"And?"

"And I hope they never do."

"But?"

"But I doubt it, because life doesn't go that way."

"That's right, it doesn't," she said, ever so gently, just as if he hadn't let her down. As if he hadn't let Luke down.

"That little baby they loved so much, that they were

cooing over and bouncing up and down on their knee while they sat across from me in my office?"

"What about the baby?"

"It will probably take them through the fires of hell one day. It could get sick, or experiment with drugs, or get bullied at school."

"That's what love does," she said, as if she was agreeing with him. "It leaves you wide-open to all kinds of pain."

"And this pretty little house wouldn't help any of that. It won't help it and it won't stop it."

"No," she agreed, "it won't. Because you don't have that kind of power."

"We're not talking about me."

"Yes, Brendan, we are—the one who builds houses, the one who chose to build houses because he always longed for a home. The one who wanted so badly for that home to protect all who enter there."

"Why are you here?"

"I've come to take you home. Not to a house. I've come to take you home to my heart."

"See?" he said with a snort of pure derision, doing what needed to be done, trying to wound her, trying to drive her away. "They were all right about you. You are a pure flake."

"Yes," she said sweetly. "Yes, I am. But I'm your flake."

"You're not my flake. I don't need a flake."

"You do. Desperately."

"What could you possibly know about my need?"

"Everything."

He scowled.

"I'm intuitive, remember? A healer. I know what you need."

Don't even ask her, he ordered himself. "What do I need?" he asked, masking his desperation with a sneer.

"You took a chance," she said. "You loved. And you felt as if it made you weak instead of strong."

Accurate, but not spookily so. He kept his arms folded over his chest, his expression cynical.

"You need a place," she said softly, "where you can put away your armor."

His mouth fell open. He clamped it shut.

"You need a place where you don't always have to be the strong one. Where it's okay to fall when the parachute doesn't open."

Now it was getting spooky.

"Where someone is going to be there to catch you."

"It sounds like a good way to get squashed like a bug on a windshield," he said.

"That's exactly how I'd want to go."

"Like a bug on a windshield?" he said cynically.

"In the service of love," she said simply. "You'll need a strong woman, Brendan. A relationship not based in her need and you providing, but based in true equality.

"Based in the recognition that, on some days, you'll hold her up, and other days, made strong by your love when she needed it most, she will hold you up.

"I'm that woman."

She sounded absolutely certain.

"I love you," Nora said with quiet composure. "And I'm never stopping. Not if it hurts me. Not if you won't let me. I'm still going to love you. I'm going to be wide open, and if it brings pain, I'm ready to accept that as part of the price of living fully, not tucked away in a cave somewhere."

He knew he had never said a single word about a cave to her. Never.

"So," she finished, her courage shining from her eyes, enough courage for both of them, "you might as well come along for the ride."

"You're crazy."

"I know," she said. "Ask Rover."

He fought the impulse to smile, but he had to fight hard.

And then she did the one thing he could not fight. The one thing that stole what remained of his strength.

She moved in close to him. She slipped her hand behind his neck and pulled his face to hers. She searched his eyes and found what she wanted there, because she smiled.

He recognized it instantly, identical to that very first smile he had seen from her when he had turned over a pile of rags in a paddock on a rainy night. It was a smile that knew exactly who he was and welcomed him.

And then she kissed him.

And he, weakened, kissed her back.

Only, the strangest thing happened. As her lips laid claim on him, his surrender became not weakness, but strength.

It felt as if she had somehow captured every one of those tears he had cried after that damn cat had died. She had captured them, and now she poured them back into his emptiness.

The energy washed off of her, and into him. Brendan could feel the life flowing back into his body, like water over parched earth.

He could feel himself opening instead of closing.

He could feel himself becoming everything he was ever meant to be, and then more. More than he had ever hoped he could be.

He lifted her slight body to him, and cradled her against his chest.

This was his home. This was what he had struggled to capture with his building designs his whole life, and this was why he had always had a sense of failure.

Because the most essential thing had been missing. Home was not a building. It was the spirit that filled it.

EPILOGUE

BRENDAN SAT BESIDE Nora in the crowded Hansen High School auditorium. They had endured the speeches, and with each one being duller and longer than the last, he wished Nora, Hansen's most celebrated citizen, had accepted the invitation to speak.

Once she had changed her column to *Ask Nora,* amazing things had begun to happen. The internet blog had been a sensation. A book of her columns and blogs had followed, and it had been on the bestseller list for eight straight months. And then she'd been approached to do a radio show.

So, as Hansen's most celebrated citizen, Nora had been asked to give the commencement address at the high school graduation.

But she had said no—it was Luke's day, not hers. Which had been a relief to Brendan, because what if the baby decided to come midspeech, and they had to leave fast?

They had long since sold Brendan's house on "the Hill."

When the acreage next to Nora's became available, they had purchased it. They had worked on the plan for the new house together. It wasn't the biggest house he'd ever built, and it certainly wasn't the grandest.

And yet it was filled with the secret that made a house something beyond a collection of sticks and stones. It was filled to the rafters with laughter and companionship and healing. Somehow Lafayette had made it in there, and so had Iggy. And the dog with three legs, who came when they called "Long" or "John" or "Silver." There was a descendant of Valentine named Cupid, and Ranger, and a small pasture that contained two sheep, Bo and Peep, and a burro named Burrito.

Nora's property had been sold at cost to Nora's Ark, now registered as a charity, with a board of directors and an army of volunteers running it. Though she still crossed the fence when a sick animal arrived in the middle of the night, even if she had not been called. She always knew a new animal had arrived, always knew when her special gifts were needed.

And more often than not, Luke was right beside her.

As each name was read out, a graduate walked across the stage.

It occurred to Brendan you could tell a lot about these kids from the way they crossed that stage. You could tell if they were shy. Or outgoing. Or plain old trouble. You could tell by the way they walked if they were going to be ambitious or complacent, if they were going to take the world by storm or just ride a lazy current through it.

"Ohh," Nora sighed quietly beside him.

He turned and looked at her, ready if need be to disrupt the ceremony, to pick up his wife, just the way he had picked her up all those years ago, and race for the door.

But she gave him a reassuring smile and placed his hand on the swell of her stomach. The baby kicked at his palm, as if impatient to make its entrance into the world. One day he or she would be crossing this stage. What would the way he or she walked say about all of them who had helped raise this child?

Brendan had deliberately chosen aisle seats. Now he glanced back toward the door, making sure the way was clear, judging how long it would take him to reach it with Nora in his arms.

But Nora and Luke had both assured him today was not the day, and for a reason Brendan still could not decipher, they knew these things. But still, he needed to be prepared. They had their way, he had his.

"Luke Caviletti."

Brendan turned his attention fully to the stage.

He had offered Luke his name a year ago, but Luke had said no. He didn't need the name to feel he was a valued part of the family. He had wanted to carry his father's name into the future.

As he came across the stage, that was what Luke looked like, a beam of pure light heading for the future. Brendan hadn't expected to feel anything at this graduation except too warm and bored, so his sudden emotion took him by surprise. He didn't try to pinch his nose, or swallow, or breathe it away. He just let it come, grateful to feel, to be alive, to have this moment of glorious pride and emotion.

He had helped raise this young man, and through the tears that blurred his vision, he could see every single thing about him.

Out of the corner of his eye, he saw the tears of joy and pride sliding down Nora's face, also. Brendan moved his palm from her stomach, took her hand in his and squeezed ever so gently.

Luke had never become what Nora had dreamed of—the popular kid who filled up their house with his friends and noise and activity.

What he had become was so much better.

He had become himself: strong, quiet, calm, certain in the gift he had to give the world. Neither Nora nor Brendan had been surprised when this young man, once terrified of hospitals, told them he would use the money Deedee had left him to become a doctor.

Luke had that same incredible quality that Nora had, the one that made people call her a healer. Only in him, it was more intense, more defined, something tangible in the air around him.

When Brendan had first met Nora, she had just lost her sister. And her fiancé. And yet despite that, she had never hesitated to be of service. She had been there for her nephew. She had provided a place of refuge for the lost and wounded of God's creatures.

Luke had that same ability to rise above what had hurt him, and use his life experience in service. He would make an unbelievable doctor.

And Brendan was learning from both of them. Village on the Lake was completed. People had moved in. They loved it there. It had won a Most Livable Community award. But now he understood exactly why all those early plans had always left him dissatisfied.

He had tried to use his work to shore up a wounded ego in service to nothing more than himself.

There was no satisfaction in that, no matter how many awards you won.

But today a different plan took center stage. He was designing a housing complex for single parents of limited income. It wasn't utilitarian or bare bones. It was beautiful.

Nora had been right. He had embraced the science of architecture with his mind, but his heart had always known it would lead him where he was meant to be. For what he really wanted was to create *home*.

Not just for him and Nora, for the baby and Luke.

No, for those afraid to dream. For those who had nothing to hope for. For those who had been abandoned, who had been crushed and were afraid.

The housing complex Mary Grant Court bore the name of his mother. Brendan loved it. He woke up every day filled with energy, excited to go to work, happy in a way he had not even known it was possible for a man to be happy.

Energy was really not the mystery he had once thought it was. You could see its power in a thunderstorm. It was energy harnessed when you turned on a light. Energy ran through each amazing thing on the planet Earth, all those invisible particles of matter moving so fast they gave the illusion of being solid.

But there was a place where energy transformed. And that place was the great mystery. It didn't remove pain; it married it. It didn't alter life experience; it merged with it. It fused with all things and became something larger than itself.

And that was when it became more than energy.

Then it became a force that could turn a pile of lumber and a load of concrete into that most blessed of places, a home.

Then it became the force that could heal the broken.

Then it became the force that could raise the dead.

Many people called it many things.

Brendan called it love.

And knew that he was the most blessed of men that he had been allowed to know it.

* * * * *

"You're relentless."

She took the plate of cheesecake he was waving under her nose.

"When I need to be." He dug in to his own helping. "Murphy and the twins are checking out some puppies at the horse barn."

"Murphy knows we can't afford a dog."

"You didn't have any pets when you were a kid?"

"A few of the families I lived with had a dog or a cat."

"Families. As in foster families?"

She nodded. "This is really good," she managed around an enormous bite.

"And you don't want to talk about it," he guessed. "The foster families, I mean."

She caught a fleck of crust from the corner of her mouth with the tip of her tongue. "Do you think your grandmother would give me the recipe?"

He smiled slightly. It was no easy task squelching the urge to kiss away the tiny golden crumb she'd missed. "She will if she figures you're gonna give me a piece, too."

A WEAVER VOW

BY
ALLISON LEIGH

First published in Great Britain 2013
by Mills & Boon, an imprint of Harlequin (UK) Limited,
Eton House, 18-24 Paradise Road, Richmond, Surrey TW9 1SR

© Allison Lee Johnson 2013

ISBN: 978 0 263 90131 3
ebook ISBN: 978 1 472 00512 0

23-0813

Harlequin (UK) policy is to use papers that are natural, renewable and recyclable products and made from wood grown in sustainable forests. The logging and manufacturing processes conform to the legal environmental regulations of the country of origin.

Printed and bound in Spain
by Blackprint CPI, Barcelona

There is a saying that you can never be too rich or too thin. **Allison Leigh** doesn't believe that, but she does believe that you can *never* have enough books! When her stories find a way into the hearts—and bookshelves—of others, Allison says she feels she's done something right. Making her home in Arizona with her husband, she enjoys hearing from her readers at Allison@allisonleigh.com or PO Box 40772, Mesa, AZ 85274-0772, USA.

For Ray and Saing.
Thank you for sharing your slice of Alaska
so generously with us.
The beauty all around you was exceeded only
by your magnificent graciousness.

Chapter One

It was the yelling that got her attention.

Murphy. It was so easy to recognize his voice. Particularly when he was yelling at a few million decibels.

Her stomach sinking like a lead balloon, Isabella Lockhart instantly dropped her cleaning rag on the lunch counter at Ruby's Café and raced for the door.

Locked.

Of course it was locked. She'd locked it herself just thirty minutes earlier. She darted back for the keys that Tabby Taggart had entrusted her with, finally spotting them on the stainless-steel work counter in the kitchen, where she'd left them after locking up the rear door.

She rushed back to the front entrance, fumbled with the lock, then burst out the glass door. Not only had the yelling continued, it was angrier than ever.

And it was all occurring smack-dab in the middle of Main

Street, right there in front of the café, where a large, dusty blue pickup truck was parked.

Murphy, please don't get into more trouble.

The whispered prayer was much, much too familiar. Moving here to Weaver had been supposed to change that.

She ran toward the truck, toward the yelling, then nearly skidded to a halt at the sight of the thin boy glaring up at a tall, broad man who was glaring right back at him.

What concerned her most, however, was the baseball bat clenched in Murphy's white-knuckled fists. If he took the bat to one more thing...

She couldn't bear to think about it.

"You damn well did know what you were doing!" The man's deep voice was furious.

"It was an accident!" Murphy yelled back. "I told you that a hunnert times!"

"Murphy!" Isabella dashed between the two males, grabbing the bat as Murphy raised it. At eleven, he already topped five feet, and only the fact that she was wearing a bit of a wedge heel kept his eyes from being at a level with her own. She tugged on the bat hard, pressing her hand flat against his heaving chest, but his grip was equally tight. "Let it go!"

His mutinous brown eyes—so like his father's that at first it had been a physical ache to see them each and every day—met hers and his knuckles turned even whiter around the wood. "No!"

She heard the man behind her mutter something, and then a large, tanned hand closed over the bat just above hers. "Give me that damn thing before you hurt someone," the man snapped, and yanked it directly out of both her and Murphy's battling grips. Then he tossed it into the cab of his truck and slammed the door shut.

Murphy's voice went up half an octave as he unleashed

a fresh round of curses that made her pale. "Dude! That's my bat. You can't just take my bat!"

"I just did, *dude*," the man returned flatly. He closed his hand over Murphy's thin shoulder and forcibly moved him away from Isabella. "Stay," he spit.

Isabella rounded on the man, gaping at him. He was wearing a faded brown ball cap and aviator sunglasses that hid his eyes. "Take your hand off him!" Whatever the cause of Murphy's latest altercation, this man had no right to put a hand on him. "Who do you think you are?"

"The man your boy took aim at with his blasted baseball." His jaw was sharp and shadowed by brown stubble and his lips were thinned.

"I did not!" Murphy shouted, right into Isabella's ear.

She winced, giving him a fierce look. "Go sit down." She pointed at the wooden bench on the sidewalk in front of the café. Her head was pounding and she had to control her own urge to add to the screaming.

Whatever had made her think she could be a parent to Murphy? He needed a man around, not just a woman he could barely tolerate.

He needed his father.

And now all they had was each other.

She pointed. *"Go."*

All gangling arms and legs and outraged male, Murphy jerked his shoulder out from the man's grip and stomped over to the bench, throwing himself down on it.

She pulled her gaze away from Murphy and looked up at the man. "I don't know what happened here—"

"Don't you have any sense at all, stepping in front of him when he's waving around a baseball bat?"

Isabella clamped down on her own temper. Whatever Murphy had done, it wouldn't help for her to lose her own cool. "Murphy would never hurt me," she said evenly, ignoring the snort the man gave in response.

She drew in a calming breath and turned her head into the breeze that she'd begun to suspect never died here in Weaver, Wyoming. She let it cool her face before she turned to face him again. "I'm Isabella Lockhart," she began.

"I know who you are."

She pressed her lips together for a moment. She'd only been in Weaver a few weeks, but it really was a small town if people she'd never met already knew who she was. Lucy had told her—warned her, really—about how different Weaver was from New York. That was why Isabella had hoped—still did—that the radical change might be the solution to her problems with Murphy. As long as she was able to hold on to him.

She focused on the man's face—what she could see of it beneath the hat and sunglasses, at any rate. "I'm sure we can resolve whatever's happened here," she continued in the same appeasing tone she'd once used to great effect with outraged prima ballerinas, "but could we do it somewhere other than the middle of Main Street, Mr., uh—"

"Erik Clay. Since there's no traffic to speak of, I don't know what you're worried about. But I am mighty curious how you think we're going to resolve *that*." He jerked his chin toward the bed of his truck.

He wasn't known for having much of a temper, but considering everything, Erik felt like retrieving that baseball bat and bashing something with it himself.

Focusing on the woman in front of him was a lot safer than focusing on the skinny, black-haired hellion sprawled on Ruby's bench.

She tucked her white-blond hair behind her ear with a visibly shaking hand. Bleached blond, he figured, considering her eyes were such a dark brown they were nearly black. It didn't seem natural that anyone with such light hair would have such dark eyes. He'd never much understood the bleached-hair deal. But even pissed as he was, he wasn't blind to the whole effect.

Weaver's newcomer was a serious looker.

"I'm sorry," she was saying. "Whatever happened, I'm sure I can make it right."

"Really?" He very nearly took her arm, but the way she'd squawked over him pushing the kid away from her kept him from doing so. Instead, he held out his hand in obvious invitation toward the truck bed. "Care to tell me how?"

Her brown-black gaze flicked over him. Her unease was as plain as the pert nose on her pretty face when she stepped over to the truck bed, which was nearly as tall as she was, and peered over the side. "Oh…sugar," she whispered.

The words he had for the damage were a lot less sweet than *sugar*. But sharing them held no appeal, considering the foul mouth her kid had already exhibited.

He reached down and plucked a baseball from amid the shards of colored glass that had once been a very large, very elaborate stained-glass window destined for the Weaver Community Church. "Your boy threw the ball deliberately."

"I did not!" Murphy screeched as he launched himself back into Erik's face. "And I ain't her—" he dropped an f-bomb as if it were a regular component of his vocabulary "—boy!"

Erik shot out a hand, halting the kid's progress even as he scooped the woman out of the kid's angry path.

"Murphy!" She wriggled out of Erik's grip and grabbed the boy's arm, physically dragging him back to the bench. "I told you to sit." She leaned over and said something under her breath that Erik couldn't make out, but that obviously had some effect, because the kid angrily sank against the bench and crossed his arms defensively over his chest.

The woman tugged at the pink skirt of her waitress uniform as she straightened. Erik quickly directed his gaze upward from her shapely rear when she turned and walked back to him.

She stepped up to the side of the truck and peered over the edge once more. "It looks valuable."

The window depicting the Weaver landscape had been a gift. An unexpected, completely unwanted gift. And it was probably wrong of him, but Erik calculated the value more in terms of personal discomfort than dollars, since the artist was a woman he was no longer seeing. And who'd likely tell him to pound sand when he approached her for a replacement, which he'd have to do, since he'd gone and donated the thing to the church, seeing how churches were more suited for that sort of thing than his plain old ranch house. Now they were expecting the thing. "It was."

Her slender shoulders rose and fell in a sigh that only served to make the curves filling out her uniform even more noticeable. Her gaze lifted to his. "If you could tell me how much the damage is, I'll figure out a way to pay you."

Erik looked away from those near-black eyes that were so full of earnestness he couldn't help but feel his anger lessening. And that just irritated him all over again. "*You* didn't throw the ball at my window. He did." He gestured toward the kid. "In my day, we pulled stunts like that, it earned us a trip to the sheriff's office."

She was fair-skinned to begin with, but he actually saw color drain right out of her face. Without seeming to realize it, she closed her hands over his arm, as if to prevent him from heading toward the sheriff's office right then and there. "Please. Not the police."

"Tell me why I shouldn't."

"He didn't mean to cause any harm."

Erik snorted, though it was a shame for such dark, pretty

eyes to show so much panic. "Really? He wound up his arm and aimed straight for my truck. I saw it with my own eyes."

"He's just a boy. Didn't you ever make a mistake when you were a boy?"

Heat was running up his arm, starting exactly where her fingers were digging into it. But it was her expression of sheer panic that had him sighing. That and the fact that he *could* remember a few ill-considered stunts from his youth.

"Relax." He eyed the boy, who gave him a sullen look in return. "He can work off the damages." Maybe that was to be his penance. Break the heart of a perfectly nice woman who'd saddled you with a stained-glass window you never wanted in the first place. In return, get saddled with a demon kid. "Out at my place."

Isabella showed no signs of relaxing, however. "Your place?" Her eyebrows—considerably darker than her whitish hair—shot up her smooth forehead as she visibly bristled. "What sort of thing are you suggesting?"

His irritation ratcheted up a notch again. "Honey, this isn't a big city filled with perverts. I have a ranch. The Rocking-C. The kid can do chores for me there."

"The *kid* has a name."

Why did Erik feel as if he was in the wrong here? He wasn't the one who'd willfully destroyed a piece of artwork worth thousands of dollars. "*Murphy* can shovel manure and haul hay and clean stalls. I figure every Saturday morning until the end of summer oughta do it." It wouldn't come close, but he wasn't saddling his peaceful existence with a delinquent for any longer than necessary.

"No *way*." Murphy shot to his feet. "I'm not wasting Saturdays with *him*."

Isabella wanted to tear out her hair. She pointed at the bench again. "Sit. I mean it, Murphy." She waited until he'd done so before looking back up at the man. "Mr. Clay, I—"

"No need for the mister, honey. Just Erik'll do."

"Fine." He undoubtedly called every female he encountered *honey.* She felt she ought to find it derogatory or something. She hadn't particularly loved being called *babe,* after all, even though she'd loved the man who'd called her that.

She blamed her scattered thoughts on too little sleep and too many months of worry. "I appreciate your willingness to work with me on this. Really appreciate it." He would never know how imperative it was that Murphy have no more brushes with the law. "But we don't even know you." She felt pretty certain that perverts—to use his word—weren't strictly the domain of large cities. "Small-town folk or not, I just can't send Murphy off with a complete str—"

"Talk to Lucy," he suggested. He didn't look amused. Exactly. But his tight jaw had relaxed just a little. It was still sharply angled, coming to a point with a whisper of a cleft in his chin. "She'll vouch for me," he added.

"Lucy *Ventura?*" She folded her arms, giving him a considering look. He was tall. Taller even than Jimmy had been, and he'd been six-three. This man was also broader in the shoulders, which—along with his chin or anything else about him—wasn't anything she ought to be noticing. Jimmy had only been gone for nine months. "You know her?"

"You could say that. She's my cousin."

"Oh." She dropped her arms and pushed her hair away from her face. Knowing that he was related to Lucy made her feel some hope that the situation could be redeemed. Not only had she and Lucy worked together in New York, they'd also been roommates for a time.

But that had all happened before Jimmy Bartholomew blew into Isabella's life.

"Here." Erik handed her the dirt-smudged baseball. It was clearly Murphy's. She recognized his scrawled signature on it that he'd added when Jimmy had given it to him. Pretending to be a big-league player, or just marking his own territory among his hoodlum friends. Whatever his reasons had been, there was no way Murphy could deny it was his ball.

She took it, rubbing her thumb over the stitching. She remembered the day Jimmy had given it to Murphy as if it had been yesterday.

Despair threatened to roll over her.

For her, Jimmy had been a whirlwind. Sweeping her off her feet one minute with buckets of flowers and outrageous displays, and proposing the next in front of his entire firehouse. But they'd never made it to a wedding.

It wasn't even three months from the moment they'd met until she and Jimmy's son were standing beside his grave.

She looked over at Murphy. When his father died, Murphy lost everyone he had.

Now he only had her because of the tenuous approval she'd received from a family court judge that placed him provisionally under her guardianship.

"Thank you," she whispered huskily. She held up the baseball between her fingers. "The ball means a lot to Murphy."

She could see Erik's jaw tighten again. "Then he shouldn't be tossing it at passing vehicles."

Another thing she could blame herself for. She'd been the one to send Murphy outside in the first place, thinking she could finish closing up the diner more quickly without him inside and underfoot, constantly complaining that he wanted to go home.

She wanted to believe that Murphy hadn't done it on purpose. But experience had taught her to be wary.

She looked along the street. There were plenty of cars slanted into the curb up and down Main, parked in front of the various businesses there. Not a single vehicle had driven by during their argument, though.

She'd wanted a place different than the city. She'd definitely gotten it. No Starbucks on every other corner in Weaver. No Starbucks at all, in fact. Just homey cafés like Ruby's that served up coffee the old-fashioned way, and no other.

She gestured toward the front door. "Do you want to go inside? We can work out the details." She wished she could see past his sunglasses. Get a better gauge on how merciful he might be inclined to be. "The least I can do is offer you some coffee." She managed a hopeful smile, even though all she wanted to do was put her head down on her arms and cry.

"Throw in a piece of pie if you've got it," he suggested as he headed around the truck for the driver's side. "And we'll talk. Meantime, I'll get this out of the middle of the road."

Murphy came off the bench when the truck engine started with a low growl. "What about my bat?"

Isabella shushed him. "Don't worry about your bat." She tucked the ball in her pocket and closed her hands over his thin shoulders, steering him toward the open door. "You're lucky he's not calling the police," she hissed. Inside, she pointed at the corner booth where his schoolbooks were still stacked. "Go sit over there and do some homework." His sixth-grade teacher, Mr. Rasmussen, was a big believer in homework. Murphy had hours of it every day.

"I'm *done* with my homework, remember?" Murphy rolled his eyes and slunk over to the corner.

How could she forget? It was because he'd been done with his homework that he'd wanted to go home. But she wasn't finished at the café yet, and she couldn't trust him to be alone yet. With no other option left for after-school care for him—she couldn't afford it—he had to come to Ruby's, where she could provide some supervision.

"Then redo it," she suggested wearily. She didn't think

she'd ever been so tired in her life. "Just sit over there and be quiet while I try to get us out of this mess."

"I wasn't doing nothing wrong."

"Really?" She gave him a look. "Like you weren't doing anything wrong when you were caught red-handed vandalizing a brownstone in our own neighborhood?"

He slid down into the booth, ignoring her.

She sighed and went behind the counter to put a pot of coffee on to brew. Then she went to the refrigerator case and pulled out an apple pie. She cut off a large wedge and popped it in the microwave to warm. If she was going to try bribery with coffee and pie, she might as well go all the way.

She was placing a large scoop of creamy vanilla ice cream on top of the pie when Erik appeared in the doorway. He was so large that he seemed to block out the afternoon sun for a moment. When he stepped inside, he pulled off his cap and rubbed his hand over his hair.

Dark blond. Lighter than the whiskers on his angular jaw. Cut short, it was thick and full even with the dent in it from his ball cap. Her mouth felt dry and she swallowed a little, looking down at what she was doing.

"Can I have a piece of that?" Murphy asked when she set the plate on top of the lunch counter.

Isabella nodded and started to turn toward the refrigerator case again.

"Please." At Erik's deep voice, she paused, looking back. But he wasn't looking at her. He was looking at Murphy, over in the red vinyl corner booth. "Please," he prompted again.

Murphy's lips twisted. "You're not my dad," he muttered, not quite low enough to go unheard.

"Damn skippy," Erik returned flatly. "If I were, you'd have enough manners to use *please* when you should, and you wouldn't curse around a lady."

The two males stared each other down for a moment.

Isabella, who'd given the whole please-and-thank-you-and-no-cursing speech to Murphy countless times, was ready to break in when Murphy grunted, "Please may I have a piece of pie?" His tone was sarcastic.

Isabella quickly nudged the plate she'd already prepared closer to Erik. "Ice cream is melting." She set up a folded paper napkin with a knife, fork and spoon next to the plate and filled a coffee mug. "Sugar or cream?"

"No thanks." With a last glance toward Murphy, he lifted one jean-clad leg over the padded red stool. "Looks great. Thanks." He slid the flatware aside and shook out the napkin, tossing it over his lap.

His ball cap was stained with God knew what; she was pretty sure it was mud caking the bottom of his jeans; his plaid short-sleeved shirt was damp with sweat and he smelled of hay. At least, she was guessing it was hay. But he used a paper napkin on his lap.

Shaking off her strange bemusement, she cut a slice of pie for Murphy, heated it for a few seconds and added ice cream to his, as well. She didn't even consider telling him to come get it. She wanted to keep as much distance between Murphy and Erik as possible.

She took it with a glass of milk over to the booth and set it in front of him. "You'll still have to eat your dinner," she warned.

He didn't answer. But his gaze flicked past her, then back down to his pie. "Thanks," he muttered a moment before he shoveled a forkful into his mouth.

Isabella pushed her hand into the side pocket of her uniform, toying with the baseball stuffed there. The pink dress was simple and clean, and she was perfectly happy to wear it, since it came with a paying job. Between it and the classes that Lucy had hired her to teach over at her dance studio, it would keep a roof—barely—over her and Murphy's heads. "You're welcome." She headed back behind the lunch counter. Having three feet of laminate countertop between her and Erik Clay seemed like a good thing. Having her hormones climb out of Jimmy's grave at this point was completely unacceptable.

"Okay," she said on a sigh. "Exactly how many hours on how many Saturdays are we talking about?" Murphy still had a few months left of school before summer vacation. And if his grades remained as poor as they were, she knew he'd be taking summer school, if it was even available. Otherwise, there'd be no choice but to add tutoring to an already thin budget. He also had to meet regularly with his therapist. It had been mandated by the court as a condition of her being allowed to bring him to Wyoming.

All of which, of course, could come to a screeching halt once their caseworker visited in seven weeks and made her final evaluation.

She blocked the thought.

Handling one worry at a time right now was about all she could manage.

"Well, now, that's a fair question." Erik tapped the tines of his fork softly against the surface of the plate a few times before he set the fork down altogether. He slowly tugged off his sunglasses and dropped them on the countertop next to the coffee mug.

Then his gaze lifted to hers, and Isabella's heart nearly skipped a beat.

Violet. His eyes were violet. Elizabeth Taylor violet. Surrounded by thick, spiky brown lashes that ought to have looked feminine but didn't. Nor did she make the mistake of thinking the color was derived from contact lenses. Not with this man.

"You bring him out next Saturday," he said, mercifully unaware of her thoughts. "Not this week. I'm busy moving stock with my uncle. But next. For four hours. We'll see how it goes from there. If he works hard, maybe he won't have to bless me with his charming company all the way through spring and summer, and we'll call it quits after a few months. If he doesn't…" He shrugged and picked up his fork again, looking as if it made no difference to him whatsoever.

She chewed the inside of her lip. It was late March. She was praying she still *had* Murphy come the end of the summer. "But if he does work steadily, you'll consider everything squared? Maybe even by the end of the school year?"

His gaze didn't waver from her face. "I won't call the sheriff, if that's what you're worried about."

She didn't care about being so transparent. When it came to Murphy, she didn't have that luxury. "It is." She wanted to look away from Erik's mesmerizing eyes but couldn't seem to.

"Got a pen?"

She automatically handed him the pen from her pocket. He leaned across the counter and grabbed a fresh napkin from the metal dispenser near his coffee mug, his arm brushing against hers. Without so much as a blink, he sat back on his stool and scratched out a few words on the napkin.

There was no quelling the shudder rippling down her spine as she whirled around, busying herself with the coffeepot that needed no busying. Without looking at him, she grabbed the cleaning rag she'd abandoned when she'd heard the commotion outside and started running it over the vinyl seats of the stools lining the long counter. When she reached Erik, she stopped and looked at what he'd written.

Four hours every Saturday through end of school year but no later than end of summer in return for destruction of stained-glass window.

He'd signed and dated it.

Hardly legalese, but she didn't care. He was Lucy's cousin and she could only hope that he was just as decent. The fact that he hadn't immediately summoned the sheriff when he could have was already more than Murphy deserved. "Do you want me to sign it, too?"

He shook his head. He jabbed the pen in Murphy's direction. "He does."

Chapter Two

"You let a set of pretty eyes and a smokin' body get to you, didn't you?" Erik's cousin Casey gave him a knowing look before focusing on lining up his pool shot. With a smooth stroke, he broke the balls, sending them rolling across the felt, sinking two. Case straightened and walked around the table, studying his options. "Otherwise, you'd have hauled that kid straight over to Max."

Max was their cousin Sarah's husband. He was also the local sheriff. "I thought about it," Erik admitted. He picked up the chalk from the side of the table.

It was a Friday night. He'd spent half the past week hauling Double-C cattle with his uncle Matthew. They were playing out at Erik's place tonight because lately Case had taken some aversion to playing at their usual spot in town. Colbys offered up plenty of pool tables as well as a cold beer and a burger. But getting his cousin over there these days was like pulling teeth.

Instead, Casey willingly drove forty minutes outta town to come to Erik's place.

Leaving that particular mystery alone for now, he thought about his encounter with the Lockhart woman and her kid the week before. "I didn't even notice her eyes—" *bull* "—or anything else about her. It was remembering the times when I could have been hauled into the sheriff's office for some stupid stunt." He chalked his cue even though it didn't look as if Case was going to stop clearing the table anytime soon. "Same as you."

His cousin grinned slightly. "Yeah, but that was when Sawyer was sheriff. He'd have gone easy."

Erik snorted. Sawyer was their uncle. A Clay through and through who put family above nearly everything. Except the law. "He'd have skinned us and hung us up to dry just to teach us a lesson."

"Or handed us over to Squire." Case was still grinning. "Let the old man teach us a lesson or two."

Squire was their grandfather. And if his sons were a hard, demanding lot, they came by it honestly enough from him.

"Dad told me the other day he thinks Squire's mellowing in his old age."

At that, his cousin finally missed a shot. "Right," he drawled. "And you didn't notice the Lockhart lady's pretty eyes."

Erik ignored that and took over the table.

"So she'll be bringing the kid out here tomorrow morning?"

"Yup." He sank a ball and moved around to the end of the table, lining up his next shot.

"What're you gonna have him do?"

"Shovel crap by hand for a few hours. Hell, I don't know. Pick rocks outta that field I haven't cleared yet." He got pissed all over again just thinking about it and he blew the shot.

Case grinned. "Just hand your money over now," he suggested as he took over the table again.

Erik grimaced and slapped a ten down on the side of the table. Then he returned his cue to the rack on the wall and went behind the wooden bar that Case, his father, Daniel, and Erik had built a few summers earlier. He grabbed a cold bottle from the refrigerator beneath the bar.

His cousin had the pool table cleared in seconds. "You want one?" Erik asked.

Case stuck the cue he'd been using in the rack. "I want a real beer. Not that prissy stuff you drink."

Erik pulled out a longneck and slid it across the bar. "Don't be sneering at my root beer," he said mildly. They both knew that if he chose to, he could drink Casey under the table. "Ordered this up special on the internet from some place in Colorado." He held up the dark brown bottle and smiled. "Home-brewed and smooth as cream. Lady who makes it is as old as Squire, or I think I'd be in love."

His cousin rolled his eyes. He took the beer and they headed up the stairs, ending up in the kitchen, where Erik had a pot of chili on the stove. He wasn't much of a cook, but a thirty-one-year-old man whose closest dining alternative was forty-minutes away tended to be able to scrounge a few things together. Between that and the frozen stuff his mother, aunts and cousins kept him supplied with, he managed well enough.

They filled their bowls and then went onto the porch that overlooked Erik's land.

"You gonna tear that old barn down anytime soon?" Case asked after he'd shoveled in most of his chili.

They leaned back in the oversize chairs that Erik had bought from a woodcrafter in Gillette, their boot heels propped on the wood rail in front of them. "Sometime this summer, maybe." The barn was the only structure still standing from when Erik had bought the property four years earlier.

He could have helped Matt run the Double-C. The Clay family ranch was the largest one in the state. But Erik had wanted something to call his own. "Gotten sort of used to looking at it." That, or he was starting to get lazy. He always had plenty of other things around the ranch to keep him busy, anyway. Chores never stopped in his business. And now his heifers were starting to calve. Another month, and there'd be more calves to deal with. Plus, he wanted to get started on the addition to his house.

The work went on and on. But it was the life he'd chosen. And the life he loved.

Casey yawned and slouched down in the chair another few inches. "So what're you gonna do about the window?"

Erik grimaced. "Haven't decided."

"Jessica'd make you another one."

"She thought I was getting ready to propose," Erik reminded. He still could hardly wrap his head around it. They hadn't even been serious. At least, that was what he'd thought. "Last month, after the whole window incident, she told me to eat glass and die." The window had been a heartfelt gift intended to pave the way for their future. She'd said a whole lot more when Erik had had to tell her how he felt—or didn't feel—but what still made Erik feel bad were the tears in her eyes when she'd said it. He didn't make a habit of hurting women like that, and he wished he could undo those few months of seeing her altogether. She hadn't been a nutcase. She'd been a perfectly nice woman. But that hadn't meant he'd been even remotely thinking marriage, now or way the hell off in the future.

And she'd flatly refused to take back the window. He hadn't wanted it. So he'd contacted the church.

"Women think about marriage all the time, I hear."

He blinked away the image of Isabella Lockhart that kept swimming into his head. He'd told Jess he wasn't looking for a wife. He wasn't all that interested in looking for a girl-friend, either.

And hookin' up for a night or two with a woman raising an angry kid like that Murphy of hers just didn't seem right. No matter how pretty she was.

He looked over when his cousin yawned again. "Keep-ing you up here?"

"Been up late all week working on a project."

His cousin worked for Erik's dad, Tristan, out at Cee-Vid. The company designed and manufactured computer games, and had made Erik's dad a millionaire several times over. But Erik had grown up knowing the business was still a cover for what his dad really was. An intelligence expert. And even though Erik and Case never discussed it, he figured his cousin's "projects" more likely involved Erik's dad's true calling than the computer games.

"Be glad Jessica lives over in Gillette," Case had contin-ued. "You won't run into her unless you make the effort." He pulled his boots off the rail and sat up. "Pretty as your face is, I'm headin' home."

"Wash that bowl," Erik said. "I'm pretty but I'm not doing your dishes."

Case grinned and headed inside the house. A few minutes later, Erik heard the slap of the kitchen screen door followed by the rumble of his cousin's ancient pickup.

Erik waved as Case drove past, and then looked out over his land. The sun was still a big, burning ball of red hang-ing in the thin clouds on the horizon. Snow could easily fall this time of year, but the fields in front of him were starting to green, and his horses were grazing in the pasture. All in all, it should've been a completely pleasant evening.

If he hadn't had to look forward to that hellion coming the next morning.

He hunched forward and thumped his boots down onto the wooden porch. Isabella would have to drive the kid out to his place. It wasn't as if Weaver had any sort of bus service. He'd given her directions to the ranch that day at Ruby's. Warned her that the road had a few rough patches along the way.

Personally, he liked the rough patches. They kept the occasional salesperson who thought they might head out his way from getting too enthusiastic about the trip. If someone drove out to the Rocking-C, it meant he really wanted to get there.

Isabella Lockhart, he knew, was from New York City. She hadn't been a dancer—Lucy had told him that—but she'd been in charge of costumes, or some such, at the dance company where Lucy had been the star dancer. When he'd been over at Lucy and Beck's place for supper a few weeks earlier, Lucy had been all excited about her friend moving to Weaver. Erik hadn't given her chatter much mind, mostly because he'd been more interested in the blueprints that Beck had drawn up for him for the great room Erik was adding to his ranch house. Now that he'd encountered the newcomer, he wished he'd paid his cousin more attention.

Calling her about it wasn't gonna happen, though. She might consider his curiosity more personal in nature than he intended. And after the mess with Jessica, he didn't need anyone making more of a man's simple curiosity than there was.

If Isabella really wanted to make things right, as she'd said, she'd have to make the trip, rough road or not.

He couldn't help wondering if she'd have the fortitude to

stick it out long enough to save her boy's hide, or if she'd decide along the way that life back in New York was more preferable and hightail it right back out of town. She wouldn't be the first person who did. Just because he'd never wanted anything else didn't mean he failed to understand that life in Weaver wasn't everyone's cup of joe.

Still, aside from the boy, the next several months were looking a tad more interesting than they might otherwise have been.

If she stuck it out.

"You gotta be kidding me," Murphy muttered, peering through the dusty windshield at the two-story house that finally appeared as they reached the top of a rise in the road.

Road was a generous term, considering it wasn't much more than two tracks in the dirt with a shorn strip of wild grass growing down the middle.

Her would-be stepson continued complaining. "This is crazy out here, Iz. Like *The Hills Have Eyes* or something."

"You're too young for R-rated movies. Especially horror stories like that one."

Murphy sat back in his seat and gave her a superior look. "I watched 'em all the time when Dad took me to the firehouse."

And had nightmares because of it, she thought but kept it to herself. "You heard Lucy as well as I did when we saw her yesterday. Mr. Clay's place is a working cattle ranch. You'll be outside, in the fresh air, exactly where you like to be."

"Yeah. Hanging with my friends, not with Bessie the cow." He made a face. "I hate it here."

"And I hated seeing you sitting in that jail cell after you broke half the third-floor windows of Mr. Goldstein's brownstone back home." She shot him a look, only to quickly turn her attention back out the windshield when the steering wheel nearly jerked out of her hands. "We're here only as long as the court allows it, Murph. Don't forget that."

"What's the difference between one foster home and another?" His shrug was uncaring, but Isabella heard the pain beneath his bravado.

At least, she hoped she heard it. It was the only way she could look past her own sorrow, knowing he didn't care that he was with her or not.

In the eight months since he'd been provisionally placed under her guardianship, she still wasn't entirely certain what was going on inside his head. While his father had been alive, Murphy had at least tolerated her. Since then, he seemed to enjoy taking every opportunity to prove otherwise.

"There's a lot of difference," she said now, deciding not to get into the distinction between being his guardian and being a foster parent. "Believe me. I know from personal experience what it feels like not having a place to belong. I saw the size of that stained-glass window, Murph. You're lucky he's giving you a chance to work it off." She had done some research online at the library and had a hefty suspicion that they were getting off incredibly lightly.

Evidently losing interest, Murphy looked out the passenger-side window and remained silent.

The entire car shuddered as she continued coaxing it along the ridiculous excuse for a road. Neither she nor Jimmy had owned vehicles in the city. She'd bought the four-door sedan from a dealer down in Cheyenne when they'd arrived in Wyoming.

Isabella had been thankful that the car had been a thousand dollars less than she'd budgeted. Which meant she'd been able to apply that toward the restitution the court had ordered for the vandalized brownstone. She'd still be making payments for some time, but it had felt good to send off that chunk.

With no small amount of relief, she felt the road beneath the tires smooth out as they drew closer to the house. It was white clapboard with dark green shutters at the windows and had a wide covered deck sticking out on one side. Not overly large, but with the ridiculously blue sky behind it, peppered with fat white clouds, it looked perfectly charming.

Somehow, it seemed to suit a man who'd cover his filthy jeans with a paper napkin while he ate pie in a café.

She followed the gravel-covered road around the side of the house. There was no obvious place to park, so she just stopped near the house. She turned off the car but left the keys hanging in the ignition. There wasn't any danger of being jacked out here in this place. "Come on," she prompted Murphy as she got out.

He swore under his breath, but shoved open the door and climbed out, too.

She looked at him over the roof of the car. "Remember what we talked about?"

He made a face. "Be polite. Follow instructions. Don't cause trouble."

She'd also told him not to curse. But she wasn't going to nitpick. "Right." She closed her door, and the sound seemed to get swallowed up in the quiet, open countryside.

"So where is he?" Murphy asked. Their shoes crunched on the gravel as they walked toward the house.

"Here." As if by magic, Erik Clay appeared. He was wearing a white T-shirt that seemed stretched to its limits over his broad shoulders and another pair of jeans that were just as mud-caked at the bottoms as the ones he'd been wearing the week before. He was also wearing a cowboy hat and leather gloves that only made the tanned wrists above them look even more masculine. "Wondered if you were gonna make it or not."

She didn't want him blaming Murphy for their lateness. "My fault. I didn't think it would take me quite this long to drive out here." She tried to aim her eyes somewhere other than at that impressive chest, but looking at his face was no less disturbing. And for some reason, those wrists above his gloves were…erotic. She finally settled for looking back the way she'd come. "When you said the road was a little rough, I had no idea." She turned toward him. "Next time I'll plan better."

His teeth flashed briefly. "Now that you're here, I'll show you around."

The desire to stay and have a tour was sudden and strong. So much so that it was unwelcome. "I can't. I have to get back to Weaver for a class."

He thumbed his hat back a few inches. "What're you studying?"

"Teaching," she corrected. "Lucy's put me on the schedule for several classes at her dance studio."

"Is that right…." He didn't seem to care when Murphy wandered away from them toward the wooden rails of the deck. "I didn't think you were a dancer like Lucy."

Isabella waved her hands ruefully. "Believe me. I'm not." Until an injury sidelined her career, Lucy had been one of the top ballerinas at the Northeast Ballet Theater. "I was the wardrobe supervisor at NEBT. But I've had enough training to teach some little girls a few basics." She also would be teaching the big girls a few things throughout the week, but didn't think tall-tanned-and-macho would be interested in hearing about yoga.

"So that's the reason for the getup?"

She thought she'd given up blushing when she was about fifteen. But when his violet gaze seemed to travel down her body, that was exactly what she found herself doing. "Um, yeah." She didn't ordinarily go around wearing formfitting jazz pants and stretchy camis that clung like a second skin. She wished she'd zipped up the sweatshirt. Doing so now would seem obvious, though. "Tap shoes are in the car."

"Tap?"

She nodded. One of her foster moms had been avidly into the activity. Isabelle had been happy enough to go along, because it meant she didn't have to stay back at home with the other six foster kids living there. When she'd been granted her emancipation a few years later and could afford it, she'd taken more classes. "So—" she gestured toward Murphy "—it *is* okay if I leave him here with you like this?"

Erik smiled a little. "Didn't figure I'd be treated to your company all the while, appealing as it might be."

She was definitely blushing now. She brushed her palms down her thighs. The diamond engagement ring on her ring finger winked in the sunlight. She tried to remember what Jimmy's wrists had looked like, and failed. "What time should I pick him up?"

"What time are you done at Lucy's place?"

"I'm only on for two hours." So far. If Lucy's business kept growing, she could end up with more classes. Which meant a little more money and a little less debt.

"Come on back anytime after that." His tone was easy. "If we're not finished, you can sit on the porch and relax a bit."

There were several rustic chairs scattered along the wide deck. Some had yellow-and-green cushions. Some didn't. Overall, the whole effect was entirely inviting.

Another unwelcome thought. Just as it was unwelcome recognizing that his deep, calm voice had a way of easing the knots between her shoulders.

"You're being very nice." Lucy had said he was nice. A very decent, perfectly nice man. And Murphy would be as safe as houses with him. "I've really got to go now, though, or I'm going to be late to my class. Murphy?" She raised her voice, looking toward him. "Don't forget what we talked about."

"Yeah, yeah." He twisted his heel into the gravel.

Hiding a sigh, she gave Erik an apologetic smile. "Thank you again for giving us this opportunity."

"Not *us*." He nodded his head sideways toward Murphy. "Him. He's the one who did it, not you."

"Yes, well, *he* is my responsibility. And I do thank you." She started edging backward toward her car. "I'll see you soon, Murphy."

Aware of Erik's gaze on her, she hurried to her car. When she started the engine and turned around to drive back the way she'd come, she could see in her rearview mirror that Erik and Murphy had not budged.

"Please let this go well," she whispered. Neither she nor Murphy could afford otherwise, whether her stubborn young ward realized it or not.

Once the faded red car was out of sight, Erik looked over at Murphy. Wearing an oversize black hoodie and blue jeans with a hole in the knee, he was still leaning against the porch, digging his shoe into the dirt. "All right," Erik said. "Your mom brought you—"

"She's *not* my mom." Murphy kicked the gravel, scattering the small pebbles. "She never married my d— She's just my guardian."

Erik decided he really should have listened more closely to Lucy's chatter. Or caved to his curiosity and called her at least once over the past week to pump her for more info, regardless of the consequences. "So where're your parents?"

"My dad's dead."

Erik stifled an oath. "Sorry. I didn't know." He studied

the kid for a moment, wondering about his mother. "How long ago?"

"Nine months." The kid lifted a shoulder that looked skinny even beneath the hoodie. "It's no big deal, dude. Am I gonna shovel cow crap or what?"

Erik figured it had to be a very big deal. Both his parents were still alive and he was glad of it, though he could do with a little less of his mother's unsubtle comments that she'd like grandchildren before she was too old to enjoy them. A crock, since he considered his mom to be pretty darn young, having passed fifty only a few years back.

He abruptly changed his mind about mucking out the horse stalls and pointed instead at the old barn. "You're gonna help me tear that old thing down."

"Then can I have my bat back?"

"Nope." He started toward his new barn. "Come on."

"Where?" Murphy's voice was rife with suspicion.

Erik's stride didn't slow. "To get some tools other than your baseball bat."

After a moment, he heard the shuffle of footsteps following behind him.

At least it was something.

"I've got a dozen women signed up for a second yoga class." Lucy Ventura sat on the edge of the desk in her small office, jiggling the baby she held against her shoulder.

Isabella swiped her neck with her hand towel. Tap dancing—even with six-year-olds—was a lot of work. "I can hardly believe a couple dozen women exist in Weaver who want to take yoga." She'd been happy to think they had enough for one class. Two would be amazing.

Lucy grinned. "You'd be surprised, Iz." A small burp filled the office. "Genteel as always, my daughter." She turned the infant around until she was sitting on her lap, facing Isabella. Where Lucy was fair, her daughter, Sunny, was dark. A mop of dark brown hair was tied at the top of her little round head with a bright red bow, and her dark brown eyes fairly snapped with cheer.

Until Jimmy, Isabella had never aspired to motherhood. Not with the childhood she'd had. Then he'd swept her off her feet, and her orderly life had flown right out the window. She couldn't help wondering what might have happened if he'd lived. What their baby—if he'd ever changed his mind about not having any—might have looked like.

An image of Murphy swam into her head. He looked like his father.

Would Erik Clay's children have his violet eyes?

She banished the errant thought and draped the towel around her neck before giving Sunny her finger. The baby latched on and yanked it around. "She's so beautiful, Luce. I can't believe how life has changed for us."

Lucy smiled gently. "Weaver's a good place to heal, Iz."

"I hope so," she murmured. Sunny's skin was as soft as down. "Murphy has a lot to heal from. He adored Jimmy."

"I was talking about you, too."

Isabella lifted her shoulder. "I'm a big girl. I'll survive, as usual."

"Surviving isn't necessarily the same as living," Lucy countered. She'd dropped by the studio only to see how Isabella's classes had gone and was dressed in a pretty sundress that Isabella herself had made for her a few years ago as a gift. "I learned that when I met Beck."

"He seems like a good guy."

"Oh, he's good all right." Lucy's eyes suddenly danced. "Anyway, what did you think about the Rocking-C? Erik's place," she prompted when Isabella gave her a blank look.

"I didn't see much of it. The road out there is terrible."

She didn't want to think about *him*. "I just hope this whole deal works out between him and Murphy."

"If Erik has any say in it, it will," Lucy assured. "I told you. He's one of the good ones."

The baby had lost interest in Isabella's finger and she moved to peer through the window that overlooked the dance studio. The room wasn't large but it was perfectly outfitted, which was typical for Lucy. "I don't want Murphy to forget that his father was one of the good ones, too." Her thumb nudged the engagement ring Jimmy had given her around and around her finger.

"You miss him."

Isabella sighed. "Sometimes it feels like I haven't had a whole lot of time *to* miss him." She exhaled again. "I loved him, but there are times I want to scream over his lack of planning." Only the fact that she and Lucy had been friends for more than a decade allowed her to admit it. "The standard life-insurance policy the department offered? Only once he was gone did I discover that he'd never updated the beneficiary from Murphy's mother." Even though, when he'd realized just how serious his situation was, he'd told her he had. If there was anything left after the medical bills, he'd believed she would need it to care for Murphy.

Lucy was wincing. "Maybe he didn't have time," she suggested tactfully. "Considering how fast everything happened. Does anyone even know where she is?"

Isabella shook her head. "Not since she finished serving her prison sentence. Jimmy had no idea where Kim went after that. Seems horrible to think of one's life in terms of money, but it would have gone a long way toward the medical bills."

"Not to mention paying restitution for Murphy's stunt."

Isabella didn't deny it. She might not have been named on the life insurance, but she was in charge of settling what was left of Jimmy's estate. She'd sold off nearly everything, except their clothes and a few other personal possessions, to take care of the debts he'd left. "He always figured he'd die in the line of duty. Not—" Her throat tightened. She shook her head. A firefighter, Jimmy had been larger-than-life. But dealing with the minutiae of real life had not been his forte. Even in the short time they'd had together, she'd realized that. And she hadn't cared because she *was* good with real life. She'd had to be since she'd been orphaned as a baby. And she'd loved him.

When the staph infection had hit after a seemingly simple scrape he'd gotten during a fundraiser for a homeless shelter, there had been nothing any of them could do. Despite Jimmy's excellent health, every treatment the doctors had tried had failed. In a matter of weeks he'd been gone; the only thing he'd left behind was his trust in her that she'd take care of everything. Most importantly, his son.

"Well," Lucy said after a moment, "you give Weaver a chance to work its magic. On both you and Murphy."

Chapter Three

Erik heard the sound of the car approaching long before it arrived.

He looked at Murphy, who was unenthusiastically pulling nails from a stack of boards. "Your—Isabella is here."

Murphy immediately flipped the heavy hammer he'd been using down onto the messy pile of boards. "'Bout freakin' time."

Erik decided to ignore the comment. "Hammer goes back in the barn on the wall with the other tools."

The kid gave him a sidelong look. They'd already had about a half dozen of what Erik was kindly considering *instructional* moments. The first one, over wearing safety goggles while they started the demo, had earned Erik a blue earful of what he could do with his orders.

Erik had heard the boy out, told him the next time he spoke like that he'd toss him in the water tank and held out the goggles. Murphy had begrudgingly put them on, possibly because he'd noticed the big metal tank was surrounded by a half dozen mama cows that didn't look particularly eager to share.

Not that he hadn't put Erik to the test again soon after. But the second time Murphy had mouthed off, Erik had pitched him headlong into the deep, cold water.

Hopefully, he'd learned by now that Erik meant what he said.

Now he just eyed the kid back, waiting for him to make his decision. Fortunately for Murphy, working in the sun had gone a long way to drying out his soaked clothes.

Grumbling, Murphy pulled off the goggles and picked up the hammer to carry over to the new barn.

Erik blew out a breath, glad the kid hadn't pushed him again. He wasn't sure what he could resort to after the tank, which was a pretty harmless punishment all in all. He didn't figure Isabella would appreciate his washing the kid's mouth out with soap, which is what he'd earned once when he was young.

Leaving his sledgehammer propped against the side of the partially dismantled barn, he started walking toward the house. Isabella was just pulling up next to it in the same spot she'd parked earlier, and he watched her climb out of her car.

He'd have had to be dead not to admire the sight.

And he wasn't close to dead.

Unlike Murphy's father, he reminded himself, whose loss still had to be affecting both the boy and Isabella.

Continuing toward her, he started peeling off his ancient leather gloves. She wasn't a widow. She and Murphy's dad hadn't been married. The boy had told him that. But she was still wearing an engagement ring. He could see it now, casting sparkles as she shaded her eyes with her hand, looking his way.

"Put your eyes back in your head, dude," Murphy muttered as he caught up to Erik and passed him by. He aimed straight for the car, not giving Isabella a single word of greeting on his way toward the passenger door. He just yanked it open and sank down on the front seat.

He saw Isabella's slender shoulders dip a moment as she watched Murphy, then they straightened as she continued closing the distance between her car and Erik.

"Did it go well enough to continue again next week?" she asked bluntly, and he felt the impact of her black-brown gaze somewhere in the middle of his stomach.

"Went fine." A lie, but what occurred while Murphy was working for him could stay between him and the kid. For now. "How'd your dance classes go?"

She shot the car another glance, but the smile she gave Erik seemed sincere, even revealing a faint dimple in her cheek that he hadn't noticed before. "Great. There's nothing like being in a studio with a bunch of little girls wearing taps on their shoes."

"I'll have to take your word for it," he said drily.

She laughed lightly. "Trust me. There're worse ways to earn a dollar."

He thought about Murphy's outraged face when he'd dumped the kid in the tank. "Probably." He wondered how long she'd been engaged. And knew that wondering wasn't one of the more productive ways to spend his time. "Next time you might want to send him with a hat," he suggested. "He didn't want to wear one of mine, but the sun's only gonna get brighter, and he'll be outside most of the time."

"I'll make sure he brings one." He easily had a dozen baseball caps, most of them gifts from Jimmy that Isabella had known he would never part with.

It was much easier looking past Erik's big body to the land around them than at the man himself. "So what, um, what sort of chores did Murphy do?" She couldn't even get him to make his bed in the mornings.

"We're tearing down that barn over there." He gestured toward a ramshackle wooden structure that didn't look like any barn Isabella had ever seen. It was a narrow, long building with half its roof and walls missing. But even partially torn down, it was big.

"Looks like a huge job. You will tell me if he misbehaves, won't you?" She'd rather deal with small insurrections along the way than an out-and-out war that might give Erik cause to cancel the entire arrangement.

"I'll tell you if something serious occurs," he said.

It wasn't entirely the answer she was looking for, but she had to believe it meant that for now, Murphy's method of restitution was still a go.

"It's pretty obvious he misses his dad."

Isabella couldn't help looking back at Erik. Beneath the shade of his stained cowboy hat, his violet gaze was gentle. And it unnerved her entirely.

"We both do." She took a step toward the car. "So same time next week?" She couldn't help but hold her breath.

"Actually—"

She felt her stomach drop.

"You don't have to wait until Saturday. Unless he's busy during the week after school, he could come out here and work."

She felt as if her brain was scrambling to keep up. "You want him to come more often?"

Erik shrugged. "He'll just work off the window that much sooner."

If Murphy were occupied even one afternoon after school, it would be one less day she needed to worry about him during those hours. But the extra driving would cost time and money for gas. "Would you mind if I think about it? Murphy's still settling in at school, and—"

"Think as long as you need to," he said easily. "You know how to reach me if you want to bring him. Otherwise, I'll just see you next week. Maybe you'll allow yourself enough time to get that tour," he suggested, "if you're interested in seeing where your boy's gonna be spending a lot of his time."

She was interested. Not entirely because of Murphy. But it was only because of Murphy that she nodded. At least, that was what she told herself. "I will." A glance told her that the boy had his feet propped on his opened door. It was lunchtime and she imagined he'd be pretty hungry after the way he'd spent the morning. "Thanks, again," she said, turning to go.

"It's going to be all right, Isabella."

She paused. "Excuse me?"

"You and Murph. You're both going to be all right."

Murph. What Jimmy had called him. Deep behind her eyes, she felt a sudden burning. Unable to think of a response, she just nodded jerkily and hurried toward the car, almost as fast as Murphy had done.

"I want McDonald's," Murphy said as soon as she got in beside him.

"There isn't one in Weaver." And she had no interest in finding out where the nearest one was. "I'll fix you a hamburger at home."

He made a wordless sound that clearly conveyed his disgust. "*Everything* here sucks. Especially El Jailer back there."

"Mr. Clay is not your jailer." He'd probably go ballistic if he thought he'd have less than a week before he had to return. Cowardly or not, she decided it wasn't the time to bring it up. "And it will continue to *suck*," she added evenly, "as long as you keep thinking that way. Get your feet down, close your door and put on your seat belt."

He did so, slamming the door with more force than necessary before yanking his belt across his thin body.

She was much too aware of Erik Clay standing right where she'd left them, witnessing everything. His evident agreeableness aside, he already knew too much about her less-than-stellar parenting attempts. Now he was seeing even more. She started the car. "You *were* cooperative with Mr. Clay, weren't you?"

Murphy shot her wary look. "Why you askin' me? He prob'ly already ratted me out."

She turned the car around, trying not to notice Erik in the rearview mirror. "Ratted you out about what?" Then she frowned, really looking at Murphy. "Are your clothes damp?"

He just made a face and crossed his arms, ignoring her.

All systems normal, then.

She hid another sigh and resolutely kept her gaze on the road. If Erik was still watching them drive away from his house, she did not want to know about it.

So why did disappointment tug inside her when her gaze flicked to the mirror despite her resolve and she saw nothing but his house?

Erik went over to his folks' place for Sunday dinner the next afternoon. His dad wasn't one much for the ranching life he'd been raised with, but they still lived on a spacious property out near the Double-C where he'd grown up. The place was crowded and boisterous. This wasn't unusual when the Clay family got together, as it did every Sunday, what with uncles and aunts and cousins and their spouses and their kids.

Erik sometimes showed, sometimes didn't, depending

on how busy he was at the Rocking-C. And while he was keeping a pretty close eye on those mama cows, today he was restless enough to want a change of scene. The fact that Lucy and Beck might be there as well was incidental.

When they weren't, though, he just had to lump it. He could have called ahead to find out for sure, but he wasn't willing to raise any particular questions over why he was so interested. So he tucked into his mom's tender pot roast, stayed through blueberry cobbler, then headed out with the excuse he wanted to get in a few hours of fishing.

Because it was one of his favorite ways of relaxing, he figured he wouldn't arouse his family's perpetual curiosity. So when he made it all the way out to his truck, he thought he was home free.

Until his mother, Hope, trotted from around the back of the house, carrying a covered dish and calling his name.

He waited, knowing there wasn't much else he could do.

"I'm so glad I caught you," she said and held up the dish. "You skedaddled out so quickly."

He took the dish from her. She'd wrapped it in a towel, and even through that, it still felt hot. He looked under the lid. Leftover pot roast nestled in mashed potatoes. "Looks like I'll be eating well this week. Thanks." He brushed a kiss over her cheek and pulled open the truck door.

"Honey, you're not still worried about the church getting that window, are you?"

He shook his head. He was resigned to contacting Jessica again. He also knew it'd be smart to give her more time to cool down first before he did. "I warned Reverend Stone it'd be a while before they'll be able to install it." Since the church hadn't expected a new stained-glass window until Erik had needed to get rid of one, they'd only gotten as far as calling meetings to discuss where it should be installed. But still, Erik felt honor-bound to deliver one at some point.

He'd cooled off enough since that ball had flown straight at his truck to appreciate the irony of his situation.

Behind her stylish eyeglasses, his mother's gaze was sharp. "Then what's bothering you?"

"Nothing, 'cept I got a rainbow waiting on me."

She just lifted an eyebrow. "That old trout you keep trying to catch doesn't bite a lick after seven in the morning and I know you're not pining away for Jessica. Perfectly nice girl, but you were no more in love with her than you were with Sally Jane Murphy in the tenth grade."

And this was what he got for not heading straight to the fishing hole and bypassing dinner altogether. Sally Jane had been the first girl he'd ever slept with. Even then he hadn't mistaken her definite appeal for something it wasn't. "That kid who broke my window is named Murphy."

She nodded. "I'd heard that."

He expected she had. Nothing happened in Weaver without the town's grapevine buzzing about it. "When's Justin get home from school?" His little brother was back east getting his master's degree in something too convoluted for Erik to even understand.

She cocked her head slightly and her long, brown hair slid over her shoulder. Just like when he'd been a kid trying to hide his broccoli in the napkin on his lap, he wasn't fooling her, and they both knew it.

"The kid's guardian is a friend of Lucy's," he added.

"Heard that, too." She smiled slightly. "I'm taking Isabella's yoga class on Tuesday evenings."

He nearly choked. "'Cause you're interested in yoga, or just checking out the newest woman of marrying age to come to town?"

She merely smiled with as much satisfaction as she had when his guilty conscience made him confess about the broccoli, and patted his cheek. "Enjoy the fishing, honey."

Then she turned on her heel and sauntered away, disappearing around the corner of the house.

Undoubtedly to spread the word among everyone still inside that her oldest boy was showing interest in the newcomer.

"Shoulda stayed home with the cows," he muttered to himself and swung up into his truck. Nothing good ever came out of trying to be subtle around his family.

He headed toward home, not bothering to maintain the pretense of fishing. His mom was right. He'd been angling for that rainbow longer than he cared to admit, and the damn thing never bothered taunting him unless it was early in the morning.

The drive home from his folks' house, though, took him straight through Weaver and right on past Ruby's. Being Sunday, it was closed. But that didn't stop Erik from wondering where Isabella was living. Maybe, like a lot of newcomers, she'd chosen the newer side of town where Cee-Vid was headquartered. There was a Shop-World out that way and apartments and office buildings, all of which Erik privately considered an eyesore despite their convenience. Or maybe she'd chosen to live in the older part of town.

And wondering at all just made him even more restless.

He passed Lucy's dance studio. Nearly the entire front of it was lined with windows, though white curtains hung in them to obscure glimpses inside from passersby. Like Ruby's, there was no activity.

He abruptly turned into Colbys's parking lot next to the studio. There were only a few people inside the bar and grill when he entered and took a stool at one end of the bar.

"Hey there, Erik," Jane, the new owner, greeted him from the other end. "Don't usually see you in here on a Sunday afternoon." Her gaze went past him toward the door. "You alone?"

He nodded and folded his arms atop the gleaming wood bar. "Give me something dark from the tap, would you please?"

She slung a white bar towel over her shoulder and moved to the taps. A moment later, she was sliding a cold pint toward him. "Get you anything else?" She held up the food menu.

"Just came from dinner at my folks'." He nodded toward the flat-screen television hanging on the wall to his left. "Mind turning that on?"

She pulled a remote from beneath the bar, turned on the television and handed the remote to him. "Choice is all yours." With a smile, she left him in peace.

Smart lady. Aside from a temporary misstep over thinking to charge for playing pool, which she'd since corrected, he didn't get why Casey had a bug up his butt about her.

He turned to ESPN and left the volume low. If there'd been anyone around who looked interested, he'd have picked up a game of pool. But he didn't feel like shooting a game by himself. Jane was back at the end of the bar chatting with Pam Rasmussen, who was dispatcher over at the sheriff's office and married to Rob Rasmussen, who taught over at the school. He easily tuned them out as he nursed his beer and watched the tube.

And then he heard the word *yoga,* and his attention zoomed right in on the women like a dog going on point.

He grimaced, turning up the volume a little, hoping to drown them out, but it was no use. He finally looked over his shoulder casually. "Yoga's a popular subject," he said. "My mother was talking about it this afternoon."

Pam looked at him, her round face wreathed with a smile. "When I called up Lucy to register for the class, she told me I'd just snuck in before she had to cut off registrations."

He grinned wryly. "Who woulda thought? Yoga classes in Weaver."

"Not just yoga. I hear Isabella's gonna teach a belly danc-ing series soon, too." She smiled wickedly. "And maybe pole dancing. Robby's not sold on the idea, but I told him it's sup-posed to be terrific exercise."

Erik tried not to let his jaw drop. And then he had to work hard not imagining Isabella wiggling her hips around in some dance-of-the-seven-veils thing...much less swinging around on some damn pole. He could well imagine conser-vative Rob's reaction to his wife doing it.

Obviously recognizing his discomfort, Pam laughed. "Blame your cousin Lucy. She's the one who hired Isabella. I was talking to Neesa Tanner at church this morning and she was raving over how much little Jenny likes her tap classes with Isabella." She swiveled her stool around to face him. "You've got that boy of hers working out at your place. What do you think of her?" Her nose practically wriggled. "She's single," she said in a singsong tone.

He made a face and turned back toward the television. Pam was the dispatcher, but even when she wasn't on duty, she seemed compelled to dispatch news concerning the resi-dents of Weaver. After a moment, he stood, dropped some cash on the bar for the beer he'd only partly consumed and headed out.

His brain could stay preoccupied with a woman just as easily at home.

"I hear she's staying at your mom's old house." Pam's voice followed him.

He stopped cold at that revelation but tried to act non-chalant. "Oh, yeah? Small world." Then, because something he didn't want to examine really closely had started zipping through his veins, he sketched a wave and pushed out the entrance.

Out in the parking lot, however, he raked his fingers through his hair, struggling with disbelief. He almost called his mom right then and there to ask why she had kept that particular nugget to herself, but fortunately a glimmer of common sense remained inside his head. Not that that glimmer kept him from driving right past that very house.

His mom had grown up there, not moving out until she'd married his dad. But she'd never sold it. Somebody in the family had always seemed to find a use for it at one time or another through the years.

The grass in the little rectangular yard was a bit overgrown, but otherwise, the place looked pretty much the same as it always had. White paint. Black trim.

And in the picture window that looked in on the living room, he could see Isabella sitting at a table, her head propped in her hands. Weariness screamed from her hunched shoulders.

The glimmer of sense faded to black. Winked out completely.

He pulled next to the curb in front of the house and shut off the engine.

She hadn't budged.

Calling himself ten kinds of fool, he got out of the truck, spotted the covered dish from his mom and grabbed it. It was still warm but no longer hot enough to need the towel. Dish in hand, he headed up the front walk and knocked on the door. From there he couldn't see through the window, but it was only a few seconds before she pulled open the door.

Her dark eyes widened and filled with alarm. "What are you doing here? I thought everything went okay yesterday."

He wanted to kick himself. "It did," he assured her quickly. The last thing he wanted was to cause her more worry. "I was just at my folks' place," he added, holding out the dish. "And since I was passing this way anyway, figured I'd deliver these leftovers from my mom." Hell. His ears were burning. "She remembers how much I ate when I was Murph's age."

Her gaze dropped to the dish, then lifted back to his face for a moment before skittering away again. "I don't know what to say."

He'd have been better off staying at Colbys and putting up with Pam. He lifted the lid. "Say you're not a vegetarian."

She let out a sudden, breathy laugh. "This is a very unexpected surprise." She reached for the dish and her fingers brushed against his as she took it. If she felt the tingling that he did, she showed no sign of it as she lifted the lid again and leaned over a little, inhaling deeply. "Smells wonderful." She glanced up at him. "But would these leftovers be yours if not for us?"

"You won't be taking any food outta my mouth," he assured her drily. "Every week I get another batch or two from someone. You're saving my refrigerator from being overloaded."

"Well, then." She smiled. "How can I refuse? I'm sure Murphy will devour it."

Erik could easily see over her head into the living room. The furniture was the same furniture that had been there for years, from the squishy, slightly worn couch to the round table in the dining area. "Where is he?" He couldn't be certain, but the papers spread across the table looked like bills.

"In his room doing homework." Her smile turned wry. "Or else just avoiding me as much as he can." She took a step back. "Would you like to come in?"

She was wearing a pair of skinny blue jeans and an oversize white shirt that hung down to her thighs. Her white-blond hair was pinned up in a messy sort of knot on top of her head and her feet were bare.

Everything about her was appealing.

Except the sparkling diamond on her finger that blinked at him like a flashing stoplight.

"Thanks, but I gotta head back home."

"Okay." Her lips curved a little, seeming only to accentuate the fullness of her rosy lower lip. "I'll be sure to get the dish back to your mother the next time I see her."

This was what he got for attributing the leftovers to his mom. "Just bring it out next time you drive Murph to the ranch." He managed not to ask if he'd have to wait until Saturday for that. He had no intention of pushing it.

"I'll make sure she gets the dish with all the other stuff I'm collecting from her," he added. "Now, go on and enjoy the rest of your Sunday," he said.

Her eyes turned bright and her dimple flashed. "I will," she said, clasping the dish to her chest. "Especially now that I won't even have to cook."

He managed a grin and turned to go.

It was all he could do not to trip over his own two feet as he strode back to his truck.

Whoever said the way to a man's heart was through his stomach had it all wrong.

All it took was a pair of flashing brown-black eyes and a mischievous dimple.

Chapter Four

The following Saturday, Isabella tried to allow more time to get out to the ranch. Erik had been kind enough to drop off those leftovers. The least she could do was take him up on his offer of a tour of his ranch.

Not that she had a single inkling whatsoever about cattle ranches. She wouldn't know at all if she was oohing and aahing at the appropriate times.

But still.

Having driven the rough stretch of road four times now, she was a little better prepared for that particular experience. She fancied that she was even beginning to learn when to maneuver to the right or left to avoid particularly jarring holes. Which made the trip go considerably faster.

But they still didn't arrive as early as she'd planned.

She just hadn't anticipated having to nearly physically drag Murphy out of bed to get him going this morning. And it hadn't helped that she'd dithered over what outfit to wear, all because she'd be seeing Erik Clay for a few minutes. That was something she had never done in her life. Not even with Murphy's father.

The boy was sprawled in his seat, his eyes at half-mast and his lips turned down in displeasure at having to spend more time with the man he called "the Jailer."

She wished she knew what to do to help him change his attitude. She'd already spoken with his counselor, Hayley Templeton, for suggestions. But nothing was working.

"I wanna go back to New York—" Murphy broke his silence with the abrupt announcement "—and live with my *real* mom."

Her hands tightened around the steering wheel. It wasn't the first time that he'd mentioned his mother. Jimmy had never lied to his son about her, though. Murphy knew perfectly well that Kim was a troubled woman who'd spent time in jail. "I know you want to go back to New York. But that doesn't mean we know where your mother is." If Isabella took him back, admitted that she had failed to provide him what he needed, he'd be placed into the foster-care system. Maybe with a better, more suitable family than her.

But guilt and grief collided inside her chest every time she thought about it.

She'd promised Jimmy.

"I'm sorry," she said huskily. "I know you miss your dad. I do, too. But going back isn't going to happen right now."

"Then *when?*"

They topped the rise in the road, and the ranch buildings came into view. It relieved her as much as it worried her. "I don't know," she said. Never, if she had her choice. Sooner, if the caseworker didn't like what she saw when she visited.

Murphy just gave that disgusted wordless grunt of his.

But he said nothing more as she drove the rest of the way

and parked next to the dusty blue pickup truck beside Erik's house. "Come on," she said as she climbed out of the car. "The sooner you get started, the sooner you'll be finished."

"Yeah, until you get out here to take me home." He slammed the car door shut and stomped ahead of her, heading toward the barn he'd worked on last week. When Isabella followed, his head swiveled around, and even beneath his Yankees ball cap she could see the alarm in his eyes. "Don't you gotta leave to go teach?"

"Yes. But not right this minute." She caught up to him. "I want to see what you're doing and say hello to Mr. Clay. He's offered to show me around the ranch."

His lips twisted. She was certain he would have said something if Erik hadn't appeared at that particular moment. Luckily he did, coming out of the partially standing barn. He had a pair of goggles dangling around his neck and a sledgehammer in his leather-gloved hand. Dusty jeans and a pair of equally dusty boots completed his outfit.

And she nearly swallowed her tongue.

Lucy hadn't told her exactly how well they grew male gods out here in Wyoming.

With nothing else covering his wide shoulders and washboard stomach but the gleam of sweat, Erik Clay looked as if he belonged on some calendar somewhere for women to drool over.

"Thought you said you missed my dad," Murphy accused in a low voice.

Horrified at herself, Isabella dragged her attention away from all that raw glory. "I *do*."

Murphy just made a face.

And why wouldn't he?

If she missed Jimmy as badly as she believed, why was she getting hot and bothered just from seeing a man's bare chest? And why had she been worried about what to wear?

"Mornin', Murph. Isabella. Beautiful morning to be outside, isn't it?"

It was beautiful. Every day the weather was growing a little warmer; winter was giving way to spring, even though snow was left in patches here and there. She mentally axed the whole tour altogether. She couldn't hang around to enjoy the morning.

Not with a man who wasn't Jimmy.

"It is lovely," she agreed. She folded the lapels of her long, purple cardigan sweater around her and avoided looking directly at Erik again. "I'll be back about the same time as last week, if that still works?"

"Ought to be fine. Murph, you know where the tools are. Get yourself that same hammer you were using last week. We're going to finish demoing the old barn this morning."

Murphy gave Isabella another searing look as he trudged off toward the other barn that was situated well beyond the house.

Isabella watched him go with an unsettling sense of panic.

"You all right, Isabella?"

She started, unintentionally looking back at Erik, only to find that he'd pulled on a short-sleeved shirt while she'd been avoiding looking at him. It ought to have helped. But the pale blue checked shirt was only partially buttoned, and the image of his bare chest seemed engraved in her mind's eye. "I'm fine," she said quickly.

"You're looking kinda peaked."

"Nothing some sunshine won't take care of." She looked back at her car. "I have your mom's dish in the car. Is there someplace you'd like me to put it?"

"Kitchen's fine."

She nodded and started toward her car. "The, um, the roast was delicious. I told your mother when she came to

my yoga class last week. I forgot all about the dish, though."
Hope Clay had looked plainly delighted when Isabella had
mentioned the leftovers that Erik had dropped off. "You
have her eyes." She cursed herself the second she heard the
words come out of her mouth.

She had no business noticing—or commenting—on any
such thing.

"I'd better give 'em back, then," Erik murmured.

She frowned, automatically glancing up at him.

He was smiling slightly. "That was a joke, Isabella."

Feeling foolish, she rubbed the bridge of her nose. "Sorry.
Guess I'm preoccupied." *Yes. With things you were supposed
to have buried with the man you were going to marry.*

"I can be a decent listener if you want to talk."

Panic bubbled inside her, which was silly. Just because
he was offering didn't mean she had to take him up on it.
She yanked open the door to the backseat and retrieved the
dish that she'd left on the floor. Clutching it to her midriff,
she closed the door. "I'll keep that in mind."

Erik hid a sigh. She was as skittish as a new filly, hanging on to the pan as if it was a shield.

"I don't want to keep you from your work," she said
quickly. "Just point me toward your kitchen."

He nodded at the house on the other side of the vehicles.
"Kitchen's in the back."

"It really was thoughtful of you to deliver the leftovers."
She smiled quickly, nervously, but her lashes kept her gaze
hidden, and then she was scurrying around her car, aiming
for the steps leading up to the deck.

Erik let her go, figuring she needed the space.

He remained right where he was until she returned a few
minutes later. When she spotted him still standing there next
to her car, her steps faltered.

"Was there something you needed to tell me about Murphy?"

"Something I want to say," he allowed. "Isabella, I'm well aware of that ring you wear."

Her eyes widened. She opened her car door, and her fingers curled over the top. "I don't know what you mean."

She wasn't talking about the ring, of course, and he knew it. "I think you do," he countered softly. "I'm attracted to you. I'm not the kind of guy who bothers hiding something like that. And I think maybe you feel a little bit of the same."

Red color hit her pale cheeks. "You're imagining—"

He lifted his hand. "Let me finish."

Her lips clamped together. Her gaze avoided his.

"Attracted or not, I see your ring. Your fiancé died less than a year ago. You're not ready to take it off. Maybe you'll never be ready to," he added, even though he hated the reality of it. "I would just feel better keeping the air clear between us. Until you want to take off that ring, or even want to start thinking about taking off that ring, I'm not going to push." He'd try, anyway. "Isabella. Please. Look at me."

She swallowed visibly, making something ache inside him, until finally she lifted her chin. Then her lashes.

And her black-brown eyes met his.

He felt the impact rock through his gut and managed a smile. "Even if you wear that ring for the rest of your life, it doesn't mean I wouldn't like to be your friend."

Her throat worked. Her gaze shied away again. "Are men and women ever really just *friends?*"

They were when there wasn't a speck of physical chemistry between them. And that damn sure wasn't the case here. But he'd do his level best to try. If only so she'd learn she could trust him. "I'd like to give it a shot," he said quietly.

She gnawed on her upper lip. "Murphy needs to be my focus. My only focus. We're all that each other has left. He—"

"Will adjust," Erik said. "I know it'll take time, but he *will* adjust. To everything, including a new life here in Weaver."

She shook her head. Lifted her slender shoulder. "Time's just it. Murphy's only provisionally under my guardianship. Our caseworker could decide at any time that I'm not good enough for the job and take him away from me."

He frowned. Of course she was good enough. Anyone with eyes in their head could see she was doing everything she could for Murphy. "Why? You were engaged to his dad. Obviously a part of their life. Does he have other family? What about his mom?" The boy hadn't mentioned her, but that didn't mean much. Murphy hadn't volunteered anything to Erik.

"His mother is around somewhere. But Jimmy—my fiancé—always had custody. They were never married and she has a lot of problems. Murphy doesn't know her at all. And Jimmy and I—" She looked away. "We were only engaged a few weeks before he became ill. He proposed a month after we met. The court is very aware of that."

He did the math. Murphy had told him his dad died less than a year ago. Which meant Isabella hadn't been a long-term fixture in the man's life at all. Yet she'd taken on raising his son. "And he doesn't have anyone else?"

She shook her head. "When Jimmy realized he wasn't—" Her voice thickened. She cleared her throat. "One of the last things he was able to ask of me was to take care of Murphy," she finally said. Her voice was a little steadier, but when her gaze flicked up to his, her eyes were damp. "Murphy's my only family now, too. I can't lose him, as well."

He couldn't help himself. He covered her hand with his and squeezed gently. "You won't."

She looked at their hands. He figured it was progress that she didn't move hers away.

"If our caseworker decides that I can't keep him on the

right path, I will." Her lips twisted sadly. "The court let me bring him here because I convinced them that the new environment would help. But here we are. We'd only been in town a few weeks when he broke that window of yours. The caseworker will be visiting before school lets out for the summer. If Murphy isn't showing signs of settling in by then, she could well decide he's better off in foster care." Her voice turned raw. "I can't let that happen."

"Then we have to make sure he settles in." He squeezed her hand once more then dropped it. He'd play the role of "just friend" if it killed him.

And sooner or later, God willing, she'd be ready to move on.

And then, all bets would be off.

He was a Clay. When they set their eyes on something, very little would stand in their way.

She studied him for a moment. "Why do you care? Murphy barely tolerates me. I can only imagine how he behaves toward you when I'm not around."

He left his reasoning out for now. "Murph and I are coming to a meeting of minds." He'd wondered if the kid would tell her about the water-tank business. It seemed obvious that he hadn't. "Trying to push me around isn't quite the same as doing it to you."

Her eyebrows yanked together. "Murphy doesn't push me around."

Erik knew she wouldn't appreciate the word *manipulate* any better, though he didn't have to stretch his imagination far to figure out that it was the more accurate term. "Push his boundaries with you, then," he amended tactfully.

Her lips compressed. Aware of a movement from behind, he looked over his shoulder to see Murphy finally emerging from the barn. The hammer was slung over his shoulder, and even across the distance, Erik recognized the measuring look he gave them.

Whether Isabella knew it or not, the boy considered her his territory.

And he didn't want to share.

Considering Murphy's situation, Erik couldn't really blame him. If he'd been a fatherless boy and some guy had come sniffing around his mother, he'd have felt the same. Murphy had to be very aware that Isabella was his only hope of having some sort of family to call his own.

Erik pulled out the gloves he'd shoved in his back pocket and slapped them against his palm. "I'll let you get on your way." He would've been happy to stand and talk with her for a month of Sundays, but he needed to rethink his opinion some about the kid. And she'd need space to think about what he'd said. "We'll see you when you come back."

She nodded silently and lowered herself into the car, only to pop back out. Her hands closed over the top of the door again. "Erik?"

It was the first time she'd said his name.

And damned if it didn't do something strange—and not entirely unpleasant—to his knees. "Yeah?"

"Thank you."

"For what?"

"Where should I start?" She lifted her shoulders. "For everything."

"You don't have to thank me. What're friends for?"

Her lips curved into a slow smile. She shook her head, looking a little bemused, then climbed into her car again. This time, she shut the door and started the engine.

He watched until she'd driven out of sight.

A friend for now. But with time and a lot of luck, he intended to be more.

A lot more.

* * *

Isabella was trembling so badly that as soon as she was certain she was out of sight of the ranch, she stopped right there in the center of the bumpy, ridged road.

She rested her elbows on the steering wheel and raked her fingers through her hair, resting her forehead in her hands.

What was she doing?

Entertaining notions of being friends—or anything else— with Erik Clay was so far off base that she needed her head examined.

The man was nice. He was decent. And heaven help her, he'd wakened every hormone she possessed with a vengeance.

Agreeing to be *friends* was about as safe as offering a pyromaniac a lit match. And about as foolish.

Knowing that he was attracted to her, too, just poured gasoline over the whole mix.

But she wouldn't—couldn't—dare let Murphy get burned in the process. And what would happen to him when Erik's interest waned? She knew perfectly well that few men were ever interested in permanently taking on someone else's child. She'd grown up seeing that fact proved again and again.

She'd simply have to set Erik straight the next time she saw him. Tell him that she appreciated his concern, and certainly his willingness to let Murphy work off the damage he'd done, but that was all. And if he repeated his suspicion that she was attracted to him as well, she'd deny it.

She'd loved Jimmy.

Feeling *anything* for another man was out of the question. "Out of the question," she repeated aloud. Just hearing her own adamant voice steadied her.

She put the car in gear and bumped her way down the

hideous path, trying to put Erik Clay behind her where he belonged.

She might as well have wished for a smooth, paved road.

"Come on." After a morning of demo work, the barn was finally down and Erik set aside his sledgehammer. There would still be a lot of cleanup, but the worst was done, at least.

He walked up behind Murphy where he was stacking the boards Erik wanted to save and flicked the kid's ball cap so that it fell forward over his nose. "Go put away the hammer."

The boy looked at him. He was obviously whipped from the pace that Erik had set. So tired, even, that the angry, defensive look his eyes always carried was absent. Which left behind only a brown-eyed, skinny kid who looked as young as he really was.

"Why? Iz isn't gonna be back yet."

"I know. I want to check one of the water tanks."

Murph's eyes widened with alarm. "I haven't done—"

"Relax. I'm not tossing you in. Just making sure it's still full." He wiped his sweaty brow with his arm. "Cows get thirsty, too. Go on. Get a move on."

"What about that?" The boy gestured at the sledgehammer Erik had left propped against the recovered boards. "You want me to put that away?"

He started to shake his head, but nodded instead. The tool was heavy. Weighed thirty-six pounds with a yard-long handle. He doubted Murphy had the strength left to carry it all the way back to the new barn.

But since Murph had asked, Erik would let him. "Just leave it against the tool chest," he said. "You don't have to hang it up on the rack."

Murphy grabbed the long handle and grunted when he swung it upward, obviously planning to carry the handle against his shoulder the way Erik usually did, only to have to take a step back when the weight of it sent him off balance.

Erik barely kept himself from grabbing it, but the heavy hammerhead hadn't come close to hitting Murphy, so he let the boy handle the matter himself. Though he did pick up the claw-foot hammer and hand it to him so Murphy didn't have to bend back down to get it.

"Thanks," Murphy muttered and turned away.

Erik watched. Waited.

Halfway to the barn, Murphy let the hammerhead fall down to the ground. He adjusted his grip on the handle and dragged the thing in the gravel behind him.

Erik hid a smile.

The hammer wasn't gonna take any harm from a little gravel, after all.

Erik went into the house and retrieved a few cold bottles of root beer, then went out to the truck and drove it over to the new barn, meeting Murphy on the way. The kid climbed in when Erik stopped, and he handed the boy one of the bottles.

Murph's eyes goggled a little. The longneck brown bottle had no label. "Is that beer?"

Erik snorted. "Yeah. I'm gonna give an eleven-year-old a beer. It's root beer."

Murph twisted off the cap and tossed it on the console where Erik had tossed his. "My dad gave me beer," he boasted.

Erik had no reason to think badly of a dead man, even one who still held Isabella's heart. But if the kid was being truthful, his estimation of the man dropped some right then and there. "Did you like it?"

The bill of the boy's cap dipped. "'Course," he scoffed. "Drank it all the time with him."

And that was a lie. Erik could hear it in the kid's voice.

He drove toward the pasture he wanted to check. "First time I drank a beer, I was sixteen. Puked it right back up." His grandfather Squire had found him and Case out behind one of the barns at the Double-C. The old man had just laughed and told them it served 'em right. "Did your dad teach you how to handle a ball the way you do?"

"Yup." The boy looked away but the lie was as clear to Erik as the first one.

He hid a sigh. Murphy wouldn't appreciate sympathy. "You play in school? Little League?"

"School."

"Weaver's got a decent community league."

Murphy's lip curled. "This dinky town?"

"Surprised you haven't heard about it." Rob Rasmussen was one of the coaches, and Erik knew Murph had him as a teacher. "They ought to be taking sign-ups soon. It goes all summer. I played when I was younger." He still did whenever enough guys could get together for a game.

Murphy's bottle halted midway to his lips. "What position?"

"Shortstop."

The boy kept drinking, studiously disinterested. "My dad was always pitcher when his firehouse played. He'd tell me 'bout it when he'd get home."

"He play a lot?"

Murphy shrugged. "I guess." He looked out the side window. "Iz was gonna marry him, you know."

"I know." Erik tooted the horn to nudge a few stubborn cows out of his path. Used to his truck, they slowly plodded aside, moving on to another patch of green to chew on.

"She's never gonna marry anybody else."

"I guess that'll be up to her, won't it?" he said a lot more easily than he felt.

He knew the kid was warning him off.

That was okay. At least it showed some protectiveness toward Isabella.

He pulled up near the tank and climbed out. "Put down the root beer and come on. No sitting around on your butt when there's work to be done."

Murphy didn't put the bottle down until he'd chugged the rest of the contents. Then he let out a loud burp and shot Erik a quick look.

"Good root beer," Erik commented blandly.

"S'okay," Murphy muttered, but when he turned to get out of the truck, Erik thought he caught a wisp of a smile on the kid's face.

Isabella had to screw up every speck of courage she possessed when it was time to drive back out to Erik's place to retrieve Murphy.

The only way she managed at all was to keep reminding herself how quickly Murphy had been ready to leave the last time. She'd tell Erik that she appreciated what he was doing for Murphy but that was as far as her interest went. She wasn't looking to add friends. There'd be no reason to linger. No reason to chat it up with him about anything else. No reason to keep thinking about his wrists or how he'd looked without his darn shirt.

But when she pulled up next to the house and parked, neither Erik nor Murphy was in sight.

She got out of the car and walked past the end of the house. Erik had said he wanted to get the rest of the old barn torn down that day, and they'd certainly accomplished that. There was nothing left but piles of wood and other rubble.

She walked across to the other barn, passing white metal-fenced pens and a tall stand of trees along the way. The steeply pitched barn was as tall as the two-story house, and considerably larger. The wide doors at the narrow end of the white building were pushed open and she walked from the sun into the shade of the interior.

A concrete floor ran down the center of the building with stalls on one side all the way to the door at the other end. On the other side, there were half as many stalls, but there was also a workbench surrounded by various tools, plus a whole lot of equipment that looked completely foreign to her.

Except the saddles. At least she could recognize a saddle when she saw one. There had to be at least a dozen of them.

She looked up. Large utilitarian light fixtures hung at regular intervals from the rafters, and she could see bales of hay and other farm implements stored high above the stalls on each side.

She'd never been inside a barn before. She'd have expected it to smell like animals. Or manure or something. But it smelled like fresh air and open fields, and everything struck her as incredibly tidy. And strangely peaceful.

"Erik? Murphy?"

The only answer she got was the faint meow of the cat that poked its blue-black head around the edge of a stall door to see who was disturbing the quiet.

She crouched down and held out her knuckles. The long, svelte cat suspiciously padded forward, sniffed Isabella's hand, then butted its head against her. "You're friendly, aren't you?" She rubbed the cat's head.

"She is when she recognizes a soft touch. Otherwise Friskie there is hell on wheels."

Startled, the cat's tail went straight up and she bounded away. Startled as well, Isabella nearly jumped to her feet and turned to see Erik standing in the doorway behind her.

Sunshine made his hair glimmer like gold.

Almost resentfully, she wished he had on a hat. Anything that would dim the overwhelming effect he seemed to have on her.

"I didn't know where you guys were. I wasn't trying to snoop."

He stepped toward her, out of that glorifying sunshine. But the violet gaze he trained on her was no less disturbing. Particularly considering the engaging way his eyes seemed to smile, even when his lips weren't. "Didn't figure you were," he drawled. "But if you're interested enough to snoop, knock yourself out."

She could feel her cheeks warming and she shifted. She'd changed into one of Jimmy's old T-shirts after she'd finished at the studio but the comfort she'd always found wearing his favorite shirt eluded her. "Where's Murphy?"

"He's inside the house washing up. And probably trying to sneak a fresh root beer without me knowing."

She shook her head. "Murphy doesn't like root beer." He considered it babyish. All he wanted to drink was cola, the same way his dad had. Now she used the treat of an occasional one as a bribe for him to drink his milk.

"Sure looked like he was drinking it when he sucked down the bottle I gave him earlier."

"I don't want him drinking too much soda. So many artificial ingredients."

"What I buy is home-brewed. Not full of the usual stuff."

"I didn't know you could brew your own root beer." Her mind boggled at the oddity of the conversation. "I guess it makes sense, though. People can brew their own beer. Jimmy tried once. Bought a kit." She smiled a little at the memory. "Stuff was swill, but he insisted we all taste it. Even Murphy got a sip. He promptly spit it out right there on the floor."

Erik grinned. "That's more like it."

"Excuse me?"

He gestured toward the opened doorway. "Come on inside. If you're not in a rush, I'll toss together some sandwiches."

She would not let herself be tempted. She needed to set him straight and be on their way. "We can't stay," she said quickly. She walked past him and out into the sunshine. He smelled of grass and sweat, and she shouldn't have found it appealing, but she did.

She quickened her step.

It did no good. He easily kept pace.

"How long have you had your ranch?" Darn it all, that was not telling him what she'd rehearsed.

"Four years. Are you going to jump like a scalded cat every time I'm around just because I told you I was attracted to you?"

She gaped at him. "Do you *always* say whatever's on your mind?"

"Pretty much," he admitted, not one whit fazed. "So?"

She pressed her lips together. She had absolutely no idea what to make of him. He wasn't like anyone she'd ever met. "I only jumped because you startled me," she said witheringly. "And I don't need more friends." There. She'd said it.

"Everyone can use more friends," he said, evidently unperturbed. "Are you really gonna teach belly dancing and pole dancing at Lucy's place?"

Frustrated, she stared at him. So far, those possibilities had only been kicked around by Lucy and her. "Possibly. Do you disapprove?" It might be to her advantage if he did.

He cocked his head slightly. His lips twitched. "It'll raise a few brows around here. But you think any man in his heart of hearts is really going to protest?"

"It's about exercise," she said flatly.

"Don't doubt it." He took a step closer.

She jerked a little.

He smiled gently. "Isabella, you've gotta learn how to relax. And I know just the place."

She shook her head. She didn't need Erik Clay telling

her what she did or didn't need. "Whatever you have in mind, forget it."

"Okay." His tone was as smooth as a peaceful pond. "But you don't know what you're missing. A spring barbecue over at the Double-C isn't like anything else you'll ever experience."

"Double-C?"

"My grandfather's ranch."

"Rocking-C. Double-C. I feel like everyone's speaking a foreign language."

"You know the fastest way to learn a foreign language, don't you? Total immersion."

She smiled despite herself. She didn't want to like him. Liking him was worse than squelching the occasional lustful thought.

Occasional?

Laughter cackled maniacally inside her mind.

"Tomorrow," he said. "Around one or so. My cousin J.D. will be there and she has a couple boys Murph's age. He's sixth grade, right?" He barely waited for her nod. "They'd be in Rob Rasmussen's class, too, then. Zach and Connor Forrest. He'll have a good time. Maybe start *settling in*," he coaxed.

"You're throwing my words back at me."

"Just being neighborly," he countered. "Offering an opportunity."

"We're not neighbors," she pointed out.

His smile just widened. "Ask Murph. See if he's interested." His tone was the very definition of reasonableness. The kind of tone she'd often used herself when someone was being completely unreasonable. "Just ask," he suggested. "If he doesn't want to go, no sweat."

"Fine," she said abruptly. "I'll ask him." It was safe enough when she knew for a fact that if it were up to Murphy, he'd just as soon sleep away his entire Sunday as do anything else. And he certainly wouldn't want to spend more time with the man he considered his jailer.

Chapter Five

"What do you mean you want to go to the Clays' barbecue?" Isabella stared at Murphy. It was eight o'clock in the
morning. On a Sunday.

And he wasn't still in bed.

He was sitting at the little dining-room table, wearing his
ancient airplane-print pajamas that his dad had given him
long before Isabella had entered the picture. He had his math
and history books open in front of him.

Voluntarily doing homework.

Had she dropped like Alice into some other dimension?

She was pretty sure she wasn't dreaming. The floor was
too cold beneath her bare feet. "I mean I wanna go." Murphy hunched his shoulders defensively and the worn pj's
stretched nearly to breaking point. "Why are you all mad
and stuff?"

She didn't want him to be defensive. She just wanted him
to be happy with this life she was trying to make for them.

"I'm sorry." She pulled out a chair and sat down opposite him. "I'm not mad. I'm surprised."

Not to mention positively stymied. She wanted—needed—to avoid Erik Clay.

Murphy didn't look at her. Just stared intently at his math book. The worksheet beside the book was only partially filled in with his scrawling handwriting.

"So? Can we go?" His lips twisted. "Or are you going to ruin that, too?"

She swallowed the blow of that. "What else do you think I've ruined?"

He slammed his book shut and shoved back from the table. "Everything!" He stormed out of the room.

A moment later she heard the slam of his bedroom door.

She propped her head in her hands and pressed the heels of her palms against her eyes. She wanted to slam doors, too.

But she was the parent here.

Or as close as Murphy had to one.

She dropped her hands. Slid Murphy's worksheet toward herself. Half the answers he'd scrawled were incorrect. She looked at the papers. He also had a history worksheet about elections and voting. Murphy had written "Who cares" in bold letters across the bottom.

She sighed again. His teachers back in New York had suggested to Jimmy that Murphy would benefit from tutoring. But Jimmy had insisted that he could handle it. That had been his motto, pretty much. He'd handle it.

But he hadn't. In their brief time together, he hadn't handled a lot of things.

She felt disloyal even thinking it.

She pinched her eyes until the burning subsided, then pushed away from the table. She went down the short hallway and knocked once on Murphy's bedroom door before she opened it.

He was lying on his bed, tossing his baseball glove in the air.

"Murphy, everything here is new for me, too." She picked up a discarded T-shirt from the floor and tossed it in the wicker basket that served as a hamper. "And I know it's been hard for you. But I'm not your enemy. If you really want to go to the barbecue, then of course we'll go."

His jaw canted. He gave her a suspicious look. "It's jus' 'cause Erik said they'd be playing a game."

"A baseball game?"

He nodded.

She let out a little breath. Of course Murphy would want to play, given an opportunity. "When did he tell you this?"

"Yesterday. While we was checking the water tank for leaks. The cows drink a lot of water."

"Do they?" Her voice was faint. She didn't know whether to be furious with Erik or grateful. She was fairly certain he wasn't the kind of man who'd use a boy to get to a woman. But she'd have to make sure.

Murphy wasn't a tool to be used by anyone.

But if that wasn't Erik's motive, why, oh why was he bending over backward to help Murphy, considering the way he and Murphy had started out?

"There's natural water on his land, too, but these cows are separated 'cause they're all pregnant. And they all gotta have salt and minerals and stuff, too. Not jus' grass."

She cautiously sat on the foot of the bed. "Do you think you might start to actually like going out to work on Erik's ranch?" If he did, maybe Erik's suggestion that she take him out there after school might have some merit. She could figure out a way to master her hormones if Murphy was going to benefit, couldn't she?

The boy tossed the glove. Caught the glove. Tossed it again.

"It's just 'cause of that stupid window," he finally muttered. "Are we going or not?"

"Yes. We'll go." She pushed off the bed, not letting herself think about how doing so might affect her. "But you have to eat breakfast and clean your room first."

His lip curled and he just grunted. But she fancied that she saw a glint of something that might be approaching happiness in his dark eyes.

It was enough to make just about anything worthwhile.

She left his room and went into her own. She quietly closed the door and called Lucy's cell phone. But all she reached was her friend's voice mail. Keeping her voice low so that Murphy wouldn't overhear her through the wall, she left a message to call. She knew her voice sounded shaky. But she couldn't help it.

As long as Lucy was at the barbecue, everything would be fine.

And then, because common courtesy dictated, she dialed again.

Unlike Lucy, Erik answered on the third ring. "Isabella," he greeted.

She cursed caller ID. And the fact that just hearing his voice made her knees feel wobbly. "Murphy said he'd like to go to the barbecue," she said abruptly. If he gloated, she wasn't sure what she'd do.

"He ought to enjoy himself. There'll be plenty to keep him occupied. What about you? Are you coming? Or do you want me to pick up Murphy on my way through town?"

She hesitated. "You'd do that? Take him even if I didn't go?"

She heard him sigh a little. "Isabella, I told you that what goes on with Murphy isn't conditional on you. Friends or more, or nothing at all. Sooner or later you'll understand that I don't say things I don't mean."

There was nothing but sincerity in his tone. She sank down onto the foot of the bed. "I'm sorry." She stared across the room at a framed photo of Jimmy and Murphy sitting on her dresser. She'd taken it the day that Jimmy finally took Murphy to his first Yankees game. His first and only game. The excursion had landed Jimmy back in the hospital for the third time in as many weeks, and that time he hadn't come out. "I'm afraid I haven't had a lot of experience with things being unconditional."

"Is Lucy's friendship conditional?"

"Of course not."

"Think of me like Lucy, then."

A laugh escaped before she could stop it. "You're not Lucy."

"Am I going to scare you off even more if I say I'm glad you noticed?"

She couldn't get more scared off than she already was. And that wasn't something she had any intention of divulging. "Murphy and I will drive ourselves out to the barbecue," she said instead. "I just need the directions."

Standing in his bathroom cleaning up after his morning chores, Erik smiled.

"It's huge," Murphy said, staring out the car window with undisguised awe.

"Yeah." Isabella was staring, too.

There was just no way to avoid it.

It was two o'clock in the afternoon. An hour later than Erik had told her to come, but she'd been determined not to look eager. Murphy was excited enough for the both of them. But now, after following Erik's simple directions, they were sitting in the circular driveway fronting the Double-C ranch house.

Erik had called it "the big house."

And it wasn't a misnomer.

Made of stone and wood, it shot off in nearly every direction. A wide porch stretched the entire width of the front. Beyond the house she could see several other buildings, and unlike Erik's place where the corrals were constructed of neat, orderly white pipe, here they were wood and seemed steeped in age and tradition.

The butterflies in her stomach she'd been battling since she'd spoken with Erik that morning multiplied. Prolific little beasts.

The driveway was crowded with vehicles parked every which way. She wedged her little sedan between a large SUV and a lethal-looking black sports car. The second she parked, Murphy was shoving out the door.

He had on his Yankees cap, and his baseball glove was tucked under his arm.

Afraid he might just well burst through the door without even knocking, she ignored her butterflies and hastily caught up with him. She closed her hand over his shoulder, slowing him down a pace before he could bolt up the shallow steps leading to the massive front door. The afternoon air was redolent with the aroma of grilling meat. It would have smelled mouthwatering on any day that her stomach wasn't clenched into knots. "Manners, okay?"

Except for rolling his eyes, he didn't deign to answer.

She let go of his shoulder and reached for the sturdy iron knocker on the door.

Isabella could have collapsed with relief when Lucy opened the door and greeted them.

"Didn't you get the message I left you this morning?"

Lucy shook her head. "Sorry. Sunny grabbed my cell phone from me last night after her bath and dropped it in the toilet. Hey there, Murphy. Looks like you're here for that baseball game Erik's been talking people into." She pointed behind her. "Everyone's in the family room," she told him. "Go on in and make yourself at home."

Isabella could see his sudden hesitation. He even started to look up at her, but he caught himself. Instead, he tilted his head cockily and strode in the direction that Lucy had indicated.

As soon as he started off, Lucy grabbed Isabella's arm and dragged her inside. "I was wondering if you were going to show," she whispered. "Erik's been pacing around like a madman."

Isabella's stomach lurched. "He said around one," she defended.

"I know." Lucy patted her arm and grinned. "I told him a woman always likes to be fashionably late."

"I'm not here because of Erik," she muttered. "It's just that Murphy wanted to come."

Lucy's grin didn't dim. She shut the door and pulled Isabella along the scarred wood-planked floor. "Uh-huh. What was your message about, anyway?"

"I just wanted to know if you'd be here." They stood in the doorway of a wide family room furnished with an eclectic collection of couches and chairs that seemed to be occupied by people of every age. She didn't see Erik, though standing next to an enormous stone fireplace big enough to walk inside was a man who looked enough like him to be his twin, except for darker hair and a slightly thinner stature.

Nor did Isabella spot Murphy. If he was already getting into mischief, she vowed to hustle him right back home again. She dragged her feet as Lucy tried to pull her forward into the room. "I was worried I wouldn't have someone to talk to. You know?"

Letting go of her arm, Lucy snorted softly. "Look at this crowd. You think there's a shortage of people to converse with? Besides, you know some of them already from your yoga classes."

Teaching yoga was one thing. Sharing the afternoon with her students at what was obviously a family affair was something else. The only family she'd ever felt comfortable around had been Jimmy and Murphy.

"Where'd Murphy go?"

Hope, Erik's mother, had come up from behind them. "Erik took him downstairs where the rest of the kids are." She gave Isabella a delighted smile. "We're all so pleased that you're joining us." She slipped her arm through Isabella's and drew her through the wide doorway. "Come along and meet everyone."

Hoping her panic was not showing, Isabella gave Lucy a look. Her so-called best friend just grinned knowingly.

"Everyone, this is Erik's young friend Isabella Lockhart," Hope introduced. She didn't have to raise her voice since to a one, everyone had stopped talking the second they'd entered the room.

"My friend first," Lucy chimed in, her voice full of laughter. She stepped around Isabella and Hope and crossed to the overstuffed leather chair where her husband, Beck, was holding Sunny. She sat on the arm of his chair, looking as if she were anticipating the opening of a brand-new ballet.

"You already know most of my sisters-in-law from yoga," Hope began. "Everyone's here except for Rebecca. She's on duty at the hospital. And Jaimie's outside with Matthew guarding the grill."

Feeling as self-conscious as she always had when she was entering yet another foster family, Isabella nodded at the women. She knew from the chatter of the women from her yoga class that Rebecca was the chief of staff at the Weaver hospital. And Jaimie, who was also in the class, lived right here on the Double-C with her husband, Matthew, and his father and stepmother, Squire and Gloria. The other women, Emily and Maggie, were smiling at her with the usual friendliness they displayed in class.

She managed to smile back, even though she'd rather have childishly hidden behind Hope's back. "It's good to see you again. Thank you for having us."

Hope squeezed her arm and gestured with her other hand toward the eldest couple in the room. "Erik's grandparents. Squire and Gloria Clay." She pointed her finger at the man with an iron-gray head of hair. "Now, you behave yourself, Squire," she warned.

The man was holding a rustic-looking walking stick between his legs and he thumped the end on the floor. "When do I not behave myself?" His voice was pure cantankerousness, but there was a crafty twinkle in his unearthly pale blue eyes.

"All the time," the woman sitting beside him said drily. She had thick, silvering auburn hair that was pulled up in a clip. She smiled calmly at Isabella. "He's particularly incorrigible with lovely young women."

Isabella's cheeks warmed. But Hope was already moving on with the introductions, ticking off a litany of names that would take Isabella forever to keep straight. "I have no idea where Erik's dad has gotten himself off to," Hope concluded.

"He's out back talking all hush-hush with Axel," Squire harrumphed. "But now that Erik's girl is here, can we get on with the grub?"

"I'm not Erik's girl," Isabella corrected quickly. But no one gave her any mind. They were too busy jumping to their feet and shuffling her along in their wake as they headed through the house. They passed through a large kitchen dominated by a huge oak table that was covered with plastic-wrapped desserts, then through the adjoining laundry room and through the back door.

Out on the deep green grass, long picnic tables had been set with red-and-white-checked cloths. She could see smoke curling out from beneath a big, covered grill.

Jaimie was standing beside it, trying to snatch away the long-handled tongs that a man—obviously her husband, Matthew—was holding above her head. "You're going to burn those ribs," she was warning. But she was laughing as she said it, and so was Matthew.

Everyone seemed to laugh a lot in the Clay family.

And if they weren't laughing, they were smiling.

Even though Isabella had long ago accepted the reality of growing up with no family of her own, everything inside her seemed to ache a little.

Then Lucy was shoving a red plastic cup into her hand and gesturing at the big metal barrel full of ice, which contained a beer keg. Next to it sat an identical barrel of ice, filled with bottles of soda, juices and covered pitchers of what turned out to be fresh lemonade when she poured some into her cup. She added a few chunks of ice and followed Lucy over to one of the tables. Baskets full of rolls and fat bowls of salads sitting in nests of ice were spread across the length of the table along with enormous platters that were waiting to be filled with whatever was sizzling on the grill.

"There's enough to feed an army here," Isabella observed. The food on the table alone would easily consume her entire grocery budget for a month.

"That's a fair description," a deep voice said, and she whirled, nearly spilling lemonade down the front of the pink sundress that she'd made the year before.

"Erik." Her voice sounded breathless and she wanted to crawl under the food table. He was holding a blue-eyed toddler with a shock of blue-black hair on his hip, and it was much easier to focus on the child than the man. "Who's this?"

"This little wild woman is Katie. She's Leandra's." He gestured toward a slender blonde standing nearby. "Have you been introduced to everyone?"

She nodded. "Leandra's in yoga." She looked around at the people who were milling about the picnic tables, choosing seats. A process that seemed to involve quite a lot of jockeying, if the decibel of voices was any indication. "So are Courtney, Sarah and Tara."

"Is that a fact?" He didn't sound the least bit surprised, though, and his violet eyes were smiling. "You look real pretty today, Isabella."

"Thank you." Her throat felt strangely tight and she looked away. "I've never seen a spread quite like this. It's pretty impressive."

"Wait until you taste the ribs," Jaimie said, brushing past her to retrieve one of the platters. "I make the best there are."

"Who makes 'em?" the man still at the grill called out. "Believe I've been the one out here babying 'em along."

Jaimie rolled her green eyes. "Don't listen to Matthew," she confided conspiratorially. "He's just getting set in his ways and we have to humor him."

"Heard that, Red." There was no heat in Matthew's deep drawl, just amusement. "You want to be helpful, sashay that pretty butt of yours over here with that platter."

Isabella pressed her lips together, watching the woman do just that, seeming to add an extra wiggle along the way.

"Ain't no proper way for a woman her age to act," Squire said as he walked over and joined them. He had a paper plate in his hand and he scooped a huge amount of potato salad onto it. But Isabella could tell by the twist on his lips that he was amused, too. "Go on and get that baby outta your husband's arms and bring 'er to me," he told Lucy. "Your man needs to hold a beer for a while."

"You mean, you want to hold your newest great-grandchild,"

Lucy countered. "He's a marshmallow," she whispered loudly to Isabella before she set off for where Beck was standing with Lucy's parents, Cage and Belle. Isabella had met them once when they'd come to visit Lucy in New York.

Excruciatingly aware of Erik standing beside her, Isabella focused on the elderly man instead. "You have a beautiful home here, Mr. Clay."

"Eh." Squire waved his hand. "Call me Squire. Ever'body does." He peered down at her. He was very tall and had obviously passed on that particular gene to his offspring. "Lucy says you used to work at that dance company with her."

"I did. She was a wonderful dancer."

"Saw her a few times." Squire turned his flinty gaze to his grandson. "You just gonna stand there like a bump, son, or be useful and set this plate down next to your grandma for me?" He waggled the plate under Erik's nose.

"God forbid I'm a bump," Erik returned drily. He took the plate. "Don't be messing with Isabella," he warned. "She's too good for the likes of you."

Squire grunted a little and gestured with his walking stick. "Get."

Isabella bit the inside of her lip to keep from laughing right out loud when Erik rolled his eyes and ambled away.

At least she could breathe easier.

Except the sight of his retreating jean-clad rear end was more than a little distracting.

Before she could be caught staring, she looked back at Squire. "I was the wardrobe supervisor at NEBT," she told him. "If you saw Lucy in one of our ballets there, she was undoubtedly wearing a costume of mine."

"That's right." Gloria had joined them and handed Squire an empty paper plate. "I saw how much potato salad you took." She tsked. "Enough to feed four. Start over with some green salad, please."

"Bossy woman," Squire complained, promptly patting her on the rump before reaching for the tongs stuck inside the salad. "Good thing I'm used to you."

Gloria laughed fondly. "Good thing we're all used to *you,* you old letch." She turned her smile on Isabella again. "Lucy tells us you're a fabulous seamstress."

"Well." Isabella shrugged, feeling self-conscious. "I get by."

"Don't let her fool you," Lucy said, returning with the baby. She slid the plate that Squire had just piled high with green salad out of his hand and handed him the sleeping infant. "She ought to be a fashion designer or something." She gestured at Isabella's dress. "Bet she made that. Didn't you?"

Isabella nodded. Her cheeks felt as if they were on fire.

"Evan's mother, Jolie, is a seamstress," Gloria inserted. "Leandra's mother-in-law," she clarified. "She has more business than she knows what to do with."

Lucky Jolie, Isabella thought. She took an empty plate from the stack and stepped aside when Jaimie returned with a platter of barbecued ribs. Despite her nervousness, Isabella's mouth watered.

"We don't stand on ceremony around here." Erik reached around her and plucked several ribs off the top of the stack and set them on her plate.

His arm brushed warmly against her bare shoulder and she looked up at him. "I can't eat all those."

His lips tilted. "You won't know that until you start. You could take less but if you ended up wanting more—and you will—I'd hate to see you disappointed." As if to prove his point, he nudged her as a mass of individuals descended on the table, grabbing ribs from all sides. And scattered among the adults snatching up food were a jumble of children, Murphy included. He was flanked by the twin boys, Zach and Connor, from his class at school, and as she watched him with some amazement, he stepped aside and scooped up another little boy so he could reach the table.

A moment later, the mass cleared.

The kids raced off, plates precariously held aloft, aiming for the farthest of the tables. Murphy hadn't given her a single glance.

Wholly bemused, she looked back at the food table.

The platters were empty except for the smoky, dark smudges of sauce left behind. The salad bowls had also been decimated.

She blinked a little. "Wow."

Erik dropped one of the few remaining cobs of grilled corn next to her ribs. "Told you."

"He also figures that whatever you don't finish, he'll have a better crack at." The man she'd noticed earlier who could easily have been Erik's twin was standing on the other side of the table. He had a smile just as smooth and easy as Erik's. "I'm Casey. Ugly there's cousin. We all know what his tricks are."

"And I know what your tricks are," Erik returned, sounding amused. His hand covered her shoulder as if it were the most natural thing in the world.

But it wasn't natural. And she barely managed not to audibly suck in a breath.

"She's got better things to do with her time than listen to your bull," he continued.

Casey's smile didn't dim. She saw the look that passed between them, but didn't have a hope of interpreting it. Not when she could hardly think with Erik's warm fingers cupped around her shoulder.

"Tricks and bull aside, I'm going to go sit with Lucy and eat," Isabella said. She sent both men a smile. "And if I have any ribs left, I'm pretty sure Murphy'll beat the both of you to them."

"Guess she told you," she heard Casey say to Erik as she escaped.

She joined Lucy where she was sitting with Beck, Leandra, her husband, Evan, and Tara. She'd barely picked up the first of the hot ribs between her fingers when Tara's husband, Axel, worked his way onto the bench across from her.

"You're Erik's girl," he greeted, stretching his hand across the table toward her. He was blond like Erik, but his eyes were brown. "Axel. Married to the prettiest girl here."

"I'm not Erik's girl," she protested again as she shook his hand. "Nice to meet you."

Erik butted Evan in the head with his plate. "Move over." When the other man slid a few inches to one side, Erik wedged himself in the tight space left between him and Isabella.

She gave him a look. "There's more room on the other side."

"It'll fill up soon enough."

His thigh was pressed against hers. But if she moved so much as an inch, he'd know he was getting to her.

Yet his smile made her wonder if he knew anyway.

"So," he asked, all calm, easy innocence, "how're those ribs?"

Chapter Six

"Come on, Isabella. You're up to bat." Jaimie was beckoning to her from the informal baseball diamond that had been set up out in an empty field behind the big house. With a John Deere cap pulled low over her nose and her red hair streaming from the back in a vibrant ponytail, she looked way too young to have grown children with families of their own.

Wives were pitted against husbands, siblings against siblings. However, thanks to their sheer numbers, Isabella—technically on Jaimie's team—had so far managed not to field *or* bat.

And now, Isabella stared with horror at the baseball bat the older woman was holding out to her.

It was the bottom of the fifth inning; the other team was in the lead by a single run. Their own team had Sarah's husband, Max, on first base and one of J.D.'s twin stepsons on third.

They were only playing five innings to begin with, and they already had two outs.

She had no personal experience with the game other than a few weeks of softball in junior-high gym class, but she'd had to sit through enough televised baseball games with Jimmy to know the situation was critical. Whoever batted next would either seal their fate or allow them to maintain a thread of hope through another batter.

So she shook her head and waved her hands, warding off the offered bat. "I'll pass. Believe me, our chances are better."

"Come on, Iz." Casey, who was also on their team, gave her a poke in the back that made her jump. "You can get out of fielding, but everyone takes a turn at bat."

"Yeah, come on, Iz," Sarah yelled from her spot out in center field. She was slapping her glove with her hand. "Give us something to do out here! I'm starting to get bored!"

"If that's a comment about your mother's batting," Jaimie yelled back, "next time you want to get a night away with your husband, you can find someone else to watch little Ben!"

"Come on, honey," Casey said from behind her. "We're all just family here." He grinned. "Of course, if you're terrible at it and we lose this game, nobody will let you live it down for the rest of your life."

"He oughta know," Erik called from his spot between second and third base. "Guy can shoot the hell out of a pool table, but he can't swing a bat for love nor money." He punched his fist a few times into his glove.

"This is not helping me," Isabella muttered, though she couldn't help but laugh. It was just impossible not to.

"Come on, Iz!"

Isabella wasn't sure where the chant started, but soon everyone seemed to be joining in. Chanting. Clapping. Cat-calling.

They were treating her and Murphy just like they treated each other, which had caused a lump in her throat several innings ago, and before the lump got any larger, she grabbed the baseball bat and headed toward the area marked off as home plate. "I'm wearing sandals and a dress here," she complained to everyone in general.

"Wardrobe's no excuse," Lucy retorted.

Isabella gave her a look. She and Tara were sitting in chairs off to one side, their infants on their laps. "But having a baby a few months ago is?" The two women were the only ones who seemed to be excused from the entire charade.

Lucy grinned. "Who knew that motherhood had such unexpected perks?"

"Come on," Squire groused. He was the umpire, though as far as Isabella had noticed, his calls generally favored whoever was buttering him up. Since that came from both sides, things tended to even out. "Stop delaying the game, girl, and get in there."

Isabella sighed noisily and moved in front of Axel, who was playing catcher. She tried to recall the dim memory of those few games from junior high and lifted the bat.

She squinted against the bright sun in her eyes, eyeing Murphy, who was standing on the nonexistent pitcher's mound, holding the ball. "Go easy on me, okay?"

He just smiled slightly and flexed his fingers around the baseball. Her stomach knotted nervously.

"Hold on a sec." Erik suddenly jogged forward to Murphy. He closed his hand over the boy's shoulder, lowered his head and said something they couldn't hear. Murphy grimaced but, after a moment, he took off his Yankees cap and handed it to Erik. Then, instead of returning to his position as shortstop, Erik jogged over to Isabella. "Sun's in your eyes," he said and dropped Murphy's cap over her head.

Something careened around inside her, and even though

she wanted to attribute it entirely to the fact that Murphy had given up his hat for *her,* she couldn't.

"Suckin' up to the batter." Casey tsked dolefully. "Trying to make sure she throws the game? How low will you stoop, man?"

Erik's gaze didn't stray from Isabella's face. "She's gonna do great."

Squire suddenly whistled, sharp and loud. "Y'all gonna play ball or can I quit this foolishness and go have my chocolate brownies?"

Erik gave her a quick wink that did nothing to help her peace of mind, then jogged back to his spot.

Isabella adjusted the cap. It really did help against the blinding sun. Then she lifted the bat and tried to envision herself as a proper ballplayer, not a thirty-one-year-old woman, wearing a pink sundress with a lightweight white sweater and flat, strappy sandals, who hadn't been up to bat in close to two decades.

Murphy's first pitch went whizzing by her with dazzling speed, right into Axel's mitt with a solid *thwap.*

"Strike one!" Squire yelled to various cheers and boos.

"Kid does have a hell of an arm," Axel commented as he straightened and threw the ball back to Murphy.

"That's what I keep hearing," she said and renewed her grip on the bat. She focused harder on Murphy and less on the ridiculous sight she must make. All things considered, she looked no less equipped to play the darn game than half the other women there.

She flexed her fingers around the bat. Waiting. Waiting.

The ball smacked into Axel's mitt again.

"Might try swinging at it, girl," Squire suggested under his breath. "Ball," he yelled loudly, to pretty much the same amount of yelled complaints he'd earned when he'd called the first pitch a strike.

She twisted her foot, setting the sole of her sandal deeper into the springy grass. A blur of motion caught her eye only a moment after Murphy whirled, and she realized Max was bolting from first base, stealing second.

Only by diving down to slide the last few feet across the green grass was the sheriff able to beat the ball that his son, Eli, handily caught.

Her pulse ratcheting up even more, Isabella tried to ignore the cheers and boos that filled the air and kept her eyes on Murphy as he caught the ball Eli threw back to him and turned to face her again. As soon as she saw his nose wrinkle a little as he wound up to launch another bullet, she started to swing.

The contact of the ball against the bat jarred all the way through her shoulders.

Stunned, she watched the ball scream past Erik, who missed even though he made a dive for it. And then the ball was bouncing out toward Leandra where she was positioned with Lucy's stepdaughter, Shelby. They'd been turning somersaults in the grass and both scrambled to their feet as the ball spun madly toward them.

"Run, girl," Squire shouted, and Isabella jumped, racing like a madwoman away from home plate. When she safely reached first base, where yet another one of Erik's cousins, Derek, was playing, he pointed out that she could have dropped the bat somewhere along the way.

She was so giddy she didn't even care about her gaffe as she turned to watch Max sail past third and follow Connor right across home plate. She jumped up and down, screaming just as crazily as everyone else on her team.

Murphy just stood there and stared, as if he couldn't believe what had happened.

Then Erik ran forward and clapped him on the shoulder,

said something that had the boy actually grinning a little, and the two of them jogged forward.

Isabella's eyes suddenly burned and she quickly bent down, swiping at her calves as if to remove some nonexistent grass stains.

There was something utterly tragic about the fact that Murphy had never had such an opportunity with his own father. Jimmy had played ball regularly with the guys from his firehouse. But he'd never included his son. And not until after he'd become ill had he finally taken Murphy to that Yankees game. He'd naturally assumed he'd have a long lifetime for them to share games.

Sarah came up beside her and bent over in the same position. Her strawberry blond ponytail tumbled over her head. "Nice job, Isabella." Even though her team had just lost, she had a broad grin on her face. "Love it when the women of this family get to surprise the heck out of the men."

Isabella *wasn't* part of this family, though. All of these people were just being kind, and even though she was grateful, particularly on behalf of Murphy, she had no business even entertaining a thought about how wonderful it must be for those who really were part of the family.

She straightened. "Thanks." But whatever else she might have said was forgotten as she was suddenly surrounded by everyone on her team, patting her back, giving high fives and moving en masse back toward the picnic tables near the house.

Isabella finally managed to extract herself from the throng when some of the women broke off to go inside to retrieve the assortment of desserts. She headed toward Murphy, who was pawing through the melting ice inside the drink barrel.

She handed him back his ball cap. "Did you have fun?"

He flipped the hat onto his head and grunted. Nodding

once, he finally extracted a tall brown bottle with no label. "Yesss." He popped off the top using the bottle opener that was welded to the side of the barrel. Without looking at her, he started to walk away.

Isabella managed not to sigh.

But after a few steps, he stopped and turned back to her. Half his face was shadowed by the cap. "That was a good hit you had," he muttered. And then he continued on his way, catching up to the twins.

A silly lump filled her throat.

"Told 'em you'd do great," Erik said, stepping up to the opposite side of the barrel. He plunged his arm into the icy water, searching around the same way Murphy had.

She gathered herself as much as she could. "What did you tell Murphy out there?"

From among the bobbing cans of soda, he pulled out another one of those tall brown bottles. "When?" He shook water from his hand.

She gave him a look. "When you got him to loan me his hat."

"Didn't say anything about hats." He popped off the top and offered her the bottle. His gaze was bright and almost as warm as the sunshine and it made her feel something inside that was entirely unwanted. "Best root beer money can buy," he added.

She automatically took the bottle from him. His fingers were cold from the ice water but the bottle was colder. "You said *something* to him."

His lips tilted slightly. "It's a guy thing."

"Seriously. I want to know."

His smile just widened a little. He shifted and reached for one of the red plastic cups, then started to draw a beer.

"You're really not going to tell me?"

He tilted his cup, letting some foam pour off as he continued filling. "I'm really not." Evidently satisfied with the head he had left, he turned off the flow and dropped the hose back into the ice. "So what sort of dessert person are you? Chocolate brownies, cheesecake or apple pie?"

She'd served him apple pie at the diner the day they'd met. He'd eaten every crumb. "Cheesecake," she allowed begrudgingly. If he wouldn't tell her what he'd said, she'd ask Murphy.

Of course, *he* didn't exactly tell her every little thing, either.

Annoyance bubbled.

As if Erik recognized it, his eyes crinkled with amusement while he took a leisurely drink of his beer. "Cheesecake's my favorite, too," he said when he was finished. "And we'd better hurry if we want to be sure of getting any. Knowing Squire, he'll have a helping or two of everything else after he's tried decimating the brownie supply."

"Good for him."

His smile widened. "You gonna get more irked if I tell you that your eyes sparkle when you're mad?"

She huffed and turned on her heel, irritably taking a swallow of root beer. It was creamy and spicy all at the same time. Utterly delicious.

She broke into a jog and caught up to Lucy.

Lucy gave her a close look. "What's wrong?"

Isabella shook her head. "Nothing." She set aside the bottle on the picnic table and reached for the baby. Holding Sunny would keep her occupied enough that she'd be able to get her head together. "Here. Let me take her for a while."

Lucy happily handed over the sleeping infant. Isabella had become more comfortable holding a baby in the weeks since she'd arrived. But it was still a little nerve-racking.

She gently grazed her knuckle against Sunny's downy-soft cheek and carried her over to one of the wooden Adirondack chairs that were scattered about on the grass. She gingerly sat. The baby slept blissfully on.

But Isabella's gaze kept straying toward Erik. He and Murphy were standing off to one side, talking with Lucy's husband, Beck, and both men were laughing. Murphy, too, had a crooked smile on his lips.

She wished for Murphy's hat back so it would help shade her eyes from the sight.

Instead, she had to satisfy herself with resting her head against the back of the chair and closing her eyes.

But nothing would help get rid of the image of them.

Erik and Murphy.

Together.

Smiling.

"She looks good with a baby in her arms."

Erik watched Murph head off toward the horse barn with Connor and Zach. He didn't have to look over to where Isabella was sitting to know what Beck meant. "Most people do."

"Don't kid me, man. Your feelings are written right on your face. You got a good hankering going on for Lucy's friend."

"Yeah, well, she's got a good longing going on for the fiancé she lost." He looked at Beck. Before the man had married Lucy, he'd already had two children—one who was now away at college and one who was just a little girl. Their mother had died before a grieving Beck had moved to Weaver. "Not sure she'll get over it that easily."

"She won't," Beck said bluntly. "Not if she loved him. But a person can realize they have more room inside than they thought. If they meet the right person, they'll feel that way again no matter how certain they were that they wouldn't. It'll never be exactly the same, but it damn sure can be just as good." He looked over toward Isabella again. Lucy was sitting cross-legged on the grass beside her, waving a brownie in the air as she chattered. "One of the hardest parts is just being able to admit that and not feel like you're betraying the person you lost."

"You felt that way with Luce?"

"You might say that." Beck's voice was dry. "Harmony and I had a long marriage," he added after a moment. "We'd still be married now if she hadn't died. But that wasn't what the cards held for us." He smiled slightly, looking across at his wife. "I have a brand-new wife I love just as deeply as I did Nick and Shelby's mom. They have a brand-new sister they adore almost as much as Lucy and I do, and there's nothing about where I am today with this new life that I regret. If I hadn't loved Harmony first, I'm not sure I'd be able to appreciate that fact so clearly." He clapped Erik on the shoulder. "But Isabella's got a boy. So be sure about what you're wanting. And she's my wife's best friend. If it's something that's gonna pass after the newness wears off, keep your sights moving. Because the two of them definitely don't deserve more pain in their lives."

"It's not gonna pass." Erik finally dragged his eyes away from Isabella and looked at his friend. "It's not gonna pass," he repeated flatly.

He knew it down to his bones. He, who hadn't been looking for a girlfriend, much less something more, couldn't envision a future at all unless she was by his side.

"Then just give her time. And space," the other man advised. Then he smiled crookedly. "But not too much space. At least that's sorta how it worked for Luce and me." Then he jogged across the grass. He flopped down next to his wife and hauled her close for a kiss that clearly surprised as much as it delighted.

Erik hid a sigh. Putting what he hoped was a casual expression on his face, he went to collect a few servings of cheesecake.

Isabella wasn't going to the dessert table.

So the desserts would come to her.

He carried the plates over. Lucy and Beck were still sitting beside her on the grass, giving each other besotted looks. Isabella's eyes were closed like the baby's.

But he knew she wasn't sleeping.

She was too tense. It showed in the nervous tapping of her pink-tipped toes against the ground.

"If you want someone to feed you cheesecake," he greeted, "keep your eyes closed. Otherwise, stop faking." He ignored Lucy's barely stifled laugh. Beck tugged her to her feet and hustled her away.

Isabella's eyelids snapped up. "I wasn't faking. I was *trying* to relax. Isn't that what this afternoon was supposed to be about?"

He took a seat next to her on the grass and held up one of the plates. "You going to tell me you don't want some of this?" Glistening red cherries were sliding off the fat wedge of cheesecake and onto the plate. "It's one of my grandmother's specialties."

Her soft lips pursed. The baby was sound asleep, stretched across her lap.

"This is something not to be missed." He waved the dessert under her nose. "She only makes it a few times a year."

She took the plate, holding it aloft over the baby. "You're relentless."

"When I need to be." He handed her a plastic fork and sat down to dig into his own helping. "Murphy's gone over to the horse barn with the twins. They're checking out some puppies. Evidently Zach and Connor are trying to convince J.D. and Jake that they need another dog. As if they don't have enough animals already." He filled his fork with cheesecake. "They have a horse rescue," he added, "and God knows how many dogs and cats already." He pushed the cheesecake into his mouth. It really was his favorite, but he was more interested in getting Isabella to enjoy hers than he was in enjoying his own. "But you know kids. Never enough pets."

"Murphy wants a dog."

Erik nodded. "Most boys do."

"So do girls," she murmured, then looked quickly down at her dessert. She took an infinitesimal amount on the tip of her fork and tucked it between her lips.

He couldn't help but smile when she groaned a little and took a healthier bite. "Told you it was good."

"It's heavenly." She didn't look at him. "Murphy knows we can't afford a dog. Vet bills. Dog food. I just can't do it." Her lips curved down. "And I know exactly how that sounds to a kid who desperately wants a pet."

"You didn't have any pets when you were a kid?"

"A few of the families I lived with had a dog or a cat. But it was never mine." She lifted her shoulder, as if it hadn't meant much to her. "I was moved frequently enough anyway that even if one of the families wanted to let me have a pet, there'd have been no point."

He forgot about his cheesecake altogether. He had a feeling he knew what she meant, making it even clearer why she was determined to retain guardianship of Murphy. "Families. As in foster families?"

Her lips compressed. She nodded, then quickly stuck a huge forkful into her mouth. "This is really good," she managed around the enormous bite.

"And you don't want to talk about it," he guessed. "The foster families, I mean. Not the cheesecake."

Her gaze flicked to his. She swallowed the bite and caught a fleck of crust from the corner of her mouth with the tip of her tongue. "Do you think your grandmother would give me the recipe?"

He smiled slightly. It was no easy task squelching the urge to kiss away the tiny golden crumb she'd missed. "She will if she figures you're gonna give me a piece, too."

Her eyes widened. She laughed. "You have no shame."

He just smiled and lifted his last forkful of the dessert. She'd laughed. It hadn't been tinged with sadness, and he felt as if he'd just won the World Series. "What can I say? I like cheesecake."

Chapter Seven

Ruby's was doing a brisk lunch business when Isabella heard the bell jangle over the door and looked over to see Erik walking in.

She quickly looked down at the coffee mug she was filling before she spilled the piping-hot brew all over the counter. "There you go, Deputy." She pulled Deputy Ruiz's check from the pad in her pocket and slipped it under the edge of the sturdy white plate holding the slice of chocolate cake she'd just served him. "Let me know if you need anything else."

The radio on his hip crackled and he reached down to adjust the volume as he slid his cake closer. "Thanks, Iz."

"Hey, Erik." Tabby, Isabella's boss, who also worked the lunch shift, greeted him. "You come in for lunch?"

Isabella looked away and focused on retrieving an order from the window behind her. It had been three days since she'd last seen him at the barbecue at the Double-C. Three days during which she hadn't been able to get him out of her head.

Not even learning from their caseworker two days ago that Murphy's natural mother had been located had succeeded in eradicating Erik from her thoughts. And it should have. The news had been more than stunning—it had been wholly unwelcome.

She gathered up the plates and carried them around the counter to deliver to the trio of women at one of her tables. From their conversation, she could tell that the young one was getting married soon, but she certainly wasn't happy about some of the details.

Isabella set their sandwiches in place. "Would you like fresh iced teas?"

"God, no." The bride shuddered and flicked her long brown hair over her shoulder. "Bring me ice water. With lemon wedges. Not slices." She somehow managed to look down her nose at Isabella even though she was sitting and Isabella was standing. Isabella had been looked down on by women considerably better at it than this girl. And with everything else on her mind, she couldn't be bothered to be either offended or amused. "Certainly." She smiled her practiced and pleasant smile before moving her gaze to the girl's companions. Mother and grandmother, she'd guessed, considering the physical resemblance. "And for you ladies?"

The mother gave her an awkward smile. "More tea would be lovely. Thank you." The grandmother nodded, as well.

Taking the offending glass of tea from the table, Isabella turned back toward the counter. Her pace faltered a bit when she saw that Erik had seated himself at the only available stool at the crowded counter instead of in one of the booths.

The counter was hers.

Which meant she'd have to serve him.

She swallowed hard and hurried around the counter. "Afternoon." She started to slide a menu in front of him.

"Don't need that." He smiled at her. "You've got a busy shift here."

She nodded. After setting a glass of water in front of him, she washed her hands at the sink beneath the counter and deftly sliced a fresh lemon into wedges. "I'll be right back to take your order."

"No hurry." As if he'd done it hundreds of times, he flipped over his coffee mug and stretched across the counter to retrieve the pitcher of fresh lemonade, which he poured into the mug.

She would rather he *were* in a hurry. Then she'd be assured of him leaving quickly.

She dropped a lemon wedge into a fresh glass of ice water, grabbed the tea pitcher along with the little bowl she'd filled with the rest of the wedges and returned to the table.

The bride took one look at the water glass and sighed loudly. "I didn't ask you to *add* the lemon to my water." She pushed the glass aside.

"Bethany," the grandmother chided, and plucked the lemon wedge out of the water and dropped it on the stack in the bowl. "Better?"

Isabella placidly refilled the tea glasses. "How are your sandwiches? Is there anything else I can get for you?"

"They're fine," the grandmother said, giving her granddaughter a steely look. "Thank you."

Isabella escaped around the counter again. "What'll it be?"

"Meat-loaf special."

She tucked away her pad without writing. Easiest, most popular meal of the day. "You got it." She refilled his water, then headed through the swinging doors into the kitchen where Tabby was dishing up a helping of meat loaf that she stacked on a mountain of fluffy mashed potatoes. She added a soft roll, two little balls of butter and a small bowl of baked beans.

"Here." The young woman held out the plate to Isabella. "Erik always orders the meat loaf when he comes in on Wednesdays," she added in explanation. "How's Bethany the B—and I don't mean *bride*—behaving today?"

Isabella took the piping-hot plate. "I gather she's always... selective?"

Tabby grinned. "That's one way to put it. My mother is making her wedding gown. The B has changed her mind several times on the style, the fabric, the trim. Mom's had to start from scratch each time, yet Her Highness can't understand why my mother is getting the teensiest bit perturbed."

Isabella wrinkled her nose. "I've dressed more than a few dancers with similar attitudes." She added to her load a plated cheeseburger and fries from Bubba and headed back out front.

She delivered the burger to the man at the end of the counter, then slid Erik's plate in front of him, along with a napkin-wrapped set of utensils. "Tabby says you order this every Wednesday."

He put the napkin on the lap of his dusty blue jeans and nodded. He'd set his faded John Deere ball cap on the counter out of his way and his gaze slid across her face like a warm breeze. "I know what I like."

How the man could make her feel flustered with just a look was beyond her. "Well." She wiped her palms down the sides of her apron and topped off his lemonade once more. "Let me know if you need anything else." Even though her automatic scan of her tables told her all was well, she took the tea and water pitchers around anyway.

When she reached Bethany's table, she paused. "How is

everyone doing? The chocolate pie is particularly phenomenal today if you're considering dessert."

Bethany huffed. "Do we *look* like we're interested in chocolate pie?"

Grandma gave the B a stern look. "I'm interested," she said tartly. "And just because neither your mother nor I are willing to break the news to your poor seamstress that you're changing the entire design of your dress again with the wedding only a few weeks away is no reason for you to take out your foul mood on the rest of us." Grandma smiled up at Isabella and her voice lost all of its steel. "Make my pie to go, if you would, dear."

"Absolutely." She'd include a little extra whipped cream, too, just because.

The mother merely shook her head wearily, so Isabella continued on her way. She could see Erik from the corner of her eye as she worked her way around all of the tables. Then she nipped into the kitchen to warn Tabby, for her mother's sake, that another design change was in the making. Tabby grimaced and immediately went over to the old-fashioned rotary-dial phone hanging on one wall and started to dial.

After Isabella quickly prepared the to-go container of chocolate pie and delivered it, she ended up in front of Erik again. He'd been steadily decimating his meal. "Mind bringing me a few more rolls?"

"Coming up." She turned back into the kitchen. It had to be a testament to good metabolism and his very active lifestyle that kept his build as honed as it was. Because it certainly wasn't from dieting. More than once she'd seen him pack away meals of a size that made even Murphy's mammoth appetite look puny.

She returned with a basket full of rolls and a small plate of butter balls.

"Thanks." He grabbed one of the rolls, split it in half,

slathered butter on it, followed by a generous helping of the
strawberry jam one of the locals kept Ruby's supplied with,
then held it out to her. "Now, you eat it."

Her eyebrows shot up. "I'm on duty."

Erik looked at the diners on either side of him. "Anyone
here mind if Isabella takes a few minutes to wolf down a
roll?"

She could feel her cheeks heating as a chorus of "No"
and "Go for it" followed. She glared at Erik. "That is not
the point."

"No," he returned calmly. "The *point* is that your uniform
is getting looser. You're losing weight. So take the roll, go
out the back door to the picnic table where I know y'all sit
for your breaks and eat it. Better yet, eat a whole damn helping of meat loaf and potatoes." He glanced past her. "Tabby.
Tell her to take a break already and eat."

"Take a break already and eat," Tabby repeated, obviously amused.

Isabella gave her a look that the younger woman blithely
ignored. "Fine," she told her under her breath. "But you can
cash out your favorite bride for me."

Then she snatched the roll out of Erik's fingers and escaped into the kitchen.

"Don't you be throwing out that roll, either," she heard
Erik call loudly. "Bubba, you make sure she doesn't."

Isabella ignored the heaping plate of meat loaf the grinning cook held out and went out the back door.

She threw herself down on one of the benches at the
picnic table and glared at the soft roll. The strawberry jam
glistened invitingly. The butter was straight from the cream-
ery in town. And the rolls—well, nobody made better rolls,
whether they were dinner rolls or cinnamon rolls, than Tabby
Taggart. She came in at an ungodly hour in the mornings to
make them from scratch.

She sighed. Ate the roll. Licked strawberry jam from her finger.

"That's better."

She couldn't even pretend to be surprised that Erik had appeared around the back corner of the building. "Are you skipping out on your check? You know, it comes off the server's pay when you do that."

He set the basket of rolls he was carrying on the table and straddled the opposite bench. He didn't bother to answer the ridiculous accusation.

They both knew he wasn't the type to skip out on anything.

"Why don't you tell me what's eating at you?"

She snatched another roll from the basket and found that he'd buttered and jammed all of the ones there, too. It only made them more tempting. A feat, considering her appetite had been pretty much nil for the past few days.

Arguing with Murphy over everything from doing his homework to moving back to New York tended to do that even when she wasn't plagued with the worrisome news that the caseworker had imparted.

"Nothing's eating at me."

"Right." His gaze was steady. And it felt inescapable, even after Isabella turned her back on him and sat facing the other direction.

She nibbled at the roll. There was a reason Ruby's was always as busy as it was. The food might be simple, but nobody with a taste bud in their mouth could deny that it was unfailingly delicious.

"I can't help you if I don't know what the problem is."

She frowned and looked over her shoulder at him. It was hard to stay indignant, knowing that he really did mean well.

He was just that sort of man.

"I'm a big girl. I'm quite able to handle my own problems."

"I'm not saying you can't. But there's nothing wrong with some help now and then. Or even just an ear, if that's all you need."

She let out a sigh and turned away again. It only meant she was facing the plain backside of Ruby's, but at least looking at white siding and a serviceable steel door didn't give her heart palpitations the way looking at him did. "When's the last time you ever needed help with anything?" He was undoubtedly the king of competence.

"Needed Murph's help to tear down that old barn," he returned reasonably.

She made a face at the white siding.

Despite everything, the dappled sunlight felt so warm and welcome on her shoulders. "Not the same thing and you know it."

"What I'd *like* to know is what's making that uniform hang on you."

A flippant answer came to her lips but she just didn't have the heart to voice it. She rubbed her forehead. Pinched the bridge of her nose. "They've found Murphy's mother," she said. It was the first time she'd said the words aloud. To anyone.

And she'd chosen him, of all people, to confide in.

She closed her eyes, shutting out the plain white siding.

She heard Erik swear softly. Then he moved around the table and sat down beside her. She could feel the warmth of him against her shoulder, but aside from that, he made no move to touch her.

And she appreciated it.

If he'd slipped a comforting arm around her shoulders or taken her hand or anything, she was pretty sure she'd just fall apart altogether.

That was a luxury she had no time for. She was a parent now. At least for the time being. Parents weren't supposed to be weak. Surely that was written in a rule book somewhere.

"How'd you find out?" His voice was quiet. Steady.

And again, she appreciated it. "Our caseworker, Monica, called me." She hesitated for a moment. "I haven't told Murphy."

"Sounds wise to me."

"Does it?" Her lips twisted. "This is *his* mother we're talking about. He has a right to know about it."

"He's eleven. And you've already said that she's never been a mother to him. I think taking time with the news until you've figured out the ramifications is just showing some responsibility on your part."

"Responsibility?" She set aside the roll. It had lost its appeal. "More like fear."

"Fear of what?"

"Losing him to her."

"Could that happen? Where is she?"

"Anything could happen," she said huskily. She'd learned that when a perfectly hale and hearty firefighter was felled by an infection. She picked at a ragged fingernail. She'd given up on paying for manicures months ago. "She's living in a halfway house in Jersey."

"Drugs?"

She nodded. "Monica said Kim's been testing clean since she got out of prison several months ago. She has a regular job managing her uncle's convenience store." Her voice turned raw. "If all that continues, it won't be long before Kim will be able to leave the halfway house." Add in Jimmy's very healthy life-insurance policy that was out of reach to Isabella and his son, and Kim could turn out to be a very attractive candidate to raise her own child. And Lord knew that Murphy wanted to be raised by his mother rather than Isabella. He told her so, regularly.

"That doesn't mean you'll lose Murphy."

Isabella looked at him. No matter how hard she tried to keep them at bay, tears glazed her vision. "Short-term fiancée versus biological mother? What sort of choice is that?"

His jaw set, looking hard. "Loving, dedicated *parent* versus woman who has never tried being a parent at all? Is she asking to see him? Saying that she wants him?"

"Not yet." Isabella gnawed on the inside of her cheek. "It's just a matter of time, though."

"Why?"

"Because she's his mother!" She pushed off the bench. "What kind of mother doesn't want her own child?" Her head ached. She knew good and well that Monica Solis would prefer to see Murphy with his biological mother if she could talk her into taking him. Not because Monica didn't approve of Isabella necessarily, but because she wanted to keep families together.

For once, Isabella wished they had a caseworker more like the ones she'd had as a child, who hadn't seemed to care much about anything, least of all her.

"This isn't all about Murphy, is it?"

"Of course it is." She brushed her hands down the front of her pink uniform and picked up the basket of rolls. "Do you want any of these?"

His gaze didn't waver from her face. He shook his head slowly.

She stepped over to one of the trash bins and threw out the remaining rolls. They couldn't be served to anyone else, and she'd lost what little appetite they'd momentarily spurred. "I have to get back to work."

"Isabella—"

"The only thing I have going for me where Murphy is

concerned is this job here and the classes at Lucy's. I don't want to lose either."

He gave her a chiding look. "You're not going to lose anything for taking a well-deserved break."

"I don't need a break!" Her voice rose and she turned away from him, tears blinding her.

"Isabella." He sighed her name and his hands closed over her shoulders, turning her around into his chest. His hands slid over her back. "It's going to be all right."

She fisted her hands between them. The desire to just lean into him was overwhelming. To let someone else do the worrying for her. But she'd never had anyone to do that for her. Not even Jimmy. She'd barely had time to adjust to his explosion into her life when he'd left it just as abruptly.

The dappled sunlight had nothing on Erik's hands, stroking slowly up and down her back. He was warm and strong and steady, and she felt she was on the verge of crumbling to dust. "What if it's not?"

"Don't think that way. Isabella, you're not—"

"Um, sorry." Tabby had pushed open the back door. "Isabella, you have a call from the school."

Isabella swiped her cheeks and pulled away from Erik's arms. She looked at Tabby, who was clearly uncomfortable. "The school? Why?" What had Murphy done now? And how serious would it be?

Enough to get him taken away from her for good, Kim or no Kim?

Erik's hand closed over her shoulder. "Don't go thinking the worst," he said softly.

"It's the principal's office," Tabby told her. "It just sounded important."

Isabella nodded. What else could she do? She put one foot in front of the other and felt Erik's hand fall away. She shivered, reached the doorway and slipped past Tabby. She was aware of Erik following but couldn't manage a protest.

Just get to the phone, she thought. *Get to the phone and deal with the latest disaster.* That was all she had to do. Her hand shook as she picked up the old-fashioned receiver hanging by its coiled cord from the wall. "This is Isabella Lockhart."

Erik came up to stand beside her. He didn't touch her. But his presence helped steady her anyway.

"Ms. Lockhart." The voice on the other end of the line was brisk. "This is Viola Timms from the elementary school. Principal Gage would like you to come down as soon as possible to meet with him."

Isabella pressed a fist to the knot in her stomach. The day that she'd registered Murphy, the middle-aged secretary had struck her as full of heavy-duty starch. She'd had no reason to change her opinion since. "Is Murphy all right?"

"He's all right. But he is in the principal's office. He's been suspended."

"Suspended," she echoed, dismayed. But at least it wasn't another expulsion. The first one had happened right after Jimmy died. She'd gotten Murphy into another school only for him to earn yet another expulsion. The third school had been harder to come by. And the brownstone incident had occurred soon after. Isabella knew then that she had to get him out of New York and away from his so-called friends there. "For how long?"

"Three days. It's mandatory. Principal Gage will explain everything when you come to pick up Murphy."

It was the middle of the lunch rush. "He's not allowed to finish out the day," she guessed. "I'll be right there."

"Thank you, Ms. Lockhart." A moment later, Isabella was listening to the dial tone.

She slowly replaced the receiver. Both Erik and Tabby

were watching her. "Guess I'll be taking a break after all," she said. She pulled off her white apron. "I'm sorry, Tabby. I know this leaves you in a lurch right when we're the busiest. But I'll be back as soon as I can." She focused on her boss and ignored the frown growing on Erik's face. "I'm afraid I'll have to bring Murphy back to the café with me."

Tabby waved a dismissive hand and followed her over to the four narrow lockers that they used to store their personal belongings while on shift. "That doesn't matter to me. Murphy will be fine here. And in the meantime, Bubba can help out front. Most everybody is ordering the special anyway." She tilted her head and looked at Isabella closely. "Are *you* okay?"

Just put one foot in front of the other.

Get to the school.

"I'm fine." She pulled her purse out of the locker.

Meet with the principal.

Deal with the situation. Just one step at a time.

She fumbled through her purse searching for her car keys. "I'll be as quick as I can."

She turned toward the back door again, only to find Erik standing in her way. "I'll drive you," he said.

"That's not necessary."

"You're as white as a sheet." Despite her resistance, he easily tugged the keys out of her hand and dropped them back inside her purse. "You're not getting behind the wheel of a car when you're this upset."

She wished she had the energy to bristle.

The truth of the matter was that she could walk to the elementary school very easily from Ruby's. It would only save a few minutes at the most by driving over there. But she didn't seem to have the energy for that, either.

And what did it matter if Erik took her to the school?

He already knew more about the situation with Murphy than anyone else in town did.

So she just nodded and headed out the back door.

A school suspension. Murphy's mother being located.

How many more signs did she need before she faced the fact that she had no more business trying to be a parent than the woman who'd abandoned *her* when she'd been a baby?

Chapter Eight

"I met with Principal Gage when I registered Murphy for school," Isabella told Eric as they walked down the empty hall of Weaver Elementary School. Their heels rang on the plain, utilitarian tile. Even though it was obvious that Isabella would have preferred that Erik wait in the truck, he'd accompanied her inside.

"He's a decent guy. Cares a lot about the kids here." Joe Gage had become principal long after Erik had attended. But his mother gave Joe high marks, and she'd know—she'd taught here back in the days that Joe had been a teacher himself, and she was now head of the school board.

"Even ones like Murphy?"

"Especially ones like Murphy." He touched the small of her back, guiding her around the corner that led to the main office.

"Hey, Viola," he said as they entered. He knew it irritated the woman immensely to be addressed by her first name. She was that way even at church. "Ms. Lockhart is here to see Joe."

"Please have a seat," Viola said properly. "Principal Gage will be with you shortly." She pressed a button on her phone and spoke quietly into it.

Erik led Isabella to the trio of empty yellow chairs lined up against the wall opposite the secretary's desk.

Isabella sat, holding her purse clenched on her lap. She stared at the round clock on the wall above the desk.

"I think these are the same chairs they had when I used to get sent to the principal's office," he observed as he sat beside her.

She made a faint sound. But then, after a moment, she looked at him. "I'm sorry. What did you say?"

He couldn't help himself. He unlatched her white-knuckled fingers from the purse and folded her cold hand inside his. "I said these look like the same chairs they had back when I went to school here."

"I'm sure you were never sent to the principal's office."

"You'd be wrong." The door to Joe's office was closed. He wondered if the man was in there right now with Murphy. Supposed he probably was. Back in Erik's time at the school, whenever he'd been sitting in the principal's office, it wasn't likely that he'd be sent back to cool his heels in class until one of his folks came to spring him. He hitched his ankle across his knee. "I don't even remember how many times I was hauled in." She hadn't pulled her hand away from his. It was just resting there inside the curve of his fingers, tense and still curled into a fist.

But her lips twisted with disbelief as she looked at him. "For what? Crossing outside the crosswalk?"

He smiled faintly. Tartness right now from her was a good thing. Certainly a hell of a lot better than that whipped look she'd had ever since she'd told him about Murphy's mother. "Smoking," he admitted. "Third grade, I think that was."

"Third grade," she echoed. "Good grief. What were you doing with cigarettes in the third grade?"

"Trying to smoke 'em," he said wryly. "And my parents had a lot more to say about it than 'good grief,'" he recalled. "Fourth grade was for getting into a fight with Wally Drysdale over who got to sit behind Cindy Schaeffer. Broke his nose."

"You had a violent streak."

"Not particularly. I'd still feel a little bad about it, except that ol' Wally took his face—that the broken nose gave an interesting cast to—out to Chicago after high school and he's been modeling underwear ever since. Goes by *Chad* now."

She didn't look as if she believed him, but her fist was starting to relax. "What was so special about Cindy Schaeffer?"

"She had the longest braids of any girl in school. And they were as orange as carrots."

"And after the broken nose, who got to sit behind her?"

"I did." He bobbed the toe of his boot, wondering what was taking Joe so damn long. "But then I tied them in a knot while we were watching a *National Geographic* film and got sent to these same chairs again."

Her lips actually curved up a hair. "You did not do that."

"Cross my heart." He thought back. "By the time I was Murph's age, the principal had my folks' phone number on speed dial."

She rolled her eyes. "Did they even have speed dial that long ago?"

"Hey. Thirty-one isn't *that* old."

"I'm thirty-one," she said. The faint upward curve at the corners of her lips disappeared. "And sometimes it feels positively ancient."

He squeezed her hand. "That's because you've had a tough year. It'll get better."

"I wish I could believe that." She sighed. Then she hopped to her feet the second Joe Gage's door cracked open.

The balding principal looked surprised to find Erik there with Isabella, but he said nothing. He merely invited Isabella into his office.

Erik knew he'd be seriously overstepping her comfort zone if he made a move to go with her into Joe's office, so he just stretched his arm across the back of the seat she'd vacated and gave her an encouraging smile.

Her black-brown gaze held his for a moment, then her lashes lowered and she hurried into the office.

The door closed once again.

Erik dropped the pretense of casualness and pushed to his feet, pacing in front of Viola's desk. "Don't suppose you'd care to tell me what earned Murph's suspension, do you?"

She gave him a pinch-lipped look. "No, I would not care to do any such thing. And you know, Reverend Stone and our church committee are still waiting for that stained-glass window you promised."

Erik gave her a look. He hadn't yet contacted Jessica and he knew he needed to. It had been a month since Murph broke the window. "Viola, do you ever find anything in life to be happy about?"

Her lips thinned. She turned to her old-fashioned electric typewriter and fed a sheet of paper into it, even though she had a state-of-the-art computer sitting right next to it. A moment later, she started clacking away, which was a sound that took him back to his childhood just as surely as those yellow chairs did.

Viola Timms had never shown a sense of humor.

The office area was too small to allow for any decent pacing. He could have gone into the hall, but he didn't want

Isabella to come out of Joe's office and find him gone. So he went back to the chairs and sat down again.

Before long, though, Joe's door creaked open to reveal Murphy—looking sullen—closely followed by Isabella. She was still pale, but no worse than before going into Joe's office. Erik stood and stayed right where he was, controlling the impulse to go over to meet her.

"Thanks for coming in so quickly, Isabella," Joe was saying. "I wish there was something else we could do, but in situations like this, my hands are tied. The school district's rules are absolute."

Isabella nodded. "We understand." Her gaze collided with Erik's for a moment before it skittered away. She closed her hand over Murphy's shoulder. "Don't we, Murphy?"

The boy hitched his shoulder. "I guess."

"There's no guessing about it," the principal said, though he didn't sound particularly heated. "Bringing weapons to class is forbidden."

Murphy sighed noisily. "Wasn't usin' it as a *weapon,*" he muttered.

"I know," Joe said. "Mr. Rasmussen said as much when I spoke to him about it. And that's why you're only getting a three-day suspension. Otherwise it would be worse." He was holding a manila envelope and he stuck out his free hand to shake Isabella's hand. "We'll be looking forward to having Murphy back with us on Tuesday."

She nodded, offered her thanks again, then hustled Murphy forward.

"Murphy." Viola held up the backpack that had been sitting behind her desk. "Don't forget this." She smiled thinly. "I've placed a sheet inside from Mr. Rasmussen with your assignments."

The boy automatically hefted one of the straps over his

shoulder, but his expression was horrified. "I've still gotta do *homework?*"

That thin smile grew even more chilly. "Unless you want failing grades, too."

"Thank you for retrieving the assignments, Mrs. Timms," Joe cut in, giving her a censorious look.

She sniffed and turned back to her typing.

"Keep up on the homework now and you won't have to do extra when you get back next week," Joe told Murphy reasonably. "Then there's less than two months of school before you'll be on summer break."

Murphy made a face. "What about my knife?"

Joe handed over the manila envelope to Isabella. "That is up to your guardian," he said easily. "Just don't bring it back to school."

"Yeah, whatever."

"Murphy," Isabella chided tightly.

He exhaled noisily. "I won't bring it again," he muttered.

"Good man." Joe clapped him on the shoulder, gave Erik a nod and headed back toward his office.

With the principal gone, Murphy jerked his head toward Erik. "What's *he* doing here?"

"Erik gave me a ride over from Ruby's," Isabella said, nudging him toward the doorway. She gave Erik a quick look from beneath her lashes as she and the boy preceded him from the office. "He was there having lunch when the principal's office called." As they walked along the halls, one of the school bells rang. Doors flew open and elementary kids of every size and shape raced out into the halls, all heading in their direction.

If Erik recalled correctly, their common goal would be the cafeteria for their lunch. He scooted Isabella to the other side of him where there was less chance of someone colliding with her.

Murphy, obviously seeing the movement, gave them a sour look. "Lunch," he muttered. "Right."

"Don't even talk right now," Isabella warned, "unless it's to offer an explanation of *what* you were thinking bringing this to school." She waved the manila envelope, then shoved it into the voluminous depths of her patchwork-colored purse.

Murphy's gaze followed the envelope. "Can I have it *back?*"

"You weren't supposed to have it at all," she told him.

Erik wanted to know what sort of knife it was and what the hell he was trying to accomplish by bringing it to school. But he held his tongue. Soon they reached one of the doorways that led them outside and to his truck.

He opened the rear passenger door and waited until Murphy had climbed into the backseat, where he slumped down. He'd retrieved a ball cap from inside his backpack and it was pulled low over his eyes.

Erik shut the door but stopped Isabella when she reached for the passenger door. "Just a second. You're really going back to work?"

She nodded. "I have to close up. Tabby leaves before I do. She's taking some online college classes in the afternoons and evenings. And cleaning up out front isn't one of Bubba's responsibilities."

He wondered what she'd say if he told her Tabby and Bubba would do exactly what Erik requested, and decided it was better to let Isabella feel some measure of control in her own life rather than know that it was actually Erik and his brother who owned Ruby's now. They had ever since his mother— who'd inherited it herself from her great-grandmother Ruby— passed it on to them years ago. "Why don't I take him out to the ranch with me?" he suggested softly.

She frowned up at him and pushed her hands into the pockets of her uniform. "This isn't your problem."

He let the sting of that roll off. "I know it's not, but that doesn't mean I can't help. And it's not entirely unselfish. I've got some fence I need to replace. An extra hand will be useful." He wasn't exaggerating. Things were getting really busy again out at the ranch, what with calves starting to drop.

She rubbed her nose. He could tell she was considering it. "Don't you want to know why he had the knife?"

"I heard Joe. He wasn't using it as a weapon." Erik was betting the kid wasn't actually violent, any more than Erik had been when he'd been a kid. "So I'm guessing he was probably showing off with it."

"Yes," she said on a sigh. "He says he just wanted to show it to Zach and Connor. It was Jimmy's Buck knife. They evidently didn't believe that Murphy had one. He took it from my jewelry box," she admitted. "But I didn't notice it was missing. I should have, but I didn't."

"You can't blame yourself for every little thing he does. He just chose to play show-and-tell at school with a banned item. Not the smartest thing he's done, but probably not the worst." He'd gotten his first knife when he'd been younger than Murph.

"No. Definitely not the worst," she agreed.

"So let me drop you off at Ruby's since you insist on going back, and take him with me out to my place. I'll make sure he gets his homework done, plus I'll have some cheap labor. You can pick him up later when you're done."

She gave him a close look. "You really want his help? This isn't because you feel sorry for me or something?"

He didn't feel sorry for her. But he also knew she probably didn't want to hear anything more about what he did feel. Not now anyway. And he did think that it would do Murphy good to be outside in the sun and not cooped up inside. He'd spent enough time with the kid to notice he was happier when he was outside and busy. In that regard, he and Erik were the same. "I can do the job on my own, but it goes easier with a few extra hands." He shrugged. "And it'll lop off more time from his window-sentence. Come and get him when you want. If you've got things you need to do after you get off from Ruby's, have at it." If he could finagle it, he'd get her to sit back and relax for an hour or two on his porch.

"Murphy sees his counselor on Wednesday evenings and I have yoga classes at Lucy's studio." She looked at her watch.

He easily revised his plans to suit her schedule. "Why don't I drop him off at his appointment, then you can do your yoga thing and pick him up when you're done? It'll give him even more time to work on his schoolwork, and it'll save you having to drive out to the ranch at all." He vowed then and there to do something about getting the road graded to make it an easier trip for her when she did make it.

A line had formed between her eyebrows. "I feel like I'm taking advantage of you."

He spread his hands. "If you want to take advantage of me, I'm your man."

Her frown disappeared. She flushed. "Very funny."

He grinned. "Can't blame a guy for being a guy." He glanced through the window at Murphy. The kid was watching them closely.

He had no illusions about Murphy. Even though the barbecue and baseball game out at the Double-C had gone over well, Erik still knew that the boy considered him, at worst, the enemy, and at best, the competition.

"What about the rest of his suspension?" Murphy wouldn't be in school for the rest of the week, or on Monday. "Have you thought yet about what you'll do with him beyond this afternoon?"

"I think I'll have to take off work." She lifted her shoulders. "I don't see any way around it. Having him hang out at Ruby's while I close up for a few hours is one thing. But all day?" She shook her head. "He'll be climbing the walls and who could blame him? But leaving him home alone is not an option."

He didn't ask her if she'd thought about what she'd do with the boy once the school year was finished and there would be every day to consider and not just a three-day suspension. Maybe she had a plan. Or maybe she was just afraid that by then the caseworker and courts would have ended her guardianship altogether.

"I can take him out to the ranch again on Friday and Monday," he offered, "but tomorrow I've got some business in Gillette." He had a load of supplies to pick up and would be gone most of the day. Since he was going, he might as well bite the bullet and fit in a visit to Jessica's studio along the way. If she refused to deal with him, he'd hunt up another glass artist to replace the stained-glass window and that would be that.

"I don't expect you to take him at all," Isabella reminded him. "This is my responsibility."

"Sounding a little like a broken record there, Izzy."

She gave him a stern look. "Nobody calls me Izzy."

He smiled and decided then and there that the nickname suited her far more than just Iz, which was what most of the folks seemed to call her. "Let's just get today taken care of," he suggested, "and we'll work on what to do tomorrow along the way."

"One step at a time."

"Exactly. So…how about it?"

She sighed deeply. "I'm never going to be able to repay you for everything you're doing for us."

"Did I ask for repayment for anything other than that window?"

"You're a nice guy, Erik Clay," she finally said. "Why aren't you settled down with a half-dozen kids of your own to keep you busy?"

"Never met anyone I was interested in settling down with," he said easily. Until he'd met her. But he wasn't fool enough to admit that out loud.

If he did, she'd probably snatch up Murph and head right back to the skyscrapers of New York.

"Well, that's something I can understand." She put her hand on the truck door handle. "Until I met Jimmy I felt exactly the same way." Then she pulled open the door. "Murphy, you're going to go out to the ranch with Erik and work there with him this afternoon," she announced.

Then she climbed in and shut the door before Erik had a chance to.

Jimmy. Always Jimmy.

Erik pushed down a sigh, reminded himself that he was supposed to be a patient man and rounded the truck to get in and drive her back to the diner.

Without Murphy waiting impatiently for Isabella to finish closing up after the last customer left, she was able to finish her tasks in record time. It was still the middle of the afternoon when she sat down at the dining-room table to review, yet again, the never-ending pile of bills. The busier she kept, the easier it was to keep her growing number of unwanted thoughts at bay.

Erik.

Murphy's mother.

The impending visit from their caseworker.

She'd organized and reorganized the bills so often she had them all memorized. And she finally pushed them all away. She couldn't pay a dime on any of them until payday, and that wasn't until Friday.

The house was too silent without Murphy around. And she couldn't help but worry that it could well be silent like that permanently if Murphy was taken away from her.

She cooked some pasta but eating held no appeal and she ended up refrigerating all the leftovers. She still had a few hours before class, so she dragged the old-fashioned reel lawn mower out of the garage and ran it over the grass. The thing was ancient, but the blades were sharp, and it didn't take long before the grass was short and tidy once again.

She put the mower away and went back inside to find her cell phone ringing. She quickly snatched it out of her purse, all her nerves ratcheting right back up. "Hello?"

"Hey, Isabella."

"Tabby." She sat down on one of the dining-room chairs and pressed a calming hand to her racing heart.

Not Erik at all.

She'd already arranged with Tabby to take off work the following day. She'd told Isabella that she'd prevail upon one of the women who occasionally worked there to fill in. "What's wrong?"

"Nothing," Tabby assured quickly. "I was just over at my folks' place. The B was there after they left Ruby's."

The bride and her ever-changing wedding gown, Isabella thought. "Did your mother tell her to take a flying leap?"

Tabby chuckled. "Oh, I'm sure she wanted to if not for her being old friends with the B's grandmother, who also happens to be married to the mayor. Anyway, I was mentioning to Mom about you being a seamstress and designing the costumes for your old dance company, and she wanted me to see if you're interested in helping her. Either with the design or just doing piecework. Whatever you're willing to do. She thinks that if she has some help on it, maybe the gown'll actually be done on time."

Isabella's fancy sewing machines and the supplies she

hadn't been able to bear parting with were still in boxes stored inside the hall closet. She hadn't sewn so much as a stitch since she'd left the dance company, and the idea of getting her fingers back into fabrics and trim was nearly irresistible. She'd never done an actual wedding gown, but she'd certainly designed enough dance costumes. "I'd be glad to help your mom."

"She'll pay you, of course," Tabby said.

"That's not necessary."

"Please." Tabby's voice turned dry. "Believe me. The B will have to pay for the pleasure out of her own pocket. That was part of the rather heated discussions they all had in my mother's living room this afternoon."

Isabella could easily imagine. "In that case," she said, "does your mom want me to call her or what?"

"Yeah. As soon as you can. I know she's anxious to get started." Tabby reeled off a phone number and Isabella scratched it down on the back of her phone bill.

"I'll call her right now," Isabella said. "Thanks, Tabby."

"No. Thank *you*." They ended the call and Isabella dialed the number she'd written down.

Thirty minutes later, she'd followed the directions that Jolie Taggart had given her to her home on the outskirts of town and was studying the sketches spread across the woman's charmingly rustic dining-room table.

The older woman was shaking her head, her hands propped on her hips. "Ordinarily, I like this sort of work," she admitted. "But Bethany has been a challenge. These are all the designs that actually made it beyond a sketch. I have bodices, half-finished skirts and fabrics that she's selected coming out my ears, only to have her turn around and decide she doesn't want any of them after all. Now she says she can't live unless she has one dress that combines elements from each one—'a perfect symphony of spring.'"

Jolie rolled her eyes. "Her words. Yet as you can plainly see, the styles are entirely different."

That was an understatement. From heavily elegant to a veritable brothel of shimmering fluff, the gowns were *wildly* different.

"I'm at my wit's end," Jolie admitted. "She wants to come back on Saturday afternoon to approve the final design and I'm completely out of ideas. I can put it all together exactly as she's described and she'll look like a clown. But it would be nice if I could manage the task without it coming to that."

"She doesn't deserve the effort," Jolie's husband, Drew, said as he passed through the room, a coffee mug in hand. He was a tall, dark-haired man with smile lines creasing his face.

It wasn't Jolie's husband who had Isabella's mouth going dry, though. It was the sight of the two men with him—Erik and his father, Tristan.

"Don't worry," Erik said the second she spotted him. "Murph's duly delivered to his appointment."

She swallowed, but nothing was helping either the dryness or the jerkiness of her pulse. "Thank you."

"We're just here to talk to Drew about some horses he's training for us," he added, as if he wanted to disabuse her of any notion that he might be there because *she* was.

She was aware of the looks passing between the others and hated knowing they were all speculating about what one of their own was doing with the newcomer in town. She'd been in Weaver long enough to understand that particular dynamic. Speculation and gossip were simply part of the backbone of the town. And that was fine as long as she wasn't the subject of it.

"Before I dropped Murph off, we had an early dinner over at my folks'," Erik added.

Isabella couldn't help flicking a quick look at Erik's father. The older man had a faint smile on his face, as if something about the entire situation amused him. "I hope Murphy didn't put you or Mrs. Clay out," she told him.

"Hope's always glad to have more mouths to feed." He sent his son a sideways glance before looking back at Isabella. "Maybe next time you'll be able to join them. There's always room for another beautiful woman, far as I'm concerned."

She found herself blushing. It wasn't hard to see the source of the blarney that Erik had inherited. And as appealing as the notion was of being included in anything to do with Erik's ridiculously welcoming family, she knew that it would be better all around to resist the lure. "You're very kind."

At that, Drew snorted. "Don't let him fool you," he advised with a grin. "Tris and I go *way* back. The stories I could tell—"

"Will have to wait for another day," Jolie interrupted. She took a sip of her husband's coffee, then pushed her hands against his shoulders. "Get on with you. Isabella's here to help *me,* not indulge you old men."

Isabella bit back a smile. One thing she couldn't do was attribute the term *old* to either Drew Taggart or Tristan Clay. They were both ridiculously handsome men who reeked of vitality.

"You indulge me just fine," Drew drawled, giving his wife a quick look. Isabella was delighted to see the older woman's cheeks pinkening.

But then her gaze collided with Erik's, and he was smiling, as if he'd noticed the very same thing, and her pulse started ricocheting around all over again. It was all she could do not to jump out of her skin when he touched her elbow. "I want to steal Izzy for just a minute," he told the others.

Jolie gave him a look. "For just a *minute,*" she warned.

He raised his hand. "Scout's honor." Then he closed his hand around her elbow again and nudged her out of the room.

"Were you ever a Scout?" she asked as soon as they were standing alone in a softly lit room that she assumed was a study, considering the wide desk on one side and the beautiful built-in bookshelves crammed with books.

His teeth flashed briefly. "Are you doubting it? I think I'm wounded."

She rolled her eyes and sighed noisily. She wasn't going to show him how easily he charmed her. It would only lead to trouble. And she had enough trouble on her plate. "What'd you want? I really want to get back to help Jolie before yoga."

"My mother said she'd be happy to keep him with her tomorrow while you're at work."

"You *told* her about his suspension?" Not that it mattered, considering how word traveled in the small town.

"I didn't tell her. Murph did."

She blinked. "He did?"

"Surprised the hell outta me, too. Announced it right in the middle of the chicken and rice."

"Why would he do that?"

He shrugged. "Who knows? My mother has an affinity for children. Always has. She didn't bat an eye, but asked him if he deserved the suspension. Murph nodded, passed the rolls when my dad asked him to, and that was that." His thumb roved over the point of her bare elbow in a wholly distracting manner. "Before we left, though, she told me to offer her services for the day if you needed them."

She shifted away from him. Far enough for his hand to fall away. Yet she wanted to move right back. It was all too easy becoming accustomed to his touch. "That was very kind of her—" so kind it made something in her chest feel tight "—but I couldn't possibly take advantage of her that way."

"Up to you. Just know the offer's open." Then he tucked a finger beneath her chin and pushed upward. "Murphy isn't the only one who needs to settle in here in Weaver, Isabella. There are people all around you who are willing and able to help you. All you have to do is be willing to accept it."

She could hardly breathe. "I'm nobody to any of them."

His eyes narrowed slightly. Dropped to her lips for a heart-stopping moment. "Don't kid yourself, sweetheart. You're definitely somebody."

Then, just when she was almost bracing for the kiss that was so evident in his expression, he dropped his hand. Stepped away.

"Don't be late for class," he said.

And then he left her standing there alone in the study, trembling.

And wishing, so, so stupidly, that he'd given her that kiss after all.

Chapter Nine

When Jolie came to find her a few minutes later, Isabella was still trembling. "Are you all right, dear?"

Isabella quickly brushed back her hair and nodded. "Fine. Sorry. Let's get back to that dress."

Jolie gave her a close look but mercifully said nothing. She just nodded and led the way back to the dining room.

Once they were settled at the table, Isabella quickly reached for one of the sketches. The one showing the most elegant dress of them all. "Do you mind?"

Jolie waved her hand. "Have at it."

Isabella began marking up the sketch with a pencil, determinedly pushing Erik as far into one corner of her mind as he would go. She replaced the severe strapless neckline with the deep halter of the gown in the second sketch. Then she lengthened the modest train to match the longer length in the third sketch. She avoided thinking about how she'd never even considered what sort of wedding dress she might wear after Jimmy had proposed. But now, she couldn't seem to stop wondering what sort of gown Erik would want to see on his intended.

Probably something traditional.

Simple.

With a hint of sass.

"She wants bling," Jolie told her, interrupting the foolish reverie. "Crystals. Beading. We don't have time to do a lot of beading."

She renewed her focus. This was about Bethany's gown. *And nothing else.* "And you say she wants something filmy and airy, to suit the season, but the only fabrics she's willing to consider are heavy satins."

"Exactly. And even if I can convince her that she'll need something very lightweight to get that airy feeling, I can't think of any that would be substantial enough to bear the weight of that much *bling.*" Jolie practically bared her teeth on the word.

Isabella thought about the scads of embellished fabrics she'd had at her disposal at NEBT. If she could call in a few favors, get her hands on some, it would ease their task considerably. "If we bead here—" she made a few more marks on the sketch "—and here, the weight shouldn't be too bad. We'll have to line it, naturally, but with the skirt constructed of several layers of translucent fabric, maybe with some subtle ruffling, she'll have the airiness. We could even do some crystals on one of the heavier underlayers—say, the satin she wants—so some shimmer would peek through. What time of day is the wedding?"

"Two o'clock in the afternoon."

She'd bet Erik would want an afternoon wedding. Followed by a big barbecue-style reception.

Stop it!

"Pretty formal trimmings for an afternoon wedding," she managed, and earned another close look from Jolie.

"Yes," the other woman agreed. "But try telling that to Bethany."

Isabella kept her gaze on the sketch. *Bethany's* sketch. "What if we switched from ivory to white? Took out the heavy satin? Would that seem more in keeping with an afternoon wedding? Maybe use a butterfly motif or something?" She tossed the suggestion out almost desperately.

"I think that sounds perfect," Jolie said. "But again... selling the idea to Bethany is the problem."

Isabella slipped into one of the chairs surrounding the table, the tiny part of her mind that was still functioning rationally skipping over the hundreds of fabrics and trims she'd once used. She grabbed the fat pink eraser from the table and went to work again on the sketch. Removing here. Adding there. She was vaguely aware of Jolie sitting down beside her to watch what she was doing. And after about twenty minutes of fiddling, she sat back and held out the heavy white paper.

Jolie's eyes widened. "Oh, my goodness. You're a genius! It's perfect."

Isabella smiled. "I'll make some calls early tomorrow morning to one of the girls I used to work with. See if she'll send me some of the embellished fabrics I have in mind and we'll whip up the basic pattern so it'll be ready when Bethany comes to see you on Saturday. Not the finished product, of course, but at least enough to give her an idea of the cut and fit. You have her measurements already, obviously."

Jolie nodded. "And with this sketch, she'll *have* to love it, too."

Isabella smiled wryly. "Well. We can hope, can't we?"

Jolie suddenly threw her arms around her and gave her an enthusiastic hug. "Oh, my darling. You are a lifesaver."

She let go and tilted the sketch to the light, studying it again. "Look out, New York fashion designers!"

Isabella laughed. She was fairly certain the real designers of the world were perfectly safe from the likes of her. But one glance at her watch told her the time had passed even more quickly than she'd thought, and she rose from the table. "I'll call you tomorrow morning and let you know what's going on with the fabrics. Then we'll get the pattern cut and stitched up in time for your Saturday appointment."

Jolie rose, too. "I feel like I can breathe again."

"Well, that's good. Wouldn't want you to stop doing that." Isabella gathered up her purse, and the older woman walked her to the door.

Whatever steadiness Isabella had regained while she'd worked on the sketch disappeared in a whoosh at the sight of Erik's truck parked outside the house next to her little sedan.

Mercifully, though, there was no sign of *him,* so she hurried to her car and drove away like the devil was at her heels.

But no matter how fast she went, she couldn't outdrive the images of weddings and barbecue receptions.

Isabella smiled and waved at the last student to leave her class before she closed and locked the entrance door.

The dance studio was entirely silent after a few hours of chattering laughter and throbbing music. Murphy would be at his counseling appointment for a while yet so she took her time setting the studio to rights again in preparation for the next day's activities. She polished mirrors, dry-mopped the floor and wiped down chairs.

The routine tasks were a comfort. When everything was as tidy as she could make it, she retrieved her sweater and purse from the office, doused the lights and left through the rear door, locking up behind her. She was parked in the lot on the side of the building, but even though it was entirely dark out, as she headed to her car she felt no wariness the way she would have back in New York. As soon as she turned the corner, light from Colbys across the way took away the worst of the shadows.

Dr. Templeton's office was on the other side of town. Isabella still had enough time to run into Shop-World and pick up a few groceries if she was quick. With her mind going over the short list of what she needed, she didn't notice the dark truck parked a few empty spots away from her car.

Not until a deep voice broke the silent night. "Izzy."

She went stock-still. Peered at Erik's tall shadow that separated itself from the shape of his truck. She'd managed to almost eradicate those silly notions that she'd had back at the Taggarts' home. Notions of kisses and weddings that weren't.

"What are you doing here?"

"Waiting for you."

An answer that did not help her state of mind at all.

"Why?" She yanked open the back door of her car and shoved her bag inside. The slam of the door sounded sharp in the night air.

"Because it's dark outside. Because Lucy needs to install a better light in her section of the parking lot. Because I can't seem to stop myself where you're concerned."

Her nerves felt frayed. Even though she damned her own foolish tongue, she couldn't manage to keep it silent. "Stop yourself from what?"

"Isabella." His voice was a soft tsk. "You're too smart to play dumb." His shadow became even more distinct and she realized he was coming around the back of her car.

She went still but couldn't move away to save her life. Not even when he stopped so close to her that she could see the gleam of his eyes and the shape of his lips in the moonlight.

Her heart climbed into her throat. She moistened her own

lips nervously. If he kissed her, she wasn't sure she'd have the strength to resist.

And what kind of person did that make her?

His arm moved and she braced herself, anticipating, waiting…

But all he did was set his hand on the top of her car. "I think you should consider my mother's offer."

It took her scrambled brain a moment to decipher the words coming out of his mouth. It wasn't what she'd expected.

Which left her wondering rather hysterically what she *had* expected. For him to profess his undying devotion to her?

She'd already had the impossible happen once—a man sweeping her off her feet.

Who could the impossible happen twice?

"You mean her offer about watching Murphy tomorrow?"

"Yeah. I think it'd be good for him." His fingers softly drummed the roof of her car. They were long. Square-tipped. And strong. She knew his fingers were strong.

Something inside her knew they'd also be gentle.

Her mouth had gone dry again and she wished she hadn't been so hasty shoving her dance bag in the backseat. There was a bottle of water inside it that she sorely needed.

It would also have given her antsy hands something to do. Instead, she wondered what they'd feel like pressed against the solid wall of his chest.

She shook herself. This was a conversation. Not a seduction. "Why? Because she used to be a teacher? I don't mean any offense, but Murphy's not likely to be particularly impressed by that." He seemed to barely tolerate any of his teachers. His latest, Mr. Rasmussen, was no exception.

"Because my mother has a way of getting through a person's defenses."

Well, that was true enough. Isabella had experienced it

herself. "Erik." She rubbed her forehead, wondering how she would ever get through to him. "I don't want to be any more beholden to you than I already am."

"My mother isn't me."

"She's your family! She might as well be you. It's practically the same thing."

"Sweetheart," his voice dropped a notch, "there's a world of difference between me and my mom."

Considering the way the blood was flying through her veins and that her knees felt positively shaky, she was well aware of that fact. "You know that's not what I mean," she managed.

His hand slid away from the roof of the car and settled on her shoulder, making her vividly aware of the thinness of the sweater she'd pulled on over her stretchy camisole and dance pants. Particularly when she felt the warmth of his thumb slowly circling the point of her shoulder. "What are you afraid of?"

If her knees went weak from his hand on her shoulder, what would happen to her if he *really* touched her?

Something deep inside her clenched, wanting and warm, even as her mind shied away.

She was still wearing her engagement ring, she reminded herself dimly. Erik had promised that he would respect that.

"I'm not afraid of anything," she returned. "Except—" Oh, heavens, his hand went to her neck and curled warmly against it beneath the ponytail she'd yanked her hair into. "Except—" What had she been going to say? "Murphy," she said thickly. "Losing Murphy."

She felt his thumb pressing gently against her thundering pulse at the base of her throat. It was unbearably intimate. "Because you don't want to be alone again."

"Yes. No." He was confusing her. "Because he's Jimmy's son, and because we're...we're family. Being alone has nothing to do with it." She'd been alone all her life, despite the never-ending stream of foster families with whom she'd been placed. Foster brothers. Foster sisters. Foster parents. She'd had them all.

But she'd still always been alone. That fact was as much a part of her as her white-blond hair. She could tint it dark brown, but underneath, that blond would still be there. Falling in love with Jimmy hadn't changed anything.

He, too, had left her. She knew he hadn't chosen to die. Hadn't chosen any of it. But knowing it didn't change the fact that he was gone.

And she'd been left behind.

"I love Murphy." Maybe she hadn't at first, but that was the reality now. "He's the closest thing I'll ever have to a child of my own and I want the best for him."

"Is there some reason you can't have children of your own, too?"

She felt the conversation spinning out of her grasp and didn't have a clue how to get control of it again. "What? Physically? No. But that's not what I meant."

"So you do want more. Children, that is."

Jimmy hadn't wanted more children. And because she'd wanted Jimmy, she'd agreed. "That's not what we're talking about!"

Erik's thumb glided slowly up her neck, and her knees felt even more wobbly. *He* would want a baseball team of children, no doubt.

"Okay," he said softly. "What are we talking about?"

Her hands rose. Fell. "I don't know," she practically wailed. "What are you doing to me?"

"Ah, Izzy," he murmured. "What have you already done to me?"

Then he finally, finally lowered his head, and his mouth found hers.

No more knees or legs at all. Just water where joints and bone used to exist.

Her fingers curled into his shoulders, grasping for support.

He tasted warm. And so welcoming that she yearned to curl into him and never think again.

When he lifted his head, she sucked in a deep breath, aware that all he'd really done was slowly brush his warm lips over hers.

Nothing overwhelming.

Nothing deep.

Nothing overtly sexual.

And she realized it would have been far less disturbing if his kiss had been exactly like that.

Sex—just good old-fashioned sexual chemistry—would have been so much easier to deal with than the strange tangle of yearnings he made her feel. Yearnings for things she'd never known.

The closest she'd ever gotten was with Jimmy. And even he hadn't made her feel this way so easily. As if she were almost whole…from nothing more than the brush of a hand. Or from a faint, crooked smile that showed far more clearly in a pair of violet eyes than it ever did on a pair of mobile lips.

Which made her feel as if she were losing Jimmy all over again.

She snatched her hands away from Erik's chest as if she'd been caught doing something horrifying.

"I can't do this," she said hoarsely and slid around him, yanking open the car door and collapsing shakily onto the driver's seat. She fumbled with the car keys, trying three times before she was able to fit the key in the ignition, only to gasp when Erik reached past her and pulled the keys right back out again before she could start the car. "What are you doing? Give me back my keys!"

"You're not driving when you're this upset."

"I'm not upset."

"You're shaking life a leaf." His voice had turned flat. "I'm sorry, okay? I shouldn't have kissed you. It was out of line."

Tears burned in the corners of her eyes. What on earth had Erik ever done but show kindness to her and Murphy? "It's not you," she said thickly. She curled her hands around the steering wheel. Even though she wasn't going anywhere. Literally or figuratively. "Erik, you don't want anything to do with me. I'm a mess. You—" Her throat constricted even more. She stared hard at the steering wheel. Struggled with the churning inside her. "You deserve more."

She heard him let out a long breath. Then he crouched next to the car door, looking in at her. "Isabella." His voice had gone from that horrible, flat tone to soft, deep gentleness that slid over her as warmly as a caress. "Just tell me. Tell me what you're feeling. Let me help you."

She pressed her molars together hard. How could he possibly help when he *was* the problem? "You don't understand."

"You don't have to be afraid of moving on." His voice was still soft. Steady. "It doesn't mean you didn't love Murphy's dad." He slid a lock of hair away from her face, tucking it behind her ear. "You know that, don't you?"

An ache too deep for words filled her. "I can't be part of your world, Erik."

His head cocked slightly. She didn't look at him, but she could feel his gaze on her face all the same. "What world is that?"

She let out a humorless laugh. "Everything. Caring parents. Big family barbecues. People who are there for each other. Who don't hesitate to stretch out a hand to someone in need, even when they're a virtual stranger. Laughter…

and hugs…and kisses and—" Her throat closed off but the word *love* ran around inside her head.

"And you can't be part of all that because you don't want to be?"

Her lips opened. Closed. She couldn't make herself answer. Who wouldn't want to be part of all that? A world that was larger than just the sum of its parts. A world unlike anything she'd ever known but had always dreamed of. "What happens when it ends?"

His palm slid along her cheek. Turned her face until she was looking at him. "Ah, sweetheart. Who says it has to end?"

"It always ends," she whispered.

"No. Not always."

She couldn't bear this. "For me it does. I took a chance. Once. And now I'm trying—badly—to raise that man's son without him."

"You're not doing anything badly. And I'm not going to die."

"That's what Jimmy thought, too." She swallowed hard. "I need my keys, Erik. I have to pick up Murphy."

For a long moment he didn't move. But then, after a moment, he slowly eased his hand away from her face. He pulled the keys from his back pocket where he'd stowed them and settled them in the palm of her hand. He was still crouched alongside the car, his head on a level with hers. "I'm going to follow you," he warned. "Nothing more. I just want to make sure you get home safely."

"You don't have to do that." She wished he wouldn't. But she could see by his expression that it didn't matter what she said. He was going to do exactly what he said he was going to do.

That was just his way.

So she carefully fitted the keys into the ignition. But she didn't start the car engine. "I'm sorry, Erik."

"Don't be sorry, Isabella." He finally straightened, but still looked in at her. "Just don't let a fear of what the future holds keep you from living life right now, either."

Then he pushed her door closed and walked around the car to his truck. He started it up. His headlights came on, but he didn't budge. Not until she finally started her own car and drove out onto the street.

He didn't tailgate her. Just followed a circumspect distance behind, his headlights a steady presence in her rearview mirror as she drove out to the counselor's office. No point in stopping at Shop-World now. She had no time left.

As soon as she pulled up in front of the office building, Murphy pushed through the door. He didn't look right or left as he ran to the car and threw himself down into the passenger seat, automatically pulling the safety belt across his body.

Isabella flicked a glance in her rearview mirror. Erik's truck was idling across the parking lot. Giving them—her—space.

Her fingers flexed around the steering wheel. She looked at Murphy. "Everything go okay?"

He lifted a shoulder, plucked at the fraying strap of the backpack he'd dumped on the floor of the car between his gangly legs and said nothing.

Isabella wished she knew what he and his counselor talked about. Did he go in there and rail about her each time? Had Hayley been able to get through his defenses enough to help him really deal with anything? The woman might have a doctorate, but she was no older than Isabella, and even though Isabella had her own standing appointment with the woman every other week, she felt more of a mess than ever.

"Are you hungry?"

He shifted. "I ate with Erik and his parents." He plucked at the backpack strap awhile longer. "His dad runs Cee-Vid."

"I heard that."

"It's pretty cool," Murphy added. Then he hitched his thin shoulders and looked out the window.

Isabella exhaled, flexing her fingers again as she drove away. "So for tomorrow," she began in a calm tone she didn't really feel, "would you rather I take off work and stay home with you, or do you want to spend the day with Erik's mom?"

He didn't answer at first. She continued retracing her route back through town, taking a cue from Erik's book and silently giving Murphy time to come to a conclusion on his own.

"I really get to decide?" he finally asked suspiciously when they turned onto their street.

"Yes."

His lips twisted. He looked away from her as she pulled into the short driveway in front of their house. "I'd rather go to Mrs. Clay's," he said and reached for the door to push it open. "She's hot."

Isabella sat there blinking in surprise as he headed up the front walk to the door.

He was eleven. What business did he have finding a woman old enough to be his grandmother *hot?*

She jumped a little when Erik knocked softly on the window beside her head. She gathered her scrambling thoughts together and climbed out of the car. "Murphy thinks your mother is hot," she blurted.

His eyebrows shot up.

Then he threw back his head and gave a deep laugh. "Well, hell. I guess there're probably a few around here who think that besides him. My old man would be first in line."

And despite everything, Isabella giggled.

Erik gave her a quick wink, then waved at Murphy—which Murphy acknowledged with a small jerk of his chin—and sauntered back to his truck.

She watched him go and didn't even realize she still had a smile on her lips until Murphy called from the doorway, "You gonna stand there all night or what?"

She hid a sigh before joining him on the front step to unlock the door.

"I don't know why you let him keep hanging around," he muttered, jostling through it too fast for her to respond.

Not that she'd have known what to say, anyway.

Murphy dumped his backpack on the table and headed down the hall. A second later, she heard the slam of his bedroom door and she looked back over her shoulder.

Erik was sitting in his truck. At her glance, he lifted his hand in a silent wave.

Only then did he drive away.

She was desperately afraid that he might be taking her heart with him.

Chapter Ten

Erik managed, only by sheer grit, not to call Isabella the next evening. He did, however, get some news of her courtesy of J.D. and Jake when he stopped by their place on his way back from Gillette to drop off an aging horse he was delivering. It had belonged to an old codger in Gillette who'd died.

"It's too bad that Murphy was suspended," J.D. commiserated as she followed Erik out to his truck after the horse had been unloaded and coddled for a few minutes by his horse-trainer cousin. "Mom was telling me earlier that he spent the day with your mom so Iz wouldn't have to take a day off work." She was carrying a covered bowl of potato salad that she wanted him to take, though he'd already refused to let him fix him a plate of leftovers from the dinner they'd just shared. "If it weren't for showing that knife to Con and Zach—" She broke off and shook her head. "I love my stepsons like they were my own, but that doesn't mean I'm not well aware of their ability to—"

"Instigate?" Jake interjected as he joined them. He was carrying their rambunctious toddler, Tucker. "Probably the mildest term I can think of to describe my imaginative sons." He and J.D. shared a rueful smile.

Erik took the chilled bowl from his cousin and set it inside his truck. Fortunately for the twin boys, their enormously wealthy father had nobody sitting around waiting to pass judgment on whether or not he was good enough to keep custody of his kids.

"I need to call her," J.D. was saying. "See if there's something we can do to help."

"The only thing Isabella's concerned about is Murphy settling in here so she can remain his guardian." Erik didn't figure he was breaking any confidences with that. Everyone in town probably knew it, even if they didn't know all of the details.

"We should have her bring Murphy out here to Crossing West. The boys can chase around and not get into too much mischief." J.D. lifted a squirming Tucker out of her husband's arms and set him on the ground. He immediately began a plodding run toward the wooden-railed fence that sectioned off an empty pasture.

J.D. grinned and took off after their son, calling over her shoulder to Erik as she went. "Thanks for bringing down the horse. And tell Iz when you see her that I'll be calling."

Assuming that he *would* be seeing her.

Erik wanted to believe it, but considering the way she'd spooked after he'd done the unforgivable and kissed her, he wasn't all that sure of anything.

With his mind elsewhere—namely on Isabella—he stayed

a few minutes longer, shooting the breeze with his cousin's husband before leaving.

Crossing West, like the Double-C, was located on the opposite side of Weaver from Erik's spread. Meaning he had to drive through town to get there.

He kept the truck on the main road. Didn't veer off to the familiar little side street by the park where Isabella and Murphy were living.

He wanted to. But he didn't.

When he reached Colbys, though, he muttered an oath and pulled off into the parking lot.

It was nearly dark.

Which meant that the lights shining from inside Lucy's dance studio next door were easily visible. He didn't know if that meant Isabella was in there teaching or if Lucy was. Either way, he turned from the sight and went into the bar and grill instead.

Seeing Casey there surprised him a little. The fact that his cousin was squared off at the far end of the bar with Jane in some sort of debate didn't. Then Case turned on his heel, only to stop short at the sight of Erik coming through the door.

"Hey," Erik greeted, and jerked his thumb toward an empty pool table.

His cousin's stormy expression cleared a little. He nodded, and they headed to the table together. While Casey racked the balls, Erik glanced back at the bar. There was no sign of Jane. He pulled a few cues from the ones hanging on the wall and handed one to Casey. "So what's the beef between you two?"

Casey took the cue and ignored the question. "You wanna break or just hand over your wallet?"

Two games later, Erik and Casey were even on the money score, and since neither was particularly interested in changing the status quo, they headed out. When his cousin approached an unfamiliar truck parked in the lot, Erik realized why he'd been surprised to see Case in Colbys. "New wheels?"

Case shook his head and averted his gaze. "Janie's new wheels. My truck's parked at her place," he muttered. Then he climbed behind the wheel and drove off, leaving Erik staring after him.

"Erik?"

He damn near jumped out of his skin and turned to find Isabella crossing the lot toward him. She was wearing those butt-hugging black pants of hers and a pale-colored camisole that announced to God and country all of her shapely assets despite the pink sweatshirt tossed over her shoulders.

"What are you doing here?"

"Realizing that the grapevine doesn't always know everything."

Her eyebrows rose. "Excuse me?"

He shook off his bemusement where Case and Jane were concerned and tried not to get caught ogling her. Not easy when everything about Isabella was a vision. "Nothing. I didn't know you taught on Thursday nights."

Her lips pressed together in a soft O as she looked back at the studio. The windows were now dark. "I don't. I met Lucy over here to talk about the new class she wants to offer."

"More yoga?"

She looked up at him, though her eyes shied away. "Um, no."

His mind careened from yoga getups to…something sexier. "The belly-dancing thing?"

She nibbled the inside of her cheek. Shook her head.

Strangely enough, he felt the need to sit. Unfortunately, the only thing around was the uneven, weatherworn pavement underneath his boots. So he shifted, shoving his fingers into the pockets of his jeans. "What, then?" But he figured he already knew.

"Pole dancing." She gave him a quick look. "And it's only because Lucy took a survey of all the women she knows and that's what they voted for," she added almost defiantly.

Even though he'd expected the answer, it almost made him choke. He pinched his eyes closed. "What's happening to the women of Weaver?" He opened his eyes. "And you're going to teach it?"

"Yes. We'll start the first class in a month or so."

"When have you *ever* pole danced?"

Her chin lifted. "When I was seventeen," she said flatly. "It was the fastest way to make enough money to get out of my last foster home. I wasn't a stripper. Or a prostitute. I just *danced*."

"I don't care if you were a stripper," he said. What she'd done at seventeen was immaterial to him.

"But you'd care if I'd been a prostitute."

His hands lifted. "You just said you weren't!"

"And you believe me. Just like that." She snapped her fingers.

What the hell kind of hole had he dropped into? "Yes, just like that." He eyed her. "Did you lie?"

"Would it matter to you?" She clutched her hands around her shoulders, and the diamond on her finger winked in the lone parking-lot light. "Make this interest you think you have in me disappear more quickly?"

He heard the door to Colbys open behind them and a few couples exited, talking loudly. He closed his hand around her arm and drew her behind his truck where at least they'd have a semblance of privacy. "No matter what you did or didn't do when you were seventeen, my interest isn't going away, so cut the bull."

She averted her gaze. "Some girls did, you know."

He wanted to sigh. For her. For women everywhere who felt pushed to such extremes. He was glad for her sake that she hadn't been one of them. "I'm sure they did. But you and Luce need to understand that having a pole-dancing class, hell, just calling it that is gonna shock some folks in a town like Weaver. Not everyone's gonna clap their hands in delight."

"That's why we're calling it 'pole dancing for fitness' and making sure that men know they can do it, too. In a class for men only, of course. We know better than to spring too much on the good citizens of Weaver, even if pole dancing has pretty much been mainstream fitness for a few decades."

Now, that *did* make him smile. "Can't think of a single man around here who'd pay good money to swing around on some pole, mainstream or not."

"It's an incredible workout. You might be surprised."

"I'll take your word for it," he said. "I'd rather wrestle cattle and hay bales all day."

Her dimple flashed.

He decided he hadn't fallen through a hole after all. "Where's your car?"

She shook her head. "The weather's so nice I decided to walk here."

"Murph?"

"At home."

"Alone?"

"I think he had a good day with your mother and I decided that an hour on his own wouldn't be the worst thing in the world. I rented a DVD he wanted to watch."

"Sounds like progress."

She nodded. "I hope so." She adjusted the strap over her shoulder, and the sweatshirt fell open even more.

Evenings and mornings were still cool, yet he was suddenly sweating. He looked toward the darkened studio for a moment and felt a drift of evening air. "So you gonna bring him out to the ranch in the morning or leave him home for the day?"

"The ranch," she said quickly. "An hour tonight is not the same as a full day. If that still works for you," she added.

Everything about her worked for him. So damn well he was in pain, and only a portion of it was physical. "Yeah," he said abruptly. "Why don't I give you a ride home?" Might as well add to his torture for a few minutes more.

Her brows pulled together as she gave him a close look. "Are you sure? I don't mind walking. It's what I'd planned."

"Of course I'm sure." He reached around her to open the truck door behind her but she shifted suddenly, and his hand landed on her shoulder.

They both went still.

His fingertips flexed. With no effort at all, he could pull her to him. If he kissed her well enough, long enough, maybe she'd forget everything except him.

God knew he could barely remember anything but her.

But she moistened her lips. Laughed a breathy, false laugh. "Sorry." She acted as if he weren't touching her at all and opened the door herself, climbing nimbly up onto the high seat.

Maybe to her it *was* as if he wasn't touching her at all. Maybe, no matter what he'd thought, believed, felt, she would only ever want the touch of the man she'd lost.

Colby's door opened again, letting out a burst of music and voices. The noise only seemed to underscore his unwelcome black thoughts.

He pushed the truck door shut, walked around and got in on the driver's side, then drove out of the parking lot. He joined the few other vehicles on Main. Turned automatically when he needed to turn. Pulled up in front of the little white house that looked pretty much the same as it always had.

One step at a time.

Just get home.

Get your act together and remember that Rome wasn't built in a day and all that bloody crap.

"Erik?"

His hands tightened around the steering wheel. "Yeah."

"Thank you."

His jaw tightened. "No problem. It was only a few blocks."

"I don't mean for the ride. Though I appreciate that, too." Her hand touched his rigid arm. "I mean for everything else."

"You're welcome." The words came from somewhere deep inside him, an automatic response due to simple training in manners by his folks when he was a kid. Because he damn sure wasn't feeling mannerly now.

Particularly when Isabella unclipped her seat belt and, instead of mercifully leaving him to his personal misery, pressed her other hand against the console between them and pushed herself upward and over to brush her soft lips against his cheek.

His grip tightened even more. There'd be new ridges in his steering wheel after this. He'd rather have no contact from her at all than this pale shadow of what he really wanted.

"Isabella," he managed carefully, "unless you want to put those lips on mine right now, you need to hustle your butt out of the truck and go inside."

She caught her breath. She was still leaning over the console. Not only did he hear that sharp inhale, but he felt it, in the push of her rising chest against his arm.

Closing his eyes against it was no help. It just heightened every other sense that was already acutely tuned to her. "I'm a patient man," he added grimly. "But at the moment I'm clean out."

She hadn't let out that breath.

And he was a drowning man.

"Dammit, Izzy." He turned to glare at her.

Her eyes were wide. Her lips parted softly as she finally exhaled. "Do you see me hustling?" Her voice was husky. Unsteady.

He felt like shaking his head to dislodge the sudden buzzing in his ears. He couldn't have heard what he'd heard. But he had.

And she proved it when her hand moved from his locked elbow to his cheek. And then those fathomless eyes of hers closed and she found his lips with her own, moving slowly, sweetly.

Temptingly.

Her fingers stroked along his jaw. "Don't you want to kiss me back, Erik?"

He wanted a lot more than a kiss. He wanted heart. Soul. And body.

But a drowning man grabs what he can.

He closed his hands around her and hauled her over the console, right onto his lap.

She gasped but didn't protest, and when he closed his mouth over hers and kissed her the way he'd been wanting to ever since he'd lied about his mom's leftovers, she gasped again. It seemed like an eternity before he finally lifted his head and hauled in air.

Isabella's heart was a careening train inside her chest. Her lips felt hot and swollen and she didn't seem to have the strength to lift her head from Erik's hard chest. Everything about him was hard. And she was so...not.

His hands slid around her waist, pulling her more tightly against him, and she nearly melted. She pressed her lips against the hot saltiness of his throat and felt the sound he made. He suddenly lifted her, though, and dumped her rather less than elegantly back into her own bucket seat.

Her hands closed around air. "What—"

He raked his hands through his hair, making the short strands even more disheveled. "We're sitting in front of your house under a streetlight." His voice was gruff. "If we don't stop, we're gonna be front-page news for sure."

The reminder served as a good, cold dousing.

"Right." Half of the customers who came into the diner already referred to her as *Erik's girl.* She corrected them every time.

A kiss didn't make her anyone's girl.

But if someone had seen them, she'd have a hard time convincing the town's grapevine of that.

She'd have a hard time convincing herself of that, too.

Every muscle she possessed seemed to be shaking, but she managed to right herself in the seat. She tugged her snug, stretchy camisole back down over her hips where it belonged. Then she pulled up the scooped neckline that had dipped dangerously low.

Her skin felt too tight. Too hot. Too everything. She'd never felt so consumed by a kiss. "I…I didn't mean for that to happen."

He pinched the bridge of his nose. "I'm sure you didn't." For the first time since she'd known him, he sounded weary.

She gnawed the inside of her lip and looked at him. His gaze was rigidly directed out the front windshield.

A calm, patient man who'd do the right thing no matter what. Who'd promised her time and space.

But she could see the strain on his face. In the tight white line of his jaw.

She hated knowing she was the cause of it.

"I do know who I was kissing, Erik," she said softly.

He angled his head after a moment and looked at her.

Even in the dim light, she could see the shadows in his eyes. He picked up her hand. Ran his finger over the engagement ring she still wore. "Do you?"

Her fingers curled, instinctively protective of the ring. Something warred inside her.

As if he understood, his hand moved away from hers. Settled on the steering wheel. The shadows in his gaze turned darker still before he looked away, and she knew she wasn't the only one feeling torn up inside.

"Make sure Murph brings his cap tomorrow morning." His voice sounded like gravel over glass.

Her throat tightened. She felt like crying.

Crying for what she knew she'd lost with Jimmy. Crying for what she feared she would lose with Erik. Even if it was only for a chance that she hadn't been able to believe she even wanted.

But all she did was nod. "I will." She quickly pushed open the truck door and slipped out, nearly racing into the house. As soon as she was safely behind the front door, she heard him drive away.

She exhaled, shuddering. Luckily, Murphy's attention seemed glued to the explosions and car chases on the TV screen. He was sprawled on the couch with a bowl of popcorn propped on his belly. It was the same spot she'd left him in less than two hours earlier.

Trying to gain control of herself, she hung her sweatshirt on the coatrack by the door and went over to the dining-room table where she'd left her notes after calling NEBT that morning. One of the girls she'd worked with there had promised to overnight several items to her. She picked up her notes and headed toward her bedroom, even though it was a few hours earlier than her bedtime.

"Shut off everything when your movie is over and go to

bed," she told Murphy as she passed him. "And don't forget to set your alarm for tomorrow morning. We have to leave extra early to get out to the Rocking-C before my shift at Ruby's."

He didn't reply, just shoveled another handful of popcorn into his mouth.

Everything normal there.

She closed herself in her bedroom and stared at Jimmy's ring on her finger.

Nothing normal here, though, at all.

"Come on, Murphy. Get up." It was still dark outside when Isabella pounded on Murphy's bedroom door the next morning. She'd already tried twice before, to no response, but this time, she pushed the door right open. She'd already showered and was dressed in her uniform for Ruby's. But he was an unmoving lump beneath the pillows

She stifled her impatience. Her head ached from too little sleep, but that was no reason to take it out on him. And she knew rising this early wasn't his particular forte. "Murph. Up and at 'em. You're going to have to eat your breakfast in the car. You know how long it takes to drive out to Erik's."

Just saying the man's name made her feel unsteady. Or maybe that was simply the result of the tumultuous dreams she'd had about him during the brief stretches of fitful sleep she'd managed last night.

She went to the aging but perfectly serviceable dresser, pulled open a drawer, grabbed a pair of jeans and a T-shirt, and tossed them onto the bed. "We're leaving in five whether you're dressed or not." She reached out and tugged the blankets away from Murphy's head.

But his head wasn't there. Only a bunched pillow. And his airplane jammies rolled into a messy lump.

Panic, cold and coppery, flooded her.

She yanked the blankets clean away from the bed, half
expecting to see him still hiding beneath them. The bed-
ding collided with the shelf on the wall, jostling it off its
bracket. Ball caps, schoolbooks and baseball cards crashed
to the floor. She barely noticed, dropping to her knees to
peer under the bed. Then she searched the minuscule closet.
Then the rest of the house, looking in, under and on top, even
though the dread settling inside her told her what she'd find.

Nothing, save a few dust bunnies and boxes from New
York that remained unpacked even after being in Weaver
all this time.

She ran to the kitchen and snatched up the old phone
hanging on the wall next to the refrigerator and jabbed the
buttons.

As if he'd been waiting, Erik answered his cell phone before the first ring could even finish trilling. "Don't tell me
you're not bringing him." His voice was strangely tight. "I'll
come drag his ass out of bed myself if I have to."

"I can't find him." Saying the words made it way too real,
and she clawed at the back door that opened onto the small
lot behind the house. She stepped outside, the long, coiled
cord of the old phone going with her. Her eyes searched the
dark yard behind the house, but all she found were more
shadows, and she sank weakly down onto the cold concrete
steps. "I can't find Murphy," she said again. "God, Erik—"

"Hang up and call Max." His voice, steady and deep, cut
across hers.

"Where would he *go?*"

"Izzy, hang up," he said again. "Just dial 911. I'm on my
way."

She shuddered and nodded, though he couldn't see her.
The phone went dead and she scrambled to her feet, going
back inside to redial.

Why hadn't she called 911 first?

Why hadn't she gone into Murphy's room the first time she'd knocked? Or checked on him in the night?

Or heard him when he left the house!

Or, or, or. The accusations streamed nonstop inside her head as she punched out the numbers. A man answered immediately and promised that the sheriff would be there in a matter of minutes.

Shaking wildly, she hung up and went back into Murphy's room. It looked as if a tornado had hit it, and this time it was all her own doing. She righted the shelf and picked up the baseball cards that were scattered on the floor, stacking them with exaggerated care back where they belonged. *Where are you, Murphy?*

The doorbell rang, startling her so badly she knocked the baseball cards back off the shelf again.

Leaving them where they lay, she raced to the front door and yanked it open. And even though she knew Murphy wouldn't have returned—much less rung the doorbell—she wanted so badly to see him that it was a disappointment to see Max Scalise standing there. His wife, Sarah, was with him, her eyes still looking blurred with sleep. "I'm sorry," she said, entering before her husband and sliding her arms around Isabella in a hug. "I made him let me come." She pulled back and gave her husband a quick glance. "I'll make coffee," she said and headed for the kitchen.

"Let's sit down," Max suggested, "and you can tell me everything." He was dressed in jeans and a sweatshirt, but he had a radio on his hip that was crackling with gibberish that she couldn't make out.

Isabella nodded jerkily and closed the front door after scanning the dark street in front of the house. She went to sit on the couch. A matter of hours before, Murphy had sprawled there eating popcorn. A few kernels were still scattered on the cushions. She covered her face with her hands and tried not to think the worst. "He's going to try to get back to New York," she told Max.

"Did he tell you that?"

"He didn't have to." She dropped her hands and stared at a tiny white piece of popcorn next to her thigh. "It's the only place he'd want to go."

Max continued asking questions, stopping now and then to respond to his radio. Did Murphy have a cell phone of his own? No. A computer? No. They didn't have a computer. He used the ones at school when he needed to. Who were his friends in New York? Isabella reeled off the names. Anyone else he might be likely to contact?

His mother. But since he didn't know she'd been found, Isabella just shook her head.

Sarah returned and pressed a cup of coffee into Isabella's hands. She knew better than to try swallowing any past the lump in her throat and merely curled her hands around the mug for the warmth.

Is Murphy warm enough?

"Izzy?"

She shoved the mug aside and barely had time to stand before Erik strode into the house and pulled her into his arms. He was big and warm and steady and she clung to him, the tears that she'd managed to keep at bay until then stinging her eyes.

"It's going to be all right," he murmured against her ear. "We'll find him, Izzy. I promise you, we'll find him."

Her fingers twisted into his soft T-shirt. "What if we don't? I went to bed early." She didn't want to face the reason why—because of that kiss. "I don't know how long he's been gone!"

He cupped her face in his hands. Brushed his thumbs over the tears on her cheeks. His violet gaze bored into hers, so steady and so certain that she was finally able to pull in a deep, calming breath. "We will find him," he said quietly.

And despite everything, despite the nightmare of the past year, everything inside her wanted to believe.

Chapter Eleven

The sun came up and still there was no news about Murphy. After taking her statement, Max departed. He had the entire state of Wyoming on alert. Locally, his department was canvasing Weaver and the surrounding areas. Sarah stayed behind and was soon joined by Tabby. The three of them began cooking up breakfast for the other folks that started showing up, as well. Erik stayed with her for a while, but he, too, soon went out to join the search.

She wanted to go with him, but he insisted that she remain at the house in case Murphy returned.

Considering Murphy had run away from *her* in the first place, she couldn't imagine why he would.

"Come on." Lucy drew her away from the doorway, where she had remained standing long after Erik had driven off. She tucked her arm through Isabella's. "You should eat something."

If she did, she was afraid she'd vomit.

She looked around at the people crowded into her small home as if she hadn't noticed them before. "Where'd everyone come from?" Half of Erik's family was there. The rest, she learned, were out looking for Murphy. Plus, several of the regulars from Ruby's had come by to show their support.

Lucy's worried expression lightened a little. "This is Weaver. And you're Erik's girl," she said, as if that explained everything.

Isabella's eyes burned too deep for tears. "I'm not Erik's girl," she said faintly.

No one listened.

Finally, rather than fight everyone who seemed to think it was paramount that she sit and have coffee and something to eat, she did.

More people came and went. Erik's grandparents. His mother, who took Isabella into her arms and hugged her as if she were no older than Murphy instead of a grown woman. "Tristan's doing everything he can, honey."

Isabella appreciated the thought, though she wasn't sure what Erik's father—who was pacing around her front yard talking on a cell phone—could do that Erik wasn't already doing.

The package of fabrics arrived from New York. Someone set it unopened on the table. Another wave of people passed through. Isabella finally excused herself and closed herself in her bedroom, just to get away from them all. She changed out of her pink uniform and pulled on a pair of jeans. But when her hands automatically reached for Jimmy's old shirt, she pulled out a black turtleneck of her own instead. She prayed that Jimmy was watching out for his son, because she'd failed miserably at it.

Then she found her purse and hunted through it for her cell phone. She needed to hear Erik's voice.

But her cell phone wasn't there. Nor was it on her dresser—or in the kitchen, or anywhere else when she went to look.

"What is it, honey?" Hope had noticed her search.

"I can't find my cell phone." Despite the turtleneck, she felt cold. "Maybe…maybe Murphy took it."

Hope's expression sharpened. She gestured, and Tristan seemed to magically appear. "What's the number?" he asked.

She reeled it off even as she shook her head. "Murphy's not going to answer it if it's anyone from here calling."

"We'll see." He headed back outside again, his phone at his ear once more.

"I need to tell the sheriff." Isabella reached for the phone on the kitchen wall. She should have thought to look for her cell phone earlier. Hours earlier.

"Tristan will take care of it," Hope assured her. "But you make any call you feel the need to make." She proceeded to clear the kitchen so that Isabella would have a modicum of privacy.

But when Isabella dialed Erik's cell-phone number, she got only his voice mail. She hung up without leaving a message.

What was there to say?

She went to sit on the couch again, too numb to do anything but stare blindly at the pieces of popcorn Murphy had left behind.

Lucy spoke her name a few minutes later. "Iz. Erik's back."

Isabella bolted from the couch and tore out the front door.

He met her halfway up the yard, catching her arms in his hands. "He's in Braden," he said without preamble. His father was standing nearby. "At the bus station there."

Braden was the closest town, but it was still well over an hour away. Her legs wanted to go out from beneath her. "How'd he get there?"

"Don't know that yet." Despite her shaky legs, he was walking her to his truck. He pulled open the door and helped her up inside, then turned back to his father.

"We've got eyes on him," Tristan said cryptically. "They won't approach until you get there unless he moves."

"Thanks." Erik shut the door and rounded the truck, leaving Isabella looking through her window at his father. The older man smiled slightly.

"What did he mean?" Isabella asked as soon as Erik got in. He'd left the engine running and he put the truck in gear, roaring down the street with no regard whatsoever for residential speed limits.

"He means he has people watching Murphy."

"*What* people?" She was glad for any help, but why it was coming from a video gamer and not the authorities puzzled her. "Was your dad a cop or something?"

"Or something." He turned the corner and they flew down the sleepy Main Street. "He'd have found Murph earlier if we'd known he had your phone."

Dismay still had her in its grip. "I should have looked," she said thickly. "I didn't—"

He grabbed her hand and squeezed. "Don't. The point is we know where he's at now. And he's safe. We can just be glad that he had the phone turned on."

It had been only minutes since she'd realized it was missing. It stunned her that he'd been located that quickly because of it. "I thought this sort of thing only happened on television," she said. "Your dad must have a lot of computers or something."

"Or something," he repeated. "Someday he'll probably tell you about a few of the things he's into." He squeezed her hand again. "If this had happened even ten years ago, a cell phone wouldn't have mattered. There wasn't really any service around back then."

She chewed the inside of her cheek, staring out the window, wishing the miles would pass even faster.

Erik was doing his best, though. The countryside was flying by.

When they got to Braden, it appeared to be only slightly larger than Weaver to her. The bus station was located in the center of town. Erik pulled up in a no-parking zone and they got out. A man wearing a cowboy hat and dark glasses was standing on the sidewalk. He'd obviously been waiting, and he gestured toward the building. "He's sitting close to the back entrance. We've got it blocked in case he bolts."

"Thanks."

The man just tilted his head slightly and ambled toward the illegally parked truck. He leaned back against the truck bed, looking casual.

Someday, Isabella might wonder over it all. For now, she was just anxious to get to Murphy. But worry about his reaction to being caught made her feel as if her feet were mired in wet cement

Seeming to understand, Erik took her arm. "Let's take him home."

"What if he runs away again?"

He seemed to sigh a little. "He won't," he promised.

She felt like crying. "You don't know that. Even if he didn't, when our caseworker learns about this—" She broke off, unable to continue.

His hand tightened for a moment, and then he relaxed his grip. "I do know that he won't run." His voice had dropped an octave. "He saw us kissing last night, Izzy."

Her heart, already dwelling somewhere in her belly, dropped all the way to her toes. Why hadn't Murphy said something when she'd gone inside?

Instead, he'd just sat on the couch, eating his popcorn. Ignoring her.

"It was just a kiss," she said faintly. Stupidly. There'd been nothing "just" about it.

Erik's lips thinned. "It wasn't just a kiss to him." He pulled his cell phone out of his pocket and hit a button before handing it to her. "Message came in last night. I didn't notice it until this morning."

A moment later, Murphy's voice blasted from the phone. Aside from every other word starting with *f,* the general slant was that Erik could take his broken window and shove it where the sun didn't shine. Murphy was glad he'd broken it and he would break everything else of Erik's he could get his hands on as soon as he had the chance.

When the vitriol ended, Isabella silently handed Erik his phone. "He didn't mean it," she whispered. "He was upset. He's scared and feeling like he's all alone."

Erik deleted the voice mail. "All the more reason for him to learn that crap like this—" he gestured with the phone in his hand "—doesn't fly with the people he *does* have." He shoved the phone back in his pocket. "Let's just get him and get out of here," he said, leading her through the doorway. "We'll work it out when we get home."

There were other things she wanted to say, but finding Murphy took priority. Inside, the station was sparsely occupied and she spotted him immediately.

He was slouched in a chair, wearing his black hoodie.

Almost as soon as they spotted him, he spotted them. He jumped up, his expression darkening. But he didn't bolt for the glass door located behind the row of chairs were he'd been sitting.

Instead, he charged forward, his gaze locked on Erik's. "What the hell are *you* doing here?"

Alarm coursed through her.

"Taking you home," Erik answered evenly.

Murphy glared even harder. The reply he gave was shockingly rude.

Isabella gasped, her stomach turning to stone. "Murphy!"

"Not physically possible," Erik answered the boy curtly. "The water tank wasn't enough? You can apologize to Isabella or you can have another lesson."

Isabella watched in horror as Murphy's fist curled and flashed out, his fledgling manliness fully offended. She didn't know what to do, but she had to do something, and instinct propelled her forward.

She heard Erik's curse.

And she felt all of Murphy's anger explode against her cheek when the blow he'd intended for Erik hit her squarely in the face instead.

From somewhere she heard a startled scream.

And after that, she heard nothing at all.

"I didn't mean to hit her!" Murphy's voice had gone up at least an octave as he trailed them into the employee break room where a clerk was hurriedly directing them.

Erik had never felt such darkness inside him in his life. He carefully settled Isabella on the ugly green couch that took up half the room and crouched next to her. Thankfully, she was already coming around, groaning and holding her hand gingerly to her face.

The clerk had disappeared and Murphy was hovering there nervously. "Is she okay?" His voice was a squeak.

Ignoring him for the moment, Erik yanked open the freezer in the corner. He'd hoped for ice but settled for a plastic Baggie full of some indeterminate-looking stuff. He yanked it out, banged it once on the counter to break it up and crouched next to Isabella. Her eyes were closed. A tear crept down her cheek. "Here." He pulled her hand away from the red imprint left by Murphy's fist long enough to tuck the plastic bag there. "Hold this against it."

"I didn't mean to," Murphy said again. His face looked pale against his unruly black hair.

Erik didn't so much as lift his hand toward the boy. Murphy was genuinely upset. But so was Erik. He gave the boy a hard look. "Go somewhere. Not far. And sit down." Erik knew his dad's associates wouldn't let him disappear again.

Hostility toward Erik was screaming from Murphy's pores when he turned around and stomped away.

"He really didn't mean to hit me." Isabella swung her legs down and sat up, trying to brush aside Erik's hands. "I'm fine. Really."

He was angry. More so at himself than anyone. She wasn't fine. Nothing was fine. "I know he didn't mean to hit you." The kid had wanted to take Erik's head off. He'd known it even before Isabella had told him he'd disappeared. "But he still did it." He gingerly drew her hand with the frozen Baggie away from her cheek. Murphy's fist had landed high. "You're probably gonna have a shiner, sweetheart."

She groaned and slumped back against the ugly couch. "I can only imagine what people will say to *that*." She pressed the bag back to her face, wincing a little. "It's cold."

"That's the point."

She opened one eye to peer at him. "I should just pay you for the window."

"Dammit, Isabella! This isn't about that freakin' window." He'd met with Jessica briefly the day before and ordered its replacement. She'd been cool, but had taken the order nonetheless, particularly after he'd told her it would be hanging in a church for half the town to see and not stuck unwanted in a closet somewhere. It would be ready in a month. The cost of the window had become moot to him. What it stood for, though, where Murphy was concerned, was a matter of integrity. And for a kid on the cusp of growing up, that was beyond price. "And handing over money doesn't solve Murphy's issues."

She lowered the bag to her lap. The welt on her face stood out redder than ever. Even though it had been Murphy's fist that connected, Erik felt he'd put it there and it made him sick.

He should have been able to protect Isabella, no matter what.

He should have been able to protect her boy, too.

That was what a man did when he loved a woman.

"The only thing that will help Murphy is being able to trust that I'm not going anywhere," she said huskily. "He's obviously got it into his head that—" She broke off. Her eyes shied away. "That something's going on between us," she finished abruptly. "What can I say? He's eleven. He doesn't understand."

"He understands more than you think. I want to marry you, Izzy."

Her eyes went wide. Her mouth rounded and her cheeks flushed. "Erik—I—"

He let out a joyless laugh. "Don't worry, sweetheart. I'm well aware that my chances on that score are slim to none."

"We…we hardly even know each other."

His jaw ached. She'd already admitted to becoming engaged to Murphy's dad after a short time. Had they known each other better? Had Jimmy looked into Isabella's eyes and seen the same things that he did? Known, in his bones, the things that he knew?

"Time's not going to change things," he said gruffly. "I already know I could spend the rest of my life happy to see you smiling at me. And that our kids would have your eyes and—God help 'em—my chin. If there're things about me you want to know, all you have to do is ask me. Or pretty much anyone else in Weaver."

She was staring at him as if he'd grown a second set of arms and a tail to boot. "There's nothing wrong with your chin." Her voice was faint.

He took the bag and pressed it to her cheek again. "Keep it there. A stubborn chin. I come by it honestly."

Her hand brushed his as she took the bag. He paced across the break room. He couldn't think straight unless there was some distance between them.

"I don't know what to do, Erik." She sounded miserable. "Murphy needs me. He hasn't even had a chance yet to trust in me, much less me and…and someone—" She broke off.

He knew where she was going. The kid believed he'd be edged out.

"I know Murphy needs you." Erik needed her, too. But Murphy was a child. Erik was the adult. He let out a long breath, clawed his fingers through his hair. "So we're going to have to make a change."

She paled again. "Change?"

"I'll pick up Murphy on Saturdays from now on. He's gonna work off that window like he agreed. All the way through the end of the school year at the very least."

She dropped the frozen bag to her lap again. "I don't understand. You still want him out at the Rocking-C? Even after everything he threatened?"

"Especially after everything he's threatened." He let out a long breath. "How else is he gonna learn a man stands by what he says if he's not shown how?"

Another tear crept down her cheek and it was almost enough to unravel him. "There's no reason for you to have to drive in and out to get him," she finally said huskily. "I know how busy you are out there, and you're already doing so much, I—"

"I don't want you coming out to the Rocking-C." He pushed out the words, cutting her off. She blinked. Her lips parted, and he wanted to believe it was pain that crossed her face, but where she was concerned, his judgment was getting too clouded.

"But I—"

"Not unless you decide it's where you want to stay for good and you're ready to wear another man's ring on your finger," he finished.

Which just had her lips snapping shut and color flagging her cheeks again. Combined with the swelling red splotch under her eye, it gave her a whole lot of color.

He crossed the room and leaned down toward her. "I told you," he said softly. "This *interest* you think I have isn't going anywhere." Then, because he was a man and could only take so much, he brushed his mouth slowly across hers.

When he straightened, she looked dazed, and he took some comfort in that.

"You need time to face that fact just as much as Murphy does." Then he nudged the cold bag against her cheek. "Keep it there," he reminded, and helped her to her feet.

They left the break room.

Strangely enough, he was no longer angry. Half-numb, maybe. Exhausted, definitely.

But at least he didn't feel like tearing something off its hinges.

Murphy was sitting on a chair close to the break room and he jumped to his feet when he saw them.

"Let's go." Erik's voice was short. He couldn't help it.

The boy didn't look at him.

The truck was right where Erik had left it. His dad's undercover crony tipped his hat and disappeared around the corner of the building as soon as they were inside the vehicle.

They drove back to Weaver in silence.

Isabella's house was empty when they arrived. Not for lack of caring on anyone's part, he knew, but because people were allowing them some privacy.

Erik saw Isabella and Murphy inside, making sure that Isabella was settled on the couch before going into the kitchen. He found a bag of frozen beans in the freezer to replace the thawed Baggie from the bus-station break room, and he took it out to her.

Then the three of them just stared at one another.

Erik knew he was the odd man out.

"Did you buy a bus ticket?" he asked.

Murphy grimaced and shook his head.

"Then what were you doing there?"

The kid shook his head. "Nothin'."

"Murphy." Isabella tossed aside the beans, looking pained. "We can't go on like this. *Talk* to me. I know you were angry about me kissing Erik, but you can't just run away!"

"Why not? You're gonna go off and marry *him*."

Isabella gave Erik a startled look. "What did you tell him?"

"I didn't tell him anything," he said evenly. "He has eyes in his head."

She looked shaken. She moistened her lips, her gaze shying away as she focused on the boy. "I loved your dad very much," she said carefully. "But he's not here anymore. And just because you and I are…having…having lives…doesn't mean I'm forgetting him. Sweetheart, every time I look at you, I see him in you."

Erik wondered if she really believed her own words or if they were only for Murphy's benefit.

"Until you don't have room for me. Just like my real mom. She still doesn't want me."

Murphy's voice was low.

And despite everything, Erik hurt for the kid. Just as much as he hurt for the rest of them.

"Murphy." Even though he flinched, Isabella rose and put her hands on his shoulders. "What do you mean about your real mom?"

He shrugged off her hands and gave them both a raw look.

"Miz Solis left a message for you on the phone last night." He jerked his chin toward Erik. "While you were out sucking his face."

Isabella felt her legs turn to water. She sank down onto the couch. "Oh, Murphy," she whispered. Why hadn't she just told him the truth about his mother being found? They could have talked it out. At least tried to. "What did the message say?"

His lips twisted. "That my ma got the 'surance money but now they can't find her again." He looked away. "She doesn't want me, either. Never did." His voice dropped. "Just like you."

"Murphy, I *do* want you!" She knew his uncertainty. His fear. Growing up, she'd felt it all herself. No child deserved this. "No matter what happens in the future, I'm always going to want you. Can't you see that by now?"

His throat worked. He jerked his chin toward Erik again. "You won't if you're with *him*."

Isabella opened her mouth to answer, but no words came to her lips. She didn't know what to say.

And she could see by Erik's expression that he knew it. His eyes stared into hers for what felt like an eternity. Then he looked toward Murphy. "I'll pick you up tomorrow morning," he said. "You've got work waiting at the Rocking-C. Be ready."

Murphy looked from her to Erik. "You got any root beer?" His voice was challenging.

Isabella started to protest, but Erik's hand moved subtly by his side and she subsided. "You gonna break all the windows in my house like you threatened?" he challenged in return.

Murphy's lips twisted. He looked away. "No."

Erik's lips twisted, too. But he didn't look away. "Then I got root beer."

And then, as if he'd done everything he could do, had taken everything he could take, he handed her the cold bag again, turned on his heel and left.

She wanted to run after him.

But she didn't.

Next to burying Murphy's father, standing there while Erik walked away was the hardest thing she'd ever done.

Chapter Twelve

"Good Lord, Isabella." Tabby stared at her with horror when Isabella walked into Ruby's Saturday morning after her tap class was finished. "What happened to your face?"

She flushed, realizing that Tabby wasn't the only one staring. The breakfast rush had passed, but there were still a half-dozen customers there and they were all goggling. Something she hadn't even considered when she'd sought the comfortable familiarity of Ruby's. "Nothing. Just clumsiness."

"More like a good right hook," someone said, earning a chorus of shushes.

Tabby had come around the counter and was peering more closely at her face. "Lordy," she breathed, and wrapped her hand around Isabella's arm as if she were afraid she wouldn't be able to stand otherwise. She drew her over to the nearest stool. "Sit down. Why are you even here?" She raced around the counter, grabbed a clean dish towel and dropped a scoop of ice cubes into the center of it, then handed the bundle across to Isabella. "Here."

Isabella dutifully pressed the improvised ice pack to her face. "Don't worry," she told Tabby. "I'm not going to ask to be put on the schedule."

"Good thing," Bubba grunted, coming out of the kitchen to have his own look-see. "You'd scare off alla customers."

Tabby shooed him back to the kitchen. She poured a cup of coffee and doctored it up with a dollop of cream the way Isabella usually drank it, then slid it in front of her.

"Thanks." Isabella took a sip. It didn't exactly steady her, but it didn't hurt, either. Truth was, she hadn't been re-motely steady since Erik had said he wanted to marry her.

Tabby dished up a warm, gooey cinnamon roll studded with pecans and set it in front of Isabella before folding her arms on the counter and leaning in. "So? What happened?"

She just shook her head. "It doesn't matter." It wasn't that she didn't appreciate the support that everyone had shown when Murphy ran away, but having them all know her busi-ness was uncomfortable.

"Honey, we can all see that was a fist that hit you."

"It doesn't matter," she repeated. And hoped to heaven that it wouldn't. She'd never taken any sort of punch. She had no idea how long the discoloration would last. But the last thing she needed was for Monica to visit and see her with the remnants of a black eye, delivered by none other than the ward she was supposed to be raising in a loving, nurturing environment. A ward who'd tried to run away.

Every other foster parent on the planet would be prefer-able to Isabella.

Her cheek felt numb, so she set aside the ice and reached for the enormous cinnamon roll. "How'd you learn to make these, anyway?" She wanted to think about anything other than Monica Solis's upcoming visit and what had occurred the day before. But she couldn't. Murphy was out at Erik's. He'd picked him up early that morning, just as he'd warned.

And Murphy had been ready and waiting.

He'd been silent.

But he'd been ready.

And twice, Isabella had completely lost her train of thought with the little girls in her tap class because she'd been so preoccupied worrying about how the two males in her life were managing together.

She realized Tabby was smiling at her. "The cinnamon rolls? Ruby Leoni is the one who started the diner. She's Erik's great-great-grandmother. At least, I think I've got the *greats* right. Ruby made these great rolls. People loved 'em. Came from miles just to have them. Eventually, Justine took over the café and started making the rolls just the way that her grandma Ruby had taught her. I started working here when I was, oh, fifteen, I guess. Somewhere along the way, it got to be my job."

Isabella never expected that the café had anything to do with Erik's family. He'd never said boo about it. "So who owns the café now?"

Tabby gave her a funny little look. She smiled slightly. "Technically, Erik and his brother. But Justin's back east at graduate school and never has been interested in things here."

"Erik *owns* Ruby's?" She was actually working for the man!

"Well." Tabby's head waggled back and forth as if she couldn't believe this was news. "Yeah."

Isabella didn't know why she was so stunned. After the past few days, what was one more surprise? "I assumed it was you and your family that owned Ruby's." Tabby was the one who ran things, after all.

Tabby grinned. "Well, I live in hope."

"You'd like to own it?"

She nodded. "Funny, too. Because I used to *drool* over plans of going to Europe and being an artist there." She shrugged. "I still paint. And Sidney—she's married to Derek—"

"Another cousin," Isabella interrupted. She'd met Derek at the barbecue, and she thought he and his wife had been at the house yesterday morning. But she'd been so numb and worried that she couldn't be sure.

"Exactly." Tabby didn't miss a beat. "She's partners with Tara at Classic Charms. She was pretty involved in the art world before she came to Weaver, and she likes my paintings. She has one painting of mine hanging in the shop and has even taken a few to a gallery she knows in New York."

"Tabby! That's amazing."

She shrugged. "Well, who knows what'll come of it. Maybe nothing. Or maybe enough that one day, I'll be able to buy this place outright from Erik and his brother."

Isabella realized she'd somehow polished off the entire cinnamon roll. "I think you ought to be selling these cinnamon rolls in the stores, too." Strangely enough, she was feeling better. Maybe that was what brown sugar, yeasty rolls and pecans secretly did for a person.

The bell over the door merrily jangled, followed abruptly by a not-so-merry "Hey!"

Isabella looked over her shoulder to see Lucy standing there, looking fit to be tied, her hands propped on her impossibly slender hips. Her friend hadn't been teaching at the studio that morning.

"I have to hear from Pam Rasmussen that somebody mugged you?"

Isabella gaped as she came down off the padded stool. "I *wasn't* mugged!" She was fairly confident no such thing had ever occurred in Weaver. Aside from Murphy running away, the town practically defined the word *peaceful*.

Lucy's sharp blue gaze lasered in on Isabella's face. "Then what's *that* all about?"

"I ran into the corner of a kitchen cabinet," Isabella said loudly, looking around at the faces avidly turned her way. For all she knew, rumors of what had occurred in the Braden bus station had already made their way to Weaver. "Clumsy, yes. Mugging? Not even!" She blew out a breath after the outburst and exhaustedly plopped back onto the red stool. She waved her arm at her audience. "You all can go on talking about somebody else now."

Lucy crossed the diner and leaned on the counter beside her. "What good's a grapevine when it gets all the details wrong?" She leaned closer and dropped her voice to a whisper. "I know you're lying," she said nearly soundlessly. "But it's okay for now."

"Goody," Isabella muttered under her breath.

Her friend gave her a quick wink then looked across at Tabby, who'd probably heard the exchange but could be trusted. "She's been baptized well by Weaver standards by now, wouldn't you say, Tab?"

"Pam only gossips about the people who belong here," Tabby provided. "She leaves the passersby alone."

Isabella let out a strangled laugh. "Gee, I guess I'm strangely comforted by that."

And she was.

Maybe she didn't have a clue how to deal with Murphy or Erik, much less the words he'd left her with.

But at least she had a town where she might possibly belong.

She and Lucy left Ruby's together and walked over to the studio. There, in the sanctity of their own office, Isabella told her friend everything. From start to finish. Including the kiss. The proposal that wasn't a proposal but a statement of fact. And the confusion. And when it was all out, Isabella sat exhausted in the chair, twisting the diamond ring around and around her finger.

"Wow." Lucy canted her head to one side. "Grief. A needy child. A new love." She ticked them off. "It never dawned on me how similar this is to Beck and Shelby and me."

Isabella made a face. "Do *not* start matchmaking."

Lucy's brows shot up and her eyes filled with mirth. "Iz, my friend, that match has already been made. I figured as much at the barbecue when I saw Erik pacing around waiting for you to get there, but I wasn't so sure about you."

"I'm glad you find it funny. The man's banned me from his ranch!"

Lucy's expression sobered as she gazed at Isabella with sympathy in her eyes. "You do understand he's doing that as much for Murphy as anything, right? If you have to choose between being around each other right now or having Murphy feel more secure, who's going to win out?"

"But that's a choice that's *mine* to make. Erik—" She broke off, not even knowing how to describe what she was feeling.

"Erik is in love with you," Lucy said bluntly. "He told you his intentions pretty clearly. But he's no fool, either. He knows you're going to turn backflips to make sure Murphy doesn't feel the way you felt growing up without a family. That choice *is* yours, and he's figured out which way you're facing. What else would you expect him to do?"

Isabella blew out a noisy breath. It was that or cry. "Why me? We've never even slept together. Why does he have to go and get interested—" she nearly tripped over the word that was so extraordinarily inadequate "—in me?"

"Why shouldn't he?"

Isabella silently lifted her hand and wiggled her fingers. The engagement ring flashed in the light.

"That is not *this*." Lucy lifted her own hand, rubbing her wedding band. "And if you'll forgive the cliché, the heart wants what it wants. Frankly, the fact that Erik hasn't slept with you speaks volumes to me. That man is seriously serious about you." She took Isabella's hands between her own, squeezing gently. "I am not discounting how much you loved Jimmy," she said steadily. "You agreed to marry him, and I honestly thought you'd never agree to that with anyone. I didn't even have a chance to meet him, because it all happened after I'd left the dance company."

Isabella smiled sadly. "You'd have liked him. Everyone liked him." He'd been gregarious and outrageous and he'd drawn her to him despite her initial resistance.

"I'm sure I would have. And I'm sure you were as happy together as pigs in clover. You were finally about to have everything you'd ever dreamed of. A family of your own." Lucy's gaze was steady.

Isabella swallowed. "Was it the man I loved or was it simply what he represented?" The notion was upsetting. "Is that…is that all Erik is? A family waiting to happen? Is the man who's in that spot interchangeable?"

"I don't know." Lucy lifted her shoulders. "That's something you're going to have to figure out." Then she nodded toward Isabella's black eye. "In the meantime, you'd better get some ice on that swollen face of yours or it's still going to look that way when that caseworker of yours comes calling."

Seeing the unopened package of fabric on her table when she got home a while later gave Isabella something to focus on while she listened like a hawk for the sound of Erik's truck bringing Murphy back. But when she *did* hear his truck a few hours later and her nerves started firing at Mach speed as she darted to the door, she caught nothing more than a glimpse of his profile in sunglasses. He stopped only long enough for Murphy to hop out and reach the door before he drove away.

Staring after his truck accomplished nothing, but she could scarcely keep from doing so, despite Murphy's noticing.

She finally closed the door when Erik turned the corner and disappeared from sight. She looked at Murphy. His jeans were filthy with heaven only knew what. She didn't want to guess, considering the odor coming off him. "Everything go okay?" she asked warily.

"Guess." He pulled off his Yankees cap in a puff of dust, reminding her strongly of an old cartoon. He also looked exhausted.

"Are you hungry?"

He nodded. "His cows are havin' babies." He plucked at his shirt, which had dark stains all over it. "We gotta wash this stuff before Monday."

It took Isabella a moment to realize that Murphy couldn't go back to school on Monday. He was still suspended. And Erik had said he'd take him.

So he would.

"He said there's no point in ruinin' more clothes 'cause next time'll be more of the same," Murphy added. "He says the heifers are already calved out and we can be glad 'cause that's even *more* work 'cause most of 'em need help their first time."

His. He. Evidently, Erik's name was not going to be uttered in her presence by Murphy. As for everything else, her young ward might as well have been speaking Swahili. She got the gist of the calving part and frankly didn't want to think too hard on the rest.

"But you…got along okay?" She studied him closely,

watching for any sign that he might be on the verge of doing something desperate.

He didn't answer. His dark eyes skipped over her face. "I didn't mean to hurt you. Prob'ly hurts, huh?"

"A little." She wasn't going to lie. But he didn't have to know just how badly her cheek still throbbed, either. "I know you didn't mean to hit me, Murphy. But you shouldn't have tried to hit Erik, either. I know you're angry and hurting about a lot of things, but you have to find a way of not lashing out. With your fist. With a baseball bat. With anything like that."

Any tolerance he'd had for the discussion obviously stopped short of that point. "Whatever." He turned and headed down the hall into the bathroom, peeling his grimy shirt over his head and throwing it on the floor as he went. A second later, his jeans followed, landing in a heap on top of the shirt in the middle of the hall.

Sighing, she gingerly retrieved the clothing and quickly stuck them in the wash.

With a *lot* of detergent. She didn't have a hope of getting out the stains. But she sure did hope to get out the smell.

On Monday morning, Erik gave a quick honk when he came by to pick up Murphy. Murphy grabbed the two slices of toast Isabella was just pulling out of the toaster for him and bolted for the door, as if he was afraid that Isabella might dare to beat him to it.

Then he was gone, and the sound of the truck died away.

She sighed, reminding herself that Murphy was the priority and not her own tangled emotions.

Then, because there was nothing else to do but continue on, she wiped up the toast crumbs and went to work.

And so it went. Through the rest of April.

Into May.

Ultimately, Bethany loved the wedding gown that Isabella and Jolie put together in record time, and when one of her bridesmaids asked Jolie and Isabella to make her wedding gown, too, Isabella found herself with yet another project to work on. But at least this time around, they had the luxury of several months and a bride who was more agreeable.

Murphy started talking incessantly about summer vacation and playing in Weaver's community baseball league with Zach and Connor Forrest. He showed up one Saturday afternoon, after Erik dropped him off, wearing a pair of leather gloves identical to the pair that Erik had been wearing that first day Isabella had taken Murphy out to the Rocking-C. He started tossing around unfamiliar ranch phrases as if he'd been born on one instead of in New York. His pale skin turned golden, and lighter strands of brown started showing up in his black hair. And one day, Isabella realized he'd shot up a good inch.

When he dropped a paper napkin onto his lap after she gave him a slice of pie for a snack one afternoon at Ruby's, she wanted to sit right down on the floor and bawl like a baby.

He was doing exactly what she'd needed him to do.

Without the complication of Isabella and Erik together, Murphy was settling in.

And every day, she missed Erik. Missed everything about him.

But this was real life. And she was supposed to be good at handling real life. So all she did was pull out the registration form Murphy had brought her for the baseball league and start filling it out.

Considering the caseworker was due to show up in a matter of days, she didn't dare let herself think that he wouldn't be allowed to stay with her long enough for the first pitch to even be thrown.

Chapter Thirteen

Erik made it until May.

It was the hardest thing he'd ever done in his life, but he'd managed not to contact Isabella once since that day he'd left her with a frozen bag of vegetables pressed against her cheek.

Not that he hadn't thought about her. Dreamed about her. Wished with every fiber of his being that he'd see her driving her little sedan up his newly graded road to tell him that she'd chosen him. Chosen *them*.

But he didn't contact her.

So it felt like a blow to his gut when he stopped in at Shop-World late one Friday night to grab some fishing gear for Murphy to use the next day and he spotted her steering a loaded grocery cart across the parking lot. He'd gotten so used to avoiding anyplace where he might run into her that all he could do was stand on his brakes and hold his breath while he watched her load the bags into her trunk before driving away.

He wanted to follow her.

But he forced himself to park and go into the too-bright, too-large store. He found what he needed—a relatively inexpensive rod and reel and a tackle box that he filled with the basics. He had plenty of his own gear that he could have given to Murphy, but the kid would more easily accept something new. He was still touchy about using things of Erik's, like a hat or a baseball glove. As if doing so meant a slight against the dad he'd lost.

He stowed his purchases in the back of the truck and drove through the quiet streets of Weaver.

He could just drive past her house.

It was late. Dark outside. It wasn't as if he would stop. Just…check that everything looked okay. That her car was back home, safe and sound, in the narrow driveway.

That was what he told himself, anyway.

And maybe he would have had the strength to do just that if she hadn't been sitting near the front picture window and looked out, seemingly straight at him, while he trolled past.

But she did. And before he knew what he was doing, he was out of the truck and striding up her walk.

She didn't move, though, and he realized that probably all she could see on her side of the brightly illuminated window was her own reflection and not him at all.

He'd reached the porch, though. And turning away— even though it would have been smart—wasn't something he seemed able to do. So he rapped his knuckles softly on the door. Barely three seconds passed before she yanked it open.

Like the first time he'd stopped at her house to deliver his mom's leftovers, Isabella was barefoot. She was wearing an oversize shirt with her hair pulled up in an untidy mess atop her head. Her eyes widened with just as much surprise now as they had then. Only, this time there was no alarm in them.

Just a brown-black pool of warmth that drew him in as surely as a moth to a light.

"Erik." She clutched a pair of small silver scissors against her chest. "Why… What—" She shook her head a little. "Is everything okay?"

Except for the fact that he was losing his mind? "Dandy."

Her eyebrows rose. "What are you doing in town this late at night?"

The scent of her filled his head. If this was what it was like after a matter of weeks, what kind of raving lunatic was he going to be after a few years? The rest of his whole damn life? "Had supper at Colbys with Case." He didn't mention going to Shop-World afterward. "Then we had a few beers and played a few games of pool."

She looked hauntingly uncertain. "I can fix you some coffee if you're in need?"

His need wasn't for caffeine. "Murphy in bed?"

Her lashes suddenly dropped. She moistened her lips and looked over her shoulder. He could see down the hallway to the two bedrooms. Both doors were open. She looked back and seemed surprised to find the scissors still in her hand. She set them aside on the small table next to the door. But then her empty hand fluttered to the top of her shirt, just where the buttons ended and creamy, smooth skin began. "He's actually spending the night with Zach and Connor. J.D.'s driving him back here around five so he'll be here when you come to get him in the morning."

Every curse he knew circled inside his head. Murphy being here would have been a helluva safety net. Knowing he was miles and miles away had Erik jumping off a cliff into dark waters. "Be prepared for him to come back with a new arsenal of tricks," he managed to warn. "The twins are notoriously mischievous."

She eyed him for a moment. "Did you already know that he was over there?"

"Good grapevine in Weaver, but not that good."

"Not that accurate, either," she said a little wryly.

"Ah. The mugging-slash-cabinet incident. I heard about that." He tilted his head. She had dark shadows beneath her eyes, but it wasn't because of the black eye. Not after all this time. Maybe she was having the same sleepless nights he'd been having. "Figured it was better than the truth."

"That's what I thought, too." She chewed her lip for a moment, then forced a cheerful smile that failed miserably. "I've registered Murphy for baseball," she practically chirped. "We turned in the paperwork just this afternoon."

"Congratulations. It'll be good for him."

"Zach and Connor are going to be playing, too."

"Well." He thought about that for a moment. "Maybe the league will survive the three of them all at once. It survived Case and me when we were young."

For the blink of an eye, her dimple showed as she smiled. He closed his hand over the doorjamb above their heads to keep from reaching for her. "Heard from your caseworker? Anything more about Murphy's—" he didn't really want to call that other woman his mother, even though she technically was "—about Kim?"

She shook her head. "I've called Monica a few times. They can't locate her at all." Her lips twisted. Considering Erik's opinion of the woman, he could only imagine what Isabella's was. "That doesn't settle anything for me, though, as Murphy's guardian. Monica will be here on Monday to meet with us, and when she learns about everything that's happened here—" She broke off and shook her head.

Murphy had mentioned the caseworker's impending visit a time or two. Enough that Erik knew the boy was worried.

He told her the same thing he'd told Murphy. "Maybe it won't be as bad as you think."

She pressed her lips together and rocked a little on her bare toes. "Or it could be worse. We're supposed to meet at Murph's counselor's office. Just one big, happy family. Six p.m. sharp."

"Nervous?"

She nodded. "You might say that."

"It's going to turn out all right."

"Well, I appreciate you saying that. But none of us knows anything for certain, do we?"

"Some things a person does know. For certain."

Her gaze skidded over his. "You're not talking about Murphy anymore," she said after a moment.

He shook his head once.

She worried the corner of her lip between her teeth. Stared back at him with wide eyes. "I've missed you." The words seemed to burst out of her, surprising her as much as they surprised him.

His hungry gaze roved over her, taking in every detail. Including the glittering ring still on her finger. "I'd better go." He gave her a nod miles on the side of polite.

She hesitated. "Right. It's late. Murphy told me how busy things are out there." She folded her arms across her chest. "C-calving and starting to build your addition and all."

The calving was pretty well done and the addition would be a few months in the making at the very least. "He's doing okay, you know," he said abruptly. "I probably should have let you know that before now. Still has an attitude most of the time, but what boy his age doesn't?" His mother had reminded him a few times of that. "He's still a hard worker and he learns fast. He's turned out to be a lot of help to me." Truth was, Erik was getting used to Murph's company around the place. Not just because of what he meant to Isabella, and definitely not because of that stained-glass window, which was finally in the church's hands and off his. But because Murphy *was* a hard worker. And he did learn fast. And he knew more baseball stats than any boy his age ought to. He had Erik resorting to hunting up arcane facts late at night on the internet just so he'd be prepared every Saturday.

"That's good." She moistened her lips. "Thanks for telling me. He's better around here, too. Has even taken to mowing the lawn on Monday evenings. I nearly fell over the first time he did it."

"I'll bet." His fingers dug into the jamb for a moment. Then he gave it a quick tap. "Well. G'night."

She smiled quickly, then stepped back and started to close the door. "Good night, Erik."

He'd made it all the way to the curb when he heard a sound behind him.

He turned to see her jogging across the small square of neatly trimmed grass. She stopped in her tracks when he did. "Are you sure you don't want to come in for coffee?"

With her pale, pale hair and the white shirt, she was like a ghostly wisp against the dark yard. But he knew if he touched her she'd be no wisp. She'd be warmth. And supple flesh and soft lips that tasted like home. "Izzy, if I come in, it's not going to be for coffee."

She hesitated for a long, long moment. And when she spoke, her voice had gone so husky it rasped over his nerve endings. "Good thing. I ran out yesterday." Then, leaving him standing there like a speechless bump on a log, she returned to the porch where she stopped. And waited.

And as she waited, she lifted one hand to her hair, holding it away from her face.

He wanted everything she had to give, and he knew that wasn't going to happen in one night.

But for now...for now he could see that at some point

during the time it had taken him to get to his truck, she'd removed her engagement ring.

Because the hand holding her hair away from her face was bare.

He strode back to the house, caught her around the waist and pulled her inside. He slammed the door shut. He barely had time to see the color ride high in her cheeks before he flattened her against the solid wood and covered her lips with his.

Her hands raced up his chest, sinking into his hair as her mouth opened under his. Her foot slid nimbly around the back of his calf. Yoga, he thought faintly, and wondered just how flexible she might be. Then, when her foot slid farther and he felt her leg twining around his thigh, his brain just plain shut off.

He grasped her narrow waist and lifted her off the ground. His hips pressed hard against hers and she gasped, arching right back against him, her other leg sliding around him until he felt surrounded by her. Holding her against him, he turned blindly and thanked his lucky stars that there was nothing complicated about the floor plan of the house. It was a straight shot down the short hall and only one turn into her bedroom.

The bed was three steps in, and he lowered her down onto the center of it.

Her halo of white-blond hair spread out around her head after she tossed aside the clip that had been holding it. Erik absorbed the sight as he knelt on the bed beside her.

Her eyes gleamed, as dark and mysterious as a midnight lake. They locked on his face while he reached for the buttons of her shirt and slowly undid them, carefully folding away the fabric to reveal the lush curves beneath. Even as he looked, her nipples, easily visible through the sheer white bra cradling her breasts, drew up rosy and tight. He could also see her pulse, beating hard in her throat, and he wasn't sure which was a more enticing sight.

But then she lifted her hands and undid the clasp on her bra. Suddenly, not even that flimsy fabric guarded her flesh from him. She let the cups fall to the sides and slowly reached for his hand, drawing it to her. "Touch me," she begged, her voice raw. "I've been dreaming about you touching me for too long."

The words undid him.

He closed his hands over her breasts. Felt her nipples stabbing his palms as he settled next to her, kissing her again. From her temple. To her lips. From the heat radiating from the base of her throat where her pulse beat furiously beneath the quick glide of his tongue. To the valley between her breasts and the velvety plane of her taut belly. He kissed her. Again and again, until he was two cells shy of desperate and she was trembling wildly.

But then her thigh slid over his, her strong leg pulling him closer, proving that her trembling wasn't the same thing at all as weakness. Soon he was on top of her, rolling aside only long enough to get the rest of their clothes out of the way.

Then he was sinking inside her and she was arching against him, arms and legs wrapping, holding him close as she shuddered wildly and cried out his name.

His name.

And with his pulse thundering inside his head, Erik finally let himself go and lost himself in the woman he loved.

He stayed long into the night. As long as he dared. J.D. was never late for anything, so if Isabella expected her to have Murph home at five in the morning, that was when he'd be there.

And Erik knew he'd better not be.

He could fight Murphy's emotional manipulation—unintentional or otherwise—but he couldn't fight Isabella's protectiveness, as well. He already felt he was holding the short end of that particular stick, even though in his saner moments he knew that things had moved too fast for all of them. Isabella's and Murphy's lives had been on a roller coaster for the past year. Adding Erik to the ride had been another loop they weren't prepared for.

But still, he lingered, lying beside her in her dimly lit bedroom, their fingers lazily lacing and unlacing, legs tangled. They hadn't slept. They'd made love again after that first fury had been spent. Slower. Longer. No less intense, but the way he'd always intended. And again she'd cried his name. And then she'd just lain in his arms and cried, holding him as if she never wanted to let go.

"I need to get out of here," he finally said. He toyed with the long strands of her silky hair.

"I know." She was lying on her back, her eyes staring up at him. "I wish—" She broke off. Sighed.

"I know," he said, and her lips curved in an achingly sad smile. "I'm taking him out fishing with me," he said, hoping the news would cheer her up. "I told him last week I would."

"He didn't tell me."

"Didn't figure he would." He flipped the lock of hair between his fingers and tickled her nose with it. "Your hair is naturally this color, isn't it?"

She nodded. "Hard to believe, but it's actually darker now than it was when I was a child. There was a boy in one of the foster families I was with who called me ghost-girl."

"He probably had a crush on you."

She made a face. "He was seven. I was five."

"How many different families were you with?"

She lazily slid the sole of her smooth, cool foot along his hairy calf. "Nine. None of them were awful. They just weren't…mine." She turned toward him. Her breasts nestled against his chest. "The best family was Nina and Howard. She's the one who took me to tap-dancing lessons. And she taught me how to sew." Her fingertips crept along his hip.

"How'd you get into making costumes at Lucy's dance place?" He was curious. But it was difficult not getting distracted by those fingertips. Or by the sweet, sweet push of her breasts against his chest.

"In addition to the *pole*-dancing thing—" her voice turned sly and she somehow managed to shimmy even closer, until he felt her breath against his collarbone "—which only lasted a few months anyway, I worked in a dry-cleaning store. It didn't pay anywhere near as well, but it lasted a whole lot longer. I started taking community-college classes at night and I worked at the cleaner's during the day. I did a lot of repairs and tailoring and such."

He was listening, but it was becoming increasingly…hard.

Her fingertips drifted from his hip to the small of his back, then up again, inching forward, grazing his belly, then back, driving him more than a little crazy.

"One of the customers was a major patron of NEBT," she went on, either blithely unaware of what she was doing to him or pretending she was.

Either way, he hoped to hell she never stopped.

This sort of crazy was okay with him.

"When I managed to save a formal gown she'd thought was ruined, she started hiring me to make a few custom things for her. Eventually, she introduced me to some people at the ballet, and by the time I was twenty-one, I was working in the costume department there. Lowest man on the totem pole, but I didn't care. And eventually, I made it all the way up to wardrobe supervisor." She suddenly shifted, sliding her thigh over his and pushing at his shoulders until he was the one flat on his back.

She knew exactly what she was doing. And as naturally

as if they'd spent a lifetime together, she wrapped her fingers around him and guided him home, letting out a shuddering breath as she settled over him and began to rock. He wanted to tell her that he admired what she'd accomplished, what she'd done in her life. But then she was throwing her head back, her fingers clenching his, and the tremors inside her set off his own.

By the time either one of them could move again, it was only a few minutes before five o'clock. And feeling about as sneaky as he'd thought he was being with Sally Jane Murphy in the tenth grade, he left the house and drove away, hoping that he wouldn't be seen by anyone, especially J.D. Fortunately, he made it out of the neighborhood with no surprises, and even though Ruby's wasn't open that early on Saturdays, the lights were on when he drove by and he pulled in, rapping his knuckles on the back door until Tabby let him in. A half hour later, with his second cup of coffee in his hand and his nerves considerably soothed by the first one, he drove back to Isabella's house to pick up Murphy as if he'd never been there at all.

The kid was sitting on the front step, waiting for him, and he probably never even noticed Izzy peeking through the window behind him. She lifted her hand in a silent wave, her gaze seeming to hang on to Erik's through the glass.

Then Murph yanked open the door to the truck and climbed up. He leaned over and eagerly snatched up the box of cinnamon rolls from Ruby's, sniffing at them while he fastened his seat belt. "Tabby's rolls, huh? She's hot."

Amused, Erik wondered what Tabby would think if she knew. "Don't you know any girls your *own* age who are hot?"

Murph shrugged. "None of 'em have—" he held up his hands meaningfully, flushed a little and shrugged again "—you know."

Since Erik's palms still felt imprinted from the wonders of Isabella's "you know," he guessed he did. "You're gonna be twelve how soon?"

Murphy picked a fat pecan off one of the rolls and sucked it from his thumb. "August first."

Erik rescued one of the rolls before the kid could devour all six of them. He took a famished bite and looked once more at Isabella—who was still standing in her window— before he drove away. He licked a sticky smear from his own thumb. "Your dad did tell you about the birds and the bees, didn't he?"

Murphy gave him a disgusted look. "Gross, dude."

"Did he?"

"Duh." The kid shook his head. "Like about two years ago."

"Well, if you're noticing how *hot* the ladies are around Weaver, you're probably not going to keep thinking it's all that gross for long."

The kid just shook his head and shoved another bite of Tabby's roll into his mouth. "Why're you in such a good mood anyway?" he asked around the mouthful.

"Who says I'm in a good mood?"

Murphy looked at him. Rolled his eyes.

Erik realized he was smiling, and right then there didn't seem any reason to stop. "Fishing always puts me in a good mood," he managed mildly.

It was the truth.

But not even a fraction of it.

Chapter Fourteen

"Well." Monica Solis tucked her silver-shot brown hair behind her ear and sat down next to Isabella in the waiting area outside of the counselor's conference room.

Murphy was already inside with Hayley. "I have to say that Weaver provides more amenities than I expected." She was a stylish woman in her mid-fifties who'd intimidated the life out of Isabella the first time they'd met. Still did, when it came to that. "Food's been good. Hotel bed is comfortable." She smiled. "Air is clear. Definitely not a bad place to visit on occasion."

Isabella knew Monica wasn't her adversary. But neither was she her best friend. "I'm glad you've been comfortable. You arrived last night?"

"Oh, I've been here awhile longer." Monica ran her hand down her narrow black skirt, wiping away an imaginary speck of dust. "Since last week, in fact. I arrived last Thursday."

Isabella's stomach rippled nervously. "Really. Why didn't you let us know? We could have had you over for dinner at the very least." And why, oh why, did Weaver's grapevine have to fail now to broadcast the arrival of a stranger in town?

"I had plenty keeping me busy," Monica assured.

Comforting, Isabella thought sourly.

She studied the closed conference-room door and tried not to fidget. Why were they taking so long in there? She just wanted this whole thing over and done with.

"I met for a while with Murphy's teacher, Mr. Rasmussen, on Friday. And then with his principal," Monica went on. "We discussed Murphy for quite some time, actually. His schoolwork. His socialization. Et cetera."

It was hard not to sink lower in her chair. What did *et cetera* involve? She'd been dealing with social workers— good and bad—all her life. Admittedly, Monica had been supportive of Isabella's request to bring Murphy to Weaver, but wariness still kept her from bringing up the knife, school suspension or anything else outright. "What'd Principal Gage have to say?"

"That Murphy was doing very well." Monica's expressions were often difficult to read, but she was obviously pleased. "He has a circle of friends, shows appropriate work habits in class. His grades could be better, but all things in due course."

Isabella found it difficult to believe that the principal would have kept the suspension out of his discussions with Monica, but why else wouldn't the caseworker mention it? "Meet with anyone else?"

"Officially? Dr. Templeton, of course." Monica's gaze drifted toward the door. "We went over her reports that I'll be submitting along with my recommendation to the judge."

And heaven only knew what those reports said. Beyond

generalities, Hayley never divulged to Isabella exactly what she and Murphy talked about. Which was why she'd trusted Hayley not to reveal to Murphy what Isabella talked about during *her* conversations with the counselor.

She finally pushed out of her chair, too restless to stay put. "What about Kim? Are you still trying to find her?"

Monica crossed her legs. "Judge Saunders believes enough expense has been wasted on that quarter." She looked at her impeccable manicure for a moment.

Isabella had the strong desire to shake the woman. She paced across the room, putting some distance between them. She wished that Erik were there.

"I also had a conversation with Mr. Clay," Monica continued, as if she'd heard Isabella's thoughts. "Erik Clay, the owner of Ruby's Café. Just a little while ago, in fact."

Isabella went still.

"Your supervisor at the diner, Ms. Taggart, gave me his number. Both of them speak very highly of you."

A bubble of hysteria floated around inside her chest. If it weren't for Tabby, she wouldn't have even known that he and his brother owned Ruby's. "Erik's been a good friend to us," Isabella said carefully. More than a good friend. He was the most decent man she'd ever met. No matter what happened, she wasn't going to regret the impulsive way she'd pulled off Jimmy's ring and chased after him. Not in light of the incredible night they'd spent together. For all she knew, it might well be the only one they had.

After he'd gone, she'd retrieved the ring from the table by the front door where she'd left it. She'd pressed her lips to the shining diamond. And then she'd tucked it away inside her jewelry case. Someday Murphy might want to give it to the girl he chose for a wife.

Monica was nodding, oblivious to Isabella's sudden preoccupation. "Mr. Clay said he'd taken Murphy fishing this weekend. It's good for him to spend time with positive role models."

Isabella smiled weakly. "Monica. Please. Just give me some clue here. Are you going to revoke my guardianship or not?" Monica hadn't said anything about Murphy running away. Or the black eye. Or even the pole-dancing classes that were causing quite the stir around town. Was she toying with her?

Monica glanced at the conference-room door again. She uncrossed her legs and sat forward. Her expression wasn't unsympathetic. "That decision is the judge's, not mine."

"The judge is going to read whatever recommendation you make and go with it," Isabella countered. "I grew up in the system." Something the caseworker knew perfectly well because she'd been the one to dissect Isabella's life in the first place when she'd petitioned for guardianship. "You're the one wielding the pen, even if you're not the one who signs the court order."

Whatever the caseworker might have said to that was lost when the door opened and Hayley invited them into the conference room.

Isabella swallowed her nerves and entered the room. It was dominated by a large oval table in the center. She chose the chair next to Murphy and sat down. "You okay?"

His shoulder twitched. "Guess." His dark eyes skittered toward Monica and Hayley. "I still don't see why we gotta do this."

Monica heard him. "Because everyone wants to make sure we're doing what's best for you, Murphy." She sat down directly across from them, and Hayley took her chair at the end.

The young doctor smiled at them both. She had a fat folder sitting next to her elbow on the table, but she didn't open it, deferring to Monica, who was the one running the show. Only after a half hour of regurgitating all the facts they already knew did the caseworker ask the counselor if she had anything else to add.

"Actually, yes." Hayley opened the folder and took out a stack of envelopes of every size and shape. "I didn't give these directly to Ms. Solis before because I wanted to share these with you, Isabella." She stretched forward to push the stack toward her. "I showed them to Murphy already. They've been coming into my office for the past week."

Frowning, Isabella slowly took the envelopes and leafed through them. Some bore postage marks. Some had obviously been hand-delivered. Some were typed. Some were addressed in pen, some even in pencil. "What are they?"

"I guess I'd call them character references," Hayley said, sounding a little bemused. "From a good portion of Weaver, and all testifying to their knowledge of you as a parent or as a member of the community. And some of them are about Murphy." Her gaze slid to Monica. "If there ever was a town who wanted two people to stay, it's Weaver when it comes to Isabella and Murphy."

Stunned, Isabella could do nothing but stare at Hayley.

"Go ahead," the other woman prompted. "Take a look."

Isabella pulled out one of the letters. It was just a single page, talking about her patient grace in the face of a challenge. She studied the signature, taking a moment to realize it came from Bethany's grandmother. The mayor's wife, of all people. The next letter was signed by Robert Bumble, who turned out to actually be Bubba from Ruby's.

There were letters from Jolie and Drew Taggart.

Lucy and Beck.

Max, who'd used his official title as sheriff, and his wife, Sarah. Hope and Tristan. The parents of some of the girls from Isabella's tap class. Even starchy Mrs. Timms from the school had sent a letter, saying that "Master Murphy couldn't find a more competent caretaker than Ms. Lockhart."

The envelopes went on and on. And even though most of the writers knew good and well about Murphy breaking Erik's window, about the school suspension, about his running away and even Isabella's black eye, not a single person mentioned any of it.

Then there were the other letters. The ones that had been hand-delivered. Written in pencil. They turned out to be from Murphy's classmates. "We don't want him to leave" was the consensus. Two in particular pleaded, "We need him to be our pitcher," which made her smile through the tears nearly blinding her. "He makes sure we play fair." She didn't have to look at the messy signatures to know they had come from Zach and Connor Forrest.

"Play fair?" She glanced at Murphy.

He shrugged. "That's what Erik says," he muttered. "You know. Like when we played that game at the barbecue. He said winning don't count unless the game's been fair."

All too easily, she could remember Erik whispering something to Murphy before he'd loaned her his cap. *A guy thing,* Erik had called it.

A *fatherly* thing was what it felt like.

Everything inside her squeezed.

She blinked hard and looked over at Hayley. She wanted to ask who was responsible for the letter campaign but couldn't get out the words. The other woman seemed to read her mind, though, and just spread her hands slightly atop the table.

Monica had been looking at her share of the letters, too, taking up each one as soon as Isabella set it aside. "If it's true it takes a village," she murmured, "Murphy's golden." She gave him a look. "Do you have anything to say about all this?"

He rolled his eyes and looked distinctly uncomfortable. "I just wanna go home. I'm hungry."

The caseworker finally smiled. "As a matter of fact, so am I." She gathered up the letters and tapped them smartly together against the table until they were more or less a neat stack. "I'd like to take these with me, if you don't mind, Dr. Templeton."

"Feel free." Hayley looked across at her and Murphy. "As long as Isabella and Murphy don't mind."

Isabella shook her head.

"Very well." Monica stood. She set the letters inside her briefcase and snapped it shut. "Isabella, I'll let you know when I've made my recommendation to the judge. Murphy, I'm very pleased to see that you're doing so well." She turned on her well-shod heel and left the office.

Isabella wanted to collapse in her chair. She looked over at the counselor. "All of those letters were addressed to you. How'd anyone know to do that?"

Hayley gave her a rueful look. "Seriously? I'm the only family therapist with a full-time practice in this town." She began gathering up her belongings. "Murphy, if you go into my office, you can get a cold apple juice or something for yourself out of the little refrigerator I have there."

"Cool." He practically bolted from the chair and disappeared through the door.

"I appreciate all your time with him," Isabella told her after he'd gone.

Hayley smiled. "This is what I do. For what it's worth, Isabella, I'm hoping he gets to stay with you. He wants to, you know."

"I don't know about that." Things had been going more smoothly, but that didn't mean they didn't still have their share of set-tos.

"Isabella." Hayley gave her a clear look. "I *do* know."

Isabella could only take that to mean that Murphy had actually shared this fact with the counselor.

She pressed her hand against the knot that formed inside her chest. "Kids should come with warning labels or something," she said huskily.

Hayley grinned. "Well, most parents have a chance to grow into the role while their babies are growing. You came into this game kind of mid-inning."

Isabella laughed weakly. Truer words had never been spoken.

The three of them left the building and Isabella drove Murphy home. The parking lot between Colbys and the dance studio was half-full when they passed, and impulsively, she turned into it and parked. "Come on," she told Murphy. "We're eating out tonight."

Aside from the meals they had at Ruby's, eating out was a rare treat, and he wasn't one to hesitate. The second she'd turned off the engine, he was out of the car, headed for the door, and she had to hurry to catch up with him.

She'd been inside the bar and grill only once before, and steered him away from the bar area toward the restaurant proper. A pretty hostess seated them, and when the waitress came by their table a short while later, Isabella even told Murphy he could order a cola if he wanted.

He chose root beer and, oblivious to the ripples that caused in Isabella's personal hell, proceeded to order the largest hamburger he could find on the menu.

He'd finished that, as well as half the sandwich that Isabella had ordered for herself, and was deep into a hot-fudge sundae when the Forrest clan entered, Zach and Connor noisily in the front. They spotted Murphy right off the bat, and soon the three boys were racing across the room toward the pinball machines lined up against the far wall.

J.D. edged her hip onto one corner of the bench seat that

Murphy had vacated. She was having no easy time keeping a squirming Tucker in her arms, and with a laugh, Jake
relieved her of the boy and accompanied him as he toddled
off after his big brothers. "I wonder if little girls are less
exhausting than little boys," she said and propped her elbows on the table.

Isabella smiled. "Couldn't tell you." She angled her head.
There might not have been a letter from J.D. and Jake, but
there had been one from their twin sons. "Did you know
about the letter-writing campaign?"

J.D.'s green eyes widened innocently. "What letter-writing
campaign?"

"Whose idea was it? Lucy's?" She wouldn't put it past
her loyal friend.

"Actually, I don't think our resident ballerina had anything to do with it. The boys came home from school last
week talking about it. I don't think they've actually seen
Lucy since the barbecue out at the C."

Which left Erik.

And if the letters had started arriving at Dr. Templeton's office last week, he'd started the effort even before
she'd run after him and invited him in for the coffee that
she didn't have.

J.D. was eyeing her closely, and she realized she was
shaking. "Are you all right?"

"I have to go." She fumbled with her purse, pulling out
enough cash to cover the bill and then some and dropping
it on the table. "It was nice to see you," she added hurriedly
before working her way across the busy restaurant to grab
Murphy. "Come on." She pulled him away from where he
was standing by the side of the pinball machine Connor was
playing. "We have to go."

"Wait a minute," he squawked. "I was watching—"

"No minute." She kept her grip on his shoulder as much

for her own sanity as to keep propelling him toward the exit. "I want to talk to you about something and it can't wait."

"Jeez," he complained, but he nevertheless went with her out to the car. She exhaled once they were in the car. She didn't know what the court was going to decide where her guardianship of Murphy was concerned. But she did know a few things. Finally, she knew a few things.

The things that mattered.

"Murphy, I love you. I love you because you're Jimmy's son. But mostly, I love you because you're *you*. And I don't want to be your guardian just because your dad asked me to be. I want to be your guardian because of *you*. Because somewhere along the way, you and I...we've become a family. It's not always pretty, but I guess sometimes families aren't always pretty. I never really knew that much about families because I never had the opportunity to know my dad. Or my mom. I just know I don't want to lose you."

He looked wary. "Yeah...so?"

She peered at him. "Have you thought about why all those letters about us were sent to Dr. Templeton? You think that happens out of the clear blue sky?"

"No." The answer was grudging.

"So why do you think someone would go to the effort of starting something like that? There were dozens of letters, Murph! And there were just as many about you from your schoolmates as there were about me."

"All right!" He threw up his hands. "All right, okay? I talked Con and Zach into it," he blurted. "I told 'em where Dr. Templeton's office was, and they got some of the other kids in the class to send letters, too. 'N' then the next thing I knew, I heard Mr. Rasmussen talking about it to Miz Timms in the office. I didn't know there'd end up being all those letters!"

Her jaw had gone slack. Mr. Rasmussen was Murphy's

teacher. And he had a wife named Pam, she thought dimly, and the dispatcher had duly dispatched. "*You* started it," she finally managed. Not Erik at all. "But…but why?"

"'Cause at least here I got some real friends," he said defensively. "And Erik said everyone needs a place where they feel like they belong, and you said you knew what it felt like never to belong so I figured if ever'body started saying we belonged we *would!* Mr. Rasmussen talked about how that sorta thing works sometimes—grassroots movement, he calls it—and—" He gave her a pained look. "Oh, jeez. Now you're gonna cry, too?"

She leaned over him, catching his face between her hands, and kissed his forehead. "And that, too," she said thickly. Then she sat back in her seat, giving him his freedom.

She was exhausted. "I want to go home." She started the car. "How about you?"

"Uh-huh." He flipped his foot up onto the dash, then just as suddenly yanked it back down again and brushed off the dusty mark his shoe had left. "You're not mad?"

She swiped another tear from her cheek and blinked hard so she wouldn't run into another car as she left the parking lot and turned onto Main. "I'm not mad." Unbearably touched, more like. Maybe Murphy hadn't told Hayley outright that he wanted to stay. Maybe she'd simply figured out he'd been behind the letter campaign.

"When do I get to have my dad's knife back?" he asked suddenly.

She'd practically forgotten about the knife he'd taken to school. She'd stuck it on the top shelf in her closet after his suspension. "Why?"

"I just wanna be able to gut my own fish with it next time we go fishing. Erik says a Buck knife'll work real nice for gutting, and he'll teach me how so's I don't cut off my fingers." His voice filled with relish. "I bet Con and Zach have never gutted fish."

"I'll call him about it," she managed faintly.

In short order, they were back at the house.

They were greeted by the sight of Erik's truck parked in front of it.

Murphy was silent for a long moment. "Guess you can ask him now," he finally said with studied casualness. Then he pushed open the car door and climbed out.

She slowly followed suit and got out herself but felt too unsteady to get much farther than that. She saw Murphy's pace slow when Erik got out of the truck. The boy gave a jerk of his chin in greeting. Then he looked back at Isabella for a moment, before he turned and went into the house.

It hadn't been a grin of glee on his face.

But a smile had been there. Small. But there.

Feeling as if she'd dropped down the rabbit hole, Isabella pushed her door closed and focused on Erik's face as he slowly headed her way. "What'd the caseworker say? Are you all right?"

She swiped her hand over her damp cheeks. For some reason, the waterworks had been turned on but good. "Nothing's settled," she told him. Though she still felt as if everything had changed. "And I'm fine. What's all this about you teaching Murphy how to use that knife of his dad's?"

"You're crying."

She shook her head. Sniffed. "I'm not crying," she lied.

He gave her a look. Brushed his hand down her cheek. Then the other. "Your caseworker called me today." His voice dropped a notch. "I wanted to let you know about it, but it was only a few minutes before you were meeting with her so I didn't have a chance."

She twisted her hands around the strap of her purse to

keep from reaching out for him. "Did you know about the letters?"

His brows pulled together. "What letters?"

She gave a watery laugh. "Oh. I imagine you'll hear about them soon enough. So." She moistened her lips. She couldn't seem to get enough of looking into his eyes. "About the knife?"

"Yeah. I told Murph I'd show him how to use it. I was younger than him when I got my first knife."

"From your dad?" She still felt she'd never be able to repay Tristan Clay for the way he'd located Murphy that horrible day.

He laughed softly. "*My* dad? Hell no. He taught me how to make computers from scratch and hack into the school's grading system if I wanted. Squire's the one who gave me the knife. I still use it."

"You hacked into the school's grading system?"

"No," he said, looking amused. "That would be wrong, wouldn't it?"

She eyed him, not knowing whether he was pulling her leg or not. "I'll give him the knife as long as you think he'll be safe with it." She didn't know why they were still talking about the knife.

There were so many more important things she needed to say....

"He won't hurt himself or anyone else with it," Erik assured. "As for the trees he'll inevitably try carving up? That's another matter."

"Erik?"

The lines beside his eyes crinkled softly. "Yeah?"

She let out a shuddering breath. "I think I'm in love with you."

He went silent.

"No." She unwound her hands from her purse. She'd spent too long being afraid. "I *know* I'm in love with you."

His gaze had gone sharp. His deep voice dropped a few notches and it washed over her like a warm, soothing wave. "I love you, too."

She bit the inside of her lip. "So what do we do now? If my guardianship of Murphy is finalized—"

"*When* it's finalized," he corrected, and brushed his thumb along her cheek again.

She trembled. "When."

His gaze dropped to her lips, then he leaned down and kissed her softly. "That's better." He suddenly straightened, turned around and strode toward the house. "Murphy," he yelled.

Murphy appeared instantly, as if he'd been hovering inside the door waiting. "Yeah?"

Erik looked at the boy for a moment. His pulse was pounding in his ears. "I'm gonna ask you something, but I want your promise first that you're not gonna pull some damn fool stunt again like when you ran away."

Murphy frowned. Erik saw the look he shot toward Isabella when he stepped warily down the porch steps. "What?"

"No dice. Give me your word."

The boy's lips pressed together. "I promise," he said after a moment. "What you gotta ask me?"

"Isabella doesn't have any parents for me to go to," he said. "She's got you." Maybe in a few decades, when their children were grown and thinking about having their own, Erik would find some amusement in just how nervous he suddenly felt talking to an eleven-year-old kid. Wanting that boy's acceptance more than he'd ever believed possible. "So it's your blessing we're going to have to have."

Murphy stared at him. He crossed his arms and looked sideways again at Isabella, who'd come up to stand beside

Erik. She pressed her hand against her mouth as she realized what was happening.

"I love Isabella," Erik said gruffly. "And I want to marry
her. I want us all to be a family. And someday, if we're lucky
enough to have more kids, I'm hoping you'll open your heart
to them as much as Isabella's opened her heart to you. But
even if you can't bring yourself to give that blessing, I'm
still gonna be here. I'm still going to love her. And I'm still
going to love you."

Murphy's eyes skidded back to Erik.

"Nobody's ever going to replace your dad," he managed.
"But you need a family. And turns out, so do I."

Isabella sniffed loudly. He held out his arm and she turned
into it, pressing her cheek against his chest. She could hear
his heart beating. It was steady and true, and she knew
there was no place else she wanted to be. No one else she
wanted by her side. Through the good and the bad. "Murphy," she said softly and held out her hand. "Everything is
going to be okay."

"What if Miz Solis says I gotta go somewhere else?"

"Then we'll convince her otherwise," Erik said simply.

Murphy looked from her to Erik, then back again. "Can
I have my baseball bat back," he finally asked.

Erik let out a strangled chuckle. "You give your blessing,
you can have the bat back. But you've still got to work off
the window until school's out."

Murphy screwed up his face, considering, and Isabella
realized she was holding her breath.

She'd finally realized that Erik meant what he said. He
wasn't going anywhere. And even if it took Murphy more
time to adjust, he still wasn't going to go anywhere.

Because he loved them.

Because from the very beginning, he'd been able to see
their future together, even when she hadn't.

But it still would be so much easier if the son of her heart would realize he had nothing to fear. Not where they were concerned.

Finally, Murphy's face smoothed out. "I guess it's okay. Long as I get my bat," he added warningly.

Then, as if he hadn't just made a momentous announcement, he headed back up the porch steps and went inside.

Isabella let out a weak laugh. "Is that it? That's all he has to say? Will I ever understand the mind of an eleven-year-old boy?"

Erik wrapped his arms around her and pulled her close. "It's a guy thing," he murmured. "And you don't have to understand him." He tilted her chin up until she was staring into his violet eyes and seeing the same future as he. "Because *I* do."

Isabella's eyes flooded. Being swept off her feet didn't have to involve lavish displays of flowers and romantic words.

Sometimes all it took was a man with a quiet smile and a heart the size of Wyoming.

"I do love you, Erik Clay," she said softly. "And I think it's time you and Murphy finally gave me that tour of the Rocking-C. A woman ought to know her way around the place that's going to be her home, don't you think?"

His lips tilted into a long, slow smile. "I do." Then he drew her up onto her toes and leaned down, pressing an even longer, slower kiss to her lips.

Epilogue

Three months later

Isabella heard the crunch of tires on the gravel and looked up from the bodice she was working fine hand stitches into. It was the height of summer and she was sitting on the porch in one of the oversize wooden chairs that she'd already come to love.

In all of the delightfulness to be found at the Rocking-C, the porch was her favorite spot.

Well, that and the big bedroom she shared with Erik. It was on the back side of the house, and she loved waking in his arms to the sunlight shining in. At least, she did on those mornings when he and Murphy weren't already out working cattle even before the sun was up.

She might have been born in New York, but living at the Rocking-C had taught Isabella that not only was she Erik's girl through and through, she was a ranching girl to boot.

At the sight of the dusty delivery truck driving up to the house, though, Isabella set aside the wedding gown she was working on and went down to meet it. She was expecting a special delivery of fabric, and she'd paid extra for the weekend delivery. Now she could start working on her *own* wedding gown, instead of someone else's. She and Jolie had already finished the design. It was traditional. Simple. With a splash of sass. And Isabella couldn't wait to wear it.

They'd set the wedding date for the first of November.

Just over three months away.

There were days that she wished it were here already. And days that she still had to pinch herself to believe it was happening at all.

As the driver was climbing out of his truck, she hurried down to greet him. But the delivery turned out not to be her box at all. Instead, it was a thin envelope that she had to sign for. As soon as she did, the deliveryman drove away, leaving her standing there holding the envelope.

It was from New York. From Monica Solis.

She suddenly turned and ran around to the back of the house where Erik and Murphy were working on the addition. They both had on safety glasses and construction belts, and despite one being big and blond and one being wiry and dark, they looked like two peas in a pod.

Erik had originally planned for the addition to be a new great room. Now it was going to be bedrooms. Three. One for Murphy that would be larger than the upstairs one he was currently using. Two more for…whoever came along to fill them.

She had to raise her voice to be heard above the noise of their hammering. "Erik!" She waved her hand, the white envelope between her fingers.

He straightened, pulled off his safety glasses and smiled

his quiet smile. "Decide you want to try pounding some nails again after all?"

Murphy snickered. The one and only time she'd tried her hand on the fancy pneumatic thing that Erik used, she'd nearly shot a nail through his foot.

Isabella ignored him, but not really. The fact that he was smiling more often, snickering more often, was music to her ears. He was twelve now and officially in junior high. He was also taller than she was, a fact that he liked to lord over her at every opportunity. And then Erik, who towered over them both, would lord it over him a little, just because it made her smile.

"It's from Monica," she told them now, holding out the letter. "You read it. I'm afraid to."

Erik set down his hammer and slid his arm around her as if he'd been doing it all of his life. As long as he continued doing it for the rest of their lives, that was fine with her. She tore open the letter and removed the sheet and handed it to him. Murphy wormed his way closer, so he could read, too.

"Hot damn," he hooted a moment later.

"What's it say? And what I have told you about swearing, Murph?"

"If ever there's a hot-damn moment, this is it," Erik said. "Monica says she knew we wouldn't want to wait a minute longer than necessary." He read from the yellow sticky note attached to the front of the document that he held. "'Legal custody of the minor child Murphy James Bartholomew is granted to Isabella Mercedes Lockhart,'" he read aloud. "Signed by Judge Everett Saunders." He looked at Murphy. "Judge signed it on your birthday. Not a bad present."

Murphy shrugged, as if—despite his initial jubilation—it was no big deal. But he was twelve. "No big deal" had become the new norm.

Isabella folded the cherished letter and held it against

her chest. Surprisingly, it had been Monica who'd advised Isabella to file for custody after her guardianship had been made fully legal back in May. With custody, she wouldn't have to report regularly to the court. Nor would she have to worry that Kim might one day appear and expect to exercise the rights she'd so willingly tossed away. In the end, all Monica had wanted was for a family to stay together that deserved to be together.

"So," Murphy said with the utmost casualness, "when you and Iz get married, what's that make you?"

"One happy man." Erik's whisper against her ear tickled. She smiled and slid her fingers up the back of his shirt, finding the spot where she knew for a fact he was particularly sensitive. She felt him jerk and then he caught her hand in his, dragging it away. "She's got custody of you." Erik's voice was just as casual as Murph's as he answered.

And she didn't buy it from him any more than she did from Murphy. She knew he wanted to adopt Murphy, as well. But that could come later.

"I guess that makes her your new mom," he continued. "So I guess that'll make me your stepdad."

Murphy was nodding. She had no doubt that he'd already put plenty of thought into that very matter, too. He rubbed his hand over his short hair. He'd gotten a buzz cut halfway through the baseball season. It made him look even older. And more like his father.

But Isabella could look at him now and not ache for what she'd lost. She'd loved Murphy's dad. And she loved Murphy. And together with Erik, they were going to see him grow into a fine young man.

As if he were reading her thoughts, Erik's arm tightened around her. He kissed her temple.

Murphy rolled his eyes. But instead of annoyance or disgust, he just looked resigned. And amused. "When're we going over to the Double-C?"

It was Sunday. And Sunday in the Clay family meant big family dinners together. Today, it was at the Double-C. Matthew was grilling ribs again and Jaimie would undoubtedly be trying to take the credit. Murph and Erik already had the baseball team lineups planned out.

"Soon as you're ready," Erik said.

Immediately, Murphy undid his tool belt. He set it next to his safety glasses on a stack of lumber. "I'm ready."

Isabella laughed. "I think a shower might be in order."

He made a face. "Don't know why," he complained, but he was already walking away. "We're just gonna end up swimming out at the hole after we smear you in five innings." Then he looked back at Erik and Isabella and grinned. "At least Megan'll be there," he said with relish. She was Sarah and Max's daughter and was a few years older than Murphy. "She's hot."

"Murphy!"

He'd already disappeared around the corner of the house.

"He thinks every girl he sees is hot," Isabella told Erik as he turned her in his arms. "What're we going to do?"

His hands settled on her hips and he pulled her even closer. Heat, never far away when he was near, bloomed inside her. "He's twelve," he said. "It's a guy thing." Then he lowered his head and took a quick nibble on her neck. She shivered, her hands tightening around the warm brown column of his neck. "He doesn't realize I'm the one with the hottest one around." He rocked her against him. "Think we've got time for a quickie in the new barn? Maybe make a baby sister for that boy of ours?"

She tossed back her head and laughed.

Oh, she did love this man. He made her feel safe. He made

her feel loved. He made her happy. From the top of her head to the depths of her soul.

She belonged to him.

And he to her.

She grabbed his hand.

And together they ran for the barn.

* * * * *

Look out for
Mills & Boon® TEMPTED™ 2-in-1s,
from September

*Fresh, contemporary romances
to tempt all lovers of
great stories*

A sneaky peek at next month…

Cherish™

ROMANCE TO MELT THE HEART EVERY TIME

My wish list for next month's titles…

In stores from 16th August 2013:

☐ A Marriage Made in Italy – Rebecca Winters

& The Cowboy She Couldn't Forget – Patricia Thayer

☐ Miracle in Bellaroo Creek – Barbara Hannay

& Patchwork Family in the Outback – Soraya Lane

In stores from 6th September 2013:

☐ The Maverick & the Manhattanite – Leanne Banks

& A Very Special Delivery – Brenda Harlen

☐ The Courage To Say Yes – Barbara Wallace

& Her McKnight in Shining Armour – Teresa Southwick

Available at WHSmith, Tesco, Asda, Eason, Amazon and Apple

Just can't wait?

Visit us Online

You can buy our books online a month before they hit the shops! **www.millsandboon.co.uk**

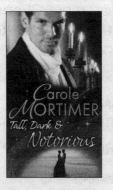
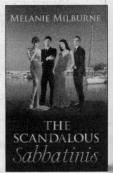

Join the Mills & Boon Book Club

Want to read more **Cherish**™ books?
We're offering you **2 more** absolutely **FREE!**

We'll also treat you to these fabulous extras:

- Exclusive offers and much more!

- FREE home delivery

- FREE books and gifts with our special rewards scheme

Get your free books now!

visit www.millsandboon.co.uk/bookclub
or call Customer Relations on 020 8288 2888